BLOOD WINE

**Other titles in the
Quin and Morgan Mystery series**

BLOOD WINE

A Quin and Morgan Mystery

John Moss

DUNDURN
TORONTO

Project Editor: Shannon Whibbs
Editor: Allister Thompson
Design: Courtney Horner
Printer: Webcom

Library and Archives Canada Cataloguing in Publication

Moss, John, 1940-, author
        Blood wine / John Moss.

(A Quin and Morgan mystery ; 4)
Issued in print and electronic formats.
ISBN 978-1-4597-0814-3

        I. Title. II. Series: Moss, John, 1940- . Quin and Morgan
mystery ; 4.

PS8576.O7863B56 2013   C813'.6   C2013-905477-4
                                                C2013-905478-2

1   2   3   4   5   18   17   16   15   14

Conseil des Arts   Canada Council   Canada   ONTARIO ARTS COUNCIL
du Canada   for the Arts   CONSEIL DES ARTS DE L'ONTARIO

We acknowledge the support of the Canada Council for the Arts and the Ontario Arts Council for our publishing program. We also acknowledge the financial support of the Government of Canada through the Canada Book Fund and Livres Canada Books, and the Government of Ontario through the Ontario Book Publishing Tax Credit and the Ontario Media Development Corporation.

Care has been taken to trace the ownership of copyright material used in this book. The author and the publisher welcome any information enabling them to rectify any references or credits in subsequent editions.

J. Kirk Howard, President

The publisher is not responsible for websites or their content unless they are owned by the publisher.

Printed and bound in Canada.

Visit us at
Dundurn.com | @dundurnpress | Facebook.com/dundurnpress | Pinterest.com/dundurnpress

Dundurn   Gazelle Book Services Limited   Dundurn
3 Church Street, Suite 500   White Cross Mills   2250 Military Road
Toronto, Ontario, Canada   High Town, Lancaster, England   Tonawanda, NY
M5E 1M2   LA1 4XS   U.S.A. 14150

1

Morning Light

When Miranda Quin woke up after sleeping alone, her mind often swarmed with languorous images. She would lie very still, hoping they'd gather into coherent memories, which they seldom did. On the rare occasions when she was not by herself, residual images would dissolve into gnawing sensations of dread or confusion, or, more infrequently, into feelings of comfort and warmth. But on this particular morning, there was nothing. It was still dark. She was drenched in sweat and lying close to the edge of the bed, with an arm draped over the side to counter being drawn into the centre. She stretched carefully and tried to differentiate one part of her body from another. She suspected she had had a bad night, but there was no rush of anxiety, there were no symptoms of excess. Just clammy flesh and a void deep inside.

Opening one eye, she tried to see the illuminated clock face. It was obscured. She sensed it must be about five. As she drifted back toward sleep the shape obstructing her view of the clock unexpectedly resolved in her mind. She raised her head, eyes wide open. Her semi-automatic lay poised in the dull luminescence. Settling back on the pillow, she tried to remember why she had put it there. She always kept her scaled-down 9mm Glock in the locked drawer of her desk on the other side of the room.

She remembered yesterday but not how it ended. Philip, beside her, was dead to the world. She reached for him under the thin cotton sheet. When her fingers encountered a slick dampness she quickly withdrew her hand. She slid naked from between the sheets and trudged through the darkness into the bathroom. Rubbing her sticky right hand against her thigh, she smelled the vague odour of almonds and rust. She switched on the overhead heat lamp and fan, which filled the room with a dull red glow and a low rumble.

Beside the shower she flicked another switch and the stall flooded with light. She swung the glass door open and reached in, turning on a full blast of water, then danced her hands into the stream, waiting for the temperature to rise as her eyes adjusted to the glare. Only then, with her disembodied arms in dazzling light while the rest of her, outside the stall, was bathed in red from the heat lamp, did she see that her right hand was smeared with blood.

We must have really been out of it, she thought.

She stepped into the shower and cleaned off the blood, then lathered her hair before reaching with the soap between her legs. She tried to focus. Her gut didn't feel menstrual; she was never early. She bent forward within the confined space of the stall as streaming lather seared her eyes. She grimaced, shook her head sharply, blinked clear, reached between her legs again, examined her fingers more carefully. There was no blood.

Miranda stood straight, rubbing her eyes with the backs of her hands.

"Philip?" she called.

The blood wasn't hers.

She called again. Silence.

And again, this time his name rising to a muffled shriek.

No answer.

Frantically rinsing shampoo from her hair, she stepped out of the shower and grabbed a huge towel, drying herself as she rushed out of the red glow into the bedroom, which had brightened with the first light of dawn. Even before she flicked on the overhead, she knew. She stopped halfway to the bed. She had seen too many corpses at crime scenes not to recognize the unnatural stillness of death.

There was no blood on the covering sheet. Only the top of his head showed on the pillow, his black hair too long for a lawyer.

She walked slowly to his side of the bed.

"Philip?" she whispered, hoping it was a stranger.

Her voice carrying his name reverberated against the walls. In her mind. In the room. Miranda pushed back the semi-sheer drapes as if natural light would help to make sense of what was happening.

Bending over, she carefully pulled the sheet away from the face of the corpse. Some of what she had taken to be Philip's black hair fanned across the pillow was congealing blood. She had to squat down to see the point of entry, where the bullet had penetrated his temple just above the right eye. She assumed there was an abdominal wound as well, to account for the blood pooled on the mattress between them.

When she leaned out of her shadow, the glazed surface of his eyes caught a flash of the morning. She reeled back. The bath towel fell and for a moment she stood naked in the middle of her bedroom, feeling unspeakably vulnerable.

Retrieving the towel, she wrapped it around her, methodically, urgently, as if it were armour, then stepped over to close Philip's eyes, hesitated, and withdrew her hand. She had tampered enough with the crime scene.

For a fluttering moment she felt disengaged, as if she were looking down through the ceiling of a film noir set, and the enormity and absurdity of the scenario were an aesthetic display. This was the way people who reluctantly returned from the dead described their own passing.

Then she felt a rushing collapse inside and from the maelstrom's rim she realized she was slipping into shock.

Clutching the towel, she moved into the living room and warily eyed the telephone, then picked up and pushed the first button on automatic dial.

"Morgan," she said when the clattering at the other end of the line subsided into a groggy expletive. "Morgan," she repeated. "There's a body in my bed."

Before he had finished speaking he knew he was on the wrong track, but it was too late to stop. "Anyone I know?"

There was a thick hum on the line.

"Miranda?"

"Yes?"

"You awake?"

"Yes."

"You're sure?"

Silence.

"Dead?"

"Yes."

David Morgan wanted to make a joke, to make it unreal. He could feel tremulations of fear and confusion in the emptiness between them. He wanted to say something funny, to move back in time to that moment just before he picked up, when he was awake enough to realize it could only be her and still half asleep, so her call seemed a welcome intrusion.

"Is it your friend Carter?" The line filled with the sounds of their breathing. "Are you okay?"

"He's been shot."

"You're sure?"

She said nothing.

"Miranda?"

"Yes?"

"You're not hurt?

"I don't know what happened."

"I'm on my way. I'll phone it in."

"I can do that."

"No, don't."

There was silence on the line, air rushing between them.

When the phone clicked off, Miranda set it down gently and walked to the bedroom door. Time slowed to a drawl. The corpse in her bed. Her lover, her paramour. In her boudoir. She liked those words. She liked the word *courtesan*. Gallic, sensual. She could never have been a courtesan. Sex was too complicated.

Time stopped; the scene, freeze-framed. Grand Guignol.

Then she felt a surge of panic. She rushed through the bedroom, now flooded with white morning light, into the red glow of the bathroom, and threw up in the toilet. Her vomit was material evidence. She flushed.

David Morgan had been up most of the night reading about antique tribal carpets. When Miranda woke him he was slumped across his blue sofa with a large book splayed open on his chest and several more on the floor beside him. Morgan was fascinated by the astonishing and whimsical beauty of weaving done by nomadic women in Persia more than a century ago, rugs that had survived practical usage on desert sand and mountain shale and now graced the walls of expensive galleries and the pages of erudite and extravagant books. Such rugs were beyond his capacity to buy, but that only made them more thrilling to study. And that is what he did. Morgan seldom read for amusement. He studied.

He was not a scholar. His obsessive enthusiasm for arcane pursuits offered a refuge from the business of homicide and helped to distract his personal demons or to keep them at bay.

Not until he clicked off the phone did he realize he was on his feet. The book had tumbled to the floor. He stood still for a moment, struggling for clarity. Then with a long sigh he strode into the bathroom, brushed his teeth while peeing, doing a sloppy job of both, and started to strip before realizing he was already dressed. He tucked himself in as he clattered through the front door to the police car outside.

He seldom drove and never brought cars home. Last night his superintendent, Alex Rufalo, had dropped in for a few drinks and Morgan sent him home in a cab, keeping the keys.

The drive from the Annex over to Isabella Street took less than ten minutes; it was too early for traffic. Morgan ran a light crossing Yonge Street. Not until he pulled up in front of Miranda's building on Isabella did he make the call to Headquarters. He was surprised to connect with Rufalo, who had obviously decided to sleep it off in his office rather than offend his wife with boozy apologies.

Morgan asked for an ID check on Philip Carter. Miranda never said, but Morgan assumed he was married.

Slogging up three flights after she buzzed him in, he thought it was time she moved. She had the resources. She owned a house in Waterloo County left by her mother to Miranda and her sister in Vancouver, but the sister signed off. Miranda was a single cop; her sister and husband were flourishing professionals. Although Miranda seldom visited the house, she refused to sell it.

She could afford better than this.

On the other hand, the stair-treads were worn Vermont marble, the wood trim was ancient black walnut, the fixtures were bronze. The place had an air of decadent longevity. It was not an unpleasant place to live, better than a high-rise. Especially since the apartments had been sold off as condos. Down-at-heels rental units, once privately owned, became shabby genteel.

Before he could knock, Miranda swung the door open and slumped against him.

Then she stood back, almost fiercely, and stared into his eyes.

He saw something in her he had never seen before; she was frightened.

He kissed her on the forehead — she would flinch or she would relax. But she seemed not to notice. He quietly turned her back into the living room, where they sat on the sofa.

"Tell me?"

She nodded. "In there."

He got up and walked into the bedroom, where the corpse had been carefully covered again. He pulled the sheet back, and as his eyes made contact with the victim's the cellphone he seldom carried beeped a shrill admonition. He let the sheet drop and turned away.

"You sure about the name?" said a voice on the other end.

"Yeah, Philip Carter. Lawyer. Just a minute...."

He walked out into the living room.

"Miranda, where did he work?" The guy was already past tense.

"Ogilthorpe and Blackthorne, Blackburn, something like that. In one of the bank towers on King Street."

Morgan repeated the information, then returning again to Miranda he asked, "Where'd he live?"

"Oakville. He commutes." Present tense.

"You got that?" said Morgan into the phone. "See what you come up with." He clicked off.

"Oakville?" he said.

"Yes," said Miranda, "and yes."

"Yes?"

"Yes, he's married. His wife is a widow. Two daughters. Oh Jesus, Jesus Lord Christ."

"Swearing or praying?"

"Both."

"Did you ever run a check on him?"

"God no! He was my lover, not my investment broker."

"So what happened?"

"I don't know. My head's swarming. We went out, I'm not sure, probably downtown for dinner, maybe just drinks, what time did I leave?"

"Headquarters? Six, six thirty."

"So we must have gone out for dinner. I can't remember."

"Where'd you usually meet?"

"Never the same place twice."

"You're kidding."

"No."

"Didn't that set off alarms?"

"It was just a game we played. It was just something we did. It wasn't a big deal."

"Well, it is now. That's your Glock by the bed?"

"Yes."

He walked into the bedroom, leaned down over the bedside table, sniffed the gun without touching it.

"You're sure it's yours?" he called to her.

She came forward and stood in the doorway. Boldly. She was playing a part. Or being played by another, an actress concealing her art from the character she plays. *It's all quite illusory*, she observed to herself.

"Of course," she said in a normal tone. "Check the desk drawer."

"It's been fired," he said. "Where's the key?"

"Centre, under the stamp-box."

He opened the locked drawer. It was empty.

"Where's the holster?" she said. "It should be there."

"You lock up your holster?"

"A lady doesn't wish to remind gentlemen callers of guns in her bedroom."

She slumped against the doorframe, depleted. She wanted Morgan to hold her.

Morgan glanced through the open bathroom door, where the heat lamp was still on and emitting a soft red glow, then he turned and eased her back into the living room.

When she was settled on the sofa he squatted in front of her. "You're going to be okay," he said.

The security buzzer sounded and Morgan pressed the release button. "They're here," he said, as if she might not have heard.

"Morgan."

"Yeah."

She started to rise, then sank back against the sofa. Squatting in front of her again, he held both her hands in his.

"Morgan, thanks."

"Hey, it's only begun. Wait till you really owe me."

"I mean thanks, you know …"

"I know."

"I didn't …"

"It never crossed my mind."

David, she thought. She never called him by his first name. No one did. He was Morgan, like she was Miranda. *It's not about gender*, she thought. *It's a personality thing. David.*

The door rattled against knuckles. She stiffened and turned pale.

Morgan opened the door.

"Hello there," said a woman of Miranda's age, poised to enter with a black satchel in one hand. She gazed into

Morgan's eyes as if assessing an extravagant purchase, then past him at Miranda and back to Morgan.

"I'm looking for a murder."

Morgan stepped to the side.

"This is it, then? Sorry, love."

She moved around him and addressed Miranda.

"I was told there was a body in a detective's bed. Never dreamed it was yours. Nice place."

She smiled at Morgan, leaned forward to kiss him on the cheek, hesitated and held out her hand, which he took momentarily before releasing his grip. Miranda did not look up; it was almost as if she were embarrassed.

"Ellen," said Morgan, his tone formal. She was not here as Miranda's friend — if she was Miranda's friend. He wasn't sure.

Ellen Ravenscroft kneeled down to place herself in Miranda's line of vision. She reached out and touched Miranda's cheek. "You're cold, love." Their eyes briefly connected. "Don't you worry. We'll get this all sorted out."

She stood up and turned to Morgan. "Now where is the body? No, you stay with your partner. I'll look in myself."

As Ellen Ravenscroft disappeared into the bedroom, a file of men and women came trooping through from the corridor. Miranda watched, and Morgan watched her watching them. Most were familiar, but each was now a stranger.

He assumed a position in front of her, a little to the side, slightly in everyone's way.

Miranda shut her eyes and it was like she was dreaming. She could hear the forensics team, medical examiners, and police personnel, but with her eyes closed they seemed a great distance away. She suppressed a rush of vertigo but refused to open her eyes, convinced that the jumble of images inside her head would reveal something, if only she could hold on. She was not trying to make a nightmare go away, she was struggling to bring it back. She wanted to be there again — inside whatever went on that she could not remember.

Morgan moved to the bedroom, but he was uncomfortable with his role as observer. The medical examiner, to the accompaniment of a photographer's flashing, in conjunction with the careful ministrations of a forensic specialist, meticulously raised the sheet covering the corpse and drew it aside, where it was folded and bagged. Even from Morgan's perspective near the door, he could see the gaping wound in the victim's gut, his innards extruding onto the bed.

"Nasty business," said Ellen Ravenscroft as she stood up and moved close to him. "Nothing showed through the top sheet. He was over on his side. The disembowelling was done in the bed after he was dead."

"Disembowelling? And the head wound."

"Executed on the spot. Bullet's in the pillow. Another pillow kicked under the bed was used as a silencer. There was a kitchen knife under the bed as well, with blood on the blade. He wiped the handle clean."

"He?"

"Whoever did this."

"Ellen Ravenscroft ..."

"Yes, love."

"You're a good person."

"And whatever makes you say that, Detective? I'm a regular bitch."

"I'm sure you are. But you assume Miranda is innocent, even though she's the most logical suspect."

"Hardly. I mean, who's innocent these days? But a suspect, no. Look, Detective, if you wanted to kill your lover, would you nail him, eviscerate him, and crawl in beside him? I can think of better ways to spend the night."

"Yeah," said a rumbling voice from just behind them. "That is exactly what you might do if you're a homicide detective and think sleeping in sludge will throw off the dogs."

"Spivak," said Morgan. "Welcome to the crime scene. This is Ellen Ravenscroft, she's the M.E."

"Yeah," said Spivak. "We've met." He was a burly man with the parched eyes of an inveterate smoker.

Spivak moved around beside Morgan and acknowledged the coroner with a wet cough.

"You want to get that looked at, Detective. You'd do better spitting than swallowing."

"You too," he leered.

No one acknowledged the joke. *Sometimes*, thought Morgan, *there's no double in double entendre.*

"I'm not yours till I'm dead," said Spivak, with the righteous sneer of the self-afflicted.

"I can hardly wait."

Spivak relished being an unpleasant cliché. He had long since forgotten what he was really like. *At least Ravenscroft is ironic*, thought Morgan. *The stereotype she animates is intentional.*

"What're you doing here?" said Morgan.

"It's my case."

Morgan said nothing. It had not occurred to him the case was not theirs.

"You have a problem with that?" asked Spivak. "Check it with Rufalo."

Morgan shrugged. "Who are you working with?"

"Him," he said, nodding in the direction of a gaunt young man Morgan had never seen before.

Spivak's last partner was killed in a car accident; a woman, a rookie, a high-speed chase. A lot of bad publicity, no liability. She was driving.

"He looks like a funeral director," said Morgan.

"He's in the right place," said Ellen Ravenscroft. "I think he's kind of distinguished."

"Maybe where you come from," said Spivak with a sneer.

Spivak is the perpetual immigrant, thought Morgan. *Born in Toronto, grew up speaking English, his parents spoke none. By identifying others as outsiders he proclaims his own credentials as a native son.*

"Yorkshire," she said, paused, and added, "*love.*" Her tone made the word seem its opposite. "Now to business," she continued. "We have a killer who was taking no chances. This fellow has been shot through the head, gutted, and for all we know asphyxiated and poisoned as well."

"Check it all out," said Spivak cheerfully, ingesting a massive wheeze.

"What do you make of this?" his funereal partner called from the bathroom doorway. Spivak and Morgan walked over to him while Ravenscroft rejoined the pathology team by the bed.

Morgan was startled when he entered the bathroom. The walls were smeared with swathes of blood that appeared to have been applied with deliberation, to deliver an indecipherable message.

"My goodness," he said.

Morgan's habitual avoidance of obscenity and profanity was known through the department and sometimes ridiculed, but never to his face.

"My goodness!" Spivak repeated.

Morgan looked at him. Spivak's eyes flicked downwards in a brief acknowledgement of something unspoken between them. He was a crude man and hard as nails, but Morgan was alpha, something to do with quietude, with his intelligence. Men like Spivak invested stillness with menace and were grudgingly deferential.

"What's it saying to us, Morgan?" asked Spivak.

Morgan reached over and flicked off the overhead light. The room fell silent. He turned on the heater-light and the low rumble of the fan spread around them in the red gloom, the blood scrawlings on the wall disappearing, merging with the shadows. He turned on the overhead and the bloody scrawl returned.

"She wouldn't have seen it," he said.

"Unless she did it herself."

Morgan glared at the burly, unkempt man — Morgan was unkempt, Spivak was scruffy.

"It's her bed, her boyfriend, her gun. She's on suspension."

"What?"

"It's automatic. And Rufalo says you're out of it, too. This is Igor, he's a mortician from Jamaica."

"Don't you be saying to he such a terrible thing, I never been to Jamaica, man," Spivak's new partner said in an exaggerated West Indian dialect. Then he turned to address Morgan. "Eeyore, not Igor," he said, and shook hands, speaking with a crisp Toronto inflection. "We're working on racial sensitivity," he continued. "So far, Spivak can't make the entry requirements for the program. I have heard a lot about you and your partner, mostly good things. My mother didn't realize Eeyore was an ass. Nice to meet you."

He seemed a nice enough kid. Morgan walked back into the living room, where Miranda was sitting on the sofa, small and alone amidst the commotion.

"You all right?" he asked.

She shrugged.

"Did you see the stuff scrawled on the bathroom walls?"

She looked at him quizzically, cocking her head like a wounded animal.

"Hieroglyphs of some sort. Written in blood."

"Philip's ..." she murmured, her voice trailing off.

A woman from the CSI unit knelt in front of them.

"Detective Quin, I'm going to need some bits and pieces."

Miranda held out her hands one at a time, and the woman pared residual matter from under her nails into a small plastic envelope.

"Did you wash?" she asked.

"Yeah, I had a shower. I flushed the toilet." Miranda seemed almost embarrassed.

"That's okay. I need to check what I can."

"There'll be powder under my nails," said Miranda. "I was on the range yesterday."

"With the murder weapon?"

"Pardon?"

"The murder weapon," the woman repeated, nodding in the direction of the bedroom.

"I guess so. I don't know." It seemed inconceivable he could have been killed with her own gun. And inevitable that he was.

"And we're going to need a vaginal scraping."

"He was my lover, for God's sake."

"Did you have sex last night?"

"I don't know."

"We'll need to find out."

"Yeah, okay. Where?"

"As soon as we can. We'll take you over to Women's."

Morgan felt for her, but it was standard procedure.

"Can you do it here?" Miranda asked.

"I can't, but the M.E. could."

"A coroner's pelvic — see if she's up for it."

The woman went to find Ravenscroft. Morgan leaned over the sofa from behind, resting his hand lightly on her shoulder.

"We'll have to go down to Headquarters," he said. "Spivak and Eeyore, they'll want to talk."

"How long?"

"What? Downtown —"

"No. How long's he been dead?" she asked.

"Five or six hours."

"Is it bad?"

"He's dead."

"Gruesome?"

"Yeah, very."

"Disembowelled?"

"Eviscerated —"

"God!"

"Yeah."

"While I slept. Oh, Jesus."

"You were unconscious, you'll need to be tested. Someone slipped you something. Given the outcome, I'm guessing it wasn't Philip."

Morgan's cellphone buzzed. He flinched at the intrusiveness. The CSI woman and Ellen Ravenscroft approached Miranda and led her into the bathroom.

When Miranda walked past Philip, exposed on the bed with his guts looping out of his abdomen, she did not flinch. She had seen worse. The bathroom, she found more distressing. Blood on the walls, taunting with unrevealed meaning. *The horror*, she thought, *the horror*, and nothing else came to her mind.

"You sure you want me to do this?" asked Ellen.

"You're a doctor, aren't you?" said Miranda.

"Fully licensed, fifteen years this side of the pond, may the House of Windsor and my own dead mother forgive me."

"So, help yourself," said Miranda, sitting on the edge of the tub.

"You'll have to drop your knickers, love."

With an annoying air of solicitude the CSI woman helped Miranda back onto her feet. She closed her eyes tight, and then opened them slowly. Curiously, she felt little grief. Rage, fear, a sense of violation, of profound loss — it was not about Philip, it was the gaping hole his absence left inside her.

Although Miranda preferred skirts, anticipating the police she had put on slacks, feeling less vulnerable that way. The CSI woman held out a bath towel, and averting her eyes she wrapped it around Miranda, who stepped out of her slacks and underwear.

"You want me to assume the position?" Miranda asked, dubiously eyeing the bathmat on the floor. Instead, she sat down again on the edge of the tub.

"Okay, spread 'em," said the M.E. "Let's see what's been happening in there."

As Miranda leaned back to brace herself, Ellen Ravenscroft hunkered between her knees with a penlight in her mouth. Miranda flinched involuntarily as the M.E. reached in with a swab.

"You had a shower, right? But no douche?"

"No. Damnit. I don't remember. Get the hell out of there."

"Just a minute, love. Okay. I'd say you had a right good night of it. Well, until, you know —"

"That's gratifying. Are we finished?"

Miranda closed her legs, stood up, and retrieved her clothes. The M.E. fell backwards on her bottom.

"Yes," said Ellen as she unceremoniously struggled to her feet while the other two women watched. "We're done."

"How long have you been doing this?" Miranda asked as she slipped back into her clothes.

"With dead people? Seems forever. I actually trained as an OB/GYN. God only knows why. Staring into the gaping maws of womanhood day in, day out, it palls after a while. So I made a lateral move to the morgue."

"You'd rather work with the dead?"

"Wouldn't we all, dear. Look at the three of us." Her glance included the CSI technician. "Women in our prime, the three witches of Caldor, whatever, guiding the departed into the underworld —"

"Is there anything else?" asked the CSI woman, edging toward the door, but instead of leaving she leaned against it as if she were afraid an intruder might overhear them.

Ravenscroft leaned close to Miranda and said in a conspiratorial whisper, "Sorry about this, love."

"Me too," said Miranda.

"I'll need a blood sample and a urine specimen, then we're finished. You threw up, didn't you, but we're hoping for traces of a knock-out drug, maybe GHB or something more potent."

"Hoping for?"

"Your alibi, love."

The M.E. took blood and without a fanfare of modesty Miranda produced urine.

"Is that everything?" she asked, turning the vivid yellow vial over to Ellen.

"You're dehydrated, dear girl. Have lots to drink, you'll feel better."

Miranda reached for the wall switch and turned on the heat-light with its rumbling fan, then switched off the main light, drenching the room in livid red. The exterior window had been painted over decades ago. The fires of Hell could not be more ominous, she thought. The three women whose life work was death stood perfectly still. She extinguished the red and they were again left in absolute darkness, except for the comical slit of illumination defining the bottom edge of the door.

She was more comfortable in the dark. Philip's blood on the walls, it was the neatness that bothered her. There was no blood on the floor, and there had been no blood on the floor of her bedroom. The grotesque message scrawled with deliberate precision was intentionally obscure, she was certain of that — the meaning was in the way it was done.

"Thanks," she said.

The other two women stepped back as she pulled open the bathroom door. Morgan was standing sentinel on the other side, facing away and framed by the busy glare in her bedroom. The body was covered with a clean sheet, like a rumpled bed.

2

The Message

Morgan and Miranda stood in the living room with Spivak and Eeyore Stritch. Morgan looked angry. Spivak seemed puzzled. He stared at Miranda with genuine concern, which was somewhat concealed behind his habitual scowl. His young partner seemed anxious.

"We've got a problem, Miranda," said Morgan. "Your friend, they can't find him."

"What are you talking about?" she said, cocking her head toward the bedroom. "You can't get more found than that."

"Yeah, you can," said Spivak.

"*Someone's* in there," Morgan said.

For a desperate moment she thought it was all a mistake, that it was someone else dead in her bed.

"His name is not Philip Carter. There was no Philip Carter at Ogilthorpe and Blackbourne, they've never heard of him."

"Morgan, what are you talking about?"

"There's no home in Oakville. No teenage daughters, no wife."

For another weird moment, Miranda felt relieved; she would not have to bear the guilt for a widow's grief or fatherless children.

"Your friend, he doesn't seem to exist."

"Is that an existential proclamation?"

"Listen to me. Philip Carter, his driver's licence, his health insurance card, credit cards, they're fakes."

"No," she snapped. "His address —"

"A Vietnamese variety store in Oakville. They met him once, he paid them, they forwarded his mail to a mailbox in Toronto."

"But you know him, Morgan. For God's sake, Philip is Philip."

"We never met."

She was incredulous. Morgan was so inextricably a part of her life.

"Never?"

"You never talked about him."

"Really!"

"Okay," said Spivak. "Enough true confessions." He motioned Eeyore to come closer then turned to Miranda. "Where'd you meet this guy?"

"In court."

"Lawyer, criminal, judge?"

"I met him coming out of a washroom."

"Janitor?"

"Lawyer."

"Women's or men's?"

"Me, I was coming out of the women's. He was in the corridor. I walked straight into him."

"In the courthouse?"

"Yes."

"You were there for the Vittorio Ciccone trial?"

"I'm a witness."

"Yeah, everyone knows you're a witness."

"It's complicated."

"Yeah, everything connected with Ciccone is complicated. Finding a dead guy in your bed, is that a Vittorio Ciccone complication?"

"Philip is a corporate lawyer. Was."

"Drug lords need corporate lawyers, especially phantom corporate lawyers."

"No, Philip didn't know him."

"It's as dangerous to be *for* Ciccone as *against* him."

"I'm neither."

"You're the link between a dead guy and a guy who kills people. You ever see him practise law?"

"No. How do you watch a corporate lawyer practise law?"

Spivak smiled, and the effort made him break into a rough, rising cough. "So tell me about the wife and kids?"

"He was married." She refused to say he was "unhappily" married. "He had two teenage daughters."

"You've seen pictures?" Spivak asked.

"He wanted to keep that part of his life separate."

"From?"

"From the part he shared with me."

"Generous man. You've known him for two months?"

"Nearly."

"Not very well."

"Who knows anyone very well?"

"Did you kill him?"

She felt rage choke in her throat and thought she was going to vomit again.

"Lookit," said Spivak. "Why would a stranger use your gun to kill another stranger, mutilate the corpse with your knife — M.E. says he was gutted post mortem — and then scrawl with his guts on your walls, and oh, yes, with you sleeping through everything, not a mark on you?"

Silence.

"And one more thing," said Spivak. "There's gunpowder under your nails."

"Am I under arrest?"

"Gawd no. I'm not even taking you down for questioning. But don't leave town, as they say. You're the prime until something better turns up. Sorry about the boyfriend."

Miranda had known Spivak for years. He wasn't a bad cop and he wouldn't get in the way while she and Morgan conducted their own shadow investigation. The kid seemed agreeable, maybe a little odd.

It was midday and they were alone. Morgan found a bottle of Châteauneuf-du-Pape in the kitchen cupboard. A recent vintage, but with a fulsome aroma. He did not recognize the label; this surprised him. He poured them each a long drink, using crystal stemware he had never seen before.

Leaning side by side against the counter, they toasted in a grim salutation to the surrounding emptiness.

After a while, they toasted again.

"Here's to old what's-his-name," said Miranda.

"Yeah," said Morgan. "To Philip."

"He brought this for a special occasion," she said. She was cupping the tulip-shaped bowl of the glass in her hand. Morgan reached over, took the glass from her, then returned it so she could properly grasp only the stem.

She offered a wan smile of acquiescence. She could feel the warmth of her lover's body, his hands, his breath.

The wine was the colour of arterial blood before it congeals. She sipped but it tasted raw, although Morgan was enjoying it.

"The prints on my gun, my prints should be all over it."

Yeah, he thought.

"Ellen Ravenscroft, Morgan, she'd jump your bones if she could."

"Or yours."

"Nonsense, she's straight. She'd eat you alive."

"Yeah," he acknowledged, gazing into the crimson depths of his glass.

"I thought I was falling in love," she said. "God, I've been stupid."

"Me too, sometimes. I married my biggest mistake."

"At least you didn't kill her off."

"Divorce; a form of manslaughter."

"How old am I?"

"Thirty-eight. Why?"

"Thirty-seven and change."

He said nothing.

"You'd think I'd learn, Morgan."

"Yeah."

"This place is a mess."

There was a stillness about her that he could feel like a shimmering at his temples. Her hazel eyes seemed resolute, her auburn hair was mussed as if she had just made love. Her lean body torqued sensually from the hips as she surveyed her apartment.

"I don't want the ghoul brigade," she said. "I'll do it myself."

A loosely knit group of volunteers who had lost loved ones to murder or suicide would confront their own nightmares by turning up after the investigators were finished, if summoned, to scrub blood off floors, scrape viscera from walls, clean furniture and rugs, do whatever had to be done. Miranda did not want to deal with the goodness of strangers.

There were professional crime scene cleaners. She had worked with them. They were good, but this was private.

"Morgan."

"Yeah?

"How come I'm alive?"

I don't know, he thought.

"Jesus," she said, "it's about me, isn't it? Philip was collateral damage. Oh Jesus Christ Lord God Almighty. This was a message to me." She smiled. "Swear and a prayer," she explained.

She looked at Morgan, a recovering Presbyterian and avowed anti-theist. It made him uneasy when she swore. He mouthed some wine and swallowed.

"Amen," she said.

"It's not always about you."

"Sometimes it is," she said, then repeated: "Amen."

The next three days went by in a blur. The minutes and hours, daylight and darkness, were undifferentiated in Miranda's mind. Morgan had taken her to his place in the Annex. Corking the Châteauneuf-du-Pape with a downward blow of his fist, he had grasped the bottle by the neck, scooped up some clothes in a bag, escorted her to the car, and driven even more carefully than usual. He was acutely aware that she disliked his driving. She always took the wheel when they were together, but this was an exception.

While she stayed with him, he slept on the sofa. Incredibly, his random collection of her clothing included changes of underwear and enough variety. But she was uncomfortable being alone in someone else's bed. She stayed for two nights and then went home because she was lonely.

Now she was gazing across the room at him in Starbucks, just down College Street from Police Headquarters. His back was to her; he was picking up a couple of cappuccinos. He turned and shambled over. She smiled. He was trying to look after her.

When the crime scene was declared open, he had gone back to her apartment and cleaned up, even scrubbed the scrawled blood from her bathroom walls.

She had been suspended with pay. He was posted to a cold case that he could work on his own, and which gave him the time to shadow Spivak and Stritch, since that was what the superintendent knew he was going to do, anyway.

"How are you making out?" he asked.

"Same as last time you saw me, eight hours ago."

"Ten. I've got an update...."

"On?"

"You, mostly."

"Shoot."

"Your prints were on the gun — which was definitely the murder weapon."

"As expected."

"And no one else's. That's okay, though," he assured her. "Your gun should have been smeared with layers of your prints. But there was only one neat cluster. At least two rounds were fired. And there were powder traces under your nails."

"We know that. I was at the range —"

"No, you weren't at the range that day. It was a couple of days before."

"Really? You checked?" She paused, trying to sort out memory from reconstruction. "Two days before? My head's more messed up than I thought — there was only one bullet wound...."

"Even Spivak agrees the prints were too neat."

"So where's the other slug?"

"Good question."

"But two rounds were fired?"

"Only one bullet was missing from the clip, but forensics are sure at least two were fired. Whoever did this was meticulous, replacing the bullet."

"What else?"

Morgan looked into her eyes and raised his cappuccino in a gentle salute.

"The kitchen knife, it was yours, it had your prints on it — of course — but no blood on the handle, only the blade."

"Suggesting what?"

"Well, there's more. Ellen Ravenscroft called."

"And?"

"She says the gut wounds don't match up with the knife. It has a serrated edge. At this point it seems a red herring."

"And? You're looking solemner and solemner. Spit it out, Morgan."

"Well, you and Philip had sex."

"Often."

"That night, I mean. I wasn't asking a question."

"And?"

"You had sex with someone else as well."

"What?"

"Seems that way."

"Then someone had sex *with me*, goddamn it. Who?"

He shrugged, almost apologetically.

"Oh my God, Morgan. Can they tell a sequence?"

"You mean who was first? No."

"It had to be Philip," she said. "Then he was killed. Then his killer ... while Philip was in the same bed." Miranda gagged but stifled the rush in her throat to retch.

"We'll get the bastard."

Even with her gut clenched and her head reeling, Miranda acknowledged to herself that Morgan had sworn. A mild expletive, but for him an indication of formidable anger. She was glad he was on her side. Controlled rage was a powerful ally.

She reached across the table and placed a hand over his. "Morgan. Since I was drugged — they've established that, right. It was a GHB cocktail. Used for date rape — does that mean Philip had sex with me while I was unconscious as well as the other guy?"

"Miranda —"

"It's okay. And it seems less likely that his killer would ... oh Jesus, it's sickening ... get off in me with a bloody corpse on the bed. No, it had to be Philip offering to share me, then he took a turn on his own, then he died."

Her eyes were glazed and her voice was tremulous, but her jaw was set firm and she looked Morgan straight in the eye as she talked. He wanted to come around and hold her, but Starbucks was a public place and intimacy was not what she needed. She needed to feel his rage as the strength of affection. She did not need pity but love.

"Miranda?"

"Yes?"

"Once we're through this —"

"There's no getting through this, there's only, you know, living with it."

He wanted to ask her to marry him. He didn't really want to ask her to marry him. He wanted to declare he would always look after her. He knew he could not always look after her. He wanted to tear her pain out by the roots. Without hurting her. He wanted to feel better about himself for having let this happen to his partner.

"Morgan, what is it?"

She was his friend. The best thing he could do was get on with the case.

"Nothing's turned up about the man formerly known as Philip Carter," he said. "We've checked with the Mounties, with the FBI, INTERPOL. Nobody's heard of him, there's no match for his prints. Total blank. One of over seven billion people on the planet."

"Yeah," said Miranda. "Not any more."

"You okay with that?"

She almost laughed. "Well, no," she said. "Not okay! On the other hand, maybe I am. If he wasn't dead, I'd want to kill him."

Morgan felt restless. He wanted to be doing things, not because he gave a damn about Miranda's dead lover, whoever he was, but for Miranda herself, to get her life back so they could be partners again.

He wanted to help her, but he didn't know where she was hurting.

Was it the horror? That would haunt the strongest of people, waking up beside a corpse with its guts spread over the mattress. Was it terror? That there might be a sequel, that she was a target? It seemed unlikely, not that it could happen but that she would let fear take hold. Was it grief for the death of her lover? He didn't think so. Whatever grief there might have been was subsumed by anger. Was it rage for Philip having used her, even if she did not understand how? Was it revulsion, loathing for Philip or misplaced contempt for herself, for the depraved sexual abuse she had endured?

Miranda sat back in her chair and then projected with a sibilant hush her deepest desire. "The son of a bitch, the one I didn't know, he's the one I want dead."

"We'll get him."

"I want him, Morgan." She leaned forward. "I want him."

Morgan had never heard Miranda talk this way. She had a cool intelligence that eliminated the emotional and the extraneous. Her mind was precise, and after three years with the RCMP following university and a decade working together on Homicide in Toronto, she knew how to use it with awesome dexterity.

"Dead won't help. We want him caught."

"Whatever. I want him dead. This is about me, not him."

She wanted to tell Morgan to let himself go, that she needed the same passion he risked on inanimate things;

she needed his ardour and fury, not spoken but felt deep in her heart and the depths of her mind.

"Okay," he said. "We're in this together."

"Not quite. I'm the one waiting for the HIV results."

"You okay?"

"Morgan, will you stop asking if I'm okay. Okay?"

Morgan felt helpless. He explained that the superintendent had given him his head, so that on the books he looked active. As for her suspension, apart from having had to turn in her semi-automatic, a pro forma procedure since it was already being held as material evidence, she was effectively on paid leave. And they were still partners.

"Rufalo's turned us loose," he said.

"And Spivak?"

"He's good. Spivak will follow up whatever leads he can get. He's promised to keep us informed. He's not a small man, we're not in competition."

"About 290 pounds of not small. With his new partner, that gives us nearly a quarter of a ton of detective on our side. And what are we up against? I've been fucked and fucked over by phantoms."

"Don't make it worse —"

"Worse! You don't like the word 'fucked'? Does it make you squeamish? Jesus, Morgan, that's what — I've been fucked. If ever a word was appropriate, that's it, that's what happened."

Neither was prone to using vernacular. *Kick ass, let's roll, just do it* wasn't them. *Fuck* was a word they avoided, both feeling contempt for lazy diction, both alive among words too much to lean on stupid expletives.

Miranda got up and walked over to order two more coffees, this time not cappuccino. Often when Morgan was alone he had double-double, but with Miranda he always took black, no sugar. He actually preferred it that way. He could taste the coffee.

"So," she said when she sat down again, "I've been ruminating for three days, perseverating, cogitating."

"Which?"

"All three. Going over and over the details. Trying for the larger picture, waiting for something to emerge. So far, nothing but details."

"Tell me things I don't know."

"Okay." She paused. "He could have had an accent?"

"Who? Philip?"

"Yeah, we'll call him Philip until something better comes up. It wasn't so much an accent as an absolute lack of inflection. It was a little unusual. You know how sometimes Europeans speak English better than we do. Germans, especially. Like that. Except he wasn't European."

"What then? How do you know?"

"He spoke about Europe as an outsider —"

"And about Canada as home?"

"Canada and the States. It was strange. There wasn't a border — Canada and the U.S., it was all the same. None of the usual Canadian edginess — benevolent antipathy — when he talked about Americans. And none of an American's blithe indifference to difference when he talked about us. I remember thinking it seemed like a borderless sensibility and that it was strange, then I got used to it. I kind of liked it. I didn't want to know too much. I didn't want the emotional risk. He could have been either Canadian or American."

"Or neither."

"Perhaps. He was very cosmopolitan."

"He knew good wines. I wonder where the Châteauneuf-du-Pape came from? I've never seen a label like that in Ontario — maybe the States. Could he have been Israeli?"

"Because he knew wines? An interesting connection! And no, definitely not."

"How can you be so sure?"

"Morgan! A lady knows."

"Yeah, okay, so, not Jewish."

"Not Jewish. Let's see, what else? Afghani? No, the Taliban never came up. So who does that leave us?"

"Where did that come from?" asked Morgan.

"What, the Taliban? I don't know, whenever I think of relations between the sexes these days, I think of them. I mean, Morgan, watch the newscasts. Countries in that part of the world treat women like a different species. Crowd scenes, throngs in the streets, and no women. A sea of beards and burnooses, and impotent fists throttling the air — and not a woman in sight unless under a shroud. And don't give me the freedom of religion crap — freedom for whom? The normalization of hatred for women, that's what we're seeing; fear and hatred of women. Even by women themselves. Especially by women themselves."

"I wasn't going to say a word. We live in parallel realities, get used to it." He paused, curious about the direction their conversation had taken. "When I think of Afghanistan, I see those giant Buddhas crashing into clouds of dust a few years ago and, you know, it makes me ashamed and I think, God save us from religious zealotry."

"An interesting prayer for an atheist."

"Have you seen the pictures, giant hollows in the rock where the statues were, gaping holes spilling rubble? I'm ashamed on behalf of humanity."

He's more concerned about statuary, about cultural artifacts, than about women in shackles of drapery, in perpetual shadows. Perhaps it's all the same.

"I made a list," said Miranda abruptly, as if the clash of cultures were not under discussion. "You know, a list of the places we went for dinner or drinks, I gave it to Spivak."

"He's already checked them out," Morgan responded. "No one recalls either of you. It's like you were never there, like you didn't exist."

"That's comforting. We were being unobtrusive, you know, too mature to flaunt our *discretion*."

"What about the last night, nothing comes back?"

"No, yes."

"What do you mean, no, yes?"

"Morgan, in the morning, there was a smell of almonds...."

"And?"

"Hand cream, there must have been hand cream in the women's washroom. I use aloe-based moisturizers at home, this was almond."

"And this tells us what?"

"That we dined at an upscale restaurant. Large. The little spiffy bistros on the list have modest little bathrooms. I'd say we went to one of the major hotels. The Four Seasons, the Royal York. Almond is very old fashioned. I'd guess the Imperial Room at the Royal York."

Before their eyes adjusted to the midday June sunshine, they had crossed the street and descended into the glossy underworld that spreads beneath downtown Toronto like an alternate universe, where weather and seasons are residual memories, office workers are on half-hour tethers, and retail is king.

From the Union Station subway stop they had direct access to the grand lobby of the Royal York and immediately found the maître d' of the Imperial Room, who had just come on shift.

"Yes sir," he said, directing himself to Morgan. "This lady was here a few nights ago."

"Really," said Miranda, "how can you be so sure?"

"Well, sir," said the maître d', still addressing Morgan, "the lady needed assistance in getting up from the table. It does not happen often, our patrons usually, ah, consume with discretion —"

"Hey," said Miranda, taking him by the arm and swinging him around. "It's me, I'm here. Talk to me."

"Yes, ma'am, of course." He turned to look at Morgan. "She was quite drunk, sir. I am sorry."

"You're gonna be a sorry soprano if you don't focus," said Miranda.

"Yes, ma'am."

"Where was I sitting? Who was I with?"

"Over there," he said, nodding to a discreet table against a far wall. "You were alone with a gentleman, and then another gentleman joined you."

"The bill," said Morgan. "We need to see the bill."

"Could I ask what for, sir?"

"You are assisting in a murder investigation."

"Really? Well, of course." The maître d' was warming to his role. "If you will please come this way," he said, and gently pulled his arm free of Miranda's grasp. He led them into a small office and rummaged through a sheaf of receipts.

"Nothing," he finally said. "There is no record."

"There must be a bill," said Miranda. "Perhaps we paid in cash." As an aside, she said to Morgan, "He had credit cards, but he always used hard currency, sometimes American."

"Of course," said the maître d'. "It happens so seldom. Yes, you are right, Detective, just so. Here we are. Giovanni was your waiter. He will be here shortly. Let me see. You had very good wines; quite memorable, in fact. A bottle of Bordeaux with dinner, very nice, Château Cos d'Estournel, 1986. Excellent choice with your boeuf bourguignon. Myself, I might have preferred a sunny Clos de Vougeot, something a little less sinister, but, well, *chacun à son goût*. And when your other friend arrived, Dom Pérignon. A magnum. Memorable, indeed. Yes, of course. Excellent. Still, I do not understand … unless you drank more than your share, Detective."

Morgan led her out into the main dining room. "Let's get Spivak on this. He can arrange a sketch, maybe, of the third man, from the waiter."

"I want to talk to him."

"The waiter? Okay."

They stood in the middle of the room, watching people cleaning up from the luncheon crowd, preparing for dinner.

"Does it look familiar?" Morgan asked.

"Yes."

"Okay," he said, surprised, "what do you remember?"

"Dancing with my father —"

"What?"

"I remember dancing with my father. We came here, just before my teens, a year before he died."

"Really."

"Mart Kenny was playing. I think he played here for years. My dad always wanted to see Mart Kenny and His Western Gentlemen, we heard him on the radio. But my mom wouldn't dance with him. She could dance really well but she didn't think he could, so he danced with me."

"Was it the same?"

"As now? It feels like it was, but, you know, memory is fickle. No, I don't remember being here with Philip. I don't know, Morgan, it all seems familiar."

She paused.

"The other man. He came before the Champagne … which is a perfect drink to conceal knock-out drops."

"You could have been drugged before you got here."

"Morgan, apparently I didn't come in staggering … and it seems like I made quite a show when I left."

They saw the maître d' beckoning them from the side of the room. He pointed toward the kitchen.

"He just came in. Giovanni."

They walked through the kitchen to a staff lounge. A tall, lean man with residual acne glanced at them and away, then again. He recognized them as police. Miranda and Morgan both knew instantly that his name was not Giovanni. There was no one else in the room. The man stood upright, confronting them, not belligerently but not intimidated.

"Where you from?" asked Morgan.

"Sienna."

"You speak Italian, then? I speak Italian."

The man's eyes narrowed. "Yeah," he said, "I do."

Miranda smiled. Morgan's bluff was being called.

"Go ahead," said Morgan. "Speak."

"What do you want?" said the man.

"What's your name?"

"Giovanni."

"When it's not Giovanni, what's your name?"

The man shrugged. "Malouf. Iqbal."

"Which?"

"Iqbal Malouf, that's my name."

"You illegal?" asked Morgan.

"A little."

"How's that?" said Miranda.

"My visa ran out."

"Recently?" she asked.

"Eight years ago. I'm married, I've got a kid. He's a Canadian, in school."

"Your wife?"

"Illegal. Lebanese, same as me. We met here."

"At the hotel?"

"Yeah."

"Have you ever seen me before?" asked Miranda.

"Sure, three-four nights ago, table by the wall. Dom Pérignon. You got drunk."

"Did you know I was a cop?"

"No. You were some guy's date."

Miranda flinched. "And the others?"

"The guy who brought you, I don't know. He was smooth, I'd say computers, maybe a stock analyst. Too calm for a broker. A tax lawyer, maybe."

"Well, thank you," said Miranda. "And the other one?"

"Never saw him before. Never saw any of you before."

"What can you tell us about him, the third person?" asked Morgan.

"Nothing."

"Think."

"Nothing."

"We're not with Immigration."

"Oh, come on, man. I didn't see anything. He was just a guy. Mid-thirties, well dressed. He didn't pay. The other guy paid, the guy who brought her."

"Me," said Miranda, exasperated with having to establish her presence again. "We came together, he didn't bring me."

"He paid. Big tip. Not too big, big enough."

"The third person, the other guy, tell us more?"

"There's nothing more."

"Immigration ..." said Morgan.

"He was Lebanese."

"Good," said Morgan. "How do you know? Did you know him?"

"No, he's not from here. I'd have seen him around. Ethnics, you know, we stick together."

"How do you know he was Lebanese?" Morgan repeated.

"I speak the language. I know."

"Did the other guy speak Lebanese?"

"No, the Lebanese guy, he just said a few words. To me."

"He knew you were Lebanese?"

"He knew I wasn't Giovanni. I was just part of the ambiance, man. We didn't have a relationship."

"You've never seen him before?"

"Like I said."

"Thanks for your help," said Miranda. "Do you think you could give the police artist a description?"

"Yeah," said the man. "But it would, you know, be generic. He just looked like a prosperous Lebanese guy about my age in good condition."

"Did you go to university?" said Miranda.

"Yes, in Beirut, engineering."

"Get legal," she said. "Do what you're trained for."

"I make more money as a waiter," he said with a shrewd grin. He smiled. "So you're not going to turn me in?"

"No," said Morgan.

"Thanks, man. Yeah, and he wore a big ring."

"A big ring?"

"Like a sports ring, like if he won the Stanley Cup or the Boston Marathon."

"A lot of gold, no diamond," said Miranda.

"Yeah, like that."

"We'll be in touch," said Morgan.

3

Strange Bedfellows

Morgan telephoned Miranda in mid-evening to see how she was doing. She was touched and a little irritated by his concern. It was warm but she was wearing flannel pajamas, purple moose printed on white. Morgan was in boxer shorts, which he wore as pajamas, and a T-shirt from Home Hardware.

"You want me to come over?" he said.

"I'm watching *Buffy* reruns."

"The Vampire Slayer? Good grief."

"It's not hepatitis, it's postmodern."

"Postmodernism is over, Miranda. Before anyone figured out what it was. "

"You watch *Survivor*."

"For the organized spontaneity."

"Have you ever watched *Buffy*?"

"Not without feeling guilty."

"For what, Morgan? Sex and death, short skirts?"

"You wouldn't understand."

They bantered for a while, then Morgan signed off and returned to his book, letting Miranda get back for the closing credits of the best show on television; she admired the moral complexity.

It is a lot easier to be right than good, in a world where irony is how things actually are.

Morgan was reading wine books. He was trying to find information on Philip Carter's Châteauneuf-du-Pape. Even Hugh Johnson didn't list it.

The label was puzzling. Like the better French wines, it stated in small print, *Mis en bouteille au château*, and there was a pen-and-ink sketch of a generic chateau. The *agent exclusif* was Baudrillard et fils, Avignon, but the chateau was not actually named. The odd spelling on the label, ChâteauNeuf, one word, capital C capital N, was peculiar, but led nowhere. The vintage was signified on a separate neck label, 1996.

It was not one of those frou-frou bottles, with the glass melted into a languorous shape, covered with fake dust as if it had been mouldering deep in the cellars for an age, like some of the more urgently marketed Châteauneuf-du-Pape found in upscale wine stores throughout Canada and the States. It was a fine wine, presented in a bottle as sleek and muscular as the wine it contained.

The grapes were unidentifiable. The wine was a blend of the pliant and the austere, sun-rich from the stony hardscrabble southern landscape, suitably named for the doughty popes of Avignon who made it their favourite drink.

Having been opened for three days, it was beginning to take on a madeirized note, but Morgan swirled a bit in his glass and found the air cleaned it up.

Suddenly, he recognized a taste, a hint on the nose, of something strange but familiar. Not Châteauneuf-du-Pape, something else. At a wine tasting once, a blind tasting, they had been given a mystery wine. No one guessed it, and it turned out to be a Cabernet Sauvignon from Lebanon, with just a touch of Merlot to soften it, and, if he remembered right, a bit of Cabernet Franc for the spice.

Morgan had attended a couple of tastings organized by the Opimian Society but found them frustrating because, while he had the nose to appreciate the flourishes in their esoteric discussions, he lacked the resources to buy their selections. He was sufficiently discriminating that he remembered the mystery wine. That pleased him.

Miranda was searching a long shot on the news of black-bearded men thronging the streets of, she wasn't sure where, angry and relieved there wasn't a woman in sight, when she was startled by a knock at the door. It must be Morgan; he had slipped by the security door without buzzing. She was pleased. She knew right now he needed her as much as she needed him. *It's funny*, she thought, *how men feel violated when someone close to them has been damaged*. It was flattering but oppressive, like they should be able to control the world.

She opened the door.

A young woman stared through her, wavered, then collapsed. Her legs splayed awkwardly to the side so that it was difficult for Miranda to drag her inside. Miranda knew she wasn't dead, not even dying. She recognized the kind of emotional exhaustion she had seen before when someone has witnessed a brutal crime against a loved one, a child or partner. Sometimes they collapse when an ally approaches to share the pain.

Miranda closed the door. The woman lay on the floor, very still. Her blond hair fanned over the hardwood, although her face rested against the scatter-rug that had bunched up under her head and shoulders. She was wearing a grey skirt and a designer T-shirt; bare legs, sandals, not a lot of make-up, well-manicured nails, clean hair, no rings, a thin gold chain around her neck, wrist wrapped around the strap of a voluminous Monica Lewinsky handbag. Her eyes were glazed, unblinking, and vacant.

Miranda stepped back. She had never seen the woman before in her life.

As she squatted down beside her, her white flannel pajamas imprinted with grazing moose struck her as weird.

"Have we met before?" she said.

No response, but the woman was conscious.

"Hey," she said, gently shaking the woman's shoulder, "do you know me?"

Miranda felt a strange surge of empathy.

"Come on," she said, trying to get a grip on the woman to help her up. "Let's get you comfortable, then we'll introduce ourselves. No? Okay."

Miranda lowered the woman's head gently against the rug and walked back into the living room. She sat on the sofa so she could see into the hallway, where the woman lay very still, breathing softly. She got up and went into the kitchen and poured herself a straight Scotch, single malt. She sat down again on the sofa, contemplating her guest.

"Can I get you anything?" she called, feeling ridiculous. After a long pause, she added, "If you want to talk, you know...."

Miranda tried to think clearly. *If I wasn't traumatized by recent events in my life, what would I be doing now? What* should *I be doing?*

She got up and walked closer as a pool of water spread slowly from under the young woman onto the hardwood.

"Oh jeez," Miranda exclaimed. "You can't pee there."

With the strength of propriety, she lifted under the young woman's torso, hunkered down, swung a limp arm over her own shoulders, and hauled her to the bathroom, the woman's legs dragging behind, inscribing a wet trail on the floor.

Miranda was shaken. She had been confident the woman was in shock of some sort and would snap out of it. Now she wasn't so sure. Then she decided the urination wasn't from poison or drugs but a natural release of the muscles, as if the woman had found safe refuge after a sustained surge of adrenalin and her body relaxed beyond appropriate limits. *It could be worse*, thought Miranda.

It did not occur to her to call the police; she *was* the police. It did not even cross her mind to call her partner. This was personal, something she had to deal with herself. That seemed logical at the moment — just the two women, both victims in a baffling and hostile world.

Miranda slid a bath towel under the woman's body, folded another, and put it under her head. Then she sat down on the floor beside her, leaning against the cool porcelain tub, and drew her knees up against her chest. She reached over and with the back of one hand gently brushed the woman's blond hair away from her face.

Her eyes flickered and for a moment Miranda thought they were beckoning to her, trying to make contact, but they went dull again.

Miranda got up, switched on the heat-lamp and fan, and resumed her position, as if she were keeping vigil. With the overhead on as well, the light in the room was tinged with amber and the rumbling of the fan filled the air with a brittle noise, like wind over dry grass.

The young woman — Miranda could see she was not a girl, she must have been in her mid to late twenties — looked radiant in the amber light, but she lay very still, almost like a corpse on display at a wake, except she was turned to one side and breathing.

Miranda touched her again on the forehead then let her fingers drift over her cheek, finding reassurance in the warmth of her flesh. Miranda stared at the woman's blue eyes, waiting for a person to appear in their depths, someone who could explain what was happening to both of them.

The web was a last resort. Morgan preferred books for such an inquiry; he wanted to turn the pages of wine books and revel in the graphic design of grapes and landscape among blocks of text in a pleasing variety of fonts. But nothing he owned showed a listing for Baudrillard et fils in Avignon or anywhere else. Nothing for a Châteauneuf-du-Pape called simply that, ChâteauNeuf-du-Pape. He realized in a satisfying small revelation that this might be its name, the Ninth Château; there was no break between Château and Neuf and there was a cap on the N. Or perhaps Neuf simply meant New and was nothing more than an aberrant spelling.

There was nothing on the Net.

This was a quandary not unrelated to the strange death of Philip Carter. It was Carter's bottle — he had to have bought it somewhere. It must have an origin, however obscure. He thought about Carter's Lebanese friend and felt a wave of revulsion sweep through his gut, but he could not conjure a connection between the hint of Lebanon in the wine and the man who assaulted Miranda.

Rising from the sofa, Morgan smacked his shin against a painted wood chest he used as an end table. It was precariously stacked with books and magazines so that its dimensions were illusory, and when he hit it a number of them clattered to the floor. While on his hands and knees to retrieve them, the faded black-stencilled lettering caught his eye. *S. Sutter, 1789.* This was on a field of thick green paint, worn and cracked by time into a lustrous patina.

Morgan paused and ran his fingers over the letters. After his parents died, when he had retrieved the chest from the shed that his mother called the summer kitchen in the home they rented all their lives in old Cabbagetown, he used it to pack the few possessions they had worth keeping, and then only for sentimental value. This was when Cabbagetown was still a slum, before it became urban chic. These were the sole remnants of his childhood among the working poor.

This was also the beginning of his interest in country antiques. When he got the painted pine box home and cleaned it up, he discovered the stencilling. After a bit of research he found it was a woman's dower chest built in the Niagara Peninsula, probably Welland County, Bertie Township, and that it had belonged to

Sarah Sutter, who married Jacob Haun in 1794. The Sutters were Loyalists during the American Revolution. Sarah's father, having served fourteen months imprisonment in New Jersey for his British sympathies before coming to the Niagara area in the summer of 1785, was refused compensation; it was judged that "he had not come within the British lines" *during* hostilities, but only afterwards in hope of recompense.

Morgan sat back on the floor, staring at the box. Why was he thinking about this? Why was he rehearsing in his mind the facts he had dug up about an antique hope chest?

He trusted his own discursiveness; it sometimes led to intuitive leaps where unlikely connections, once made, would suddenly seem inevitable.

Was it the chest itself, with the traditional bracket base, the rural Pennsylvania Chippendale coping, the austere slab face with its tiny lock opening, the thick, worn paint, or was it Sarah Sutter, whose father established Sutter's Mill in early Toronto before the American invasion? No, it was Niagara. Something about Niagara.

Morgan got up from the floor and wandered distractedly into his kitchen, where the ChâteauNeuf-du-Pape stood open on the counter. He poured himself two fingers in a brandy snifter and swirled it vigorously, then held it to his nose and inhaled a deep draught of the pungent aroma, redolent with sunbaked soil and ripe fruit.

As he closed his eyes to savour the smell of the wine, wheels clicked into place like a slot machine coming up with a winning set. Lebanon and Niagara, unexpected locales for the origin of fine wines, and a mysterious wine labelled as ChâteauNeuf-du-Pape but not from the Avignon region — these connected.

He had heard of the millions to be made in counterfeit wines but he had never taken the rumours seriously. Not because he did not think such things happened but because it seemed a frivolous crime, relatively harmless to all except those willing to pay exorbitant prices for exquisite small pleasures.

Suddenly, he envisioned Miranda's assailants as operatives in an international conspiracy of epic malevolence, concerned with illicit wine trade on a major scale.

He knew of a twenty-four hour wine merchant in Rochester who had the best fine wine offerings in the northeast. He called and got an assistant manager who assured him, yes, they did carry ChâteauNeuf-du-Pape, some very good vintages, and could give a reasonable discount by the case, along with a lower invoice, if required, to offset excessive Canadian tariffs.

Miranda heard the telephone ring. She was still sitting on the bathroom floor. She had been there for four or five hours. She could remember time expanding as if she were an observer watching two women, neither of whom seemed familiar.

Post-traumatic stress disorder; the observing Miranda knew about such things and even thought it might be an appropriate term, perhaps for both women. It didn't mean anything — it was not a diagnosis, it was a description.

She could envision Morgan on the other end of the line giving his Clint Eastwood scowl, which would shift too quickly into a sly Kevin Spacey grin and then, because no one was answering, his face would collapse into a Jack Nicholson sneer or a Mel Gibson smirk, or, if he could muster it, a blue-eyed Paul Newman smile, even though his eyes were deep brown.

No, that sequence would be if he thought she was in bed with her lover. He would have another set of faces for this, whatever was happening now.

He doesn't know how he looks, she thought. *Maybe nobody does.* For the most part he was stone-faced, displaying only the subtlest nuances of character, like all the great screen actors. Some people thought he was cold. Others thought he was cool.

He was only forty-two, but she never thought of him in terms of young actors like Ewan McGregor or Brad Pitt. They had not yet done enough in their lives to transcend the roles they played. And never like Al Pacino, De Niro, or Hoffman, who were inseparable from their roles.

The phone kept ringing in a monotonous jangle, like a giant insect blindly searching its prey.

Morgan was childish, sometimes, but only with her. He would recite bits of nursery rhymes or schoolyard jingles, sometimes delightfully, absurdly obscene, always inappropriate, although he almost never swore. *You can take the boy out of the schoolyard,* she thought, *but …*

Time passed, and she could hear voices and a key rattling in her door.

Then Morgan was beside her. The building caretaker who let him in had gone back to bed. Morgan touched her, and she touched the blond woman's cheek.

"Hello, Morgan," she said.

"My goodness, it stinks in here," said Morgan.

"I'm okay," she said. "You were going to ask if I'm okay. I'm okay. This is my friend, she's okay."

"You're not," said Morgan. "I'm going to call an ambulance."

Suddenly, as if she had been slapped in the face or jarred with defibrillators, Miranda returned to herself.

"Morgan! No ambulance, no cops." She placed her hand around the back of his neck and drew herself upward as he rose to his feet.

"My God," she said. "I'm stiff."

"And who is this?" said Morgan. "You're both filthy."

"I'm okay, Morgan. I'm okay. Let's get cleaned up here."

Morgan turned on the shower and in a surreal, almost balletic sequence of movements, he and Miranda got the young woman into the streaming water, where Miranda, still in her pajamas, stripped off the woman's soiled clothes and handed them out to Morgan, who tossed them in the tub and then went for a bathrobe, which they wrapped around the young woman, who appeared conscious of what they were doing but did nothing to assist. He took her into the bedroom and spread her out on top of the sheets, noticing there was still residue around her wrists, possibly from duct tape, then he returned to assist Miranda, who was tangled trying to get out of her drenched moose-grazing flannel pajamas. He helped her into and out of the shower then towelled her off before wrapping her in a clean white beach towel and leading her into the bedroom to sit on the edge of the bed beside her erstwhile companion.

"Why are you here?" said Miranda ingenuously, implying it was a pleasant thing to have him drop in, but a bit of an intrusion.

"I wanted to talk about wine. When I called, there was no answer — who is this? She obviously needs help? So do you —"

"And you're here, Morgan. She came to me, I'm the help she was looking for. We'll help each other, Morgan. How can I help you? You want to know about wine? You're the expert, but I'll tell you what I can."

"Miranda ..."

"She came to me, Morgan, because she needs me. Philip sent her."

"Philip!"

"I know he's dead. I'm not confused. But she's a link between him and the man who killed us, killed him."

"How do you know?"

"Statistics. Logic. How often does a discombobulated blond turn up at your door, how often does a corpse turn up in your bed? Both extremely unlikely. The chances of these two events happening in the same week to the same person, astronomically unlikely. Ergo, it's magic, or there's a causal connection."

"We've got to call Spivak, see what he can make of her. We've got to get her to a doctor. Does she talk?"

"Call Ellen Ravenscroft."

"What?"

"Call Ellen Ravenscroft, she's a doctor.

"She's a coroner, this woman's alive —"

"Morgan, are you with me on this? She came to me. Not to the police, not to the hospital, she came to me."

Morgan reached out and felt her forehead. Miranda leaned against the pressure of his hand. He stood up, and bending over her, he lowered her back onto the bed beside her new friend, who had closed her eyes and seemed to be asleep. Miranda closed her eyes as well and drifted off as he watched her.

He wandered out into the living room and down the

hallway. The floor was sticky with drying urine. He got a sponge-mop from the kitchen, dampened it with a little water and some vinegar from under the sink, and cleaned the floor from the hall through to the bathroom. He put the mop away after rinsing it and stood in the bedroom doorway, surveying the strange scene of the two women asleep on the bed.

He started back to the living room, then turned and taking a light blanket from the back of a chair, he covered the sleeping women, tucking the blanket close around them as if they might catch a chill, even though the night air was seasonably balmy. Through an open window he could hear the ambient hush of the city.

When the security door buzzed, he let Ravenscroft in without checking to see who it was. She had been surprisingly cheerful when his call wakened her. He met her at the door.

"Thanks," he said softly.

"You're welcome," she said. "Where is she? And there's no point in whispering, we'll have to wake her up anyway."

Ellen walked into the bedroom and flicked on the overhead. "My God!" she said. "There are two of them?"

Morgan had not told her about the stranger. He had said Miranda seemed to be suffering from post-trauma shock and had asked for Ellen by name.

Miranda stirred, and without opening her eyes mumbled, "Hello, Ellen Ravenscroft."

"Hello, Miranda Quin. And who are we in bed with this time?"

Miranda's eyes flashed open. She glared at the medical examiner, then shut them again and smiled. "She's my friend."

"And what's your friend's name?"

"I don't know."

"Can your friend talk? I think she's awake. Are you awake, Miranda's friend?"

The woman's blue eyes flickered then stayed open, clear but expressionless. Ellen pulled back the blanket and scowled at the strange array of bathrobe and towel covering the two women.

"I gather this was your doing," she said to Morgan.

"Yeah," he said.

"Very gentlemanly, Morgan. Very modest. But perhaps a sheet would have been enough. It's sweltering under there. You go on out to the living room and I'll see what I can do with these two. Come on, love," she said to Miranda. "We'll start with you. Up you get."

As Morgan left the room, the M.E. was struggling to get Miranda mobile. From the living room he could hear thumping and bumping but could not imagine what, exactly, was going on.

After a surprisingly short time, Miranda and Ellen emerged from the bedroom with the stranger between them. Ellen had dressed both in baggy sweatshirts and pajama bottoms. Morgan got up and Ellen helped the two women to the sofa, where they sat side by side, both looking dazed as if they had just woken from a long sleep.

"I've checked them over," said Ellen, addressing Morgan as if the women were not there. "Miranda's fine. I mean physically. They both are. I think we might try a tranquillizer."

"I don't do tranquillizers," Miranda snapped.

"But then again, perhaps we won't try a tranquillizer," said Ellen, pausing, "on either of them. Goldilocks here is in deep shock. She may have been sedated, but everything's working fine. I'd feel better getting her to a hospital —"

"No hospital," said Miranda.

"— or not. I don't think she's in any danger. I don't think either of them are."

"I think we're both in danger," said Miranda.

"If someone was trying to kill you — " said Morgan.

"— we'd be dead."

"Did you check her bag?" Ellen asked.

"No," said Morgan. "What bag?"

"In the hall," said Ellen. "It's not Miranda's."

"Not my taste," Miranda explained.

"And I figured it's not yours, Morgan. Therefore, it must be Miranda's new best friend's. It's blond-appropriate."

Miranda smiled.

Morgan retrieved the bag from the floor of the hall. He brought it back into the living room and set it on the glass-topped coffee table. All three women leaned forward, anxious to see what was inside. Morgan realized this was the first sign the stranger had shown of interest in anything not bottled up in her own skull.

He pulled out a gun, dangling it carefully from the trigger guard. He sniffed it then set it down gingerly on the glass.

"It's been fired," he said. "Fairly recently."

He removed item after item from the bag, setting each on the table in a random display. Mostly it was cosmetics and toiletries. There was a wallet and change purse, both empty. In the shadowy depths at the bottom was a large crumpled-up wad of used tissues.

Morgan turned to the young woman. "What's your name?" he asked. They were stunned when she responded.

"I think Michelle," she said. Her cobalt-blue eyes began to take on personality, as if she were finding her way inside toward the light.

"How do you know Miranda?" he asked.

Her eyes flicked in Miranda's direction but she said nothing.

"What happened?" Morgan asked, speaking in a voice intended to project gentle authority. "Where'd you come from, why are you here? What's your last name, Michelle?"

She directed a conspiratorial glance at Miranda. "I'm tired," she said, trying to get up from the sofa. "I'd like to sleep."

"Me too," said Miranda, rising and helping the young woman. "Thanks for coming, Ellen. I'll call you in the morning. Night, night."

She began to lead the woman who called herself Michelle into the bedroom.

Morgan stopped them. "What's going on?" he said.

Miranda looked into his eyes, asking for patience. "Will you stay?" she said. "Sleep on the sofa?"

"I think I killed a man," said the strange young woman.

"We'll talk in the morning," said Miranda.

She looked at Morgan and shook her head slowly, as if to acknowledge her friend was delusional. Morgan walked Ellen to the door as the other two women went into the bedroom.

"What the hell was that?" said Ellen. "She killed someone?"

"I don't think so, I don't know."

"She's been through something major. You should get her downtown."

"Yeah. I want Miranda in better shape when we do. It's not going to change anything, letting them sleep."

"They're not friends, you know, Morgan."

"I know, but Miranda needs her, and they seem to connect. I'll be right here."

"You want me to stay?"

"No, I'm fine. Thanks for coming. I'll call when we get this sorted out."

"Good luck. You all right?"

"Fine, just fine."

"G'night love," she said, leaning forward and kissing him on both cheeks. She walked out, pulling the door shut behind her.

Morgan went back to the glass coffee table and picked up the Lewinsky-esque bag. It still felt heavy. He prodded the large clump of soiled tissues at the bottom with a ballpoint then turned the bag up and emptied it over the table. A wad emerged slowly, breaking free from where it had adhered to the inside of the bag, and then rapidly unravelled across the glass, a flurry the colour of diluted blood.

Morgan's eyes focused on the massive gold ring before his mind could grasp that he was looking at a severed human hand. Unmistakably male. He was surprised at how cleanly it had been cut away at the wrist and how little blood there was at the stump end. He was surprised at how well-manicured the nails

appeared, with their cuticles neatly done, the edges
evenly curved.

They were sitting in an anteroom of the psychiatric ward
of a hospital. Outside, they could see rooftops of other
hospitals that lined University Avenue in a stalwart display
of public health-service efficiency. It was mid-morning,
the June sky a radiant blue with cotton clouds hovering
in random swatches as if smog were only a rumour.

Miranda listened as Spivak berated Morgan with
enough exaggerated indignation to make it obvious he
was not actually angry, just frustrated.

"You sat there! You sat there all bloody night long,
staring at a bloody disembodied hand. With a smoking
gun on the table. With a homicidal amnesiac. You didn't
call in? What the hell were you thinking? They needed
their beauty sleep?"

"Yeah," said Morgan.

"Did you nod off yourself, is that what happened, did
you stretch out and you were so goddamned laid back
you fell asleep?"

"Yeah," said Morgan.

"Morgan," said Miranda.

"No, I didn't. I was thinking."

"You and your goddamned thinking —"

"You should try it," said Miranda.

"Thank you, Detective," said Spivak, turning to
Miranda. "You're quite alert after a good night's rest."

A doctor came through locked double doors and
approached Spivak's partner. They talked and Eeyore
Stritch walked over to the others by the window.

"She's fine," he said. "They're going to release her after lunch."

"She doesn't know who she is," Morgan exclaimed.

"Can't arrest her for that," said Spivak, joining them at the window. "But for a severed hand in her handbag, we could hold her for that."

"On what charge?" said Miranda.

"Committing an indignity on human remains," said Eeyore Stritch.

"We don't know if the rest of the guy's dead," said Morgan. "Maybe he gave it to her. Chopped it off as a keepsake."

"Yeah, well, I'll want to know where she is," said Spivak. "Don't lose her."

"She's not with us, she's not ours," said Morgan.

"She is now."

"We're running the prints on the hand," said Eeyore Stritch. "So far, nothing local, not in Canada. We're running a DNA comparison, too, to see if there's any connection with your guy, Miranda."

"Which one?" said Miranda.

Morgan said, "What about her prints?"

"We're running them as well."

"And the gun?" said Miranda.

"No, well, we should hold her on that," said Spivak. He hacked repeatedly into a handkerchief then continued. "It's illegal, carrying a discharged weapon, concealed."

"It wasn't concealed," said Miranda.

"It was in her purse."

"Yeah."

"That's concealed."

"Debatable," said Miranda. "What about prints? Were there bullets?"

"On the gun? No prints —"

"Why would she wipe it clean, then put it back in her purse?"

"And no bullets, it was empty."

"You don't even know how recently it was fired."

"She's not licensed."

"You don't know that," said Miranda. "Her ID is missing."

"It's not registered."

"So the gun is illegal, she's not. You saw her wrists, somebody duct taped her wrists. She was a victim."

"Detective," said Spivak, "we're not charging her with anything yet. You two keep an eye on her. Morgan's still on the force —"

"I'm suspended, not fired."

"We'll come back for her," said Morgan.

"Whatever. Keep in touch." Spivak nodded to Eeyore Stritch and the two of them sauntered down a corridor leading to the elevator, leaving Morgan and Miranda facing each other in silence.

After a time, Miranda got up and paced around the room, then returned to sit beside Morgan.

"Why didn't you call in last night?"

He shrugged.

"Why not? What were you thinking?"

He grinned. "You needed rest."

"Why, really?"

"I'm not sure." He stretched awkwardly against the hospital settee so that he could reach into a side pocket of his pants. He pulled something out, clutched in his fist. Holding his hand out toward her, he slowly unclenched his fingers. Lying in his palm was the massive gold ring. Slowly he closed his fingers over it and started to slide it back into his pocket, then changed his mind and held it out to Miranda. She held it in her cupped fingers, hefted it as if testing for weight, then dropped it into her purse.

4

The Winery

Morgan signed out a car but Miranda was driving. They sped along the Queen Elizabeth Way. Traffic was light; it was early afternoon. Morgan leaned around from the passenger seat, straining his safety belt to address the blond woman in the back.

"You remember me, do you?" he said. "From last night."

"Yes, of course," she said. "You were at Miranda's place."

"And what about you, why were you at Miranda's place?"

"I don't know. I don't know how I know her name."

"How did you get there?"

"I don't know. Where are we going?"

"Do you recognize where we are?"

"Yes, sure. We're on the QEW on the way to Niagara."

Morgan glanced over at Miranda, who registered with a rise of her eyebrows that the woman calling herself Michelle did not say Hamilton but Niagara. Most people would say Hamilton; Niagara was down the escarpment, the landscape leading to the Falls. Only someone familiar with the area would call the highway the QEW and see it as the route to Niagara.

Morgan had waited in the car outside the hospital while Miranda went in to take charge of the young woman. They did not want to intimidate her, but when she got in the car she casually acknowledged him and settled back comfortably, prepared to be driven wherever her custodians might take her. Her blue eyes seemed clear and very dark inside the car; her pupils dilated to bring the interior into focus.

When she looked out the window to take inventory, her eyes became lighter, the colour of chicory by the roadside. She was hauntingly beautiful, Morgan thought. But she did not seem to have nightmares bottled inside; rather, she seemed almost empty.

"You sure you're all right to drive?" he said, turning to Miranda. "I don't mind."

"Morgan, I'm fine. Where are we going?"

"I told you I talked to Millennium Wines in Rochester last night. I called back this morning and got Forrest Sherwood, the owner. Seriously, that's his name. He buys the Châteauneuf from a wholesaler in Buffalo. The wholesaler told me he buys only from reputable importers. But in this case he has a numbered company to deal with. Turns out it's registered in the Bahamas. Dead end to the paper trail. Only when I told the Buffalo wholesaler I was a homicide cop, we leapfrogged into real memory — he recalled having seen the guy who usually drives delivery. Unmarked truck, that's not uncommon. A jobber. But he said the driver works for Bonnydoon, a boutique winery near Niagara-on-the-Lake."

"That's a boutique town," said Michelle from behind them. "It's cute, like a life-sized miniature."

"Yeah," said Morgan, "so I hear."

"And we're on our way to check out Bonnydoon?" Miranda asked.

"We are."

"Is Sherwood Forrest going to change the name of his store?"

"What are you talking about?"

"Millennium Wines. Now that 2001 is here, even the mathematical purists have to admit we're in a new millennium."

"Did you ever see the movie?"

"What, Kubrick's *2001*? Yes, I had a crush on Keir Dullea, no, on Hal, on the disembodied voice. I found it very erotic."

"You are strange," said Morgan and turned to the woman in the back seat.

"Why Michelle?"

"What do you mean?"

"It's not your name, why Michelle?"

"How do you know?"

"You split the syllables. If it was your real name, it'd be worn, you'd slur it together."

"Really? Then what is my name?"

"Why Michelle?"

"It's from *Buffy*."

"What!"

"Sarah Michelle Gellar, she plays the slayer."

"You watch that, too?" Miranda exclaimed over her shoulder.

"And you can remember who plays which, in relation to

what, but you don't know your own name?" said Morgan.

"I seem to have been traumatized in a highly selective way, Detective."

The Bonnydoon Winery turned out to be mostly warehouses, storage sheds, and a private airstrip running between rows of vines. Set back against the escarpment, looming over the modest vineyard, was a rambling house of extravagant proportions designed for a mountainside on Vancouver Island or the California coastline. Lots of glass, cement columns, cedar beams.

There was no one around when they pulled up in front of a shed marked THE OFFICE. For a few minutes they sat in the car.

"Just what is it we're looking for?" asked Miranda.

Morgan released his seatbelt and turned to the woman in the back seat.

"Does this look familiar?"

She seemed subdued but not frightened. "Maybe," she said. "I remember an airplane."

"Were you on it?"

She closed her eyes. "I can hear it, I can't see anything."

"Come on, let's look around."

The three of them got out and stood together near the front of the car, waiting for someone to come out of the office or down from the house.

Michelle leaned against Miranda, but Miranda edged away so she had to stand on her own. The young woman closed her eyes and her nostrils twitched. She opened her eyes.

"I've been here. I recognize the smells. Turned earth,

gasoline, sulphur, sun-heat on cedar, stewed fruit, gravel, gunpowder, damp cement."

"My goodness," said Morgan. "You're a wine taster by trade."

"You think so?" said Michelle.

Miranda cocked her nose, trying to differentiate the smells. She had no doubt Morgan was right. For Miranda the various odours ran together in a blur. For Michelle it seemed like a DNA code of the place.

"I've been here," she repeated. "I remember a small plane. I remember feeling my stomach pitch, I was on board. I must have been blindfolded. I can hear the engine, I can feel the vibration. I can hear shouting over the engine noise."

She sat down unceremoniously on the gravel drive with an inelegant and childlike lurch. She was dressed in new clothes that Miranda had bought for her at a funky shop on Yonge Street just over from the hospital. She had insisted on wearing a skirt, although Miranda had provided her with slacks as well. She wore a T-shirt that proclaimed the beauties of Toronto and displayed the CN Tower like a soaring phallic icon rising hard by the clam-shaped SkyDome. Miranda had not shaken it out to see the design when she bought it. She bought three the same, in different colours. The clothes were Miranda's size. The skirt fit perfectly. The T-shirt was tight.

"What?" said Miranda, leaning down. "Michelle?"

"I'm trying to remember. My name is Elke."

"Elke?"

"I am from Stockholm. I have been speaking English since I was a small child. I studied wine in London and New York. I was here last night."

Morgan was surprised, not that she had been here before but that she was Swedish. He prided himself on a good ear for dialects and accents. Once she had explained, he could detect a slight Scandinavian lilt, but so vague it might be generational, something picked up from an immigrant parent or even a grandparent.

"What else do you remember?" said Morgan.

She did not respond. Morgan and Miranda helped her to her feet. They walked over to the office and Morgan tried the door. It was locked. He gave it a loud thump but there was no response.

"Let's walk," he said. The three of them would have appeared from a distance to be strolling arm in arm. In fact, Miranda and Morgan were supporting the young woman, whose body seemed to be reacting to memory fragments at a visceral level that her mind could not deal with, aroused apparently by the smells and perhaps ambient sounds of her surroundings. Sometimes she would shut her eyes and nearly swoon, so they had to brace her upright, and then she would try to stride out as if they were holding her back.

By the end of the runway, near the open-sided aerodrome, they wheeled and then walked back to the first of the warehouses. The sliding door was ajar. They slipped into the gloom inside and stood still for a moment, waiting for their eyes to adjust to the muted light.

There were a series of vast cement cisterns down the centre and large fibreglass tanks or casks stacked high along both side walls.

"Not here," said the young woman suddenly and marched out the open door, with Morgan and Miranda trailing behind.

"What's not there?" asked Miranda.

"That's where they mix their wines. I wasn't in there."

"Mix?" Morgan asked, struck by what seemed an odd term.

"Yes. The casks were filled with a Cabernet blend from Lebanon, I imagine."

"Are you sure?"

"Yes, I'm sure. And the cement vats, that's where they're mixing the Lebanese import with local wines."

"Is that legal?" asked Miranda.

"I don't know, I'm not from around here. I've never been to Niagara-on-the-Lake. Maybe I saw it on television."

They entered another wine shed, much like the first. The blond woman's nose twitched. She walked around like a cat sidestepping unseen obstacles, catching odours hovering in layers and channels as she slowly passed through them. Miranda and Morgan watched.

She returned to their side. "It doesn't make a lot of sense," she said.

"What?" said Morgan.

"Rhône. They're simulating a Rhône valley blend, the southern Rhône around Avignon. I'd say they've created a Frankenstein monster, an Ontario-Lebanese fake Châteauneuf-du-Pape with the seams and scar tissues disguised."

"Disguised by what?" Morgan was intrigued. If this is what he had been drinking, Carter's ChâteauNeuf-du-Pape, it had seemed superbly blended."

"Chemicals. And a master blender. It's like having perfect pitch, there's not a formula, it's instinct."

"So, if it fools the experts," said Miranda, "then what's the difference?"

"But it doesn't, that's just it. When is a Rembrandt not a Rembrandt? Simple, when it's recognized to be by someone else."

"Well, thank you," said Miranda. "I think there's no doubt you're in the wine trade. It shouldn't be too hard to track you down —"

"When is Elke not Elke?" said Morgan.

The other two ignored him.

The end warehouse was different from the others. It had a loading dock on the side and there were power lines running in, suggesting industrial machinery. On the outside, it had the same asphalt shingle siding. Probably all these buildings had been used for apples and cherries, peaches or pears, before the orchards were torn up to plant vines.

Inside were stainless steel tanks and pipes and a complex of belts and wheels, racks and tracks, for bottling, labelling, packing wine in wooden cases, each clearly stencilled with the imprimatur of Baudrillard et fils, Avignon, designating the contents as ChâteauNeuf-du-Pape, with the vendage, 1996, stamped on neck collars in washed-out ink.

"So this is the set-up," said Morgan, fascinated. He picked up a loose label lying on a bench and examined it closely. It had a serial number in blue ink stamped under the sketch of the generic chateau. "Were these bottles individually numbered?"

"Yes, of course," said the blond woman. "That would confirm their value, especially in the New World, where individuality is at such a high premium."

"What do you think they'd sell for?" asked Miranda.

"Maybe eighty or ninety dollars a bottle, American."

"So, a thousand dollars a case. A thousand cases, a million dollars."

"I would imagine they sold many, many more," said the young woman with authority. "Thousands upon thousands, in the American market — I think if you check out lading bills for Bonnydoon Winery we'll find they exported far more than they could produce from a paltry vineyard like this."

"So why is no one around?" said Miranda.

"I think maybe they've had a shake-up in management," said Morgan.

Michelle, or Elke, as she now chose to be called, walked over and stood near the base of a giant stainless steel vat. She moved a little to one side, as if trying to catch an elusive sound floating in the air. She closed her eyes and opened them several times, then she smiled almost shyly.

"I was right here, I was taped to a chair. Duct tape, I can hear it being stripped from the roll. Nothing over my mouth. My eyes were covered. I didn't scream. I could hear the steel tank, listen, you can hear the faint pulsing of fermentation, no, not fermentation, this would be the final product ready for bottling. You can hear the air pressure against wine on steel … something, I can hear something."

Miranda stood close beside her but could distinguish no sound emanating specifically from the stainless steel.

"My name is Elke Sturmberg. I know everything now. I work in New York. I work for an auction house. I know who I am. I know I was here, strapped in a chair. There is a disconnect. I was in Rochester, then Buffalo, then a small plane, then I was here."

Morgan retrieved a chair from the edge of the scene and set it down beside her. She lowered herself onto the chair with her eyes closed, almost as if she were enacting the role of a clairvoyant. Suddenly she shivered and slumped down in the chair, overwhelmed by her vision.

"What is it?" said Miranda, the sharp rise in her voice betraying her close identification with the woman's overwhelming anxiety.

Elke Sturmberg reached up without opening her eyes and grasped in the air for Miranda's hand. She seemed to be jolted from within by a series of graphic revelations.

Gradually, she sat more upright in her chair. They waited. She opened her eyes and began to speak. "There was screaming. At first I thought it was me. I might have screamed too. No, I was silent, trying to block out the sound. It was penetrating, a man screaming. There was a loud crash, like an axe against wood, then the screaming stopped. I think he passed out."

"And what happened to you?" asked Miranda.

"I waited. I could hear the sounds of a body being dragged."

"What does that sound like?" asked Morgan.

"It just does," she responded. "Breathing, voices, scraping, rustling —"

"Could you make out what they were saying?"

"Not much English. It was another language. Not European, nothing distinguishable."

"And then?" said Miranda.

Elke seemed to retreat inside herself, then flinched. "A shot, there was a gunshot."

"A pistol? The gun you were carrying?" Morgan asked.

"No, a rifle."

"Not a shotgun?" He wondered if she knew the difference.

"A rifle," she said.

"Okay. Then what?"

"A man rubbed his hands all over me."

"How do you know it was a man?"

"You know! He touched my breasts, ran his hand up my skirt —"

"Did you scream?"

"No, I was frozen. Then he stopped."

"Did he go inside your clothes?" Miranda asked. Swabs had been taken in the psychiatric ward, but there was no evidence of sexual assault.

"No. It wasn't — it was, there was something cold about the way he touched me, clinical. Like he was doing a gender inventory. He was detached."

"Did you think you were going to be killed?" Morgan asked.

"No, I did not think I would die. I thought they would hurt me. I wanted to die."

"But instead, what happened?" said Morgan.

The young woman got up and walked around.

"We'd better call in the Provincial Police," said Miranda. "And Spivak, he'll need to know what we're up to."

"What are we up to?" said Morgan.

"Good point," she said.

"No point," said Morgan. "No point in bringing in reinforcements just yet."

Miranda realized, as far as Morgan was concerned, that this was their case.

"Okay," she said. "We've got a villain copping a dispassionate feel, we've got a chopped-off hand, that was the sound of the axe. We've got a rifle shot. What about the pistol? You said it had been fired recently. Maybe not here."

"Sounds of a body being manhandled before the gunshot, not after — is that right, Elke?"

"Yes, it echoed but it was like a dull 'thunk.' I couldn't tell where it was coming from."

"And did you hear clambering?" Morgan asked.

"What?"

"On metal?"

All three of them looked at the steep steps leading up the side of the largest stainless steel tank, following them to the top with their eyes, where they could see a closed hatch.

Miranda was first to start up. The other two stood back. When she got to the top, she leaned down and tried the hatch.

"It'll open," she announced.

She hesitated, then swung the hatch up and reeled back from the fumes bursting free. She squatted down to look in, letting her eyes adjust to the darkness. The tank was half full. She reached around and found a measuring rod, then extended it down until it touched a shadow. As she prodded, the rod broke in half, and the shadow shifted. A dead man's face drifted slowly into the disk of light below her.

She gazed at the corpse turning in the murky darkness, struggling to make sense of her conflicting responses. The stump of a wrist protruding from a shirtsleeve confirmed this was the man with the gold ring. Her assailant, he was dead. But she did not feel vindication or relief, only anger and a vague sense of renewed violation.

"What you got up there?" called Morgan.

There was a large bullet hole in the dead man's forehead. A humane gesture? she wondered. To stop him from drowning? Not through the chest, he would have sunk. Was it to relieve the pain of his amputation? Or was it someone guaranteeing his death? The work of a professional? An expression of contempt? Redundancy born of indifference or hatred?

She stood up and took a deep breath. "I think we'd better call in the appropriate authorities," she said.

"My phone's in the car," said Morgan as she rejoined them on the ground.

"Mine too," she said, "in my purse."

The three of them walked to the door and as Miranda stepped into the sunlight a rifle shot rang out and the wood in the doorframe exploded into splinters at the level of her heart. Morgan reached past Elke and dragged Miranda off balance, back into the tangled shadows as all three lay sprawled on the floor. There was another shot, then another. Then there was a resounding silence as each listened to their own breathing, to the pounding in their chests, as they tried to assimilate what was happening.

Morgan's Glock semi-automatic was at home in the Annex, secure in a locked drawer of his desk. Miranda's was in police custody at Headquarters. They were not used to firing weapons — they were not used to being fired at. Homicide is about dead people, at least the kind of homicide they usually investigated — which were crimes that might draw public attention, murders among the depraved, the very rich, the irretrievably disadvantaged.

"Now what?" said Elke.

Morgan rose to his feet and peered through a slit by the door. "I'd say, given how the bullets hit the frame, they were coming from the direction of the house." There was another explosion and he ducked. A new hole appeared within inches of where his head had been.

"Do you think they know you're the police?" said Elke.

"If they do, I'd say we're just part of the clean-up on their way out the door," said Miranda. "They're closing down business."

"And if they don't?" asked Morgan.

"Well, same thing, I guess."

"Either way," said Morgan, "they'd rather we weren't here."

"I think they'd rather we were dead," said Miranda.

"I don't know," said Morgan. "So far, they're just shooting to announce their presence — and to test for return fire. I suppose if they did want to get rid of us, there'd be room to dump us in there with your —" He stopped. He was about to say glibly, "your friend."

Miranda caught his eye. She smiled and threw him a mock kiss. "Okay," she said. "How're we going to deal with this situation? You're the action figure role model, the testosterone kid. You lead us, Morgan. We'll follow."

"Where's job parity when we need it?"

"You two aren't taking this very seriously," said Elke, sweeping her blond hair away from her face. "You may be used to being shot at, but I'm a civilian."

"I've never been shot at before in my life," said Morgan. "Not intentionally. And I've never shot anyone."

"Great," said the blond. "So am I in charge, then?"

"We'll handle it," said Miranda. "We're just thinking how."

Morgan peered out through the crack, scrunching his face against the wood to get the best view. "They're coming, they definitely want us dead. Three of them. Two are carrying rifles. One's a machine gun of some sort, the other's an assault rifle."

"Oh my God, my God," said Elke.

"Praying, Morgan. Not swearing." Miranda smiled. "You got any ideas?"

"They're stopping at the car, opening the doors. They know it's a cop car. They're looking over here. One's motioning to the others to circle around."

"The back door, is there a back door?" said Miranda.

"Too late," said Morgan.

"No," she said. "Open it." She reached over and took the blond woman by the arm. "Come on," she ordered. "Up here."

Morgan swung the back door ajar, then scrambled up the steel stairs after the two women. Miranda lifted open the hatch in the top of the tank.

"In you go," she said to Elke.

"No."

"You go, Miranda, I'll lower you," said Morgan. Miranda held out her arms to him and he dropped her slowly into the fetid gloom of the tank, letting her go when he could reach no farther. There was a splash and a single cough.

"Okay," she said as she pushed away the dead man, who had been drawn close by her body's displacement of the murky fluid.

Voices outside were closing in fast. Elke grasped Morgan's arms and let herself be lowered until she dropped into the wine, totally immersed before surfacing beside Miranda. They were both sculling to stay afloat.

Morgan swung over the edge, and hanging from one hand he pulled the hatch cover down before letting himself drop beside them in the darkness.

He was just tall enough that his feet reached the bottom, and as they heard the shed door crash open he took one of the women in each arm and held them still with their heads just above the surface.

Suddenly a machine gun shattered the air. Crashing sounds, deafening. The firing was random, in anger. The men out there thought they had escaped through the back door. The machine gun rattled like chains in a bucket, and light holes appeared all around them. The body of the man with the gold ring thrashed about. They could hear wine gushing, splashing, more holes opening up beneath them in small disks of light.

They huddled with the corpse in the bottom of the tank as the wine level dropped to a brackish pool in the bottom, and then the splashing stopped. There was silence, then they could hear the roaring of an engine. A plane was landing or taking off.

Morgan whispered, "I think they're gone. You two all right?"

There was no answer. He shook Miranda. She looked at him in the mottled light and smiled wanly.

"I think I've been hit."

"No!"

"How's Elke?"

The blond was staring at them in stunned disbelief. Then she whispered softly, "I didn't know things like this happened."

"They don't," said Miranda. "Not usually."

Morgan checked her over in the stray shafts of light that seemed to be dancing in the fetid air, so that the stainless steel walls flashed eerily, like the inside of a furnace.

"Flesh wound," he said, looking at the raw tear on her thigh. "You're just grazed, you'll be okay."

"Oh, God," she said. "What a pain. At least it's antiseptic, you know, the wine ..."

"I think we're on fire," said Elke.

Faint columns of smoke were wafting through the holes in the stainless steel.

"We're on fire!" said Morgan. "They've set the shed on fire. Let's go, let's get out of here before we're roasted alive."

"Steamed," said Miranda, correcting him. Inane quips. It was a way of dealing with the adrenalin rush.

"Yeah. Here, I'll have to boost you up. No, your leg — Elke Sturmberg, you get to be hero."

Miranda tried to help brace Morgan as the other woman shinnied up over his shoulders.

"I see England, I see France," said Morgan.

"Morgan!" Miranda snapped. "This is serious."

His head poked out away from Elke's skirt.

"I am serious, damnit." He shifted his attention to the woman on his shoulders. "Reach. It pushes up, no straight up. Give it a whack. Another."

"I can't reach, Morgan."

"Hang on," said Morgan. "Miranda, steady me."

Smoke was streaming in through the holes, and rays of bright yellow light danced against the walls and over their saturated clothes and wine-drenched flesh.

Morgan leaned against Miranda and stepped up onto the corpse, which let out a grisly moan.

"I've got it," Elke yelled as light flooded in from above. "Push!"

Morgan heaved and she swung up and in a flurry of legs clambered over the edge. Immediately she started coughing. She braced herself and draped her upper body down, reaching for Miranda.

Morgan lifted Miranda. When he clasped around her thighs, trying to hoist her up, she screamed involuntarily. He had squeezed her wound. The corpse rolled and they both fell on top of it.

"Please!" the young woman shouted. "Hurry! Miranda!"

On the second attempt, Morgan got a better grip and hefted Miranda high. Elke caught her hand. They hoisted her up and over the edge.

Elke reached down again, farther this time, Miranda holding her from falling. Morgan stretched but fell short of her grasp. She wouldn't be able to take his weight anyway.

"Get the hell out of here," he shouted. Both women were choking from smoke. Flames raced through the rafters just over their heads. Debris was falling, some of it past them into the tank, where it sizzled and popped. The heat inside the tank was almost unbearable. "Get out," he shouted again. "Miranda! Go!"

He sank down against the corpse.

"Morgan, grab!"

He looked up. Miranda's slacks were dangling through the smoke.

He stood up, stood on the corpse, balanced, shouted, lunged, grasped the blood- and wine-soaked cotton, snagged his fingers into the fabric until his nails seemed to pull out of his flesh. The two women pulled with everything they had. Suddenly, he felt a hand on his wrist. He could not relinquish his grip on the slacks. Two hands on his wrists, drawing him over the edge.

The three of them tumbled their way down the steel steps and raced out the open back door, Miranda running in spite of the bullet wound on her leg, Morgan choking on smoke. The young blond was laughing hysterically at the unexpected achievement of being alive. They fell together in a huddle on the ground. Morgan and Miranda picked up the laughter and they all were laughing, lying on the ground, with billows of smoke drifting overhead.

Then, in a break in the smoke, they heard a turbulent roar separate from the fire and looked up to see a plane immediately above them. It banked, circled, and came back low, swooping so close they could feel the wind off the prop. Bullets riddled the earth all around them, none finding its lethal mark. Then the plane flew up, and waggling its wings, soared over the escarpment into the setting sun, and they were alone with the dull roar of the fire as the smoke in the stilled light of evening spiralled high into the air.

5

Mr. Savage

"We nearly drowned. We nearly suffocated in wine fumes. We nearly burned to death. We've been riddled with bullets. Miranda, your leg has been riddled with bullets. We've nearly been decapitated with a propeller. What's next?" Morgan looked cynical, smug, and wretchedly dirty.

They stood by the open trunk of the car. Miranda was being helped into the slacks she had bought for Elke after having water from a plastic bottle slopped over her wound, which was just a graze but quite bloody, and then having alcohol and a bandage applied from a first aid kit. The two women changed into the extra T-shirts. Morgan took off his shirt and tossed it in the dirt, retrieving an old police windbreaker from the depths of the trunk.

He slid into the passenger seat to call for help. Undoubtedly neighbours would have already phoned 911 and volunteer firefighters would be on their way. He wanted to make sure the police came as well. He wanted to make sure Spivak knew what was happening; he felt the need to be grounded in a world he knew.

Miranda opened the driver's side and turned with her injured leg stretched away to lower herself onto the seat. Elke had a grip on her shoulders. Just before contact with the seat, Morgan lunged, reaching out and twisting in the air so that he lifted against her with one of her buttocks in each of his palms. She squealed indignantly as she reeled away into Elke's arms and the two women staggered backwards.

"Morgan, you fool! Have you lost it?"

"Stay back," he yelled.

"Damn, that was undignified, Morgan!"

"Back off," he declared vehemently as he strode around the car. "Over there." He pointed to a picnic table a couple of car-lengths away. Both women were frightened by his weird behaviour. "Over here," he repeated, walking to the table himself and flipping it onto its side.

When all three were behind the table, he picked up a brick-sized boulder and heaved it towards the car, swinging underarm. It fell short. He picked up another, the same size. Stepping out well in front of the table, he put all his weight into the throw, and while the boulder was still in the air he dove back over the table. There was a split second pause, then the boulder hit the driver's seat and there was a teeth-jarring explosion as the car lifted into the air and disintegrated, descending in a rain of fiery debris.

"That's it," said Morgan as the raging din subsided. "That's enough for one day. You guys okay?" Neither woman said anything as all three rose to their feet and surveyed the damage. Morgan was still in wine-stained pants and Elke in a wine-stained skirt. Miranda's clothes looked a bit dusty but clean, in stark contrast to her face and arms, which, like the exposed flesh of the other two, were smeared with wine residue, filth from the fire, and particles of exploded stuffing from the car seats.

"No wonder they flew off unconcerned about whether they shot us," said Miranda.

"Yeah," said Morgan. "They didn't leave much to chance."

"Morgan ..."

"Yeah?"

"Don't say 'what's next?'"

They could hear a siren off in the distance, coming from somewhere down near Lake Ontario. They turned and walked toward the house. Morgan needed a phone, Miranda wanted to sit somewhere comfortable and wait for medical assistance, Elke was anxious to clean up. They were sure the house was abandoned. People don't fire off machine guns and torch sheds or explode police cars and then go back to the dinner table.

They were astonished, then, when as they reached the garden gate that opened onto a lawn in front of the house, the main door slowly began to swing open. All three dropped to the ground, rolling to the side for cover behind shrubs, which of course would not stop bullets but might obscure the shooter's view. They waited. The door seemed to groan on its hinges, although it was a massive slab of glass framed in cedar. There were no shots. The cicadas in the meadowlands between the lawn and the vineyard trilled loudly in anticipation of nightfall. Flames from the fires behind them had subsided, but the car remnants and the crumpled shed smouldered, and columns of smoke rose straight upwards and pooled in clouds overhead.

There was a sudden blast and the burning shed exploded in a renewed swirl of smoke and flames.

A creaky voice called over their heads. "Hello…?"

Morgan glanced across at Miranda under her shrub, massaging her thigh above the wound. She nodded.

"Hello…?" he called.

"Is that you, Mr. Savage?" The timbre of an old lady's voice, ancient but strong, shaped the words in the air, but still no one appeared in the doorway.

Morgan stood up behind his small cover of greenery, head and shoulders exposed. "No ma'am, it's us."

"Well, who's us," said the old woman, stepping into the light so she was framed by the door opening. She was diminutive, stooped, but with her head tilted erect. "Who is it?"

"You don't have a gun, do you?" said Morgan.

"Yes, I do," came the answer, then a pause. "It's upstairs. Do you need it? It's only a shotgun to scare away birds."

Morgan stepped out onto the walkway.

"You stay there, now," said the old woman. "I'm not to have visitors."

"Well, could you step down here, ma'am, a little closer. We're the police."

"You look like filthy rag-tag brigands," she said.

"I'm sorry," said Morgan, "but we've had a bit of trouble."

"And haven't we all," said the woman. "Do I smell something burning?" she asked, moving out under the trellis in front of the door. "Where's Mr. Savage?"

"Could you come down here where we don't have to shout?" Morgan asked.

"You don't have to shout, young man. I can hear you."

"Could you come down here, please?" said Morgan patiently. Elke helped Miranda rise out of the shrubbery and they stood by his side.

The woman slowly made her way to confront them, feisty but anxious, and to ease her anxiety they stepped back outside the gate, then pulled it shut between them. She seemed unconcerned by the fires down the slope that had leapt now from roof to roof, so there was an awesome conflagration, with flames and smoke obscuring the eastern horizon.

"Did they fly away?" she said.

"Who?" Morgan asked. "Was that Mr. Savage, is Mr. Savage your son?"

"Oh, no, dear, I wouldn't call my son Mister," she said, smiling radiantly. "We don't have any children."

"You and Mr. Savage?"

"No dear, Peter and I, we don't have children."

"Peter is your husband?"

"Yes, dear. Peter passed away. Mr. Savage looks after me."

"Really," said Miranda.

"May I go in and clean up?" Elke asked the old woman, reaching over the gate and taking her by the hand. "I really need to use your bathroom."

"I'm sorry, dear. Mr. Savage said I wasn't to leave the house."

"But may we come inside?" said Miranda.

"Mr. Savage didn't say not to come in. He told me I wasn't to leave."

Sirens wailed in the background as fire trucks bumped over country roads, tracking the fire by sight. Cars were pouring down the long laneway as volunteers arrived before their equipment. Several had already pulled up but kept their distance from the fiery sheds, their headlights redundant in the clear evening air. The house was to the west of them, in shadow with the setting sun glaring from behind the escarpment. From down by the fire, no one could see the curious group negotiating by the garden gate.

"You see, my husband died after we tore up the orchards. It broke his heart. But Mr. Savage insisted. Mr. Savage owns the property, you see. It was in my husband's family since 1791. But we have no children — are you all right, dear?" She interrupted her narrative on seeing the bloodstain spreading on Miranda's thigh. "Perhaps they can help you." She indicated the activities down by the sheds. "I never know what's going on down there. I don't leave the house."

"Mr. Savage doesn't like it?" suggested Morgan.

"No, he does not."

"And where is Mr. Savage, now?"

"He told me to stay in the house," said the old woman. "I'm Mrs. Peter Oughtred. Peter was a Haun on his mother's side."

Miranda felt dizzy with pain and blood loss. Elke helped her to sit down on the grass outside the gate. Morgan's concern for her reflected in his voice.

"You'll have to let us in, Mrs. Oughtred, my partner needs help."

"What was all the noise, was that you? Did you make those loud noises? I heard explosions down by the winery. I stayed in the parlour. I was watching television."

"Mr. Savage told you to stay inside?" Morgan asked.

"Yes, he did," she responded. Her voice quavered with exasperation. She had told him this already.

"And Mr. Savage owns Bonnydoon Winery?"

"He built this house for us. They tore down the old house and built this one in its place. Peter never liked it."

"No?" said Morgan.

"We had the parlour and the bedroom downstairs and the kitchen and a bathroom."

"But it's a huge house —"

"Yes, and they needed the rest."

"When did your husband die, Mrs. Oughtred?"

"Three years ago. I've been here alone since then."

"With Mr. Savage?"

"Mr. Savage comes and goes, sometimes by car and sometimes by airplane. He makes sure I have supplies. I can clean up after myself. Peter was ninety-four, I'm ninety six. He was a year older than me but I'm older now."

"Does Mr. Savage have a first name?"

"I'm sure he does."

"Would you mind telling me what it is?"

"No, I would not mind at all."

Morgan waited. "Uh, what is it?"

"I don't know, dear. Mr. Savage is Mr. Savage."

Morgan paused. "Was your husband a vintner?"

"Oh no, we're farmers. We had orchards. These vines are only four years old."

Morgan looked around at the firefighters. An ambulance had arrived. It was sitting on the edge of the scene in case of an accident. An OPP car was lumbering up the laneway.

"Police are coming," said Morgan to Miranda and Elke. "Provincials. There's an ambulance, let's get Miranda down there."

He stopped and turned back to the ancient Mrs. Oughtred. "My name is Morgan, ma'am. I'd like to talk to you again. We'll have someone look in on you. I don't think Mr. Savage will be back."

"Well, of course he will, he owns everything here until we both die. He promised me when Peter passed away, Mr. Savage promised I could stay until I died too."

"He did. Well, I'm sure you can stay. Don't worry, we'll track Mr. Savage down."

"He always comes back."

"Mrs. Oughtred —"

"Now you go along with your friends, Mr. Morgan. They don't look too steady on their feet. And you all should wash up, you know. You don't make a very good impression."

She waved at him with a hankie in her hand, even though he was just on the other side of the gate. Apparently unconcerned about the billowing smoke and flames behind him or the frenetic activities of the emergency crew, she turned and started walking back to the house. Morgan trudged down the walkway, glancing back at the old woman as he caught up with the other two. She was already at her door, and when he looked around next she had gone in and shut it firmly behind her.

As they emerged out of the gloom of the escarpment a cluster of police, firefighters, and medics surged up the slope towards them.

"We must really look like we need help," said Miranda.

"We do," said Elke. "We've been through hell."

They stopped, leaning against each other, waiting for the emergency crew to reach them. Morgan turned and looked back at the house.

"She was determined to stay," he said.

"Mr. Savage told her she could, until she passes away." Miranda looked back as well.

"Mr. Savage told her to stay inside." A tremor of horror crossed his face.

"Morgan?"

"My goodness!" he exclaimed.

"Morgan, no!"

Miranda shouted at him as he swung around, took a stride back towards the house, stumbled, and as he was rising to his feet the entire escarpment exploded into a blistering, deafening inferno. For an instant the house was outlined in flame, as if it were hovering against a fiery backdrop, then it smashed into a billion points of light as the shock waves hurled Morgan and Miranda and the blond woman down the slope toward the emergency crew huddled on the ground against the blast, with the burning sheds behind them.

Nothing seemed to move for a suspended instant, until the cicadas resumed their urgent thrumming; then the entire scene burst into a flurry of activity. It was like a war zone in the aftermath of a bombing raid. Flames billowed against the oncoming darkness and smoke curled in mindless strands through the thick, acrid air. Men and women, some still dressed from work, scurried around, drowning smouldering fires, gossiping, trying to figure out what had happened. Told there were two deaths, a body in a tank in the wine-shed debris, and old Mrs. Peter Oughtred in the inferno where the house had been, they summoned the Fire Marshal from Niagara-on-the-Lake, and the OPP officers took charge.

6

The Rocking Chair

Three hours later, Morgan and Elke Sturmberg were sitting in an interrogation room at Police Headquarters in Toronto. They looked like they had been soaked in a red-wine marinade.

"Miranda's on her way," said Spivak. "They're just getting her bandaged up. She's got a change of clothes in her locker. You want coffees, I'll get you coffees." He sidled out of the room, letting the door swing sharply closed behind him.

Morgan smiled across the table at the young blond.

"Don't confess to crimes you're not proud of," he said. "We're being observed. Of course, they know I know we're being observed, so maybe they're not bothering. Sometimes a room like this is just a good place to talk."

"Do you ever torture people here?" she asked.

"For confessions? No, not often."

"Good," she said. After a moment, she declared, "I remember pretty well everything, but I don't remember driving to Toronto. Why would I go to Miranda's?"

"It's a mystery," said Morgan. Then looking up at the mirrored wall, he said, "Spivak, where's the coffee?"

The door opened and Miranda hobbled in on her own. Then Eeyore Stritch came in, carrying three coffees precariously balanced, and set them on the table.

"I'm gonna live," said Miranda as she sat down.

"Good," said Morgan. "Saves me the trouble of finding a replacement."

"Detective Quin," said Eeyore Stritch in a funereal tone once they got settled. Miranda braced herself for whatever was coming. "The hand, the man in the vat, he wasn't the one."

"The one what?" she responded.

"The one who raped you."

Miranda flinched. Nobody had used the word *rape*. Philip may have got her into bed under false pretenses, but that fell into the realm of seduction. As for the semen deposited by his killer, that had somehow seemed more an infusion, absolutely disgusting but not sexual assault. She was, as she told Morgan, fucked. Rape seemed something else, demanding at the very least the awareness of the victim.

"It wasn't him?" She was baffled.

"We did a rush job on the DNA. It shows the man in the vat and the man who — did that to you — were different people."

"Why did you assume they weren't?" said Spivak, who had just come into he room. He knew by the ensuing silence he had asked a compromising question. "Explanation?" he demanded.

Miranda fished into her purse for the gold ring and dropped it with a resounding clang on the table.

"What's this?" said Spivak.

"The waiter at the Imperial Room told me the man with Philip was wearing a gold ring, very ostentatious, an eye-popper."

"So …?"

"Well, this ring," said Morgan, cocking his head towards the ring on the table, "it might have been, how would you say this, on the hand that came in by itself."

"My hand?" exclaimed Elke.

"Not yours exactly," said Morgan. "The one in your Monica Lewinsky handbag."

"It's a knock-off."

"What the hell are you talking about, Morgan? You saying this ring was on the dead guy's finger?"

"On his severed hand, not the one still attached. The guy in the vat and the guy at the Royal York are one and the same. And the hand in the bag, it was obviously his."

"For Christ's sake, Morgan. You took a ring off a dead man's hand, you gave it to your partner for a keepsake. What! What's going on here? You're both sick."

"A severed hand. We didn't know for sure he was dead," said Morgan. "It was a connection. We thought sooner or later it might give us a lead. Apparently it's not going to."

"I thought we were in this together," said Spivak.

"Yeah," said Morgan. "Sorry. It seemed like a good idea at the time."

"Jesus, Jesus, Morgan."

"Expletive," said Miranda to Morgan. "Not prayer."

"What the hell am I going to do with you two! Lady," he turned to Elke, "do you know who you are yet? That would be helpful."

"I seem to have been abducted."

"No shit," he said. "Do you know who the hell you are? Where do you come from?"

"She does," said Morgan. "But not how she got to Toronto."

"Does anyone?" said Eeyore Stritch.

"What?" demanded Spivak, wheeling on him. "What?"

"Know how they end up in Toronto …" Whatever wit there might have been in his comment dissipated like unacknowledged flatulence. He chuckled to himself. Miranda liked him for that.

"Okay," said Spivak. "Either we're working together or we're not working together."

"We're working together," said Eeyore Stritch, who thought Spivak was addressing him.

"Yeah," said Morgan. "Sorry, I thought — recovered memory syndrome. If she held onto it, maybe she'd remember things."

"And I do," said Miranda. They waited.

Miranda shut her eyes for an uncomfortably long period, then flashed them open. "His face, in the wine tank, that was the man with the ring. Philip met me in the lobby of the Royal York. He was there first, reading a paper. We didn't have reservations. We never made reservations. We went in for dinner. Halfway through, the man, the other man, joined us. He didn't eat. Philip ordered a bottle of Dom Pérignon. The two men, they weren't friends. They knew each other, and they were keyed up about something. Maybe they quarrelled."

"Now we're getting somewhere," said Spivak, who seemed to have forgotten the purloined ring.

"Was there any evidence of her door being jimmied?" Morgan asked.

"Her apartment door? Miranda's? No," said Stritch. "But a pro wouldn't leave any marks."

"So here's what happened," said Morgan. "The ring-man doctors Miranda's drink. Philip thinks it's the Dom Pérignon, he walks her out of the dining room with as little fuss as possible. They get her to a car, a taxi. Have we checked taxis? Philip takes her home. The other man disappears."

"How do you know?" said Miranda.

"The semen, it wasn't his. Now let's say Philip takes you home. You make love ... correction, he has sex. Remember, he doesn't know you're drugged. He just thinks you've had too much champagne. You pass out ... but, you know, maybe you're already doing it by then —"

"Doing it!"

"Making love ... pathetic, but not totally degenerate —"

"Says you," said Miranda. "I think it's despicable."

"He falls asleep beside you. Someone else, apparently not the man with the ring, another man breaks into your apartment —"

"Condo."

"Condo, right. You two are out cold. The third man gets Miranda's gun from her desk —"

"How did he know it was there?" asked Miranda.

"Where else would it be? He jimmies the drawer, takes out your Glock in its holster, right?"

"Right."

"He puts a slug through Philip's head, another through his gut —"

"Through his gut?" Spivak interjected, not anticipating Morgan's hypothesis.

"Yeah."

"Okay."

"Okay. To this point, he's been neat and efficient."

"Right," said Spivak.

"Then he — he fucks Miranda."

"Steady," said Stritch.

"Okay, it's my word," said Miranda. "Go on, Morgan."

"It's not too messy, at this point. The sex, it's not about writhing around, he makes a deposit...."

"Yes," said Miranda, envisioning it happening to someone else. "Then?"

"Okay," said Morgan. "No, at this point he hadn't shot Philip in the gut. Just through the head. Using the pillow to muffle the sound. Now he takes Miranda's hand, he puts the Glock, which he'd wiped clean, in her hand, he twists her arm around and pulls her finger on the trigger — the gun goes off against Philip Carter's abdomen."

"And?" said Miranda.

"The intruder, he puts the gun on the bedside table. It's not convincing, he thinks. He needs it to look like she did it. Why would she shoot him in the gut? He gets a bullet from the desk drawer, puts it in the clip. Sets the gun back down on the table with only one bullet missing. We know two were fired. He's smart and cold, he's a foreigner, he wouldn't know the extent of forensic discovery. He rolls Philip's body away from Miranda, on top of the sheet, and with a knife he's carrying he goes after the slug inside the corpse. He's wearing one of Miranda's plastic aprons. Check, I'll bet there's one missing. When he gets the bullet, Philip's guts are slopping out of his body. The guy thinks the mess will reinforce that she's crazy. He goes to the bathroom, washes meticulously. Gets her kitchen knife, slicks it with blood. Dumps it under the bed, not too obvious, he thinks. Goes back into the bedroom, covers the two of them. Starts to leave. Sees the holster where he set it beside the bed. Returns it to the desk, sees it's flecked with blood — no, he fired one of his shots through the holster. That's it. The other was through the pillow. He has to take the holster with him."

"Why through the holster?" asked Eeyore, who was mesmerized by Morgan's narrative.

"To muffle the sound. His first shot was through the holster. Otherwise he would have used the pillow for both."

"What about the blood on the walls?" Miranda asked. "How does that fit into your grand scenario?"

Morgan's face took on an introspective scowl, brow furrowed, eyes squinting, then he pronounced it was one of two possibilities.

"Either he was trying to show how hysterical Miranda was when she killed the guy, I mean, something to go along with disembowelling him and then climbing back in beside him with his guts hanging out. Or. I think there's another side to this guy. Fastidious, yes, and absolutely cold-blooded. But pathologically driven to assert his own personality, no matter how necessary it was to conceal himself from discovery."

Spivak started a deep-chest rumbling smoker's cough. Conforming to social custom, the others tried to ignore him, despite the fact that he was dying by increments.

"It wasn't a matter of hiding, it was important to direct our sole attention to Miranda as the killer."

"Why?" said Eeyore Stritch.

"Don't know."

"I'd say it was both," said Miranda.

"Both?"

"Yeah, leaving an indecipherable scrawl — that would imply my dementia. I think you're right, Morgan. It's not a message, it's a signature."

"Sounds likely," said Spivak, whose face was now flushed red.

"That's exactly how it was!" exclaimed Elke.

The four detectives turned to her simultaneously, surprised she was still in the room. They had forgotten about her as Morgan's account unfolded, and now she seemed incongruous, an outsider, her presence compromising. Spivak began coughing again.

"Pardon?" said Stritch. "How *what* was?"

"The way you described him," she said to Morgan, "that's the man they took me to, after they picked me up in Rochester —"

"Picked you up!" exclaimed Spivak.

"Abducted. In the parking lot outside Millennium Wines. I was driven to Buffalo. We met someone in Buffalo, they dumped me into a plane, they flew me across the border to Bonnydoon. The man there, I know it was the same man who was at Miranda's, he moved exactly the way you described him. I didn't see him, my eyes were covered. They taped me to the chair, then the man in charge, the man you described, he chopped off the ring-man's hand. He touched me. They dumped the ring-man in the vat, someone shot him. I know it was him. You described him exactly."

"He didn't actually describe him at all," said Spivak.

"She knows it was the same man," said Miranda with strident authority. "It was him."

"So then how did you get to Toronto?" asked Stritch.
She looked at him blankly.

Spivak arranged for a car to drive Miranda and Morgan home, after dropping off Elke Sturmberg at The Four Seasons on Avenue Road. It was midnight when they pulled up in front of Miranda's condo. Morgan insisted on helping her in and told the officer who was driving to go ahead. He would walk home from there.

"That's how we get a reputation, Morgan. It'll be all over Headquarters by morning."

"Do we have a reputation?"

"You know we do."

She buzzed her own number at the door before turning the key in the lock to open it. He looked at her quizzically.

"You're very strange," he said.

"It scares the burglars away."

"Have you ever been burgled?"

"No, see, it works." She leaned on his arm as they made their way slowly up the worn marble stairs. "The apartment never seems so empty when I get there, knowing the buzzer's already been buzzing. It's like I envision a warm, welcoming space with sound waves still reverberating, even when it's dark."

Morgan smiled at the poignancy. In common with anyone who lives alone, he knew the exact moment of loneliness that waits like a chilling embrace when you first return to an empty home.

When they got to her door, he took the key and opened it, reaching inside to switch on the hall lights.

The bulb was out. They walked through into the living room, where he flicked on the overhead.

"Okay," he said. "You get to bed, you must be exhausted. It's been a long day. How's your leg? You all right?"

"Morgan, relax. My leg's fine." She stood back and looked at him. She shook her head in mock exasperation.

"You're going to walk home like that!" she said. "Have you any idea what you look like? Come in and we'll see if we can't get you fixed up. You'll get arrested for vagrancy."

Hobbling into the bedroom, she came out a few minutes later and tossed a pair of khaki slacks at him.

"They were Philip's. They'll fit."

She disappeared again and came back with a sweatshirt.

"It's mine, it's extra large. It'll be just right for you. Sorry, I don't have any underwear your size. How about socks."

She dropped back into the bedroom and returned with a pair of thick work socks. She also had a pair of old-fashioned blue knickers in her hands.

"Better than nothing," she said.

"Not bloody likely."

"It's up to you. They're clean. I wouldn't tell."

He hefted the khakis in his hands, looked at the knickers, and shrugged.

"Why don't you change in the bathroom? Have a shower while you're at it. I can wait. I'm too wired to sleep."

While Morgan showered, she stood in the bathroom doorway, watching him openly, then made her way to the toilet and perched on it to talk to him.

"This is action central," she shouted.

"What?" he responded, trying to locate her position from the sound of her voice.

"My shower, this is where the action is."

"You want to join me?"

She leaned forward from the toilet and gazed around through the streaming glass.

"Very tempting, Morgan." She paused as if considering the possibility, then added, "But not tonight. There have been enough disappointments for one day."

He turned off the shower. She got up and handed him a towel over the stall door as she walked out into the bedroom.

"Can you hear me?" he called.

"Yes, you don't have to shout."

He walked into the bedroom, clutching his towel and the small bundle of clothes.

"It's all yours," he said. "I'll change in here."

She looked at him and smiled. It would be easier for her in the bedroom but she did not want to deflate his gesture of gallantry. She went into the bathroom but left the door open so they could talk while he dressed. She undressed.

"I'm sorry about the old lady," she said. "Mrs. Peter Oughtred. Do you think she had a first name?"

"Yeah, it'll go on her gravestone. Along with her maiden name."

"Isn't that an awful phrase."

"What?"

"*Maiden name*. After seventy years of being Mrs. Peter Oughtred, she'll revert to Jane Smith, or whatever. I don't think she had a clue what was going on there at the Bonnydoon Winery. What do you think he called her?"

"Who?"

"Peter."

"Mrs. You know, I bet he called her the Missus." He paused. "Can you hear me?"

"I can't for a minute, Morgan. Pour us a couple of drinks. There's Scotch in the kitchen." She turned on the shower. He walked to the bathroom door, stood admiring her through the wet glass for a moment, leaned in, and flipped on the heater-light and fan, which emitted a rumbling glow, pulled the door shut, and wandered out into the kitchen, socks in hand, leaving the silky blue knickers crumpled on the end of the bed. He changed his mind, went back in and retrieved the panties, folded them neatly, and stuffed them in his back pocket. Let her think he'd worn them!

When she came out, hair in a towel, wrapped in the terrycloth robe that Elke had been wearing less than twenty-four hours before, Morgan was in the kitchen, sitting back in an old Boston rocker that Miranda's grandmother had passed on to her when she was a child, with his feet up on the seat of another chair. She picked up her Scotch and sat down near him on the floor, stretching her wounded leg in front of her.

Morgan started to get up.

"No," she said. "I'm better here for a bit." She leaned back against the wall.

"So, what do you think of our Elke?" she asked.

"She's very attractive in an ethereal sort of way."

"That's not what I mean, Morgan!"

"Oh. Well, I think there's a lot we don't know. I think there's a lot she still doesn't know."

"What are you saying?"

"You can remember what happened to you, right? It was fuzzy before you were doped, but it came back. Drugs and trauma obscured things for a time —"

"And you think she's been through more than me,

and that's why she's drawing a blank."

"She recalled everything up to Bonnydoon. It's not amnesia. She phoned New York from the station. She got a bit confused, she called her ex-boyfriend. Then she sorted it out. She called her boss at Beverley Auctions, she's their wine expert, that's big bucks. Her boss told her to stay at The Four Seasons on the company tab. What am I missing?"

"Her childhood in Sweden, her early experience with sex watching Ingmar Bergman films, no, I think you've covered it all."

"Until the disconnect, between hearing the ring-man executed in the wine shed and turning up on your doorstep with his hand in her purse."

"And a gun."

"A smoking gun."

"So, there's got to be a major traumatic experience in there, you figure, more than being abducted across an international boundary and bearing witness to murder?"

"Yeah, that's what I think," said Morgan.

"And she ends up at The Four Seasons on an expense account. Tomorrow she'll shop."

"Envious? Yeah, but Spivak told her not to leave town, not without us, so she's gotta have supplies."

"From Yorkville, Hazelton Lanes, already."

"So she's trapped in the most fashionable part of the city. She hasn't much choice."

"Trapped? The thing about The Four Seasons, Morgan —"

"It's very expensive."

"Elegant."

"In an expensive sort of way."

"What else is there?"

7

The Four Seasons

Morgan walked through the cool of the night along side streets over to the Annex neighbourhood. The residual June heat gathered a thin layer of glistening moisture on the sidewalk and on the meagre rectangles of grass in front of houses standing shoulder to shoulder along the way. Only Yonge Street was alive at this late hour, and he hurried across it as if the gaudy lights and the night people threatened contagion.

He stopped in front of his house and surveyed the scene. The street was lined on both sides with huge silver maples. Some homes were single-family, but most were multiples, converted either to apartments or condominiums.

Condominia?

His own place was part of a rambling nineteenth-century agglomeration of stonework and brick with turrets and gables and gingerbread trim, a modest mansion that had been reconfigured as a jigsaw cube of modular dwellings with two-storey windows knocked through the

"You ever stay there?"

"With Philip? No. We had dinner. Met for lunch once. But for … private times … we came back here."

"Always?"

"Yeah. Don't look so shocked."

"I'm not shocked. Disappointed, maybe."

"Jealous."

"No, I'm a grown-up. Disappointed *for* you that it couldn't have been better."

"Is that genuine sympathy, Morgan? Or condescension?"

"Yes," he said, with careful equivocation.

There was a long pause. They were friends. Neither felt rancour for breaching bounds of propriety. As partners used to being together in soul-draining crises, their rules of intimacy were elastic. There was no urgency, as there might be between lovers, to resolve the differences between them.

"Morgan, know what I think?" Miranda eventually said.

"What?"

"I think you should knock that back and go home."

"Yeah."

"We're meeting her for breakfast. Maybe she'll put it on her tab. We need a treat."

"Okay," he said, getting up from the old rocker and, after a futile flick of the light switch, walking down the dark hall. "See you tomorrow. Nine o'clock."

"Too early. She won't be up."

"Nine thirty."

He stepped out into the illuminated gloom of the corridor, drawing her door shut behind him.

Good quality footage from a high perspective showed their car wheeling into the brightly lit portico; two doors opened, the driver's and the back passenger-side door. Elke Sturmberg emerged and gazed around, then stared straight up into the camera before waving the doorman back and the driver away. She leaned down and made a gesture of goodbye through the car windows. As the car pulled away she stepped towards the door and out of the camera's scope.

"Okay," said Morgan. "What about inside, is that on tape?"

The security man switched to a second screen that was keyed up to begin playing a few seconds before the exterior shot lost track of the blond.

"Nothing," said Spivak. "She didn't make it through the door. There's a blind spot close to the building. The camera's trained on the cars, not the people coming in."

They turned away and walked back into the sumptuous lobby.

"Did you interrogate the people on the desk?" Miranda asked.

"No," said Spivak. "We thought we should leave that for you."

"You didn't know we were —"

"Sarcasm, Miranda," Morgan interjected. "Detective Spivak has of course interviewed everyone concerned. Detectives Spivak and Stritch are doing their jobs very well. We, if we're co-operative, will observe and pick up what we can, and contribute what we can, whenever possible."

Spivak nodded benevolently, not quite sure whether Morgan was being deferential, defensive, or bitchy. It didn't seem to matter very much which it was.

Eeyore Stritch was leaning to look beyond his partner into the dining lounge, admiring the brunch buffet.

"What do you think?" said Miranda. "Dutch treat."

"It's expensive," said Morgan.

"Not for what you get," said Spivak, folding his arms across his protuberant gut. "It's all-you-can-eat."

"Yeah," said Morgan. "Dutch treat."

"Right on," said Stritch, revealing beneath his usual gravitas a hint of the sensual enthusiast.

Eating here, this is a measure of our confusion, Morgan thought as they waited for the maître d' to seat them. *We've gone through Dante's Inferno with a woman who turned up out of nowhere with a smoking gun and a severed hand and bonded with Miranda. An old woman died, a million-dollar wine conspiracy has been brought down, a winery has disappeared from the face of the earth. The stranger, a beautiful blond, has also disappeared, presumably only from Toronto. Why not have a good meal?* The words did not come to him with such clarity, but the sentiments did, the review of events scrolling by through his mind like a film on fast-forward.

Superintendent Alex Rufalo hovered over the four detectives, who were seated at two pairs of back-to-back desks just outside his office. He gave them a gloomy smile.

"Detective Quin, you're not here," he said. "And you other three? I came in for some peace and quiet. You turn up after Sunday brunch at The Four Seasons, your star witness is missing."

"Nope, she's not," said Spivak, struggling to suppress a burp.

"Not?"

"She's missing, but she's not a witness. Well, she's a possible witness, maybe, but we're not sure of the crime."

"Would you like to clarify that?" said the superintendent, turning to Morgan.

Morgan had eaten moderately from every food group represented, including shellfish, crêpes, salads, and pastries.

"That's pretty much it," he said. "We've got a witness, but no crime; we've got a crime, but no witness. We've got crimes, witnesses, victims, but no suspects."

"And no leads," declared the superintendent. "Four of Toronto's finest, and we have chaos."

"Three," said Miranda. "I'm not here."

"Well, I'll tell you what," said the superintendent, pausing for emphasis, "you three get down to some serious brainstorming. Since you're not here, Detective Quin, you can referee. I'll be in my office."

As he retreated through his door, the others relaxed. *There is something inherently Presbyterian about people like us*, thought Miranda. *We feel guilty for having a sumptuous meal, even though we paid for it ourselves, and it's Sunday, for goodness sake, we're not on company time.*

But, of course, cops, like priests, work twenty-four seven, regardless of the hours they punch in on the clock. The superintendent, like a bishop, was a reminder of their commitment, as well as their fallibility.

"You were right," she said, looking at Morgan.

"About what?" Spivak demanded, as if he were being left out of something important.

Morgan shrugged.

"The apron," said Miranda. "An old plastic apron of my mother's. It's missing. And a pair of rubber gloves from under the sink."

"So the killer dug it out of the guy's gut," Spivak muttered, "while you were lying there. Nice."

They talked, arranging known facts into a variety of scenarios. When a coherent pattern refused to emerge, they concluded there were not enough facts.

They drew a chart on a chalkboard and stared at it.

Morgan recalled the old woman, how she lived blithely in the midst of a wine conspiracy of epic, and, as it turned out, deadly proportions. People died over wine, and the old woman died when the scam closed down. And she understood nothing that was happening around her. "Maybe we've got it wrong," he said.

"What?" said Miranda. "It's not about an international wine conspiracy?"

"Yeah. No, it is, but we've been caught up in our own perspective, like old Mrs. Oughtred. Mr. Savage is playing us...."

"Who's Mr. Savage?" said Stritch.

"Sort of the generic bad guy," said Miranda.

"Exactly," said Morgan.

"What are you talking about?" asked Spivak. "Make sense."

"There's a bad guy," said Morgan, "who killed Philip Carter and assaulted Miranda. There's a bad guy who tortured and executed the ring-man, there's a bad guy who blew up the winery and old Mrs. Oughtred, and there's a bad guy who has been running the wine fraud, using the old lady's place in Niagara to blend fake Châteauneuf-du-Pape and smuggle it into the U.S.

Maybe they're all the same guy, maybe not."

"And?" said Spivak, feeling he was missing something or being left out.

Morgan stared at him then made a leap from one track to another. "We've been assuming the man who killed Philip Carter framed Miranda so he wouldn't be caught."

"Yes," Miranda said. "And?"

"But what if that was his purpose from the outset?"

"What?"

"To set you up for a fall. The man called Philip Carter, he was collateral damage, not you."

"Why bother?" said Miranda. "I wasn't the one connected to Bonnydoon."

"But maybe this wasn't about Bonnydoon."

"What, then?" demanded Spivak impatiently. "Why go after Miranda? What about the semen?"

"This guy is meticulous and inevitably imperfect."

"Imperfect?" Miranda queried.

"Yeah, too careful," said Morgan. "Imagine you're him, you make mistakes, then you cover them — or you're so careful you don't see them happening. The semen? It never occurred to him you would be checked. Why should you be, you're in bed with your lover, you killed him. The rape kit's irrelevant. He knows about killing, he doesn't know forensic procedures."

"Why go after her?" Spivak repeated. "What's the connection?"

"Ciccone," said Morgan. "Why Miranda, why now? Vittorio Ciccone."

"I doubt it," Spivak proclaimed. "Ciccone needs her."

"You testify next week?" Morgan asked.

"Tomorrow. I did the preliminary nearly two months ago, explaining how I knew him, how we 'connected' through the Ferguson case."

"Ferguson?" Stritch asked in a quiet and sombre voice, not wanting to intrude on the strange thought processes going on around him, yet needing at least minimal information to keep up with the exchange.

"A little girl, raped and murdered by her stepfather —"

"Okay," said Stritch. "So, why would Vittorio Ciccone want to get rid of his best chance for acquittal?"

"Maybe somebody else did," said Morgan. "An enemy in the wine trade."

"Then why kill Philip, why not me? Why not keep it simple?"

"I don't know."

"Why would Ciccone have any interest in wine?"

"I just think he does."

"Come on, Morgan," said Miranda. "Compared to the millions in drugs, a few bottles of fake wine are small-time."

"Maybe," said Morgan. "Although Elke Sturmberg figured there was big money in a quality wine scam." He paused. No one else said anything. "It's like we've got a contour map with no names on it. There's no key, and we're just assuming north's at the top of the page."

"I think I've found your key," said the superintendent, emerging from his office. "Not exactly found, since she's disappeared, apparently without a trace —"

"Elke Sturmberg?" said Miranda.

"There's a report on my desk. I just got to it. A John Doe was fished out of the Humber late Friday night, riddled with bullets."

"Wiseguy," Spivak suggested. "Biker?"

"Connected with our missing blond," said Morgan.

"Seems the slugs they dug out of the cadaver were from the gun we found in her purse."

8

Tim Hortons

When Miranda walked along Isabella Street on her way home after the fallout from Elke Sturmberg's status shifting from missing to wanted, she was distracted. She did not notice the warm evening air, the trees rustling softly overhead, the occasional passerby, nor did she notice the black limousine parked in front of her building until she was beside it, and then she paid it only passing attention.

She had studied language in university, linguistics and semiotics, and she often amused herself among words while on another level engaging in subliminal deductive analysis, working her way toward the resolution of a criminal conundrum. When Vittorio Ciccone's voice called to her quietly through the open window in the back of the limousine, she was wondering about the directionality of prepositions. Why do Torontonians walk "along" a street like Isabella that runs east-west, but "down" a north-south street like Yonge or Avenue Road? Do New

Yorkers walk up and down the avenues, but along, no across, the grid of numbered streets in Manhattan? Are some prepositions longitudinal and others latitudinal?

"Miss," the voice hissed. "Miss Quin." She did not hear the summons with the falling sound of her own name.

The driver got out of the car and called her. "Hey you, Miss Quin."

She wheeled around and, responding to what seemed a sinister situation, her hand swung back to where her semi-automatic would be if she were carrying it, which she was not.

"You're on suspension," said the voice she recognized as Vittorio Ciccone's. He knew she had been reaching for her gun, even though she never in actuality had drawn on anyone who was not in the midst of a criminal act.

"Mr. Ciccone." She leaned down and looked through the window, where he was sitting in shadow. "We shouldn't be talking."

"It's legal," he responded. "I asked my lawyers. They said it was legal. I'm a free man, still innocent, on bail. You're a temporary civilian, a witness on my side."

"Not on your side," Miranda countered. "I'm not doing you any favours."

"Oh, but you are," he said. "And there are people who do not like what you are doing."

"Cops? Some don't like it, they want to see you go down."

"Get in, we need to talk."

"Thank you, but no. We're not friends. I don't like what you do. If the jury overrides my testimony, that's fine with me."

"You would see an innocent man go to jail," he laughed.

"You have a strange way of defining innocence."

"And you have a strange way of determining guilt, Detective. Okay, you stay there. But listen to me."

"I'm listening."

"There are people who want me put away."

"Many," Miranda responded. "Are you surprised?"

"Besides cops, besides the righteous. There are very bad people, they want me out of the way."

"Why not kill you, it couldn't be that hard."

The man in the shadows laughed again. "Because then there would be much bloodshed, it would not be pleasant. You know about vengeance. It is a tradition. Many would die. And worse, there would be publicity. It is bad for business. It is easier to have it done legally — well, not so legally. Those two cops trying to take me down, they will be looked after, I am sure, one way or another. It is easier to have the state do the dirty work."

"So, what are you telling me, Mr. Ciccone?"

"Call me Vittorio, Miss Quin."

"Call me Detective, Mr. Ciccone."

"These bad guys, they have already tried to, shall we say, remove you from the process, destroy your credibility."

She was not surprised he knew about Philip. People like him have a way of knowing what happens whenever it concerns them, whether leaked in the courthouse or the confessional. But the same question she asked Morgan came to mind.

"Why not kill me, why kill my ..." she paused, "my friend?"

"In spite of what you might think, I do not know everything."

Miranda squelched her response and edged away from the car.

"Miss Quin," he called, trying to restrain her with sincerity. "Detective Quin, we each have our codes of honour, and I, like you, in my own world I am an honourable man."

She wanted to ask him how many addicts had died for his honour, how many prostitutes, how many derelicts, what human detritus crawled the streets for his honour? But she said nothing.

"I am here to thank you," he said. "I am here to warn you. This is not a threat. I am on your side, even if you are not on mine. There are people who will try to get at me through you. They have tried already. They will try again. I have a bodyguard posted." He leaned forward into the light and nodded toward a car parked on the other side of the street.

Miranda looked across, incredulous. "You are having me guarded?"

"Just until my trial is over. Then you're on your own."

"No, Mr. Ciccone. That isn't how it works. Gangsters don't cover cops. I am on my own right now. The guard detail goes!"

"You hurt my feelings, Miss Quin."

"Sorry."

"You put me in danger."

"No, Mr. Ciccone, you put yourself in danger."

"I do not expect to die in prison. It is you who will keep me out."

"No one expects to die in prison, that's what crooks have in common, the smartest, the dumbest, you're all going to beat the system. But you know, Mr. Ciccone, the prisons are full of people like you."

"Goodnight, Miss Quin. I will call off my guard. I am sure you do not have a death wish, and you will be careful; forewarned is forearmed. You will be wary, for my sake."

"For my own, Mr. Ciccone. Good night."

Miranda buzzed herself in and walked slowly up to her apartment on the third floor. When she got there she walked through to her bedroom without turning on the lights and looked surreptitiously out her window. A man got out of the car in the shadows across the street. He walked over to the limousine and bent down to converse with Ciccone in the back seat. She saw the flash of a cigarette lighter, then the driver of the limousine got out and, without turning to address the guard at the rear window, walked along Isabella toward the glaring lights of Yonge Street.

It all seemed strange to Miranda, some kind of an impenetrable play being enacted three storeys below.

The guard returned to his own car across the street, climbed in, and drove away. The limousine sat there, stolidly filling the loading zone in front of her building. She turned and got ready for bed, using only table lamps, as if she did not want to draw too much attention to herself from the vantage of an observer on the street.

Before she crawled onto her bed, sliding the top sheet to the side because it was too warm to be covered, she glanced out the window again. The limousine was still there. Vittorio Ciccone was not taking any chances; he would stand guard himself. The trial was set to resume in the morning. He wanted her there.

Miranda woke just before dawn, as she often did when she had a lot on her mind. There was a flashing red light pulsing through her room. At first she thought she was dreaming and closed her eyes tight, trying to make the light disappear. She rolled over slowly onto her back, then opened her eyes again and tried to assimilate the significance of the light coming through her window from outside.

Must be a cruiser on the street, she thought. *It's June, no snowplows, wrong colour light.*

She got up and looked out the window. The police car was parked behind the black limousine. The flashing lights filled the street with surreal activity as buildings wrenched into waves of garish red struggled vainly to retreat into the shadows.

The scene was exactly the same five minutes later when Miranda emerged from her building, dressed but dishevelled.

One of two uniformed officers got out of the cruiser as she walked around the limousine, but when Miranda flashed him her ID he recognized her and said nothing. The window on the far side was open. She bent down and could see Vittorio Ciccone sitting in the shadows. She took a flashlight from the officer and shone it into the car interior.

Ciccone stared straight through her. He had a single bullet hole in the centre of his forehead. It was like a third eye weeping a small strand of blood.

The other officer got out of the cruiser and walked over to them. "I've got a make on the limo," she said.

"It's Vittorio Ciccone," said Miranda.

"Yes," the officer said, doing a double take, then recognizing Miranda. "Detective Quin. You live here? It is Ciccone. At least, it's his car."

"It's him," said Miranda. "I do live here, yes. Third floor. And yes, he was visiting me."

"Visiting you!" said the first officer incredulously. "Aren't you involved, you know, in the big murder trial?"

"Yes, I do know. Yes, I am. Was. The trial's over. The jury, it seems, is redundant."

"Yeah," said the second officer. "It's more efficient this way."

Another cruiser pulled up, then an ambulance, which immediately called for the coroner's black maria. A third cruiser arrived. The superintendent got out and walked over to Miranda, who was sitting on the cement step of the walkway leading into her building. The uniformed officers had been deferential, but wary. They knew she was connected to Ciccone; they knew she and her partner were clean.

"Superintendent," she said, looking up.

"Detective Quin."

"Glad you could make it."

"I was still in my office."

"Sorry about that," she said. There were rumours he and his wife were having problems. He had been working odd hours, sometimes not going home at all.

"Ciccone was here to see you, was he?" he asked, ignoring her sympathy.

"Yeah." She rose to her feet. "I mean, why else would a gangster be parked in front of my place in this part of Toronto, dead or alive."

"What'd he want?"

"You look like hell, Alex. You should go home."

"What did he want?"

"He wanted to look after me."

"Look after you?"

"I was a valuable commodity. He had a guard posted to keep an eye on me. I think it was the guard who killed him."

"What makes you think that? Where's the driver?"

"You'll never see the driver again. The shooter let him walk."

"You actually saw this happen. The guy's been dead six or seven hours."

"At least. More. We talked. It was late evening. Just getting dark. It was dark by the time I got upstairs. Say, nine thirty. I looked out the window."

"And you saw him get shot."

"I saw the so-called guard walk over, and they conferred. There was a flash, I thought it was a lighter."

"Vittorio Ciccone didn't smoke."

"Yeah, I know that. Clean living. No drugs, only the best wines, a gourmand. I didn't think of that at the time."

"This was nine thirty. And you were going to bed?"

"Yeah, Superintendent, like you I keep odd hours."

He did not respond, so she clarified. "Alone, to read, watch a bit of TV, whatever. I didn't keep looking out the window. I saw the shooter's car drive away. The limo stayed. The driver walked. I slept."

"And he was worried about your safety."

"He was worried about going to prison. He didn't like the irony, doing life for something he didn't do."

"Well, you're off the hook. Someone's done you a favour."

"That's what he said, that I was doing *him* a favour."

"Were you?"

Miranda felt herself rise in fury, then she relaxed. Alex Rufalo knew her better than that. He was being rhetorical, trying simply to make a connection.

"Yeah," she said. "Check my Swiss bank account."

He grinned at her, which surprised him. Since being promoted to superintendent he tried not to smile in public.

Morgan took a while to assimilate what she was saying. He was just getting up when she called, before going back to bed. He was groggy; he had stayed up reading but he couldn't sleep in. There was too much on his mind, a mixture of arcane information about the world distribution of rare wines and facts about the mysteries exploding around them without a coherent pattern of demolition.

"This does not make life easier," was his initial response after a series of barely audible groans.

"It does for me," Miranda responded.

"No trial."

"No more bodies in my bed. Ciccone confirmed your suspicion that I was, in fact, the target, not Philip."

"To keep you from testifying?"

"Yeah, or at least to destroy my credibility. Killer-cop love-nest, cop exonerates crime boss, a simple equation — bad cop, crime boss goes down."

"There's still the wine connection," said Morgan.

"Not if Ciccone was the ultimate target."

"Especially if Ciccone was the target."

"What do you mean?"

"Your man Carter, he and his friends at the Ninth Chateau —"

"The what?"

"ChâteauNeuf-du-Pape."

"That would be the pope's new palace."

"Or his ninth. Anyway, he's the link."

"The pope?"

"No, Carter."

"How do you figure?"

"Carter didn't seduce you for nothing."

"No, he didn't. Seduce me. For nothing."

"There's too much coincidence, Miranda, to be a coincidence."

"Go on."

"Carter was after something. You were a project. Sorry, but you were. It was all too elaborate for a sordid seduction scenario. He was after something big."

"You're the last of the Romantics, Morgan."

"And what did you have worth the effort? Sorry, this isn't personal."

"Well, of course it's personal."

"Let's just imagine he was after something else, in addition to ..." He let his voice trail off, then started up again. "What would that be? Answer: Vittorio Ciccone."

"Let me think about it, Morgan. Go back to sleep."

"I'm getting up, you're the one going back to sleep."

"Okay. Meet me in an hour. Starbucks?"

"Tim Hortons."

"Which one?"

"Near the Summerhill subway."

"Yeah, in an hour."

Morgan got there before Miranda. He liked going to Tim Hortons. His father used to talk about hockey in the old days, when Horton was a star. Ordering a double-double and a honey cruller made him nostalgic for a past he never knew. It also made him feel like a bit of a rebel. If Miranda had arrived first, he would have ordered coffee with milk and maybe a cinnamon bagel, or bag-el, as they insisted on calling it.

Miranda came breezing in, dressed casually, carrying a large bag. "Why here?" she said when she got a coffee and dutchie and joined him.

"Hockey," he murmured. "My dad."

"What?"

"Nothing. You're looking," he looked at her appreciatively, "very nice."

"Thank you," she said, flashing an uncharacteristically demure smile.

"So," he said, warily, "let's talk business."

"Okay," she responded. "I'm going to New York."

"City?"

"Where else?"

"Elke Sturmberg?"

"Of course."

"You know what I don't get? If they were prepared to blow up the whole operation at Bonnydoon because she knew too much, then why not just kill her too?"

"Morgan, even with a felony of this magnitude, people don't arbitrarily kill people. They don't just leave a trail of bodies."

"No? I count four so far. How many constitute a trail?"

"Let's say Elke was on to them, and she was brought back to Mr. Savage. At Bonnydoon."

"To be interviewed. Then why not toss her body in the vat with the ring man?"

"Good point," said Miranda.

"Maybe they knew the man in the vat would be found, even after the explosion, maybe they wanted him to be found."

"Why?"

"I don't have any idea," said Morgan. "But let's say they did. And let's say they did not want to have Elke's body found."

"If in fact they wanted to kill her. Maybe she's part of the conspiracy."

"You don't think that."

"No. It wouldn't make sense," said Miranda.

"Then, somehow, she ended up at your place. Now she's disappeared. Maybe they've got her again."

"No way. You saw the surveillance video. She looked straight into the camera. She was in control."

"Then why go back to New York?" Morgan asked.

"Because."

"What makes you so sure?"

"Maybe I identify with her," said Miranda. "I know how she thinks."

Morgan gazed at her across the table. When she glanced away, his eyes did a quick inventory. He drew in a deep, appreciative breath. He did not like to acknowledge she was a woman, but he was always aware.

"That only goes so far, you know."

"How so?"

"Well, she's a cold-blooded killer and you're not."

"You mean the dead guy in the river? Why cold-blooded?"

"Six bullets."

"I'd say that's hot-blooded, an expression of panic or passion."

"And I'd say it shows clinical detachment, more like a gangland execution."

"Just because she had the gun doesn't mean it was her."

"Well, let's go way out on a limb and say it was. Then she'd know we'd be after her. Then she'd run away. So, my question is, where does a woman like that disappear to? She's high-profile. With her looks, her credentials, her experience in international trade — people like her don't just vanish."

"No, Morgan, they go to New York."

He couldn't tell if she was joking or affirming her mission.

"I think if she's haunted by what she can't remember," Miranda continued, "she'd return to home base, she'd go back for security. She knows people there. I'm betting she's not even hiding."

"Call her."

"What?"

"Call her."

"Where? In New York?"

"That's right. At her job. Beverley Auction House. Or at home, she'll be listed."

Miranda took a cellphone from her bag, dialled New York information, dialled again, and asked for Elke Sturmberg."

"I'm sorry," was the response, "she hasn't been in for a few days. May I take a message?"

Miranda rang off. There was no point trying her apartment, but she tried anyway.

"Hello," said a familiar voice on the answering machine. "This is Elke and I am not able to come to the —" The voice was cut off by another version of the same voice, laid over the first message: "Mine is alive, you will know where I am." Then a pause, then a beep.

"Good grief," said Miranda. She called the number again and held the phone up for Morgan to listen.

"Yeah," said Morgan. "That's cryptic."

"Her boyfriend, her ex. Remember she called him from Headquarters by mistake, or so she said."

"She hung up when he answered."

"Exactly — her ex-lover is alive. Mine is dead. That message wouldn't mean much to anyone but me."

"So he's your contact. You don't know his name."

"But I will. I have to get going to catch my flight. Be a good friend, track down his number from last night. I'll call you when I get to the airport."

"You sure you're allowed out of the country?"

"Don't ask, don't tell. As far as you know, I've retreated to the family homestead in Waterloo County. There's no phone."

She stood up, leaned over, and kissed him on the forehead with a mildly patronizing flourish so that he wouldn't think she was being too intimate. She walked out, heading for the subway. She hadn't noticed his double-double or commented on the cruller.

9

NYC

Morgan was not surprised when Miranda didn't call from Pearson. Catching commuter flights is always a hassle, and he thought how easy it would be to lose track in the wait-and-hurry of airport protocol. Still, she would have to get in touch sooner or later, since he knew where she was going in New York and she did not. He had had no trouble tracing the ex-boyfriend's number. His name was Ivan Muritori. Spivak had already been in touch with NYPD and passed on his address, along with the request that Elke Sturmberg was wanted for questioning. There was not yet a murder warrant, since the superintendent hoped to keep things on a courtesy level. She was to be picked up and strongly encouraged to return to Toronto of her own accord. If she failed to cooperate, the complicated procedures of arrest and extradition would begin. At this point, Elke Sturmberg was still a free agent.

***

Miranda's cab pulled in to the Best Western on 38th Street near the exit to the Henry Hudson Tunnel. It was cheap, clean, and so narrow that its walls seemed formed by the adjoining buildings, as if it had none of its own. She had stayed there before and recommended it to friends. She would rather spend money on restaurants or shows, although she abhorred musicals. The room was merely a place to unpack, to wash up in, to sleep.

She assumed Morgan would spend the day in the office so she waited to use the hotel phone to call him.

"Morgan!" she said ebulliently, "I'm here, New York, New York, and you're not. Did you get my address —"

"The ex-boyfriend's? Yes, and —"

"What's his address? What's his name?"

"Unlikely as it sounds, Ivan Muritori. He lives on West 58th, just over from the Inn on the Park —"

"Good, good, what number? It'll be one of those brownstones, won't it? Very, very expensive."

"Miranda."

"Yes."

"Catch your breath. Let me talk. At the present moment there is a crime in progress at Ivan Muritori's condominium, a hostage situation."

"Oh my God! You're kidding."

"No."

"Now! Really?"

"Yes."

"Right now?"

"Right now."

"He's holding her hostage! My God, I thought he was an accountant."

"He is an accountant. Listen. It's her, Elke, she's holding *him*."

"Get real!"

Morgan said nothing. The line hummed. She could hear herself breathing, she could hear the background sounds of Police Headquarters in Toronto.

"Morgan, Morgan, you still there? Seriously, what's happening?"

"Listen," he repeated. "He tried to turn her in. NYPD wanted her for questioning. When they came for her, she put a gun to his head."

"But she hasn't killed him, you said hostage."

"Yeah, it's a standoff."

"I'm on my way."

"Call me," he said. "Let me know how it works out."

"For sure. Why did the New York police want her?"

"For us. I don't know how he knew."

"I'll call."

Miranda's cab wheeled up to the police cordon blocking off the street. The cabbie asked her if she was sure this is where she wanted to be. "Absolutely," she responded, leaving him a big tip.

She got through the first barrier with no problem, simply by flashing her police identification.

The command centre was behind a phalanx of cars directly across from the ex-boyfriend's brownstone. She walked up to the man in charge and showed him her ID.

"You're out of your jurisdiction, lady," he snapped. "Stand back."

"I know the woman in there, and you're out of your depth. Boy, I —"

"Around here you don't call a black man 'boy,'" he snarled.

"Where I come from, you don't call a cop 'lady.'"

He glowered.

"And," she continued, "where I come from, 'boy' is an immature man."

He grimaced. Both of them recognized they had let primal sensitivities obscure the crisis at hand. He shrugged.

"Yeah," he said. "How're you gonna help us?"

"I know her. Let me talk to her."

"Like, you're friends?"

"I know her."

He begrudgingly handed Miranda the cellphone, as if he could not think of an alternative course of action.

"She's all yours."

"You're telling me she's on the line right now."

"What line? Lady, she's there," said the commanding officer, making the sign of a phone by waggling his hand, thumb and baby finger extended, then added, "Detective."

"Quin."

"Yeah. Clancy."

"Clancy?"

"Yeah, don't you know all cops in Manhattan are Irish?" He smiled broadly.

Denzel Washington, she thought. *Damn, that's essentializing, but damn, he's good-looking.*

"Are you listening, Elke?" She had wanted Elke Sturmberg to overhear, to warm to the familiar voice. "It's Miranda. I've come down from Toronto to see you. Morgan couldn't come with me. He's working."

"Are you working?" said Elke, sounding like she was talking from a great distance away.

"Me, no, are you kidding? You know I'm not on the job." She lowered her voice, but Clancy could hear. "You know I'm on leave, like, you know what for. Yours is alive, remember. Let's keep him that way. Do you want me to come in?"

"Do you want to come in?"

"Sure."

"No guns."

"No guns, I'm Canadian."

"You're what?"

"I don't carry a gun these days, you remember?"

"Yes, I'm glad you're here."

Miranda walked slowly up the steps of the brownstone and through the massive front door. Whispers moved through the crowd of police behind her as explanations were passed around about who she was. A relative, a professional negotiator, a cop from Toronto? Miranda opened the apartment door enough for a wedge of light to fall through into the hall.

"Elke? It's me."

There was no answer. She pushed the door so that it swung all the way open. Elke was sitting on the floor in the shadows. Her hostage was on a chair in the bright afternoon light streaming aslant from the west through the south-facing front windows. Sharpshooters across the street could see him but not her. The curtains were open wide so that outside, the observers felt exposed. She seemed to know what she was doing.

"Elke, are you all right?"

"What about me?" said Ivan Muritori.

"Shut up," said Miranda.

The ex-boyfriend hostage looked startled but acceded to what he assumed was police strategy.

Miranda walked slowly into the shadows until she was close to Elke and their eyes made contact. She squatted down in front of her, directly in the line of fire. Elke flicked off the safety. Miranda felt a cold shiver run up her spine. She lowered herself to the floor so that she was sitting, as if they were lounging at a sleepover before dimming the lights and telling each other secrets.

"Miranda?" Elke broke the silence.

"Yes."

"I remember."

"What?"

"What happened on the way to your place."

"You tell me about it, but why don't you put the gun down."

"No."

Miranda held out her hand passively, as if she were indicating she wanted the potato chip bowl or a refill of wine.

Elke stiffened and flicked the gun in a menacing thrust at the air.

Miranda shifted her gaze. "Why are you holding him? I thought it was over."

"It is over. I dumped him, he didn't dump me."

"Why did you come here?"

"I figured it's the last place they'd look. Everyone knew it was over."

"They? Everyone?"

"Whoever is trying to kill me."

"Elke, why not let him go. I'm here. You wanted that. We'll talk, we don't need him listening."

"I can't."

"What?"

"Let him go."

"Why?"

Miranda shifted around so that she could see the ex-boyfriend was tied crudely to the chair with a belt and a couple of ties. There was something vaguely comical and incongruous about him. He was wearing slacks and a polo shirt. He looked like he should be in jogging shorts or a grey flannel suit. He looked like he was sulking.

"He's an accountant," said Miranda.

"That's what he says."

Miranda got up and walked over to him, glancing out the windows at the formidable array of police in flak jackets with rifles at the ready. She wanted to establish a three-way rapport, to get Elke thinking of him again as a person, not a weapon or shield.

"So, Ivan," she said. "You're an accountant."

He tilted his head back and looked her straight in the eye. "Yes," he said in a confessional tone. "That's what I do, I crunch numbers."

"Ask him who for," said Elke from the shadows.

"Who for," said Miranda.

"Confederate Union Insurance."

"They play both sides," said Miranda.

"What?"

"Confederate. Union. Civil War. They play both sides."

The significance of the name had obviously never occurred to him.

"Ask him who else he works for," said Elke.

"Who else do you work for?"

"Nobody, she's nuts."

"I wouldn't call a distraught woman with a loaded gun pointed at my head nasty names."

"Sorry. Sorry, Elke."

"Scumball, scumbag. Creep," said Elke, getting up and stepping momentarily into the light before realizing her tactical error and slipping back into the shadows.

Miranda moved around the room until she was close to Elke again, but still in the light. "What is it, what's he done? This isn't because he turned you in?"

"For a start, yes it is. I came to him for help."

"And I tried," said Muritori.

"What happened?" said Miranda.

The ex-boyfriend started to talk, but Miranda squelched him.

"I want to hear from Elke."

"I got here late Sunday. I took the bus from Toronto. I'm sorry I took off like that. I just knew I had to get away. I didn't have any money. I telephoned Ivan, he sent me cash but Western Union wouldn't turn it over, no ID, so I hustled enough on the street, not far from the hotel. I asked a couple of business travellers for a few bucks. Canadians are generous or dumb — actually, they were visiting Americans. What the hell, they said, she's not a hooker. She just wants money. So they each gave me fifty bucks. I asked for a little more. They thought it was funny. They gave me enough for bus fare. I'll pay them back. I told them I'd been dumped by my boyfriend, we'd come up from New York."

"What about the border?"

"I wasn't asked for ID at the border. I'm blond."

"Okay, so our friend Ivan knew you were coming."

"I did," said Ivan over his shoulder. "The police came, they told me she was wanted for questioning."

"Shut up, Ivan," said Miranda.

"So when I got here," Elke continued, "he didn't tell me they were after me, that he was supposed to call them if I turned up."

"And what happened?"

"He thought I was in the shower. Only I don't trust Ivan. I was listening from the bedroom. When he called in the NYPD, I took his gun from the bedside table —"

"He keeps a gun beside the bed?"

"This is New York," said Ivan, defensively.

"So even accountants have guns," said Miranda.

"Especially accountants," said Ivan, trying to make a joke.

"Shut up, Ivan," said Elke.

"So when the police arrived, you had a gun to his head. What were you figuring, Elke? What's your next move? You're in a bit of a corner."

"Yes, so it seems. Any suggestions?"

"For a start, you can let me go. You've got her." He nodded in Miranda's direction. "Hold her as your hostage."

"He's got a point," said Miranda. "Not very gallant, but he does have a point. Why don't you let him go?"

"Because he's a crook."

"Elke, you can't hold him because he's a crooked accountant. Half the accountants and lawyers in the Western world would be held accountable at the end of a gun if that's how it worked."

"He's with the mob."

Miranda nearly choked. There was something so incongruously naïve about the blond woman's declaration, Miranda had to suppress laughter.

"Come on, Elke, I told you that's ridiculous." The ex-boyfriend had no compunction about expressing his contempt for the accusation. "That's absolutely beyond possibility."

"No," said Elke. "He is, he works for gangsters, he's a bookkeeper for the Mafia."

"I'm not even Italian, I was adopted!" he shouted. Despite the pathos or wit, it crossed Miranda's mind that there could be an element of truth in what Elke was saying.

Miranda again stepped in front of the gun. "Whether he's Al Capone or Al Pacino, you can't hold him hostage forever. You're not going to kill him."

Elke flourished the pistol and Miranda stood her ground.

"What's going on, here, Elke? Try to explain."

"I killed that man in Toronto."

"You what?" Ivan stifled a shriek.

"That's why they want me, dummy."

"You killed a man."

"Six bullets," said Miranda to Muritori. "The NYPD didn't tell you that?"

"They said they wanted her for questioning, they said it was a serious matter, they said I'd be helping her by calling if she contacted me again, they said it would be better for her."

"They said, they said, didn't you think, dummy?"

"Don't call me that, Elke."

"Dummy."

"Okay, you two," said Miranda. "You're beginning to sound like you're in love."

"Did you really kill someone? With a gun, you shot him?"

"With a gun, I shot him, yes."

"Enough!" Miranda snapped. "You've got an army out there, they want to shoot someone, too. We have a situation here. They're not going to wait forever. The city needs them, and they'll want to clean this mess up and move on. So. It's time, Elke. Let him go."

To Miranda's surprise, the blond woman emerged from the shadows and, standing fully illuminated within sight of the marksmen poised outside, she handed the gun to Miranda and proceeded to untie her hostage. Then she reached out for the gun again. Miranda backed away, gently. Elke could force a shooting and Miranda did not want that. Elke moved back onto a sofa and sat down, as if she were prepared to resume an interrupted conversation.

Ivan Muritori stood up tentatively. He started to edge toward to door, brushing his hands over the front of his crotch, holding them poised furtively. Miranda noticed that he had wet himself.

"Hey, champ," she said. "Why don't you change clothes before you go out to meet your public!"

Heartened, he walked into the bedroom.

Miranda picked up the cellphone. "Clancy?"

"Yeah. You coming out?"

"Give us a minute."

"You got it. You all right?"

"Yeah —"

A gunshot shattered the room. Miranda, gun in hand, dove toward Elke, covering her with her body as the sofa tipped over on its back. She assumed the shot had come from outside. No glass was broken. Another shot exploded from the bedroom doorway. She rolled away from Elke across the floor, firing in motion. A single shot.

She squeezed out another, then her gun jammed. She lunged behind a chair. Nothing moved. She could hear Clancy's voice. The cellphone lay out in the open.

Two more shots shook the room. There was silence, then Ivan Muritori emerged from the bedroom, clutching the second gun he had retrieved from his arsenal. He stood still for a moment. He seemed to assume they were both dead. Miranda held her breath. She could hear her blood pounding. He walked into the hallway. He opened the massive front door, still brandishing his pistol.

The entire scene fell absolutely quiet, as if someone had switched off the soundtrack in a movie. A single shot rang out, and for a split second there was silence. Then a riot of explosions filled the air as rifles and handguns rhymed off innumerable shots into the body of Ivan Muritori.

As suddenly as the lethal clattering started, it stopped. Again there was silence.

Then it was broken inside the apartment by a voice on the cellphone.

Miranda picked up the phone, simultaneously checking to see if Elke was alive.

"Toronto! You okay?"

"Yes," said Miranda. "We're both okay. Don't come in."

"She still holding a gun on you?"

"Don't come in. Everything's under control. Give us a few minutes. Have your army stand down. Danger's over."

"Roger that. Well done."

Miranda had helped Elke to her feet while she was talking. They looked at each other like comrades at arms. Miranda's leg was throbbing from her bullet wound that until now she had forgotten about, although it had ached on the plane coming down. Together they sank back against the closest wall, sliding onto the floor.

"Your accountant had two guns!"

"He's a mobster."

"And only two bullets in one of them, or it jammed. A very strange ex-boyfriend."

"That's why I broke it off."

"You nearly broke a lot more than that. You're lucky to be alive."

"That's a subjective judgement."

"Well, yes it is, Elke. Being alive is subjective, that's the way it goes. Now tell me about the man in Toronto. I want to know before the NYPD get to you."

"Is he dead?"

"Who? Ivan? Yes, I would imagine he is. Were you holding him to avoid talking to the police about the shooting?"

"No. Once I remembered, I wanted to talk. To you, not them. I'm your problem, your jurisdiction. I figured you'd call my answering machine. I tried to leave a message. I knew they'd be watching my place."

"Exactly. So what happened. We've got a few minutes."

"He betrayed me. I wanted to hurt him. Thank you for coming."

"Pick it up from Bonnydoon, we haven't got long."

10

The Mob

It came back to me on the bus. I was trying to sleep. You know what it's like on a bus, you're droning along, wheels humming, and you're half awake and you lose track of where you are. It came back in images, but not as you'd imagine, not in random order on a scale of intensity. It came back in chronological sequence, like I was watching an old-fashioned movie.

You remember I was in the wine shed, the bottling shed at the end. I was blindfolded, taped in a chair. I told you I heard someone, the others called him Mr. Savage. He chopped off the screaming man's hand. Or someone did it on his order. They mostly weren't speaking English.

I had flown to Rochester to check out a wine source. We had cases of vintage Châteauneuf-du-Pape from an estate I couldn't track down. I couldn't get a price on it. We always publish an estimate of what something will bring at auction. This was a mystery wine, and the paper trail traced our lot through a retailer in Rochester.

So, there I am at Bonnydoon when I hear a gunshot. I could picture what happened. I was blindfolded, but I could hear the body fall into the vat.

"Get rid of her," said a voice I assume was Mr. Savage's. In English. Then he said something in another language, and then he said, "Not here." Then he said in Italian, "I don't want her found. She disappears."

He was speaking in three languages.

I was blindfolded, but the blindfold slipped off. It didn't seem to bother them. As far as they were concerned, I was already dead.

He dumped my purse, motioning to another man, who picked up a severed hand. There was a gold ring. It seemed like the flesh was still pulsing. It seemed like it was alive. He wrapped it in tissues and dropped it into my bag. He scooped up my stuff, removed identification cards and papers, then dropped the rest into the bag.

"The hand," he said, then he said something in another language. Then in Italian, he repeated, "She disappears."

He leaned over me. I could see every pore in his face. He was breathing through his nose but I could smell his breath; it was sweet and minty. He ran his hands over me, not sexually, not so you'd know it. Even the crudest groper wants a response, but it was more like he was assessing a slab of meat at the slaughterhouse or trying to embed anatomical details in his memory, knowing I was going to die.

He stopped, or he was stopped. I'm not sure.

Mr. Savage told someone in Italian where to find you. Miranda Quin, he said. He gave your address on Isabella Street and spoke as if he were repeating known information. I got the impression the man he was talking to was supposed to find you and kill you. You were the main event. Your death. Mine was a nuisance, yours a necessity. Your name, your address, they were seared into my brain.

I was placed in a car. It was night. I could see lights in the big house up behind the vineyards, the house where the old lady lived.

My hands were taped at the wrists. I had gloves taped over my hands. They didn't want fingerprints. My ankles were taped. The driver taped them after I walked to the car. He ran his hands up my legs. God, men are pathetic. He had a chance, he took it. I didn't have tape over my mouth. I had not said a word since they picked me up in the Rochester parking lot. Nothing. Mute. I whispered in his ear as he was leaning over me, "Fuck you." It startled him. He flipped my skirt to prove his power then smoothed it down to prove gentility.

Gentility! The guy was going to kill me.

We drove. The scenery, the highway signs — everything I saw — was intensified by the terror. I recorded every detail in my mind, I jammed my head with facts.

After we got on the main highway, I started talking to him. In Italian. He answered in Italian but switched to English. His Italian was worse than mine. We talked in English. We might have been on an arranged date. Like I was from out of town, visiting his relatives.

We drove along the Queen Elizabeth Way, the QEW as he called it. I told him I had to pee. Badly.

It was his car. A big brutal sedan. He swore he would kill me.

I said, that's what you're going to do anyway. I'm going to pee and I'm going to throw up in your car.

He told me to wait, we'd be stopping soon. At a building site. I could pee there.

I insisted, sooner. He pulled over then realized he'd have to free me legs and my arms too, or else hold up my skirt. By now we were friends in his mind, he had too much respect.

We were almost in Toronto. He pulled off at a sign for Lake Shore Boulevard. We circled around and he parked at the base of a bridge. A sign said it was the Humber River. I remember everything.

I really did have to pee. I was losing it. By the time he got my legs free, I thought I'd wet my pants. I was squirming, so he panicked and cut my wrist tapes. I started to drop my drawers, and he turned his head away, I grabbed his gun tucked in his belt right there in front of me. He turned his head back — he looked so surprised.

I pulled the trigger. And again and again, it just kept firing. It was empty before he hit the ground.

He was looking up at me like he was disappointed, only he was dead.

I got in the car. The keys were still in the ignition. I dropped his gun, I guess, into my purse, then I backed up carefully so I wouldn't run over him. I stopped when the headlights picked him up. I got out of the car. He looked unnatural, lying there. I pushed him over into the river. I tried to finish peeing, but I couldn't. I had to go but I couldn't.

When I got to a subway, I dumped the car. Left it parked on a side street. Asked directions to your place, to Isabella. I had to rescue you. I had to connect. That's about it. You know the rest.

Do I? thought Miranda. She took a deep breath. The story was consistent with the facts. The woman wasn't accounting sufficiently for the amnesia, but then, Miranda supposed, the thing about amnesia is you forget what it's like when it's over.

"If Ivan betrayed you, why hold him hostage, why not just walk out? You had the gun, you could have left."

"The police were here before I knew what to do. It was instinctive. I wanted to hurt him. I don't just mean he betrayed me, calling the cops. Miranda, he set me up."

"Set you up?"

"Rochester. Ivan set me up to be killed."

"Elke, why on earth — you were there to find out about a shipment of Châteauneuf-du-Pape, somebody's wine cellar you wanted to auction."

"But did I say where it came from?"

"Yes. Someone's estate. Originally from upstate New York."

"It was an estate Ivan told me he was working on."

"Not surprising. He was in the insurance business. He's lying riddled with bullets outside the front door. Doesn't that …" she searched for the right word, "… engage … engage your interest?"

"Here's what I think," said Elke, ignoring Miranda's question. "I think he tried to use me. Let's give him the benefit of the doubt — he's dead — let's say he didn't know it was counterfeit. He just wanted to dump a bunch of wine. Fifty cases, a good year on the Rhône, say $200 a bottle, that's $120,000. So, let's say he really does moonlight for the mob —"

"The mob!"

"Gangsters, bad guys, Tony Soprano —"

"He's into garbage, that's where the big money is."

"Let's say I'm right."

"Okay."

"Somebody in the mob pays him off in wine, he doesn't know how to sell it, he turns to me. Then what happens? I find there's no such wine and no dead guy, no estate being cleared. So, I trace the wine back to Millennium in Rochester. Dead end. I go there to find out their supplier. You with me?"

"Yes."

"Meanwhile, the gangsters freak out. He wasn't supposed to get caught. He was supposed to pay off a jobber, unload the wine through a few select stores with mob connections. That's how these things are done. But he was greedy, he tried to sell it through me. ATF don't care, in stores it's only a few bottles at a time."

"ATF?"

"The Feds. Alcohol, Tobacco, Firearms. Whatever, it's a government agency. But me, I was going to blow the whistle. Not intentionally. I'm just good at what I do."

"So good, they figured if you knew, you needed to be eliminated."

"Exactly, Miranda. These guys don't fool around. They probably wanted to get rid of Ivan as well. When they saw you and Morgan and me back there at

Bonnydoon, they figured the word was out. Everything was already wired for just such an occasion. They blew everything up."

"No question the house was a bomb, set for maximum destruction."

"Yes, in case things went wrong. There must have been evidence in the house, records and things."

Miranda smiled at the younger woman. "Come on. Take my arm. We'll walk out together."

"Thanks for being here," said Elke. "You came a long way."

"Not so far," said Miranda. "Toronto's about the same distance away as Cleveland or Raleigh, North Carolina."

"Thanks anyway."

They stood in the shadows inside the open door. Miranda could feel Elke's breast pressing against her arm as she leaned into her for support.

"Coming out!" Miranda shouted. The street was in shadow now, and there was a flurry of restrained activity. Then everything stopped. The two women stepped into the open. The stoop was brilliant with splattered blood. They stood still.

Clancy walked up the steps, followed by two cops swathed in bulletproof armour. He reached out and took Elke's arm.

"No," said Miranda. "It wasn't her." She could not stop herself. She pulled Elke away from his grasp.

"It was him," she said. "He was holding *her* hostage."

"Say what!"

"It was him, holding her! Ivan Muritori. He forced her to say it was her, the other way around, but he was going to kill her. And say it was self-defense. When I went in, he had the gun on her. He was sitting in the open so you could see him. He kept her out of sight."

"Jesus!" said Clancy.

Miranda was astonished by what she was saying. Elke was stunned into silent compliance.

"He had us both, he was going to kill us together."

"Where'd the other gun come from?" said Clancy, running all the known facts through his mind, still dubious but not antagonistic.

"It was his," said Elke. "They were both his. It was in the living room. In a desk drawer. I told Miranda, I told Detective Quin."

"She distracted him, I went for the gun," said Miranda. "You heard the shootout. We were lucky. He took off."

"Yeah," said Clancy, "you were lucky. What took so long, after he came out?"

"I was hysterical," said Elke. "Detective Quin talked me down."

"I know her," said Miranda. "We've shared some pretty bad things. We need her for questioning. There's no way she did the killing in Toronto, but we need her to process the details."

What Miranda knew was that Elke's execution of the man under the Humber bridge was a reasonable act of self-defense, but if she admitted Elke's involvement, the NYPD would have no option but to arrest her, and Miranda did not want that.

"Yeah, well, we need her here, too,"

Miranda felt her heart sink, but he continued.

"She might help us figure who killed this guy." He nodded toward the ambulance with the back door still open, where Ivan Muritori's corpse lay under a plastic shroud.

"Who killed him? It wasn't us? Didn't you? Didn't he go down in the proverbial hail of bullets?"

"He did," said Clancy, "after a sniper picked him off from somewhere across the street. It was a perfect hit. Our guys were focused on the guy coming through the door. He's waving a semi-automatic. Pop goes a shot. He drops. Before the guy hits the ground, our guys let loose. Reflex. Once the shooting starts, take no chances. But we didn't fire the first shot, and neither did he. It was a hit."

"The mob!" said Elke.

"The mob," said Clancy. "It was professional, definitely the mob."

11

The Mausoleum

The funeral of Vittorio Ciccone was the social hit of the season. Visitation at the mortuary on Danforth Avenue was overwhelming. They were forced to farm out other jobs to competitors just to accommodate the turnover of those coming to pay their respects, those coming to be seen for personal and professional reasons, those needing to participate in an event larger than anything else in their lives, those who wanted the assurance that he was dead, which would come only by seeing him lying in state, a neat cosmetic plug in the centre of his forehead.

At the cemetery, the service and those attending were more refined. Holding the wake and visitation near where the deceased had grown up, an Italian area surrounded by Greeks, had been his wife's idea. It was in deference to his humble beginnings. It was also her idea to celebrate the burial service in front of their family mausoleum in the most exclusive part of the most exclusive cemetery in the heart of the city. Etched into the marble lintel over the mausoleum door was the name "Ciccone." The mausoleum was empty, built — bought, actually, with dynastic aspirations, the size of a small house with granite walls, no windows, and a massive door. Successive generations of the family would find their way here, eventually, where she and Vittorio would preside through eternity. It was all happening a little sooner than they had anticipated, but this was no reason to skimp on the grandeur of the event.

Morgan had never seen so many black limousines. A rock star had tried to enter the cemetery in a white limousine but was turned away at the gate. He was forced to walk in from the street. Limousines likely had to be brought in from Hamilton, Oakville, and Oshawa. Morgan arrived with Spivak and Stritch and walked in. There were police in street clothes here and there throughout the crowd, all of whom seemed to Morgan, themselves included, to be passively intrusive.

"You ever see so many fur coats?" said Spivak.

"Not in June," said Morgan.

"I didn't know people still wore black to funerals," said Stritch in a tone suggesting he approved.

"Yeah, well funerals are not all alike," said Spivak, "even if we're equals under the sod."

"Some are more equal than others," said Morgan. A smile crept over his face as he observed the obsequies. "That's quite the tomb; it looks like Vittorio Ciccone will rest high until hell freezes over."

"Or until the damn thing falls down, then they'll bulldoze it into the ground," said Spivak, registering satisfaction at the prospect. *I wonder if he's heard of Ozymandias?* thought Morgan.

The casket lay on a gurney disguised with a white satin skirt, surrounded by rows of folding wooden chairs sitting on artificial turf, except in front of the mausoleum, where there were banks of flowers arranged in descending waves, like floral surf rolling out of the crypt.

"You know what's funny about this lot?" said Morgan.

"Yeah, everyone's here," said Spivak.

It was true, there were city councillors, Bay Street brokers, members of various hospital boards (Ciccone had been a generous benefactor), representatives of major cultural institutions (Ciccone was a patron of the opera and of the ballet and gave considerable sums to theatre groups), there were bar musicians, recording artists, Rosedale neighbours who preferred to believe the Ciccone family were in construction, and representatives of several large unions, whose members were employed at Ciccone construction sites.

People not there included bikers, who had paid their respects by showing their colours at the funeral home; drug addicts, at least those who had degenerated to the point where they were unkempt derelicts; streetwalkers who would turn a trick for the price of a fix, call girls who would shoot up with weekend thrill-seekers from out of town or workaday addicts from the business district, hookers who had not yet lost their looks; and social workers who battled night and day the horrors of the mean streets most Torontonians drove through unknowingly or by accident.

Powerful members of the church and the legal profession were there, Morgan observed, even while pro bono lawyers and priests who ran shelters were absent.

"Everyone is here," said Morgan, repeating Spivak's assessment. "But you know what?"

The three of them were standing off to the side in front of some manicured shrubs, the only members of the force not trying to blend in. There would be a few Mounties there as well, because of the drug connection, but they would be invisible. Spivak and Stritch waited for Morgan to answer his own rhetorical question. They knew from his tone he was on to something. None of them were in a hurry. They were here for the duration.

"Look around," said Morgan. "Find me a gangster who is not here."

"Well, if they're not here ..." Stritch's quibble trailed into contemplative silence.

"Think about it," said Morgan. "Name me a big-time crook, a Mafia boss, a rival gangster ..."

"What's your point?" said Spivak, who recognized the funeral of Vittorio Ciccone as a mandatory event. "Who would stay away?"

"That is the point," said Morgan. "If it was a Mafia hit, don't you think the offending faction would avoid the proceedings?"

"Not really," said Spivak. "I think they might come to gloat. Or as a display of supremacy. Or to begin organizing the succession."

"Look at Frankie Ciccone, Spivak. She's radiant. The grieving widow — even gangsters grieve. But she's a smart woman, she knows the business. And she's showing no signs the killers are here."

"A good-looking woman," Stritch observed.

"What else!" said Spivak, as if there were no alternative for the wife of someone like Ciccone. Then he turned to Morgan, speaking confidentially as if Stritch were an outsider.

"She's savvy. If the assassins are here, she'd know it, you'd see it on her face."

Morgan suppressed a smile. Spivak had said exactly what he had said, in almost the same words. Spivak was waiting to see what conclusion would be drawn from their shrewd observations.

"The gunman worked for the Ciccone family, but he was from Italy, an Albanian refugee, right?" Morgan looked at Spivak for agreement.

"Yeah. Who told you he was from Albania?"

"I heard it around."

"Who from?"

"I called a friend."

"Just a guy you know."

"A friend, we went to school together, Jarvis Collegiate."

"No shit! I went there too."

"Before my time."

"How old are you!"

"Younger than you, Spivak."

"Everyone's younger than me. Look at this guy." He nodded toward Eeyore Stritch. "I knew his father."

"I thought you were Jamaican?" said Morgan, turning to the other man. "You're living a lie."

"I'm not Jamaican, man. I keep telling you that," he said in a rolling West Indian cadence. "You guys can't tell an accent."

"Maybe if you shaved your head," said Spivak as he started coughing.

"That's racial stereotyping," said Stritch. "I don't call you a slap-head Slovak —"

"The shooter," said Morgan. "He had no connections with the local community, he was taken on by Ciccone as a favour."

"To whom?"

"We don't know. Nobody knows. That's the thing, nobody knows."

"So where are you going with this?" said Spivak, between hacking and trying to breathe. "Goddamn it," he said. "I gotta quite smoking." He took a slow, shallow breath. "You're saying what?"

"Well," said Morgan, "if it wasn't the bad guys who killed Vittorio Ciccone, then maybe it was the good guys."

"Shit, Morgan," exclaimed Spivak. "It's one thing to set him up for a fall, if that's what those bozos in Hamilton were doing, but killing him, man, that's nowhere, that didn't happen."

"Why not? If Miranda's testimony was gonna get him off —"

"Then why not kill Miranda?"

"Because she's a cop. I'm saying, if cops were in on this, they'd go for the direct hit. There'd be heavier repercussions if they killed another cop, a good cop, than if they exterminated a bad guy."

"No, Morgan. Any cop devious enough to hire a hitman knows there are an infinite number of replacements for Ciccone, just waiting for their turn to step up to the plate."

"It sounds plausible to me," said Stritch.

"I'm not saying it's not plausible, for Chrissakes, I'm saying it didn't happen." Spivak glowered at his partner.

In the background, the rows of chairs were filling with Ciccone family and close associates. A solemn hush spread through the cemetery as a priest stepped up to the head of the casket. They could not hear what he was saying. Then he nodded to Frankie Ciccone and she nodded to someone else, and a hundred white doves were released from the shadows behind the mausoleum to rise in a fluttering melee of feathers and thumping air into the bright June sky. There was a gasp from the crowd expressing amazement, amusement, and an outpouring of grief.

"Be hard to top that," said Spivak.

Just then a bugler hidden from view inside the crypt started playing Taps, which echoed within the stone chamber and emerged in a resounding cacophony of thunder and brass. Without a break, the bugler switched to Reveille and as he did so emerged from the shadows to stand full-throated in the doorway of the tomb, engulfed in flowers, and the notes rang out as crisp and clean as a prayer.

"Yeah," said Morgan, "or that."

The service proceeded, but instead of the obsequies ending with the casket being lowered into the ground, it was hoisted on the shoulders of six burley pallbearers who stood waiting as a passageway was cleared through the flowers, then started to carry it into the crypt, but stopped when someone realized their load was being carried too high to clear the lintel. Excessively efficient attendants had already removed the satin-covered gurney, and the pallbearers had to lower the casket from above their shoulders, a more cumbersome task than might have been expected as they struggled to avoid the indignity of allowing Vittorio's head to rise higher than his feet. One of the pallbearers stumbled but the other five recovered equilibrium and he sheepishly rejoined them as they disappeared with the casket into the dark shadows of the mausoleum.

After they came out, the priest and Frankie Ciccone and her stepchildren, who were adults, their mother having died when they were in their teens, went into the dark chamber. One by one, the priest and then each of the four grown children came out and, after a considerable time, the widow emerged and the great door, molded in the manner of one of the Ghiberti doors on the southernmost side of the campanile in Florence, was swung shut with a heavy clang and the giant key turned to lock it in place until the necessity should arise for another Ciccone to join Vittorio. His first wife, who had been born in Toronto, was buried in Tuscany where her people originated, outside the town of Arezzo.

Morgan walked down to where the last few guests were mingling, some of them reading the cards on the floral arrangements and hoping to have a word with Frankie Ciccone, although she was being shielded by the cluster of pallbearers who now acted as a barricade, letting though one or two at a time as the widow indicated by the most subtle of eye movements. Morgan stood off to the side, surveying the scene. Spivak and Stritch had gone back to Headquarters. The remaining police presence had vanished.

Frankie Ciccone was sitting on the edge of her folding chair, comforting an elderly woman dressed in habitual black. Her children had gone back to the house where immediate family was gathering for a small reception. She glanced through the barricade and caught Morgan's eye. She dropped her eyelids in a subtle gesture and allowed the hint of a smile to compress her lips.

Morgan tilted his head to the side in a restrained expression of sympathy.

Her entourage knew Morgan was a homicide detective. He was seldom involved directly in the family's affairs. In the interpenetrating worlds of crime and the law, people know each other. No one was surprised when the widow rose to her feet and walked in his direction. In fact, the others fell away to let the two of them converse in private, off the record, on a one-to-one basis.

"David," she said.

"Francine. Sorry for your loss," he said.

"Are you here professionally?"

"Yes and no."

"For the no part, thank you."

"I am sorry, Frankie."

"Me too. He was a bastard, Morgan, but he was a great man."

He smiled at the grieving widow. She truly believed her husband could be ranked in death with bishops and senators and business tycoons. While alive, it had been enough that he lived in their neighbourhood. Now she envisioned him as their peer. By the fact of his death, if not the manner of his dying, she as his widow had been moved up the social scale. From here on she would be concerned with family philanthropies, not business.

"He did a lot of good things, David."

Morgan shrugged without rancour. This was not the time for aspersions. "You've come a long way since J.C.V.I.," he said.

"Jarvis Collegiate and Vocational Institute, rah rah rah. Yeah. Do my roots show? Just thinking about it makes you want to burst into songs from *Grease*."

"You spend more time at *Les Mis* and *Phantom* and *Cats,* I hear."

"Yes, David, I do, or I did. Vittorio loved those shows. Myself, I'd rather watch John Travolta and Olivia Newton-John, over and over, but there you are."

"There you are," he agreed. "Are your people any closer to finding the Albanian?"

"My people? No, they're not. And yours?"

"No leads."

The pallbearers were standing in a cluster, making a show of not paying attention to the widow and the detective. They were at a level in her husband's organization where it would not have occurred to them it was anything but business.

The remaining mourners had wandered off, some to spend a contemplative hour among the graves, complimenting themselves on being alive, reading tombstones and monuments, enjoying the flowers and trees, most to pursue the daily details of their lives.

"How's your partner?" asked Frankie. "I heard Vittorio was the second murder on her watch in a week."

"Yeah, plus two down in the Niagara Peninsula. You know about them?"

She looked up at him and smiled at his apparent naiveté. There was a hard line between gossip and business — especially gossip that concerned the execution of her husband. She did not answer.

Morgan for the first time noticed the rawness around her eyes and recognized her genuine grief, obscured by her composure and the elaborate funeral rites she had orchestrated.

"Let's meander for a bit," she said to Morgan, taking his arm.

They walked along a winding pathway up out of the mausoleum quarter and into more modestly occupied terrain, talking quietly. The six pallbearers followed in a cluster behind them at a discreet distance.

"Do you hear from Lucy?" she asked.

"My Lucy? No...." The two women had met at university, where all three of them shared a class in forensic psychopathology. Morgan and Lucy did not get together until after they graduated, after Morgan returned from nearly two years in Europe, finding and losing himself, and had briefly enrolled in graduate school, before dropping out, taking a diploma in criminology, and joining the police force.

When he and Lucy were married, they received a sterling silver tea service from Vittorio and Francine Ciccone, which they returned with a conciliatory note. Ciccone was still on his way up then, and a newly remarried widower. Jarvis Collegiate and their Cabbagetown childhood were a long way behind both David Morgan and Francine Ciccone. Lucy had grown up safely in Scarborough.

From time to time, he and the gangster's wife crossed paths — not that they were in the same social circles. They were always polite and quite formal with each other, meeting in the foyers of theatres, amid the bustle of significant public events — and invariably there was an exchange between them, flashed in a glance, that acknowledged they might have been lovers, might have been married, had things been different. Even in grade nine, there was chemistry between them.

Morgan was a loner — that's what she found attractive — and she was poised for success, and he found that exciting. But what attracted them to each other was what kept them apart.

She talked about her stepchildren. She and Vittorio never had any of their own. That would have been an insult to his first wife. When Frankie explained this, Morgan was baffled. She said it matter-of-factly and went on to claim that was the only way he held back. She had never felt, otherwise, anything but the best — she was his absolute true love. It was her he wanted to spend eternity with, in their mausoleum. He had no desire to join his first wife in Arezzo.

"I must leave in a minute. There is a reception at the house."

She stopped, drawing Morgan back in mid-stride. Reaching into her purse, she withdrew a card and handed it to him.

"It has my number on it. Call me."

"Unlisted, I imagine."

She looked up at him and smiled, and then her eyes turned hard. "I can't help you on this, David. But you can help me. I want Vittorio's killers. I know who they are. I want them dead. Then I will be a Rosedale widow, which in this world is not such a bad thing to be."

"The Albanian connection?"

"Nothing, David. I can say nothing more." She leaned up and kissed him on the cheek. "You may not be a great man, David Morgan, but you are a good man."

She released his arm, turned, and walked over to her burly entourage without looking back. He watched as they disappeared among the rows of tombstones, down into the valley of the dead, where the mausoleums were clustered side by side, as close as houses in suburbia.

Back at his desk, Morgan found himself ruminating about what Frankie Ciccone had said. He was not sure whether to feel insulted by her compliment, with its implied limitations, or flattered by what some might take as an insult, coming as it did from a mobster's widow.

No, he thought, *I have never aspired to greatness. God knows I am a humble and sensitive man.* He chuckled to himself. *As for being good, I think that's something someone does, not what someone is. By that measure, sometimes I'm good, sometimes not so good.*

The telephone rang. It was Miranda.

"How's New York?"

"Fine, they want us around for a bit."

"Doing what?"

"Waiting, mostly."

"You still at the Best Western?"

"No, I've moved in with Elke. She lives in the Village, a loft. She's doing all right for herself."

"You sure that's a good idea?"

"You mean, her life might still be on the line?"

"Yeah, that too. I meant maybe you're too close for your own good."

"I don't think she's in any danger. The wine scam's over and done with. Anyway, I'm off duty, remember."

"And living with a prime suspect."

"Staying with! And she's not a suspect."

"About as close as you can get, come on."

"Morgan, there's more than you know."

He backed away. He trusted her judgement, especially in matters like this. If she knew things he didn't, then her call was okay.

"Is the NYPD aware you're on leave?"

"Yes and no. My friend, Captain Clancy, he's running the investigation on the ex-boyfriend's execution. He knows. Everyone else in New York assumes I'm working."

"And he doesn't think it's strange you're staying with Elke?"

"Like I said, there's more than you know. He thinks I'm acting as her bodyguard until we can head back. He's grateful."

"Did you say execution?"

"When?"

"Just now. You said the boyfriend was executed."

"That's part of what you're not caught up about. I told you he was gunned down outside his brownstone, and that Elke wasn't implicated, that I covered for her. Well, we figured the ex was picked off by a sniper setting off a police barrage — it was a major shootout, no one would have paid much attention to a guy with a smoking gun. But the dead man never fired a shot. He was riddled like a sieve — by the time they got him to the morgue most of his blood had drained out, even without a heartbeat. The medical examiners had a hell of a job sorting out the slugs in the guy's body, but they found one that didn't match."

"It was a professional hit."

"Looks that way, for sure."

"And Elke? They buy that she wasn't the hostage-tak

"No reason not to. I'm the only living witness. F and I had time to talk and, Morgan, I'm convi

the ex-boyfriend was behind her abduction and the attempt on her life."

"You're doing a lot of that these days."

"What? Talking?"

"Being a witness. I just came back from the Ciccone funeral."

"How was it?"

"Big."

"Vulgar?"

"Extravagant. I'd say opulent bad taste. I was talking to Francine Ciccone."

"How's Frankie?" said Miranda, who was acutely aware Morgan had known her in high school.

"She's holding up well. It becomes her, being a widow. She was born to grieve with a smile. She's doing fine."

"Morgan, I can tell. You never told me! You used to date, didn't you? It's in your voice. Didn't you?"

"No way. But we thought about it. That was a long time ago. She's okay, I like her."

"Talk about dangerous company."

"So when are you coming back?"

"Clancy wants us to hang around. Did it register, what I told you? I think the ex-boyfriend set Elke up to be killed."

"Yeah, I've been thinking it over. Who would want to take out a high-living accountant? He must have been on the Mafia's payroll."

"You're on the right track, Morgan. I didn't believe it at first. His face didn't show enough character to be a bad guy. Turns out he did the personal tax returns for a bunch of mobsters. Nothing illegal. He moonlighted doing the accounts for some very tough people. He wasn't breaking any laws. But he screwed up; he tried

to sell some wine he had received as a legitimate payout. He sold it the wrong way. Big trouble. His ex-girlfriend, Elke, was about to expose the scam."

"Blow it up."

"So to speak. He thought he could squeeze out of it by offering up Elke as a sacrificial lamb. Some lamb! She had already broken off the romantic side of their relationship when she discovered whose taxes he was doing, and because he was, in her words, shallow as a mirror and dull as a dildo."

"Very precise. I wonder why she took up with him in the first place."

"Yeah, well, she didn't associate the confusion about the ChâteauNeuf-du-Pape with his mob connections, she took him at his word that it came from an estate his insurance company was settling. When she couldn't sort out the provenance, she went north on the ex-boyfriend's insistence to track it through your friend at Millennium Wines. She never got beyond their parking lot. By the time she did her escape back to New York, she had it figured out. She was not happy with the guy, Morgan. He had set her up to be killed. She didn't flinch when he died. It hardly seemed to register."

"I want to tell you about the funeral. There was no one *not* there."

"That's appropriately cryptic."

"No, there's something going on. It wasn't a hit by the mob, I'm sure of that, and it wasn't our guys, but it was a professional job."

"Do you think the elusive Mr. Savage is involved? You once suggested Ciccone might have deadly enemies in the wine trade."

"Yeah, you're not the only connection between Philip Carter and Vittorio Ciccone. Since the mob in New York has a lethal interest in the Ninth Chateau, almost certainly the Ciccone family does as well. Mr. Savage is pivotal. But he seems to be independent from either New York or Toronto. Bonnydoon, maybe that's where I should be looking, in the ashes, sifting the debris —"

"I?"

"We. The death of Vittorio Ciccone. Would you believe I've been assigned to the case?"

"You're kidding."

"No, before I left for the funeral, I had a talk with the superintendent. You're on it too, when you get back."

"I'm being reinstated?"

"Yeah, you're not a suspect in Philip's death. You're a victim."

"You're telling me."

"He was just playing it safe."

"Who?"

"Rufalo."

"Okay. Gotta go, pizza's arriving. Elke just got out of the shower. She's waving at you. Take care."

Click.

Morgan stared at the phone in his hand. He was strangely lonely without Miranda around.

The phone rang again, startling him so that he nearly dropped it.

"Morgan, it's me. You don't think it was a Mafia hit, right?"

"That's what I figured from the mob presence at the funeral, that's what Francine was trying to tell me."

"So, Morgan, what if the sniper who killed Ivan Muritori wasn't working for them either? Why would the mob bother killing a hapless accountant? For blowing a counterfeit wine operation by accident?"

"If not, then, who?"

"We'll have to think about it. Bye-bye, gotta run, pizza's getting cold."

Click.

12

The Warehouse

An hour later, Morgan was still sitting at his desk when Spivak and Stritch asked if he wanted to join them for a hamburger. As he rose to his feet, another detective, a large man with close-cropped hair, nudged Morgan as he walked by. It might have been friendly, possibly not.

"Hey, Morgan."

"Bourassa."

"We're going for a burger, want to join us?" said Spivak to the other man.

Bourassa looked at Morgan and shrugged. "No, I'm busy."

He started to walk off, then turned and faced Morgan squarely, an arm's reach away. "Your partner — too bad about Ciccone, I guess if she was bought, the sale fell through."

Morgan looked up at the big man, his face expressionless.

"So, Morgan, the necrophilia thing."

"Shut up, Bourassa!" Spivak snarled.

"You got a corpse in your bed, that's what they call it."

Spivak glanced at Morgan. Stritch walked around beside the larger man, anticipating trouble, surprised at Morgan's apparent passivity. No one had openly spoken about Miranda being a witness for the defense. Most felt she had no choice, no one envied her position, and most shared her relief that the Ciccone murder let her off the hook. Bourassa was not known as a dishonest cop but he was a moral simpleton. Morgan knew that. He stood still, transfixed by the other man's appalling ignorance.

"No guts, Morgan?"

Morgan pursed his lips in a tight smile and narrowed his eyes. A personal insult was not about to set him off. Why give Bourassa the power?

"Myself, I'd rather have the black guy here than a fucking skank for a partner."

Morgan's fist shot out straight into the man's face, smashing his flesh against the bone of his skull. Bourassa's head snapped back, but his huge body remained upright. A small stream of blood slipped from the corner of his mouth. Blood filled his nostrils and sheeted over his upper lip, dripping across his chin and down the front of his shirt. His eyes glazed and he blinked as he tried to bring Morgan into focus.

"I am a sensitive man," said Morgan as he turned and walked away. Over his shoulder, he added, "I have a good partner, and so does Spivak. We both have good partners." And as he walked through the doorway, while rubbing his knuckles to bring back the feeling, he repeated, more to himself than to an audience, "I am a sensitive man."

Bourassa remained immobile. Spivak glanced at Stritch, who was staring in the direction Morgan had gone with amazement, then he looked over at the superintendent's office and caught Alex Rufalo quickly averting his gaze to the papers on his desk.

When Morgan returned to his desk with a coffee, the superintendent called him into his office. Morgan approached unapologetically, not sure how much of his spat with Bourassa had been observed.

"He's a good detective," said the superintendent, skipping the preliminaries.

Morgan shrugged.

"You think he's dumb and a bully."

Morgan shrugged again.

"He's uncomplicated, Morgan, and he's tenacious. If he was a dog, he'd be a bull mastiff. You want him on your side."

"Isn't he?"

"That's the point, Morgan, he is. The man would take a bullet for you — you know why? Because you're a cop."

"Yeah."

"After your little debate out there, he saw my door was open. He came in covered in blood and told me it was his fault. He won't tell you that, he'd rather push your face in it, but it's over."

"Hey," said Morgan, "this is why you get the big bucks. We're cool."

"Yes, you are," the superintendent said. "Go home."

"Okay."

' "And oh, you're on the Humber River shooting, you and Quin."

"We're doing Ciccone."

"We found the car where your blond friend said it would be. Lots of prints, turns out there's a Ciccone connection. Dead guy wasn't on the payroll, but he sometimes worked for Vittorio. She may have killed him in self-defense, but there's more to it than that. We need the whys and wherefores."

"Yeah, they're elusive little buggers."

"What?"

"The whys and wherefores."

Rufalo smiled. Morgan had the feeling that the superintendent believed he had handled the Bourassa situation the best possible way, with cool forbearance and the surgical use of force. That's how he had, in the preceding few minutes, come to assess his own behaviour.

"We've got the RCMP and CSIS involved for jumping the border, the Provincials on board for the two deaths at the winery, the local fire marshal for the way the old lady died. The American border people. The NYPD. Maybe the FBI if Elke Sturmberg was really abducted. Maybe New York State Troopers, maybe the CIA, who knows. You up to it?"

"Yeah, they won't get in the way." Morgan played tough when it was politically expedient or ironically amusing.

"Yeah, well, don't cross Spivak and Stritch, they have the lead on the dead guy in Miranda's bed. Did you talk to her? She wants to play it low-key down there. She'll bring the Sturmberg woman back without an extradition warrant once they're finished with her. So, go home, get some rest."

"You too, boss."

So Morgan went home, made himself a sandwich supper, cracked open a bottle of authentic Châteauneuf-du-Pape that he had picked up on the way, and settled back to read for awhile. He usually read non-fiction. You can't make up stuff as interesting as real life, he figured.

Part of him recognized the absurdity of that. He had read the great novels in university and in small ways they had changed him. He read facts now, and they changed nothing. Still, he was at a place in his life, not old, no longer young, where he wanted to fill out his mind, not discover new parts of himself in parallel worlds.

He picked up Francine Ciccone's card from the coffee table where he had dropped it when he emptied his pockets. She was one of the few links to a childhood for which he harboured little or no nostalgia. They both grew up in Cabbagetown, both were from the sub-class known as the working poor, families with sufficient income to pay rent, sufficient stamina to hold menial jobs, and sufficient diversions, mostly beer, tobacco, and television, to keep them humble amidst the affluence surrounding their small and sometimes brutal lives.

When her name appeared in the social columns, or when her husband was featured in stories relating to drug wars and crime syndicates, Morgan would remember the times they walked home from public school together, not talking, but perfectly in tune, like two reeds vibrating in the wind. And when they got older, they sometimes gossiped or kidded about, both of them knowing romance was a dead end, both of them determined to get out of the ghetto, knowing they would get in each other's way.

At university, they occasionally had coffee, and as scholarship students they sometimes worked together at Robarts Library. Mostly, they avoided each other. It was better like that.

When the phone rang, he knew it would be her. Still, he waited until she spoke to be sure.

"David?"

"Francine."

"Did I catch you at a bad time?"

"No, not at all. Is your reception over? You must be completely worn out."

"David, I am going to give you an address. It's a warehouse in the east end, off Queen Street. I want you to go there."

"Frankie, what are you talking about?" he asked, but he knew. "You found him?"

"Listen to me, David. You go to this place, do it tonight." She gave him directions to the warehouse. Her voice sounded crisp and efficient, but strained from the exhaustion of entombing her husband, of losing a man who must have seemed immortal and, in spite of the trial, untouchable. *There are certain things,* he imagined, *you have to believe. Suddenly, he's gone. She's a woman of immense resources or she wouldn't be where she is, but it must be tough.*

"David," she paused. "You're not disappointed in me?"

"We do what we do, Frankie. Are you disappointed in me?"

"For being a cop?" She laughed. "I always thought you'd end up a professor. They're the best at disguising their past. No, I admire you. I read about you sometimes, I hear things. I think you're living the life you always wanted, even when you didn't know it."

"You too, Francine."

"Go now, and call me sometime."

"How'd you find him?"

There was a moment's silence while she considered whether to answer. "He was afraid of the border. He was trying to drive west, I suppose to Vancouver, or around into Minnesota, but once you get north of Superior, all roads converge. The fool, he thought wilderness spaces would give him refuge, but the north made it easier to track him. We know people up there."

"Is he alive?"

"Yes, Morgan, or there wouldn't be a rush, would there?"

"Thanks, Frankie. Is there a gun?"

"It's with him. You'll get a conviction. I want him surrounded in the penitentiary, night and day, by people loyal to Vittorio. Every minute of every day for the rest of his life, they will make his life hell. He will be glad when he dies, that's what I want."

Morgan felt a chill run through him. *Frankie Ciccone is a woman used to getting what she wants. In this case, it's the same thing I want*, he thought, *although the flaying of the shooter's flesh until the meat of his body shrivels in the sun would please her most, and for myself, it is enough the man gets taken off the streets.*

"Frankie, thanks."

"For what? I've forgotten already why I called."

Click.

Morgan stopped in at Police Headquarters on College Street for a car. He picked up his Glock semi-automatic from the gun locker and tucked it into a sheath-holster against the small of his back, which he regretted when he got into the driver's seat since it dug in and forced him to slouch while he drove. He did not tell anyone where he was going. The superintendent had gone home and Spivak and his partner were not around. Bourassa was at his desk, working late, possibly working on an alibi to explain to his wife why his face looked like a tub of poutine. Morgan would have preferred to have Miranda with him for backup, but she was hanging out with her friends in New York.

He turned into a dark side street by the warehouse. There was a bare bulb gleaming over the small door to the side of the loading docks. There was a light on a pole casting shadows against brick walls and a tall wire fence. The night sky formed a canopy of brackish illumination overhead. But the impression was of darkness, not light.

He could see a dull glow in the transom over the entry. When he pulled open the door his eyes were met by a sea of gloom, highlighted in the centre by a man sitting in a chair with a lamp shining on him powered by a long extension cord running off into the murky shadows.

Morgan stood still, listening.

The man seemed aware of him, although he was blindfolded. Morgan took a few steps forward and the man shrank into himself, trying to hide in plain view. He was terrified. He must have thought Morgan was one of the Ciccone people, coming back to finish the job.

Or to torture him. Morgan could see he had been brutally beaten. Dried blood was scabbed on his face, and brownish-red stains had seeped through his clothing and congealed on the surface. There was a plastic bag taped across his lap with a gun inside, the gun he used to kill Vittorio Ciccone. From the pool of blood under the gun, Morgan suspected he had been castrated or had his penis cut off. His mouth was bound with duct tape. He was struggling to breath through his nose.

Morgan knew when he ripped off the tape what he would find. The man gagged and spat out the end of his penis, coughed and vomited over himself.

Morgan saw a hose attached to a tap on a wall. He walked over and uncoiled it, turning on the tap. He walked back and hosed down the man in the chair.

He lifted the blindfold away from the man's swollen face.

"This is your lucky day," he said.

The man looked at him without comprehending.

"You speak English?" Morgan asked.

The man looked frantically about but said nothing.

"You're Albanian, right? Al-bay-nee-yah, right?"

No answer.

"You're going to need help, buddy. Help, hospital, yes?"

The man's eyes registered an indeterminate response.

"So you do speak English. Okay, I'm police, polizia, guardia, cop, you understand?"

The man shook his head, and Morgan could see he nearly blacked out from the effort.

"You do understand, good. You killed a bad man, yes? In this country we do not kill, even people who kill people. Even bad men like Vittorio Ciccone."

The man taped to the chair flinched violently at the name of the man he had murdered.

"Relax! I'm one of the good guys."

The man blinked quizzically.

"You are a professional, right? Right."

The man acknowledged with a nod.

"Well, you screwed up, my friend."

There was no response.

"We need to talk," said Morgan. "It's better here. Too many people downtown. Police. Friends of Ciccone. Lawyers. You don't have many friends, my friend. You need a doctor, understand, doctor, hospital. Better we talk a bit first, you understand?"

"Yes."

"You understand. Good. I'm your only way out of this mess."

"Good."

"Yeah, good."

"*Si.*"

"Okay, my friend. My goodness, you do look dreadful. A professional hit man. I'd expect better."

"I wear Armani, Giorgio."

"Not tonight, my friend. You look like a bucket of shit. But enough with the chatter. What I need to know is, who hired you?"

"Hired me? Paid me money?"

"Yes."

"I do not know."

"Good night, my friend," said Morgan, turning and walking towards the door. "Good luck," he called over his shoulder. "*Ciao amici.*"

"*Per favori!* Police, you come back."

Morgan stepped out into the yard and pulled the door shut behind him. A car parked down the street started up and cruised by, turned around, and drove slowly back out to Queen Street. Morgan made no attempt to hide.

He felt the reassuring pressure of the semi-automatic against the small of his back.

He heard a racket and went back inside. The man in the chair had tumbled it over, trying to break free of the tape holding him down. Morgan heaved him back into an upright position.

"Has your English improved, my friend?"

"Yes."

"Then let's talk."

The man glared at him through swollen eyes.

"I've got lots of time," said Morgan. "I'm not the one bleeding to death through my pecker. Doesn't look like they lopped off too much. You won't need more than what's left in the pen. Except for favours."

Morgan stopped. He thought, *I am a sensitive man,* and he almost laughed aloud. *What on earth am I doing? There's been too much going on, too much death. This man needs help. If you can't help your enemies, what kind of a person are you?* He was genuinely upset with himself.

"I will tell you," said the Albanian.

"Yes!"

"All I know. You will take me to hospital, please."

"Yes, I will. You talk …" Morgan began to feel for the tape ends to release the man from his chair. "You talk to me, we'll go to the hospital, okay. Same time."

"I am from Albania."

"Not the life story. Who hired you?"

"That I cannot say."

"Why not."

"Because then I will die."

"You will die."

"Yes."

"They will kill you."

"Yes."

"And the Ciccone people, they almost killed you, yes?"

"Yes."

"And you are afraid the police will kill you, yes?"

"Not police. This is America."

"No, this is Canada. But yes, no, the police will not kill you."

"That is good."

Morgan had the man's feet free and stood up to release his hands. "We cannot protect you if you don't tell us. Who hired you? Who are you afraid of now?"

"Me," said a voice behind Morgan. He wheeled around to confront a man who held a gun pointed directly at his head from twenty feet away.

"And you are?" said Morgan with as much calm as he could muster.

"This man's employer."

Morgan knew who he was. There was something cold in his voice, so mechanical, it had to be the man behind the murderous chaos at Bonnydoon, the man who violated Miranda.

"And what do you think you're going to do now?"

"I am going to kill you," said the man, smiling. "First I am going to kill my former employee. You have met, yes. This is Branko. Then you must die, as well, I'm afraid. You are merely a nuisance, Mr. Morgan. But he is a liability."

"You know me?"

"Of course. And you know me."

"You are the man with the bloody signature."

"Signature? Interesting. I thought of it more as a trademark. You know, then, I am as good as my word. I will kill you both and wash my hands in your blood."

"And you know — it won't end here."

"No? Do you think I am afraid your partner will chase me down? She is in New York, she is staying with the lady from the auction house, the one with the dead boyfriend. I suppose they have that in common, they both have dead boyfriends. I know much about both of you, Mr. Morgan. I think she will not be so formidable without you. She may have to die too, of course, but that will not be your concern."

As the man clicked off the safety, Morgan lunged away from the chair to the side, toppling the Albanian, who went sprawling in the opposite direction. Morgan rolled in the air as he fell, grasping his gun from the back holster and sliding the action before he hit the cement. A shot rang out. It was his gun; he had fired instinctively, a single shot.

Mr. Savage stood his ground as if a bullet were of little concern. Morgan held his gun on him as he rose to his feet. Mr. Savage held his gun on Branko, the Albanian. His fingernails gleamed like talons. His lips were pulled taut against his teeth in a menacing smile, the overhead light glistening on his thick black hair.

"Well, Mr. Morgan, we seem to be in a proverbial standoff. How very quaint. Of course, I have men surrounding the building. If you kill me, they will kill you both. Perhaps we should negotiate."

"Negotiate?"

"Yes. It is Branko I want. You walk out of here. It is over."

"And Branko?"

"He dies, of course. Either way, he is dead."

"And what's your guarantee for my safety?"

"My word."

"Mr. Savage."

"Yes, Mr. Morgan."

Absurdly, Morgan thought of the childhood rhyme, "Liar, lair, your pants are on fire," but what he said was: "No deal. Any other offers on the table?"

"None, not that I can think of. I'm afraid I must call my people."

"You do that!"

"You are not afraid."

"No, Mr. Savage. Because you're here with only one man, the driver of your car. He is outside, yes, and I'm betting he won't come in. Others are not so oblivious to their own destruction, or perhaps not as committed to your cause. I think if he thinks you're down, he will quietly leave."

"You do not know us very well, Mr. Morgan."

"Us?"

"It is of no concern." Savage fired his gun, a single shot through the head of Branko the Albanian.

Morgan was startled. He held his aim directly at Savage. He could execute the shooter, but there was nothing he could have done to prevent the shooting. Savage turned slowly toward Morgan, certain the detective would not shoot first.

"Now, Mr. Morgan, the equation has changed. There are just the two of us, no?"

Morgan said nothing.

"No? Nothing to say?"

"I do believe I will kill you," said Morgan. "Whether I die or not."

"You may be right, but I think not tonight. I am going to leave now," Savage said, lowering his gun. "You will not shoot a man in the back and you are not foolish enough to follow me. And you were quite right, Mr. Morgan, I would have shot you had you capitulated. It would have been easy. But, of course, you would not have left him behind. Goodnight, Mr. Morgan."

Morgan stood transfixed. After the other man passed through the door, he bent down to confirm that the Albanian was dead.

He wondered, as he walked out to the car to call in, *Is it possible Francine set me up, with Branko the Albanian as bait?*

Sitting in the dark of the car, he wondered if either of them had come all that far.

13

Washington Square

After a day of waiting and shopping, Miranda was outfitted for the fall and frustrated by the apparent lack of progress in the Ivan Muritori shooting. Back in Elke's loft, the two women busied themselves reading old copies of *Vogue* and *Bazaar*, making fun of the models as a plastic androgynous subspecies evolved for the purpose of displaying unwearable clothes.

"The fashion industry is dominated by the male homosexual sensibility," observed Elke. "Gay men design the clothes and clothe the models, they do the make-up, the hair, the layouts. Page after page of shiny pubescence. Have you ever seen so many boy-chests on girls, little wee breasts tucked out of the way in folds of fabric. And girl-chests on boys, bony and hairless, with collagen lips. God, it's amazing."

"You are disturbingly articulate on the subject," said Miranda. "You think about this a lot, do you?"

"Yes, of course. I read *Vogue* regularly. I subscribe.

And I pick up *Bazaar* almost every month, or *Elle*. I am fascinated. So are you."

"Yeah," said Miranda. "I guess it's like watching the Olympics to pick up pointers for a walk in the park."

"You are quite cynical, then, where I am amused."

"Are you?"

"I am objective. I think the fashion industry is unhealthy."

"You're saying homosexuality is an illness."

"No, the illness is that other people submit to the gay aesthetic."

"Which itself is okay?"

"Not if it means denying their own."

"Yeah," said Miranda. "Maybe we should all wear burkas."

"And bend to an even more sinister tyranny!"

"Sinister?"

"Yes, don't you agree? Christians and Jews and Muslims fear women's sexuality, but Muslims fear women the most."

"You're in a feisty mood! We were on safer grounds talking about fashion."

"Miranda, there is nothing we cannot talk about if we are reasonable."

"Let's be reasonable and talk about nothing."

"Back to *Vogue*, then."

They chatted easily together, but Miranda was aware of a shift in their relationship. Here, Elke allowed a slight Swedish accent to preen in her diction, while before it had been suppressed to a negligible cadence. She was at home in the worldly milieu of Manhattan. On her own side of the border, Miranda had been dominant. Here it seemed uncertain whether she was Elke's custodian, or

Elke was her host in a city where Miranda had little status or power of her own.

They decided to go out for dinner, and while they were getting ready the phone rang. It was Captain Clancy. He wanted to come over and talk but agreed to meet them at an intimate restaurant he suggested in Greenwich Village, not far from where they were staying.

Both took time with their minimalist make-up, and both wore skirts. Miranda decided to break in her Cole Haan sandals. They had cost a couple of day's pay and their workmanship was both subtle and striking. Although they were flats they made her feel taller. Both women were self-conscious after their cultural analysis of *Vogue* and its kind, so they were dressing up fashionably casual. The irony amused Miranda, and the paradox seemed a challenge for Elke, if only in a minor key.

As they walked through Washington Square, Miranda gazed about her in wonder. This was the version of America she admired the most, this was New York as the imaginary place in her mind where romances bloomed and were broken and clever people shared ideas with bitchy and self-deprecating wit. An urban garden embraced by converging streets lined with handsome low-rise buildings, with a backdrop of skyscrapers hovering amidst the foliage overhead, and the din of traffic, the overheard conversations, the strident cheerfulness of the park denizens, all made her think an evening like this must be special.

Morgan would like Washington Square, she thought. The world has many centres, and this awkward park, smaller than a farmer's meadow, was among the most vital. A triumphal arch and a dog-poop compound, stone chess boards, and a fountain pool meant for wading, benches and grass and flowers. George Washington seemed more comfortable here as two modest statues than on Mount Rushmore or embodied in the gargantuan obelisk in the city bearing his name. It was here he seemed most human, and his dreams for a new order most accessible. For a moment she thought of herself as American.

She was looking forward to dinner. She was looking forward to going home, to getting back to work.

Clancy was waiting at the bistro, at a table on the sidewalk under an awning. Miranda had teased Elke on their way that she and Clancy would make a good couple.

"Come on," Elke had said, slowing to an ambling pace. "You're not serious?"

"Yes, I am. You'd be beautiful together."

"You think so, really? He's a policeman."

"And? What are you saying?"

"You and Morgan are different."

"Me and Morgan! Morgan and I, we're not a couple."

"You so much are."

"No."

"You wait, sooner or later."

"No. Not."

"You like him."

"What's not to like. Morgan is good-looking. If you like strength of character in a man's face, he's personable, kind of shambling and a little unkempt. He's very bright, he has an undisciplined but exciting mind, and he can be silly. He can be very sweet. He's tough, in a good sort of way."

"Not that you've thought about this."

"No."

"And you think Clancy — we don't know his first name — you think we'd make a striking couple, is that it? Black and blond, the nymph and the stallion."

"Interesting you think about yourselves that way."

"He doesn't."

"You do."

They were walking slowly now, strolling.

"He doesn't wear a wedding band."

"You noticed."

"So did you. What about you with him? Both cops. But that wouldn't be fair to Morgan's future. No, I'll have to take him."

When Clancy stood up as they approached the table, Elke's first words were to ask his name.

"Clancy, like I said. Solid Irish."

"Do you have a first name, we were wondering?" said Miranda.

"Yeah," he answered as the two women sat down, giggling like teenagers.

"What is it?" said Elke.

"I don't use it much."

"Is it Harold?" asked Miranda.

"Harold, no, why Harold?"

"I've never known someone called Harold before, not in real life."

"You still don't. It's Seymour."

Both woman laughed. Laughter is the best way to relieve and express sexual tension, Miranda recalled having read somewhere as she tried to rein in her glee.

"That's why I don't tell people my name," said Clancy.

"It's a perfectly nice name," Elke assured him. "Seymour."

"Yes?"

"No, I was just saying it, 'Seymour.' It's an interesting name."

"I take it you two have had a good day."

"Yes," said Miranda, collecting herself. "We have had a very good day. What about you. What kind of progress?"

Clancy held his hand up casually, indicating they should eat first, then catch up on business. "Try the moules. Very savoury. I assume you want wine. I held off until you got here. Let's have a bottle. You name it — red or white? Lets have white, a French Chardonnay, Chablis, it goes with the moules."

"Nothing like a take-charge guy," said Miranda. "Are you married?"

Her question threw him off stride. He glanced from one to the other, knowing he had been the subject of conversation between them, possibly the object of a joke.

"Not presently," he said.

There was an awkward hush at the table, none sure whether they were still playing or if somehow things had become serious.

"No," said Miranda, "I'm not either."

They both looked at Elke.

"Never," she announced, as if it were a point of pride. Then realizing they both knew about her recent love life, she added, "Nearly, but ... I've made some mistakes."

Now the mood at the table was solemn, confessional.

"Haven't we all," said Seymour Clancy.

The conversation switched to families. Elke described her childhood in Stockholm and her siblings who still lived there. She came from a family of doctors who spoke English in the home, partly to nurture their worldliness and partly as a game, because it was both useful and fun. Her parents had died in a boating accident in northern Sweden, at their cottage near the border with Finland.

Miranda talked of growing up in small-town Ontario. A village, actually, but only a mile across the Grand River flats from the town of Preston, now Cambridge. To her, saying she was from Waterloo County had the same emotional resonance as being from Stockholm or New York. Yet somehow her childhood seemed less authentic. Perhaps it was the inborn parochialism of Canadians as a legacy of Empire. Perhaps it was personal.

Seymour Clancy described Queens and being black in a mixed neighbourhood. He spoke proudly of defending his peculiar name, half Jewish, half Irish, yet anger crept into his voice as he described its origin in the traditions of slavery. Being Jewish, being Irish, those are religious ethnicities, he explained. Being black in America, that's history.

Over coffee, the conversation shifted to Clancy's case.

"Do you know was he a real Mafioso?" Elke asked.

"His day job with Confederate Union was completely legit," said Clancy, who went on to reaffirm what they already knew, that he did tax returns for some of the New York mob. By the time the numbers reached him, and the paperwork, everything had been laundered. He did nothing more than confirm the arithmetic and provide a stamp of approval, his signature the proof of his clients' participation in responsible citizenry.

"There has to be more," said Miranda. "Assassination? I mean, there are easier ways to punish an accountant for screwing up."

"It isn't the books he screwed up," said Clancy, "it was the wine operation."

"Now, here's the problem," said Miranda. "The wine thing, it was a boutique swindle. A few million dollars and some connoisseurs with their noses out of joint."

"Did you try it?" Clancy asked.

"The ChâteauNeuf-du-Pape? I thought it was good, actually — but what do I know about paying the price of a Broadway show for a bottle of wine?"

"What's your point, then, Detective?"

"These guys, they're into big money, measured in the hundreds of millions. Why get so upset over the small change?"

"Yes," Elke agreed. "It's not just him, they wanted to kill me, they blew up the old lady, there's a lot going on."

"And they killed the man with the ring."

"And the man in your bed!"

"Wait! Let's run through it all again," said Clancy. "Don't forget your partner, they tried to kill him."

"What! Who? Morgan?"

"You didn't know?"

"What? Tell me, what are you talking about?"

"Have you been talking to your partner today?"

"Yes, this morning. He called me at Elke's to see if I was okay. My cellphone is shot. He called her number. I told him I was fine. He sounded relieved. I liked that. He was worried. I told him not to worry, and that we were on our way out the door, heading for Saks. He said, 'Why not?' And that was it. So, what did he forget to tell me?"

"He was set up for a hit, that's what his boss told me. Someone called Alex Rufalo, you know him? Very polite, sounds overworked."

"Yeah, he's our superintendent in Homicide. What happened?"

"In a warehouse. Mexican standoff. The shooter got away. After killing the guy who killed Vittorio Ciccone."

"Mexican standoff, what's that?" asked Elke.

"Two guys with guns on each other," said Miranda. "There's no way out. They both die."

"But Morgan's okay, you talked to him," said Elke.

"Yeah, well so is the other guy," said Miranda, relieved that Morgan survived but angry at being kept in the dark."

"But the Albanian who shot Vittorio Ciccone, he's dead," said Clancy.

"The Albanian?" Miranda was perplexed.

"Didn't you ever wonder about your boyfriend?" said Clancy, shifting to address Elke, bringing the conversation back to familiar territory.

"Ex, he was my ex-boyfriend. About what? His standard of living. He had a good job. I knew he did contract work on the side. We weren't living together. My place is nicer than his. I wouldn't have given it up."

"You didn't like him very much, did you?"

"He was clean-cut and expedient. Sometimes that's what a girl wants, Captain Clancy."

"When she's too busy for love?"

Elke stopped. She seemed to be considering the implications. He looked at her gently.

"No," she said. "You're never too busy for that. I am not shallow, Detective, I am a reasonably attractive blond in a city enthralled with blonds, and he kept the wolves at bay."

"Yes, you are," he responded, "at least —"

"At least what?"

"Reasonably."

"Attractive? You can say it, Detective."

"Yes."

"Excuse me," said Miranda. "I'm here."

The other two sat back and gazed at her as if she had burped.

"Pardon?" said Clancy.

"You too," said Elke, "in a brunette sort of way. Very, reasonably. You are."

"Thank you," said Miranda. "Back to business?"

"Yeah," said Clancy, still turned toward Elke. "He wasn't what you'd call a high flyer?"

"He lived a little beyond his income, like most of us. I'm not even sure he knew who he was moonlighting for."

"No?"

"He had some files spread out on his desk. I recognized several of the names. From the papers. Gangster's names. He seemed surprised. I honestly don't know if he knew. We had a big argument. He said who they were made no difference. I said it did."

"You broke up, then?"

"Not that night. I think he actually asked his clients if they were Mafia."

"You know that?"

"Well, he told me they assured him they were legitimate businessmen. I think I was more appalled by his naiveté than anything else. We tapered off after that."

"You make it sound like getting over a cold."

"Yeah, it sort of was like that. Then he came around to the office."

"Beverley Auctions in the Village?"

"No, the main office, forty-seventh floor, Chrysler Building."

"And that's when he unloaded the wine on you?"

"It seemed reasonable. He'd profit, we'd profit. Why not."

"Okay," said Miranda, her frustration showing in her voice. "We're back to the big question: why knock the guy off? The punishment doesn't fit the crime. He was naïve, yes. Stupid, maybe. Convenient, apparently. But he wasn't a threat to the Mafia, and the wine operation wasn't that big."

"Yeah," said Clancy. "So there you are. The most dramatic event in the guy's life was his leaving it."

"But there's more to the story," said Miranda. "There has to be."

"We've come up with nothing, no leads at all. No rumour."

"What rumour?"

"No rumour," said Clancy, "that's the point. Usually, when there's a mob hit there's, it's hard to explain, an awareness. It moves through the air like radio waves, and you know they did it, and why. There's no rumour with this one. Dead air."

"You think maybe it wasn't them?"

"It was a professional job."

"But perhaps not by one of theirs."

"Who else?"

"I don't know," said Miranda. "This is your jurisdiction."

The three of them ambled over to Washington Square after dinner and paused in the night shadows under the arch to say goodbye. Seymour Clancy was going in a different direction by subway. They had enjoyed their evening together and none of them wanted it to be over, yet there was no real reason to linger, except for the comfort of one another.

Out of the blue, Miranda exclaimed, "It's about drugs."

"What?" said Clancy, furtively looking around them. "Someone's going to think you're trying to score, man. What are you talking about?"

"You think Ivan Muritori was involved in drugs?" Elke whispered incredulously.

"No, but I think the international mob is, that's their mainstay in business."

"And?" said Clancy. "What's new?"

"An epiphany. There has to be a connection between the drug trade and the wine scam, if only to account for the body count."

"Okay," said Clancy. "What is it?"

"I said epiphany, not a full-scale revelation. I just know there has to be something more to the wine thing than wine, and drugs seem the logical answer."

"Counterfeit wine as a front for drug trafficking, it doesn't seem too bright. I mean, usually you hide behind a legitimate enterprise. Why compromise?"

"That's just it!" said Miranda. "We figure that out, we've got this one made."

"Which one would that be, Detective?"

"Well, the murder of Ivan Muritori, for starters. Let's say he stumbled on the drug connection, then, to use your word, the whole operation was 'compromised.'"

"Yeah," said Clancy. "And if we make the connection, the whole ball of wax will unravel."

"What does that mean," said Elke, "the whole ball of wax?"

"It's an idiomatic expression."

"I know that, but what does it mean?"

"That the knot will unravel."

"Why wax, why not string?"

Miranda could not decide whether Elke was being disingenuous or using wordplay as a flirtation device.

"It's time to go home," she said.

"Goodnight, Seymour Clancy," said Elke with a mischievous innocence that belied her responsibility for taking as hostage a man who was subsequently filled with more holes than a rusty colander.

"Good night, Miss Sturmberg," he responded with playful formality. "Good night, Detective Quin. We should wind up our end of things in the morning. We'll want you both available to come back to New York if anything breaks."

"For sure," said Miranda.

They turned in opposite directions and within moments were lost from each other in the motley shadows and lights of the Square. Miranda and Elke walked along in silence, Miranda absorbed with the implications of her "eureka" moment when the scale of the crimes being covered up suddenly fit with the crimes being committed. She felt a slight chill despite the warm June weather. It was getting late and her new T-shirt, an expensive parody of a souvenir with the New York skyline embossed in a surreal wave following the contours of her breasts, was not quite warm enough. She glanced at her companion, who seemed lost in contemplation, whether about the wine trade, her recent harrowing adventures, or Captain Clancy, Miranda could not tell.

* * *

A black limousine was parked by the steps leading into Elke's building. As soon as she saw it, Miranda had a gut-wrenching sense of déjà vu, but they were halfway up the steps before she heard the summons she had been anticipating.

"Detective Quin."

Both women stopped in their tracks. Elke started to lunge forward but Miranda held her firmly by the arm.

"Don't," she said.

She turned around and walked down to the car.

"Are you talking to me?" She thought of Robert De Niro. She nearly repeated herself, shifting the emphasis in her delivery to sound menacing. Morgan would have liked that, the silliness.

"Yeah. Tell your friend to come down here. We're not going to hurt you."

Since there was little option, Miranda reassured Elke, and the two of them stood by the car, waiting.

The driver got out and walked around. He opened the door and a man with a vaguely familiar face emerged. He was shorter than either of them, and stocky; old enough that the absence of a paunch was noteworthy, still young enough to convey physical menace. He had a faint scar running down the side of his face from temple to chin, arcing clear of his eye but marking his cheek with a thin, cruel line.

Miranda had seen his picture. "You are a friend of Vittorio Ciccone," she said.

"Yes, poor Vittorio, may God rest his soul. And in that mausoleum of his, I'd think he would. Welcome to New York, Detective Quin."

"What can we do for you, Mr...." She searched for his name.

"Call me Soprano," he said. "I'm from New Jersey."

"Mr. Sebastiani," she said, remembering. He was the biggest name in New Jersey, in his line of work.

"Wonderful. Call me Carlo. And this is Miss Sturmberg. I am pleased to meet you both."

"And what is it we can do for you, Mr. Sebastiani?"

"I would like you to come with me."

"And if we refuse? No, I don't suppose that is an option."

"To refuse is an option, Miranda. May I call you Miranda? To avoid the inevitable, that is not an option. You will come, please. You will be safe."

Miranda looked at Elke. The other woman's shoulders slumped in a submissive posture. She had been through this before. The horrors of her experience in Canada seemed to be flooding back, and it was all she could do to stay on her feet. Miranda reached out and took her arm. They turned toward the brownstone as if they were going to climb the steps, but the driver stepped in front of them.

"I'm the police," said Miranda.

"Canadian," the driver said. "You're a long way from home. No gun. You guys carry Glocks. Semi-automatic. Women usually carry the scaled-down model."

"It fits better in a purse with all our make-up," Miranda responded. "You've studied the habits of female police officers?"

"I used to live in Toronto. Worked for Mr. Ciccone."

"Really. Then you know we don't ride with your kind by invitation."

"Maybe this time you should make an exception." He looked past her to Carlo Sebastiani. "Mr. Sebastiani, you want I should help them along."

"That's Brooklyn," said Miranda. "I thought you were from Toronto."

"What's Brooklyn?"

"I quote, 'You want I should help them along,' that sounds Brooklyn to me."

"The cadence is Yiddish," he said.

"The cadence, my goodness."

"What, you think bad guys are uneducated? Not all of them. I started working for Mr. Ciccone while I was a student at the University of Toronto. You went there too, before my time, so did your partner."

"You know a lot about us."

"It's my job. I'm not from Toronto. I went up there to study."

"And you define yourself as one of the bad guys."

"Lady," he said in a Brooklyn accent, "doing what I do, you ain't one of the good guys. In a Manichean world, if you ain't good, you're bad."

"Excuse me," said Carlo Sebastiani from inside the car, "if I'm not intruding, both of you shut the fuck up. Get in the car, all three of you. Now."

"And if we don't," said Miranda.

"If you don't, Tony shoots you. Tony, show her your gun. And you know what, anyone watching out their windows, the lights will go out. Nobody sees anything. That's how it goes."

"Very convincing, Mr. Sebastiani."

"Carlo, I told you to call me Carlo." He smiled, Tony smiled.

They both looked more menacing when they smiled. Miranda took a step toward the car. Elke stayed close beside her.

Carlo Sebastiani leaned forward. "Ms. Quin, look up the street. You see those two men by the newspaper boxes? They are carrying guns. Look down the other way. See that car parked there? There are two guys in the front seat. Two guys don't sit in the front seat together unless they're, you know, fruits, or cops, or — do you know why else? Because they, like those other two, they're waiting for you. They've been waiting a long time. They saw you go out, they saw you cross Washington Square, they saw you have dinner with Captain Clancy, one of New York's finest, and I mean that with no irony whatsoever, and they've followed you back here. Actually, like us, they anticipated your arrival back here, they got back before you did. Now what do you think of that?"

"You followed us?"

"They followed you, we followed them."

"They're not yours! What do they want?"

"They want you dead."

"Dead?"

"Both of you."

"Dead," said Elke. "Miranda, aren't you getting tired of this?"

"Yes," said Miranda. "I am. I really am." She returned her gaze to the men in the car. "And what's your role in this?"

"For the time being, I want to save your lives."

"For the time being?"

"Nothing in this life is certain, Detective, nothing is forever. At the moment, we are allies."

"Allies?"

"For want of a better word. Tony, help the ladies into the car. Use minimal force, but it's time now. Our friends will be anxious to proceed. And Tony, as soon as they're in, get us the hell out of here, if you please."

"Yes, Mr. Sebastiani." He touched each woman gently on the arm and each clambered in past Carlo Sebastiani. Before they had fastened their seat belts, Tony was behind the wheel. He jammed the gas pedal to the floor and the limousine hurtled straight towards the parked car with the two men in the front. The other car burned rubber, spinning to the side as it careened over the curb and up onto the sidewalk to avoid being smashed. It was over that fast. The limousine cruised crosstown and turned down lower Fifth Avenue, turned at 26th Street, rolled back up Eighth, and stopped.

"What?" said Miranda, "is that the end of the ride?"

"If those clowns stopped to think," he said, ignoring her question, "I'm not going to let Tony use a car that costs this much as a battering ram. He was bluffing. Tell the ladies you were bluffing, Tony."

"If that's what you think, Mr. Sebastiani."

Miranda felt there was an element of banter between them, something suggesting a bond running deeper than the price of a car which, she was certain, could be replaced overnight. She suspected the formality, addressing his boss as Mr. Sebastiani, was for her benefit.

"How did you lose them so easily?" she asked.

"This is our part of the world," said Tony over his shoulder.

"That's enough, Tony," snapped Sebastiani, as if the driver was about to reveal family secrets.

"Do we get out here?" said Miranda. "We can take a cab back to the loft."

"No, Miranda. That would not be a good idea. These men, they want you dead. Do you understand that? I do not want you dead right now, do you understand that? And do you understand that, ultimately, I don't give a rat's ass if you live or die?"

"Then why," she did not want to consent to the idea of being rescued, "why this?"

"Let's say it's for Vittorio. I owed him. You were good to my old friend. I know, you did not want to be good. I have been told you are an honest cop. My friend on the Toronto Police Force, you might know him, his name is Pierre Bourassa. He is an honest cop. Incorruptible, so he tells me. That's what he says about you. He upset your partner, he wanted to know about you. He is not subtle, Pierre Bourassa. Mr. Morgan, he vouched for your honesty."

"Vouched?"

"Yes, so I was told."

"You are in communication with the Toronto Police force on a daily basis?"

"No. But these are special times. I know Bourassa. We went to law school together. Both failed. He became a cop, I became what I was meant to be."

"A gangster."

"The word has a certain ring to it."

"And 'these are special times.' Would you care to explain?"

"No."

Miranda felt the interior of the car was like a bathysphere and the surrounding street scene, gleaming softly through the smoked glass windows, was another world. The limousine door opened and Tony crawled into the spacious interior to squat and face them. Suddenly he had a black hood in his hands and whipped it over Miranda's head before she had time to respond. Her fists flailed and then strong hands grasped them together and snapped handcuffs over her wrists.

"Elke," she said, in a muffled voice. "Elke, you'll be all right."

Elke said nothing.

"Carlo!" said Miranda. She paused. "Very interesting. I appreciate, you rescued us. Now take the goddamned hood off before I …" After another long pause, she said, "I'm amazed you failed out of law school. Must have screwed up the ethics part. So what now."

"Now, my dear, we go for a ride."

"I've seen that in the movies. It never ends well. Going for a ride usually means, well, going for a ride."

"Yes, it does, Miranda. In this case, to a safe house as my guest. The hood is to protect you. I think it is better if you don't know where you are."

"And how long am I going to *not* know where I am? When do we get turned loose?"

"All in good time. Meanwhile, you will be safe."

"Who were those guys?"

"Your assassins."

"Okay, Carlo. Who were our assassins?"

"Men who want to kill you, that is all you need to know."

"No, it is not all I need to know."

"Detective, it *is* all. Please sit back, enjoy the ride. Tony, let's go."

Miranda could feel Elke's thigh pressed against hers. It was strangely comforting. She listened to the cross streets, counted the lights they stopped at, and within a couple of minutes was thoroughly disoriented. Then she felt the car descend and heard a sustained rush of air. She knew exactly where she was, in the Hudson Tunnel, on their way to New Jersey.

14

The Safe House

After an interminable drive, the car slowed and wound its way through a series of gentle curves. They must be in suburbia, Miranda thought. Expensive suburbia, with streets laid out in sweeping geometric patterns. She had not heard a sound from Elke since before the hoods were put on.

"Elke?" she said.

There was no response.

"Elke, do you really think there's a gay cabal to subvert femininity?"

"What a bizarre question, given our present condition," said Elke.

"Well, do you?"

"No, I was just playing the devil."

"Meaning what?" said Miranda, who was incredibly relieved her companion was responsive.

"If you two are talking in code, it won't help," said Carlo Sebastiani. "As the saying goes, 'resistance is futile.'"

"That's not a saying," said Tony from the front seat as they pulled into a driveway. "That's the motto of the Borg."

"The Borg?" said Carlo Sebastiani. "What the hell are you talking about?"

"*Star Trek*," said Miranda.

"Shit," said the Mafia boss. "Seven of Nine. Yeah, great tits, I've seen her, what, you think I'm culturally illiterate?"

"Too sophisticated, Carlo. You've got more on your mind," Tony responded with companionable grace. "That's why you're the boss."

"Fucking right," said Carlo.

"What on earth are you people talking about?" said Elke impatiently. "What's a seven-of-nine?"

Miranda heard automatic garage doors roll open, the car shunted forward, then the decisive rumble as they closed. *This is it*, she thought.

By the time Tony had climbed into the back and removed Miranda's cuffs and hood, Elke's were already off. Carlo Sebastiani held them in his hands as if they were lingerie. He waited for the women to get out first, admiring them as they squirmed out of the confined space.

Stepping from the garage into the house, Miranda was surprised. Far from being a place of confinement, it was an opulently appointed suburban house with gleaming hard furniture and plush soft furniture, all in earth tones with a few strategic accents of brilliant colour. Waiting for them in the living room was an attractive woman in her early fifties who rose to her feet, kissed Carlo in a familiar embrace, greeted Tony as a friend and smiled at the two women, waiting for an introduction.

"This is my wife," said Carlo, with an awkward gesture to the woman whose imperial demeanour left no doubt about her status.

"Pleased to meet you, I'm Linda. You're going to be staying with me for a while."

"I'm Miranda, this is Elke. I'm a Toronto police detective."

"I'm a stay-at-home empty-nest New Jersey housewife," said Linda Sebastiani. "Sit down, make yourselves comfortable. Tony, will you find Carmen, have her get us some drinks. So, Detective, how do you like New Jersey so far?"

There was more menace in the woman's charm than anything Miranda perceived in her husband's obvious expressions of power. Miranda looked around. There were no bars on the windows, no guards posted at the doors, no attempt to stop her from taking in the details of their surroundings.

But, of course, she thought. *There is a front garden and hedges. I could never identify this place from the street in a million years. As for breaking free, even if we got away, where would we go? We don't know where we are. New Jersey. That covers a lot of territory.*

The maid came in and took orders for drinks. Miranda asked for a Scotch, straight up.

"Of course," said Sebastiani, "if you would prefer wine?"

"Let me guess," said Miranda. "You have ChâteauNeuf-du-Pape at perfect cellar temperature."

"Yes, we do, and as you say, it should be slightly cooled, enough to show a bloom on the bottle. Am I right, Ms. Sturmberg?"

Elke, who had seemed distracted to this point, either through fear or possibly frustration at yet another intrusion on her normally quiet and esoteric lifestyle, responded with surprising vivacity. "Yes, that is definitely best. I would always serve up a blended wine at cellar temperature. By the grape, I'd go cooler or warmer, depending."

"On what?" asked Linda Sebastiani with genuine interest.

"On the grape. Beaujolais, which is Gamay, I might even chill. A Merlot, just below room temperature. Something heavy like Hermitage, which is Syrah, or an Australian Shiraz, if they're good, I'd rest them on the table for half an hour before opening to let them warm, then let them breathe for another half hour before pouring."

"You are in the wine business, of course," the other woman noted.

"Yes, I am."

"And what do you think of our contribution to wine culture?" Carlo Sebastiani asked.

"Italy's, it's —"

"No, no, Ms. Sturmberg. I am a patriot. Italy is, as a poet once said, a creation myth. I am a proud and loyal American. I am asking about our ChâteauNeuf."

"You are a patriot who sells counterfeit French wine to a gullible American public," said Miranda.

"Do not confuse honour with honesty, Ms. Quin," he snapped back.

"Carmen," said Linda in a voice sufficiently strident to interrupt the conversational flow, as she clearly intended, "would you bring up a bottle of Bordeaux from the cellar, say, Château Mouton Rothschild."

"Yes, ma'am. What year would you like?"

"Our guests are special, let them decide."

Without hesitation, Elke chimed in with, "Nineteen forty-five, that would be nice."

"Bring us a nineteen forty-five, then," said Linda.

"You have it!" exclaimed Elke. "Really?"

"Of course," said Linda. "Carmen, you will open it, please, and leave it on the sideboard. I'm sure my friend would like it to breathe."

Miranda was fascinated to see how Elke's passion for wine displaced her sense of imminent danger or social propriety as the virtual prisoner in the home of a family of gangsters.

"This is a nice place," she said. "Perhaps I could use your phone."

"Thank you," said Carlo. "We only use it now and then, for special occasions. Think of it as a family cottage. It is a safe haven from life on the mean streets — and the main streets. It's nice. But, of course, as anonymous as a one-dollar bill. Even the police don't know about this place. And no, you may not use the telephone."

"Captain Clancy is going to miss us. He'll know by morning."

"He will know you are safe."

"No way!"

"What?"

"He's not on your payroll?"

"As you say, no way. But he understands certain things, he will know not to worry."

"What is going on here?" Miranda demanded.

"As I said, my dear, I am a patriot."

"You are a hoodlum."

"They are not mutually exclusive."

There was an awkward lull in the conversation. Miranda watched Linda Sebastiani for any sign of empathy, something she could play on. The woman seemed serene, the only one in the room not agitated by the silence.

"So," said Carlo. "You want to talk about wines?"

"I would like to know why we're here."

"If you knew, you would not be here."

"Say again?"

"If you understood the situation, you would be at home. You would be back in Canada."

"Canada," said Linda, savouring the word as if she were trying to identify an unusual flavour. "Toronto. Yes, you must know Francine Ciccone, the poor woman."

"Poor woman, I doubt. I know who she is. I've met her husband."

"Who is dead."

"Yes. I'm sure you know the situation between us."

"Yes, I do. Sometimes, despite what my husband says, honesty and honour come together. It was a good thing you were trying to do for Vittorio."

"It was not for Vittorio Ciccone. It was simply what happened."

"And your partner, he is an old friend of Francine's." Linda said this as a statement of fact.

"They were in school together."

"And college," said Linda. "Did you know Tony went to the same university? It was in Toronto, am I right?"

"Yes, and you?"

"Wellesley. Outside Boston."

"Did you graduate?"

"Yes, Detective."

"*Magnum cum laude*," exclaimed her husband with pride.

"*Magna*, not *magnum*," said his wife gently. "Carlo studied on the streets of New York and did his graduate work in Toronto, but not at the university."

"Vittorio," said Carlo, "he was my professor, eh." He seemed proud of knowing to add *eh* to the end of his sentence.

"I thought you went to law school?"

"Carlo!" exclaimed Linda.

"Yeah, that's just something I say."

"I didn't think Bourassa studied law," said Miranda.

"Ah, but he did. I didn't. He failed out."

Miranda glanced at Elke who, after her initial display of terror, seemed to be settling in as a houseguest. Whatever her post-traumatic response to yet another harrowing event, it had quickly passed. She had her eye on the '45 Château Mouton that the maid had brought in, opened, and set on the sideboard.

"Normally, I would insist such a bottle be opened in my presence," she said, addressing Carlo.

"You'll just have to trust me," he responded with a good-natured shrug.

"If you'd sell plonk as Châteauneuf-du-Pape," said Miranda, "why wouldn't you re-use a Mouton bottle for special occasions like this?"

Surprisingly, Elke rose to the defense. "It isn't plonk, Miranda. That's the ironic part. If they — you guys — had marketed your Ninth Chateau as a legitimate blend, you could have done very well, won a few prizes, sold it for twenty or thirty dollars a bottle, built a major business."

"Yeah," said Carlo, "we could have. But we didn't. You want a swig of this?" He got up and grasped the Mouton by the neck.

"Be careful!" Elke exclaimed. "You'll stir up the sediment, you'll bruise it."

"If there *is* sediment," said Miranda, still dubious about the wine's authenticity.

Carlo held the bottle up against the overhead light. The others gathered around him, taking turns gazing into the sombre opacity inside the base of the green glass.

"Looks real," said Elke. She turned to Miranda. "Have you any idea what it's worth, do you know what we're drinking?"

"A lot?"

"A whole lot."

"As in, how much?"

"Ten–fifteen thousand. One bottle sold at auction a couple of years ago for $31,000 U.S. dollars."

"Thirty-one thousand!"

"Yes."

"Dollars!"

"Yes."

"Mr. Sebastiani, you make it almost worth being your captive."

"Our guests," said Linda softly, as if clarifying a minor social faux pas.

Miranda nodded to her in a gesture of temporary acquiescence and held out her glass.

Carlo poured, and in fact handled the Mouton with great delicacy. He looked around him.

"Here, Tony. Where's your glass. Carmen," he called. She emerged through a door from the dining room. "Get a glass, you gotta try this."

Just as Miranda was beginning to like this man, he exclaimed, "It's worth more than she makes in a year!" The maid put down the glass she had picked up, smiled, and with the vaguest intimation of a curtsy, she eased herself out of the room.

"Immigrants," said Carlo, "no taste!"

Elke held her glass lightly by the stem, filled to just below the widest part of its bulge, leaving room for the wine to breathe. She swirled it in slow motion and pressing the rim to her nose, drew in deeply. Then she held the glass away from her, examining the wine against the light.

"Beautiful brick colour," she said. "Perfect nose. Ripe blackberries, bitter chocolate, vanilla, dried grass. It has a depth beyond words."

She placed the glass to her lips. The others watched in anticipation. She took a sip, swirled it in her mouth, breathed through her open mouth, mouthing the wine, and swallowed.

"Thank you, Carlo. That is an experience to die for — not literally."

The others drank, each imitating the procedural details of Elke's tasting, and all shared her sense of wonder. For a few minutes the perverse dynamics of their relationships were obscured by their pleasure.

Then Miranda set her glass down. She addressed Carlo. "You're not really interested in wine, are you?"

"You are mistaken. I love a rare, good wine like this."

"But you have no interest in making it. The winery was a cover, right? You and Vittorio Ciccone, others from New York, the ChâteauNeuf-du-Pape thing was an elaborate bit of distraction."

"Why would we do that?" said Carlo. "We are not in the habit, if you are referring to me and my business associates, of simply amusing ourselves."

"I meant distraction as — never mind. Then what?"

"What, what about what?"

"You've got us here as prisoners, and it has something to do with counterfeit wines. Don't we deserve an explanation?"

"It is not necessary."

There was dead silence.

"Perhaps you are tired," said Linda. "I will call Carmen. She will show you to your room. I am afraid you will be sleeping in a suite downstairs. Do not be alarmed, the room is well appointed, but it has no windows to distract you. Don't you agree, Detective Quin, windows, they can be a distraction."

Miranda ignored her. She was annoyed for letting the woman's social skills, her husband's generosity in sharing the incomparable wine, distract her from the gravity of their situation.

"It is about drugs," she said abruptly, turning directly to Carlo.

He said nothing, but he set down his glass with wine still in it, as if the best wine of the last century no longer held his interest.

"You're making a big mistake, Carlo. You can't keep us here forever," she said, feeling vaguely uncomfortable for uttering clichés. *The Mounties will come to our rescue,* she thought. *I'm a Canadian.*

"Tony," said Linda, indicating the decision was hers, "take the ladies downstairs, please." Then, in a more congenial voice, she added, "Breakfast will be served at eight fifteen. Carmen is especially good at breakfasts. Good night."

She turned to address her husband privately, making it clear their visitors, or prisoners, were no longer of interest.

Miranda turned to Elke and nodded their assent, and both followed Tony along a corridor and down a staircase into the secured suite below ground level. The door was so thick, it seemed like they were entering a vault.

"Soundproof," he noted. "I hope you'll be comfortable."

"Thank you," said Elke as if he were their host for a weekend visit.

"I'd better take your purses," he said.

"Oh, come on," said Elke, plaintively, "there's stuff in there I need."

"You'll find everything necessary in the bathroom," he said, and took Miranda's proffered bag and then Elke's, and motioned them to enter.

They stepped into what looked like a moderately expensive hotel suite, complete with matching cabinets for the television and mini-bar.

"The bathroom's in there. The thermostat's here." Tony indicated the thermostat by the door. "There's lots of fresh air pumped in to make up for no windows. There's kinky stuff in the drawers there, in the dresser, if you two want to play. Handcuffs and leather. Enjoy yourselves, think of this as a holiday retreat."

"Thanks," said Elke, walking over and sitting on one of the twin beds. Then, provocatively, she added, "Since you can't stay, you'd better go. See you in the morning, Tony."

She smiled. He smiled back.

Tony closed the door and locked it from the outside. Miranda noticed there was a steel bar that could be bolted across the door from the inside to make the room virtually impregnable. Why, she could not imagine, unless even crime bosses need a safe room.

Miranda checked out the bathroom and came back into the bedroom. She couldn't shake from her mind the image of the final exchange between Elke and Tony. She was responding to something indefinable, and it sent a chill shooting through to the bone.

The two women explored. There were cotton pajamas neatly folded on each bed, along with toiletry kits like the ones airlines give away in business class. Miranda picked up her kit and pajamas and went back into the bathroom. She had a shower and rinsed out her underwear. She used the hair dryer to dry her hair and returned to the bedroom. Elke was slouched against the backboard of her bed, stripped down to her panties and bra.

"My turn," said Elke. "You didn't use up all the hot water, did you?"

Miranda shook her head and pulled back the spread. She drew the sheet up around her, then as Elke stepped into the bathroom, she hopped out and opened the TV cabinet, and climbing back in, she directed the remote control wand at the screen and switched on CNN.

Talking heads. American politics. Terrorism in the U.K., either IRA or a group called al-Qaeda, both claimed the credit. Weather, then a panel of talking torsos arguing vociferously from fixed opposing perspectives.

Elke emerged, towelling her hair. Miranda switched off the television.

"I don't like those things, those driers, they give you split ends."

"Elke?"

"Yes?"

"I'm going to ask you a question."

"Yes, of course."

"Actually, it's not a question. But perhaps you have an explanation. You were not wearing a hood, were you, in the car. You weren't manacled with handcuffs?"

Elke walked around to the far side of her own bed. She glanced up at an air vent, then back at Miranda, who understood they were being observed. Then she thought about Elke, waiting in her underwear for her turn in the shower. Was she being modest, or teasing? Were they being watched in the shower as well? Was Elke conscious of an audience? There was a lot about Elke more important than her mode of undress that concerned Miranda right now.

"Elke? Did you hear me?"

Elke turned her head halfway toward Miranda, and she seemed to be smiling. Than she stripped off the bedspread and stretched out on top of the sheets.

"Goodnight, Miranda."

Miranda did not answer. Her mind was racing. She reached over and turned off the bedside light. There was the glow of a night-light seeping out from under the bathroom door. If Elke Sturmberg was not blindfolded or tied down in the car, it was because she knew these people. The implications ran rampant through her head. How was this woman connected to New Jersey gangsters, to the Mafia?

Miranda settled her head deeply into the pillow, prepared to stay awake through the night. She felt profoundly betrayed. She was not afraid of Elke, but suddenly she recognized Elke as part of a frightening conspiracy. Questions roared through her mind. Did Elke arrange for their abduction? Was her work at Beverley Auctions a cover? Was she involved in the drug trade? Did she set up Ivan Muritori to be killed? Did she execute the man by the Humber River in cold blood? That's what Morgan had intimated. Did she have anything to do with Morgan's ambush? Did she lure them to the winery in Niagara to be killed? No, she ended up with them in the bullet-riddled vat. What was her Canadian connection? How come she knew the landmarks west of Toronto — was it because she was registering details in response to her terror, or something more sinister? Why did she end up at Miranda's apartment? With a severed hand in her Monica Lewinsky knock-off handbag?

The last thing Miranda thought as the hollow silence of the soundproof room closed around her and she drifted off to sleep: *Damn her, she peed on my floor.*

She peed on my floor.

15

Old Friends

Morgan fell asleep on the blue sofa. The television was flashing indecipherable images when he peered through squinted eyes, trying to read the time on the digital display on the VCR below the screen. It was exactly three in the morning, as if the clarity of curvilinear digits had awakened him much the same way old-fashioned clocks used to click in anticipation of the alarm going off. Three, zero, zero. As his eyes brought the read-out into focus, the final digit transformed to a one. He sat upright and fumbled for the wand, turning off the television. The time panel remained illuminated. It was the only light in the room. He had had the presence of mind, before falling asleep, to turn off the reading lamp.

It had been an unsettling day and he had denied himself closure by not going upstairs to his bedroom to sleep. He was wearing boxer shorts, which meant he had got himself ready for bed before settling in on the sofa. He wore boxers as summer pajamas, never as underwear.

He had been under restraint. It was only the direct orders of the superintendent that had kept him away from Francine Ciccone. Most of the day he had spent in the office, correlating forensic information from the various plots and subplots that followed from Miranda's discovery of her lover's corpse in her bed. He was searching for the grand scenario, something that would tie all the details together in a coherent account.

That's how Morgan's mind worked. He was inductive, he would accumulate facts and impressions and gradually or suddenly a pattern would emerge. That was how he thought of himself, thinking. Miranda was deductive. She would pick up a detail and extrapolate from it an entire narrative. That was how he thought of her, thinking. Part of the mythology they shared was the assumption their minds worked in opposite but complementary ways.

This was a bit of a joke around the department. For the most part, their colleagues thought of them thinking exactly alike. They cultivated the myth of difference but worked so well together precisely because they were not. In spite of the dissimilarities in character, sex, experience, and disposition, they were very much the same.

He had called her in the morning at Elke Sturmberg's apartment in Greenwich Village. Inexplicably, when she got on the line, he decided not to tell her about his experience at the warehouse. It seemed like an imposition.

"You okay?" he had asked.

"Sure, of course. We're off to Saks Fifth Avenue in a few minutes. And Elke wants to show me some shops too small to advertise in *Vogue*. How're you doing?"

"I'm fine," said Morgan, reassuring himself as he spoke that he was telling her the truth. Last night seemed far away, like a Bruce Willis movie he had watched on the late show, while at the same time reading one of his esoteric books, perhaps on Ontario country furniture.

"You're sure?"

"Yeah, you're the one in the war zone." *Goodness*, he thought, *what a cliché*. He had been every bit as much under fire in Toronto the Good.

"Well, the war's over. The NYPD want us to stay around for a bit, though. Clancy, he's running the show, he's easy with the hostage situation, that it went down like we said —"

"But it didn't?"

"Not exactly. But, you know, Morgan, Elke was caught in the middle, she did what she had to do. The bastard sold her out, he was going to have her killed."

"Really?"

"No, but he sent her off to Rochester, he set her up to take the fall for exposing the wine scam ... and she ended up in the wine marinade in Niagara."

"And she executed a two-bit hoodlum under the Humber Bridge."

"Morgan, she's in the next room," said Miranda in a low voice. "We can argue the fine points later. The fact is, explanation, exoneration, she was the hostage taker, but she was also the victim — it would have been compli-cated to explain to Clancy. I just cut through the red tape. The woman is innocent, except maybe of overreaction."

"Blonds are usually the victims."

"What does that mean?"

"I have no idea."

"Well, she is ... both. And she's taking me shopping."

"Why not."

"Exactly!"

"You take care in the big city. Don't spend too much."

"See you in a couple of days. Don't solve any murders without me."

"Later."

Morgan picked up the phone on impulse, then put it down. He should call her back, let her know what had happened. He had spoken to Clancy at the NYPD; he'd pass it on. She would be furious, finding out about the warehouse standoff second-hand. He set the phone down gently. He got up and walked to the bathroom, washed up, climbed up into the darkness of his sleeping loft, and got dressed. It was three fifteen in the morning.

Morgan ambled through the muted light of the city at night, from the Annex down to College Street and across, past the monolithic Police Headquarters building, admiring the rectilinear tumble of rose-coloured granite and gunmetal steel that surged against the sky as he walked closer and passed by in front. At Jarvis, he paused. Ahead and to the south lay Cabbagetown, now one of the chic addresses in the city, but when he was growing up, as the name suggested, derived from the staple of boiled beef and cabbage eaten by denizens of the largest Anglo-Saxon slum outside England, it was a far different place, a curious mixture of tenements, tumble-down townhouses, and prized restoration projects. A short distance to the north was another world entirely, one enclosed by walls of privilege and power.

Morgan turned north and, still well before sunrise, he found himself in the heart of Rosedale, surrounded by fine homes, manicured front gardens, strolling over red brick sidewalks under the spreading canopies of towering silver maples along the narrow boulevards and winding streets.

A cruiser pulled up beside him and a uniformed officer asked what he was doing.

"Walking."

"Walking? Where's your dog? Have you got ID?"

"Yes."

The uniformed officer got out of the car. His partner got out the passenger side. She had her hand draped casually over her gun, not menacing but wary.

"Let's see it."

"What?"

"Your ID. What're you doing, walking around here, this time of night?"

"Would you be asking that anywhere else?"

"Okay, my friend, up against the car, hands down, spread 'em. Now, carefully, reach in, get your wallet, hand it to my partner."

Morgan was neither amused nor angry. He was interested, curious to see how the situation would develop. He handed his wallet to the officer standing at his side.

"David Morgan, you're us. Gaffield, ease up. He's a detective, Homicide."

Gaffield, who had a strong hand firmly on Morgan's shoulder, did not release his grip.

"Find a picture," he said. "Photo ID. Check his driver's licence."

"Gaffield!"

"Could be stolen...."

"Gaffield. I recognize him. Detective Morgan. You know, one of ours."

Gaffield let his hand drop from Morgan's shoulder. "Yeah, okay. Sorry, Detective. You never know."

"No, " said Morgan, "you never know. Have a good evening, both of you." He turned away and walked off. The cruiser caught up with him and rolled along at his pace with the window down.

"You might want this," said Gaffield, holding out Morgan's wallet.

"You're not supposed to take the wallet," said Morgan, retrieving his wallet.

"You can't be too careful," said the officer behind the wheel. It was the woman now. They had switched.

"No, just doing your job."

"Goodnight, Detective."

Morgan did not respond, and the cruiser slowly pulled ahead, then sped up around the next corner and wheeled out of sight. Morgan stopped and looked around. He was in front of the Ciccone house. He had, he knew, been coming here from the beginning, from the moment he woke up on his blue sofa.

There was a low wall and a thick hedge across the front. No attempt had been made to secure the premises; it was not necessary in Rosedale. People did not go around invading other people's houses. Break-and-enter specialists avoided the neighbourhood. Virtually every property was equipped with alarms and surveillance devices, somewhat undermining the illusion of invulnerability but emphatically discouraging burglary.

Morgan slipped though the front gate, which was secured by a simple lift-latch. Set back to the left was a carriage house over the garage. He knew there was a couple living in the carriage house. They were not servants.

People like the Ciccone family are jealous of their privacy; they do not allow domestic help to stay overnight. The couple was married, with no children. The woman managed the household and was Frankie Ciccone's confidante, and although their relationship lacked parity, it was not reciprocal. Her husband was a specialist in protection. He would take a bullet for the Ciccone family, or dispense one if necessary, without a moment's hesitation.

While the Ciccones might be considered more vulnerable than most of their neighbours due to their business interests, for the same reason they were protected by their reputation from criminal invasion.

Morgan understood that the four children had moved out. Frankie and Vittorio lived alone. Frankie, now, on her own.

He walked stealthily, but in the open, around to the French doors at the back. There were no signs of a dog, no bare spots on the lawn or gnawed lower branches on the shrubs. He pondered the locked door for a moment, amused that even people in their line of work should trust the naïve conventions of home security. *And they are conventions*, he thought. *People will design elaborate locks on their doors, bolt their windows closed, and assume a pane of glass, one eighth of an inch thick, will keep out intruders. They will install elaborate alarm systems and only set them when they go out. They will leave on a light downstairs when they retire for the night, almost as a talisman to keep burglars at bay, as if they were afraid of the light the way children are afraid of the dark.*

Morgan selected a glass pane in one of the doors that was directly over a small Persian carpet on the hardwood floor in the dining room. He tapped it sharply with his elbow, there was a slight crackle, and the shards of glass fell quietly onto the rug. It was a Persian Qashqa'i, he noticed as he reached through into the light coming from the kitchen and unlocked the door. He could see the fixed red beacon on the alarm across the room and knew it was not armed.

He was fascinated by the presumptive carelessness of the Ciccone family. He thought of the hubris that brought down kings and felt a mixture of righteousness and regret.

Walking across the thick broadloom of the living room to the base of the stairs, Morgan admired the furnishings. Frankie had come a long way, in some respects. This was, so far as he could tell in the dull light streaming in from the street, in very good taste, of a particular sort. Not his taste, no personality (more *House Beautiful* than *Architectural Digest*). Given the over-the-top funeral, Morgan figured she had professional help with the house décor. He gave her credit that at least in this context she recognized her own limitations.

By the time he reached the top of the stairs, all whimsy had dissipated. She had set him up to be killed, using their friendship as the lure. He was irritated with himself for being stupid and hurt by her betrayal. He was sad, but he was angry. He paused in the hallway, his hand on what seemed most likely the door of the master bedroom.

What was he here for? Certainly not to harm her physically. He wanted to confront her, face to face. Just so that she would know that he knew what she'd done. He did not expect remorse or an apology, but he thought perhaps she might be humiliated for having sold herself out — not him, but herself. What satisfaction that would bring was uncertain.

He turned the knob slowly and pushed the door open enough to slip into the room. He could smell the delicate fragrance of feminine vanity. As he moved away from the door, he felt it swing slowly shut and sensuous strains in the air seemed to gather behind him. Without turning around, he knew she was there. The bed was empty, and he could smell the oiled steel of a revolver cocked close to the back of his head.

"Francine?"

"I thought it might be you, David."

Neither of them said anything. Neither of them moved. He caught the scent of her warmth in the air. She moved very close to him. He could feel the muzzle of her gun pressed against his skull just behind his left ear. He could smell something else, and he was certain it was the smell of the ocean, the salt of her tears.

"Francine," he said, gently. "Do you want to talk?"

"You dropped in for a chat, David? How considerate, you're here to console the widow."

He said nothing.

"This is very cozy, and so wonderfully private. Did you know I sleep naked, David? Is that why you came? Or is it to gloat: crime doesn't pay, she'll end up in bed by herself. And she did. Is that it? It's been a long time since I've had a midnight caller, David. Vittorio and I slept in separate rooms. How did you pick my door? The Lady or the Tiger? The tiger is dead."

"Francine, take the gun away from my head."

"Do you want to turn around? Do you want to look at me naked? Is that what you always wanted...." Her voice trailed off. She did not at all sound like the confident widow at the cemetery, nor did she sound like a woman who had tried to arrange Morgan's death. She sounded desperate, needing to be assured that with the death of her husband she was still a woman. She sounded infinitely lonely and lost. *This is the worst time of night to be alone,* he thought, *waiting on your own for the sun to rise.*

He turned slowly until his eyes connected with hers and she let the revolver descend to her side. He placed an arm around her shoulders as he took the gun in his hand and, setting it down, he led her to the bed. He fluffed out the top sheet in the air and eased her back against the pillows, then drew the sheet up to her shoulders and tucked it around her. He traced the back of his hand across her forehead and softly brushed hair away from her face.

She lay very still with her eyes closed, then opened them unblinking and looked solemnly up at him. When he smiled, she smiled back.

He sat down on the edge of the bed and continued to caress her forehead, letting the backs of his fingers flow gently against her skin until it relaxed and the lines faded and her face glowed in the soft illumination from the night-light seeping under the bathroom door.

Frankie Ciccone let her eyes flutter closed and she drifted into a deep sleep. Morgan lowered himself onto the floor and sat leaning with his back against the bed. His mind was filled with a lazy swarming like bees on a cloudless day, and no idea came to mind worth holding as he slipped into a light slumber.

When Morgan woke up, the room was filled with sunlight, and Frankie was lying on her side with her hand draped over his shoulder.

"Close the curtains," she whispered.

He got up and drew the drapes closed, shutting out the light. He went into the bathroom for a few minutes then emerged to find Frankie had drawn the sheet down and was waiting for him.

Neither of them said a word. Morgan stripped off his clothes and lay down beside her, pulling the sheet up over them both.

Frankie drew him on top, spreading herself so his weight rested on his knees. They kissed passionately. She whimpered and he held her close under him, her breasts pressing deeply into the hardness of his diaphragm. He nibbled against her neck but she took his face between her hands and held it aslant to her own and kissed him deeply, drawing his mouth hard-soft against hers and at the same time shifting her weight to draw him into her. They rocked gently for a long time, their mouths locked and their bodies merged in warmth.

After a while, time gathered force and exploded in a shared orgasm and they were outside the moment, waves rushing through bodies and brains in a receding sequence of pleasure until their synergy subsided and they rolled away, still joined at the loins, and stared into each other's eyes.

Neither of them spoke when Morgan got up, and gathering his clothes went into the bathroom to shower and dress. When he came out, Francine was wrapped in a silk kimono and she had opened the curtains again so the room was flooded with light.

There was a complete English breakfast for two waiting on a side table by the window. Francine poured Morgan a coffee. She poured herself tea. They ate in comfortable silence, like an old married couple.

When they finished, they both sat back. It was time to talk.

"You think I betrayed you, I know that." She spoke as casually as if she were commenting on the weather.

"Yeah, maybe that's what I thought."

"Do you still think so?"

"Maybe."

"Morgan, Vittorio and I were happy."

"It didn't cross my mind you weren't. You're tough, you wouldn't be here otherwise."

"Because we had separate rooms, doesn't mean, you know."

"I know."

"Right now I'm angry at him, can you understand that?"

"For leaving?"

"Yes, for leaving me."

"It wasn't his choice. What happened, what went wrong with the warehouse thing? You tortured the guy, you cut off his pecker, you wanted him arrested."

"We wanted him arrested, yes. But the last part, that wasn't us."

"It wasn't you who ambushed me and killed him. Was it Mr. Savage?"

"He isn't one of ours."

"And you're not his?"

"No, of course not."

"But he is a very powerful man."

"He is."

"Why?"

"I can't explain.

"You can't, or won't?"

"Both. If I could, I wouldn't."

"Before — you talked about Vittorio's killers. More than one. Who? How many?"

"You've got the Albanian."

"Dead, yeah. We've got him. He's the shooter. But who else is involved, what's Savage's connection?"

"I told you," she said, almost plaintively.

"You can't or won't say. Let's put it on the line, Frankie. The Ciccone family is boss. Yes?"

"Yes."

"But someone is playing you, right."

"Playing us?"

"Like you're the pawns, just like us, black and white pawns, robbers and cops, but someone else is game-master. This Mr. Savage, he's playing both sides."

"Morgan, I know too much about my husband. He would come in here sometimes in the dead of night and crawl in beside me and we would talk until dawn. He trusted me — not just with business secrets. He trusted me with his emotions. He told me everything. He is dead, but I could still hurt him. I won't do that."

"I'm not asking you to betray your husband. It would take more than me to bring down organized crime. And the emotional thing, that's between you and him. I know being dead doesn't mean it's over, not until you're both dead. I know that. But I need to get to Savage. There's a contagion of killing, and it's got to stop. You have to help me isolate him, bring him down."

"I can't, Morgan."

"Or won't?"

"I can't."

"Can you at least explain why not?"

"You know how the business works. We're a confederation of independent families. Usually, we co-operate. Collectively, in Canada and the States, we turn over more in a year than most countries. But we're not a single entity, Morgan, we aren't a collective."

"And you're up against something that is?"

"Something like that."

Morgan recognized she was not going to reveal more through that line of questioning. He looked across the breakfast table at her. *This might have been us*, he mused. He knew she was thinking the same thing. Not with regret, neither with regret. They each had to find the way out of Cabbagetown on their own.

"Why did you hire the Albanian?" he said. "He was working for you."

A flash of unspeakable horror crossed her face. The abomination of his charge was beyond comprehension.

"Me! To kill my own husband! You think I arranged Vittorio's death?"

"No," he exclaimed, realizing until that moment the idea might have been lurking in the back of his mind. "Absolutely not!"

"What then? You sure know how to break the mood."

"I meant the Ciccone family. Frankie, there's no mood. We're not —"

"No, we're not. It just happened. I'm glad. Now we know what we've been missing. I took advantage of you."

"Seducing the prowler?"

"And of course, you took advantage of me?"

"The grieving widow."

"Which I am."

"I know."

"You're a good lover, Morgan."

"We're good together."

"And gracious, too." she said. "It wasn't me who hired the Albanian."

"Vittorio?"

"Yes. Branko appeared one day with credentials. He was a refugee in Italy, with experience in the business from Albania. A lot of them moved into the region around Taranto. He came recommended by a cousin Vittorio never met. It seemed reasonable to give him a chance."

"Kind of like social work, was it?"

"Yeah, something like that."

"So, he could have been inserted by whoever, ready to take out Vittorio whenever they wanted."

"Yes, so it seems. But Vittorio trusted him. He was the logical man to guard your partner. Vittorio's life depended on it."

"That's heavy irony, Frankie. What about the driver?"

"He disappeared. He'll come back some day. Guys like that, they don't get far on their own. He'll come back and pay the consequences. He was a coward, nothing more. He could not have saved Vittorio, so he saved himself. He walked away, but he'll come back."

"And take his punishment."

"And renew his loyalty."

"And what about the man under the bridge?"

"Gianni. He did odd jobs for us. He was a nice kid."

"Who was about to execute Elke Sturmberg in cold blood."

"Elke Sturmberg, the blond, is that her name?"

"You know that already."

"Maybe."

"And instead, she killed him."

"So I hear. Gianni wasn't working for us, not then."

"For Mr. Savage?"

"I couldn't say."

Morgan started to rise from the breakfast table, then sank back in his chair. It would be difficult to imagine a more congenial setting, he thought, in stark contrast to their conversation about murder and betrayal. The sun played across the yellow and white gingham tablecloth, glinted off the flatware and plates. He could still pick up the womanly scent in the air when he flared his nostrils and drew in a few deep breaths.

"You all right?" she asked.

"I've got to go," he said. "About last night?"

"It's okay, it was good."

"No, I mean the night before, in the warehouse."

"Yes."

"That wasn't you?"

"You still need reassurance? It must be hard to trust so little, David. I promise you, it was not our people. We wanted the bastard arrested, we wanted him doing hard time, like a rat in a maze. *Our* maze."

"The penitentiary, you think it's yours?"

"Some of Vittorio's associates call it 'the college.'"

"Lovely." He rose to his feet and stood still for a moment, admiring her in the morning light. Her eyes, still a little swollen from grieving, looked sleepily exotic. He stepped around, leaned down, and kissed her.

"Goodbye, Francine."

"You take care, David Morgan. See yourself out."

"What about ..."

"No one will see you. I have never been unfaithful to my husband. What I do now is up to me. They understand that. Maria will come up the back way when I call. My couple in the carriage house, they will be busy, they will not notice you leaving."

Morgan went out through the front door. He could hear voices in the kitchen. He felt reasonably sure no one saw him as he ambled down the flagstone walk and through the gate to the street — at least, no one connected with the Ciccone family. It was eight thirty in the morning. Other people in Rosedale were leaving their houses for work or school or their appointed rounds of civic responsibility and personal well-being. A pleasantly unkempt man emerging onto the sidewalk among them was of no more than passing interest except to the conspicuously unobtrusive pair hunched in the front seat of a car parked up the street.

Morgan turned and walked directly toward their car. As he approached, they drove off, looking away. He noted the licence number but knew it would lead nowhere. He shrugged and reversed his direction, figuring he would take the subway home.

16

Ladybug, Ladybug

At virtually the same time as Morgan wakened on the blue sofa and responded to the call deep within that led him to Frankie Ciccone's bedroom, Miranda's eyes flashed open. In the darkness of the room, the illuminated digits of the clock shone like a strange temporal beacon. Three a.m. She looked across at Elke, who was lying on her side in deep shadow. Elke had slipped off her underwear and draped it over her headboard. Her pajamas lay in a crumpled shadow on the floor. Miranda rose and went into the bathroom. There was a strong enough glow from the night-light coming under the door that she could find her way without stumbling. In the bathroom, with the door closed, she switched on the overhead light, then, assuming there was a camera observing her, she turned it off again.

After using the toilet, she flushed, and then stepped into the shower. The showerhead was fixed to a vertical slide to adjust the height. She tapped the bar with her fingertips. The Sebastiani family did not stint; it was a heavyweight hollow steel rod. Even in the semi-darkness, it was not difficult to slip the bar free. It had a good heft as she slapped it quietly against the palm of one hand.

Turning off the night-light, she crept out into the blackness of the bedroom. She could hear the sullen hush of the soundproofing as she moved close beside Elke's bed. She raised the steel rod, but only to reinforce a sense of power. She lowered it, placing it carefully on top of her bed.

She reached to where the headboard should be and clasped Elke's brassiere in her hand. In the muted darkness she knew she had to be sure of her moves. Holding the brassiere between her teeth, she let her hands slowly descend and hover over Elke's invisible form, moving slowly within the radiant heat of her body without touching, until she was sure where she was.

Miranda suddenly clasped the other woman's arms and slid her hands down to her wrists, clasping tightly. Even before Elke yelled, Miranda had the brassiere wrapped around her wrists, binding them tightly together. Intuitively, she swung the woman's body around and jammed her open palm against her mouth to stifle Elke's protestations. Then she said in a calming voice that it was only her.

"Elke, I want you to be very quiet. I'm going to take my hand away...."

"What are you doing?" Elke hissed in the darkness.

Miranda replaced her hand over Elke's mouth, gently this time. She waited. She wanted to know if anyone would respond to Elke's yelling. After a few minutes, she took her hand away again.

"It seems I'm right, no one is paying any attention. And the room is definitely soundproof — that's sinister."

"Miranda, I —"

"Shut up!" Miranda again placed her hand over the woman's mouth, this time pressing her lips hard against her teeth. "I do not want to hear from you. Nothing, not a word. You are a dangerous woman." Even while she spoke, Miranda could feel the sense of outrage rising within her at Elke's lethal duplicity.

"Mrmmmmmmmmmmpfh —"

Miranda gave her a sharp rap against the side of her jaw. The other woman fell silent, apart from the sound of her breathing, which was rapid, as if she were on the verge of a panic attack.

Miranda groped around until she found Elke's blouse and twisted its fine material into a makeshift rope, which she used to bind the woman's ankles.

She did not want to risk using the overhead. Someone might check the monitor. She went back into the bathroom and turned on the light, then returned to the bedroom, closing the bathroom door all but a sliver, which provided sufficient illumination for her purposes.

Still in her pajamas, she made her way along the walls of the room, starting at the bathroom door and working her way around. She was feeling for the coolest wall, an exterior wall. As she expected, given where the other doors were and what she remembered of the general layout of the house when Tony brought them down, it was behind the headboards of their beds.

Walls, she assured herself, *are a convention. We are imprisoned behind cement blocks. Oh please God, may it not be poured concrete*. Cement blocks break easily with a sharp blow against the hollowed chambers. When she was in her early teens, she had helped her father build a garage beside the house in Waldron. They tore down the old garage and burned the wood. Then they poured cement for a floor. When the wall was going up, she carried blocks to him, one at a time. She was astonished at how easily he split them to fit the corners with a few taps from a cold chisel.

"They're not built to resist sideways pressure," her father had explained. "They'll hold up more weight than we could ever put on them, but from the side, they'll crack without hardly trying."

"Could you kick them in?" she had asked, and before he responded she gave the blocks behind him a good kick with the side of her foot.

"Well, there you are," he said when she let out an agonized shriek. "You made the damn wall move. What a girl!"

Still doubled over to help assuage the pain through histrionics, she managed to catch a glimpse of a gaping seam in the damp cement. She had moved the blocks a good half inch. But, damn, as her father would say, it hurt.

"Now there's a lesson for you," he said, rubbing her scalp like a puppy's. "Windows and walls are conventions. They work only because we believe they work. So go on, get us a beer. One Labatt's, one ginger."

She could see them both in her mind as two people, sharing things. She could see herself the way she had looked in photographs as a teenager, and him, vividly remembered as long as she did not try too hard to focus. If she did, he became blurry. He died a year after the garage was finished.

Miranda felt along the surface of the wall, tapping with her fingers every few inches. She picked up the hollow steel bar and gouged into the drywall. The sharp edge penetrated easily. Using the bar, she pried slabs of drywall away, leaving thick strips of wooden lath exposed with Styrofoam between them, covered with a thin sheet of plastic. Pulling off chunks of the insulating foam and strips of plastic, she exposed cement blocks.

"Damn," she mumbled, "that's good."

After tapping to see where one of the blocks at eye-level was thinnest, she drove the bar with all her strength against the cement. The steel reverberated in her hand, sending pains shooting through her arms and up the back of her neck.

She changed her approach. Retrieving towels from the bathroom, she draped one over the block, pinning it in place against some of the remaining Styrofoam. Then she wrapped another towel around the bar to protect her hands, and again lining up the weak point on the block, she drove the steel home, straight into the cement. It cut through like the cement was ice cream.

Using the bar as a lever, she pried away a large chunk of the block, then repeated the procedure, over and over, until she was drenched in sweat and cement dust, and there was a hole in the wall the size of four blocks. Outside, there was a pressure-treated green sheet of wood that already had holes punched through it here and there by the time she had removed the cement. The wood was harder to open up than she expected; she could not get a grip to pry and it was flush up against dirt, outside, making it resist blows from her steel rod, which, by now, was dulled at the edges.

Suddenly the last hold on the wood gave away, and her tool sank deep into earth, which came sliding down over her in a soggy avalanche. She had calculated the height correctly and had opened the hole just below ground level. She stood amidst the earth and detritus, proud of herself. The clock read 4:37 a.m. Elke Sturmberg, who had been a silent observer, looked dismayed in the half-light.

Miranda took her clothes into the bathroom and showered quickly — in case the sounds of water running disturbed anyone upstairs, it would seem like nothing more than a toilet flushing. She dressed, checking herself in the mirror. She wanted to look presentable once she got out. She had no identity, no money, and she would need to rely on the charity of strangers.

Back in the bedroom, she carried a chair over to the hole in the wall. Then, peering into the darkness, anticipating the filth and abrasions when she climbed up through the ground, she stripped to her underwear. She put her clean clothes and sandals inside a pillowslip. Picking up Elke's pajamas, she paused then slipped out of her underwear and added it to the pillowslip, put on the clean pajamas, paused again, went back into the bathroom, donned her own filthy pajamas as an outer layer, and prepared a clean, damp towel, which she stuffed into another pillowslip, which she then put inside the first. Satisfied she had the resources to make herself presentable, she smiled. Standing on the chair, she tossed her bundle up and out, then, before climbing through the hole, she looked back at Elke.

She was surprised to see an indecipherable look on the other woman's face in the gloom, something between terror and incredulity. But Elke said nothing. Miranda nodded, then turned and clambered out into the pre-dawn air.

When Seymour Clancy picked her up at the Teaneck Police Station in New Jersey, he was astounded to hear that Elke might have been complicit in the abduction, but even more that Miranda had left her behind.

"You're a cop, you should have brought her in."

"That's easy for you to say. I don't think you grasp the human mole thing."

"You crawled through some dirt. Good, and if you're wrong about her, she's in deep trouble about now."

"She is, trust me."

"In trouble or guilty?"

"Both."

"Well, we'd better find her, hadn't we, and sort out where you both fit in to the grand scheme of mayhem and murder?"

Was he implying Miranda had been complicit in the hostage drama, she wondered, or was he just as confused as she was? "They told me you'd know where we were," she said.

"Meaning what!"

"No, no, Sebastiani insisted you're as honest as I am. Only he didn't put it that way. He did say you'd know enough not to worry."

"We didn't even know you were gone."

"And might never have. Elke would have turned up safe enough, with a sad tale of my mysterious demise. She's good at spinning tales. Or would she simply say I unaccountably vanished? Sometimes least is best."

"Or less is more." He seemed to chuckle at a private joke as they slid into his car. He handed her a crumpled bag with a nondescript fast food breakfast sandwich. "Here," he announced. "I had mine on the way. The coffee's yours." There was a cardboard cup in a holder attached to the dashboard. "I hope you can find your way back. It's what they call a safe house, meaning we're not supposed to know about it."

"Do you?"

"No."

"That makes it pretty secure. Look, with Elke, I had no idea where I was. I knew I'd need help and I didn't know how she'd be, whether she'd make a scene if I flagged down a car. I just didn't know, I had no reason to trust her."

"You're reading a lot into eye contact between her and your Tony guy."

"Intuition, yeah. But when I questioned her, she didn't deny it. She wasn't blindfolded, she wasn't handcuffed. I'm sure of it. She played me, she's played me through bloody hell and back."

"Finish the damned McMuffin, I don't want crumbs in here. We're going to pay the Sebastiani family a social call. I've got a feeling there's no such thing as a safe house. You were a guest in their family home, and I use the word *guest* advisedly. Pressing charges for abduction would not be a good idea."

"Why not?"

"Because they've got lawyers, they've got lawyers for their lawyers. You could be hanging around New Jersey for the rest of your life. Remember, you're not in your own jurisdiction."

"As I'm constantly reminded."

"You'd have to lay charges as a citizen, which you're not. You're a foreigner."

"So much for the world's longest undefended border."

"New Jersey isn't a border state. And it's foreign territory, even for a New Yorker from Queens."

"Gotcha. Let's go."

"Do you need to stop for clothes?"

"Clothes?"

"Clothes, do you want to change? You're still wearing your clothes from dinner. Simple skirt, designer T-shirt, very nice, but very last night."

"Are you offering to buy? I don't have any money … do I smell? I washed my underwear. I'm a bit scuffed up, but I'm not dirty, Captain Clancy."

"You smell just fine, Detective."

"I'd take a pair of new shoes," she suggested, looking down at the garden mud on her designer sandals. As they drove she rubbed them clean with a couple of tissues. They looked almost new.

When Clancy pulled through the open gates of the Sebastiani estate, they were surprised at the easy access. He parked close to the steps leading up to the massive front door. Miranda had not seen the house from this angle before, having emerged from her garden burrow around the back into relative darkness and slipped away over a wall into a neighbour's yard before making her way to the street. The first car that had come along was a taxi, relieved to have a return fare at such an ungodly hour, the driver only a little disconcerted to be told she wanted to go to a police station, where he would be reimbursed, with tip, which he was.

"Looks quiet," Miranda said.

"Looks can be deceiving. Remember, we're just making a social call."

"And if we all pretend, then that's all it is," said Miranda. "Let's do it."

There was a long delay after they heard the chimes through the door, then it opened and Carlo Sebastiani smiled broadly in greeting. He was wearing a loose-fitting silk kimono over his clothes.

"Hey," he said with forced bonhomie, "good to see you, good to see you. How are you? It's been a long time."

"Carlo," said Clancy, glancing sideways, curious to see how Sebastiani's bravado would affect Miranda.

"You're a bastard," said Miranda quietly.

"Of course. Sorry, I'm busy, now." Carlo was speaking in an unnaturally loud voice. The scar running down the side of his face was livid.

"Is Elke here?"

He turned and called into the house. "Linda, it's Elizabeth, she wants to talk to you, she's in a rush, she can't come in."

"Elizabeth?"

"Carlo?" His wife's voice came to them from a long way off.

"Linda," he shouted. "Get the fuck out here!"

There was no question things were wrong.

Miranda said in a whisper, "Why Elizabeth?"

"You're a fucking Canadian, aren't you? She's the Queen."

"Oh," said Miranda. "I didn't make the connection. Are you okay?"

"Yeah," he said. As he spoke, he loosened the belt of his kimono so that it draped open. Around his waist were sticks of dynamite in a webbing and an electronic device at the front.

"Okay, don't move," said Clancy.

"No shit," said Carlo Sebastiani.

"Remote detonator," Miranda observed.

"Yeah." Then, in a loud voice, Carlo summoned his wife again, but she was already just behind him.

"Now play this very carefully," he said. "They'll take us all out if they have to. They don't want that. But they'll do it. He will. There's one of them in here. Now listen," he said, doing up his robe, "in a minute I'm going to walk back into the living room. The guy there, he's wired like the Fourth of July. Linda's going to go with you. He's not going to like it, but he's got me, that's what he wants."

"He wants you to speak louder or it's fireworks," said Linda. "He's really pissed off he can't hear. He can hardly see you, Carlo. Don't mess up."

"No, baby, I'm not gonna mess up," he said, then in a loud voice, he declared, "it's good you dropped by. Take care, I'll tell Tony you called in. I've gotta go now. We're pretty busy."

"Is Tony in there?" Miranda whispered. "Where's Elke?"

"Tony's with the blond, he's gone for the day," he responded so his captor could hear.

"Is he with Elke?" said Miranda, projecting her voice.

"Yeah, you know those two, they could be anywhere."

"No," said Miranda in a whisper, "I don't think I do."

"You take care then," he said loudly. "Go on, get outta here."

Leaning forward, he whispered to Miranda, "The Chateau Mouton '45, you liked it. It was good, right? It was a fake. You think about that."

Carlo bent down and kissed his wife, just brushing her lips with his own, then he pushed her out through the door. She tried to resist but Miranda and Clancy grabbed her by the arms and walked her down the flagstone steps to the car as the door shut with a dull thud behind them.

Inside the car, with Linda in the back seat, the three of them sat for a moment in stunned silence. Linda seemed shaken, not at all the controlled and controlling executive wife of the night before.

"What's happening?" Clancy asked her.

"Let's roll," said Miranda in a voice that did not seem quite her own, as if she were a character caught up in pulp fiction.

"No, you can't leave him," said the other woman. "They'll kill him."

"What do they want?" Clancy asked. "What's it all about?"

"He wants a meeting?"

"Who?"

"The man in there."

"Is it Mr. Savage?" Miranda asked.

"Mr. Savage? No. I think he works for Savage. That's who wants the meeting set up."

"Savage wants to meet with Carlo's associates?" said Clancy.

"The bosses," said Linda. "He wants to meet with all the bosses."

"And you think Carlo's going to cooperate."

"No. Carlo is a dead man," said his wife.

"How so? Won't he —"

"Don't you see, the man knows I'll call and warn them. That's what he's thinking right now."

"What Carlo is thinking?"

"And the man, they both are."

"And will you?" Miranda asked, realizing that a warning to his friends would guarantee her husband's execution.

"Yes," she said. "Carlo would want that."

"Where's Tony?" asked Miranda. "Is he downstairs with Elke?"

"Yes, I think so. He went down, came up to tell us you'd escaped — gone, I should say — and he went downstairs again to be with Elke. But he must have heard the man come in. He came back up. He came down the corridor, the man shot him. I think in the leg. He staggered backwards, we could hear him fall down the stairs. The man went down and came up again. Either Tony was dead and he didn't find Elke, or Elke dragged Tony into the secure room and bolted it from the inside."

"They could have climbed out my rat hole," said Miranda. *Mole hole*, she thought.

"No, Tony was hit for sure. I saw him go down. They're still in there. Please, we've got to do something."

"Like what?" said Clancy. Turning to Miranda, he asked, "Any suggestions?"

"The longer we're parked here in the open, the more dangerous it is for Carlo," said Miranda. "The man is going to get spooked. Pull out of sight, then we call for reinforcements."

"I don't know," said Clancy as he started the car. "More troops and the guy knows we're the enemy, for sure. Boom! He turns failure into modified success."

"And that won't be pretty," said Miranda. "But if we stay here much longer, he's going to figure we're the enemy anyway. I suggest a strategic retreat."

As Clancy shifted into drive, every pane of glass on the car suddenly crazed into shattered opacity, a split second before the tremendous thud that reverberated in a deafening explosion as the house surged into fire and flame, smashing them violently against the inside of the car as it lifted from the blast and skidded over onto its side.

For an interminable instant, everything seemed quiet, as if the billowing smoke and the flames shooting through the broken windows and fissured walls of the house were images in a documentary film with the sound suppressed for dramatic effect. Like watching war on CNN with the volume turned off. The car rocked gently on its side. Miranda opened her eyes. She was dangling awkwardly, suspended by her seat belt and shoulder harness, hovering above Clancy, who was ominously still. She could hear a strangled moan like an animal dying coming from the rumpled shadows in the back seat.

She snapped open the seat belt clasp with one hand, grasping the armrest of the door over her head, but she could not stop herself sliding down onto Clancy's inert body.

The car was not on fire, but they were close to the house. Once it burst completely into flames they would be roasted alive. She rolled sideways and reached into the back seat, feeling around, trying to orient the tumbled limbs and body of Linda Sebastiani into a coherent form. Her fingers found the woman's face, and her fingertips slipped across her lips, touching her, feeling for a response.

"Linda, Linda?"

There was no answer. She could feel movement beneath her. She looked down and could see Clancy's eyes open. He was looking straight upwards, Miranda was standing, scrunched over him. He was staring up her skirt.

She remembered what Morgan once said about hoping on his deathbed the hormones were stirring enough to appreciate the femaleness of his nurses.

As she shifted about, trying to help Clancy, the lines of the schoolyard rhyme pounded through her mind, the lines Morgan had declaimed inside the wine vat with Elke climbing over his face.

As she struggled to extricate Clancy from between her legs, she kicked off her sandals and reached down to check for breaks in his body, protruding bones or rips in his flesh, knowing there was not the option to wait for help, that she had to try moving him, removing them both from the car even if it meant risking spinal cord injury.

Neither of the other two spoke. Miranda changed tactics. She hoisted herself upwards, stripped off her T-shirt, wrapped it around her arm, and jammed her shielded elbow upwards, breaking through the shattered window sagging above her. She struggled back into her T-shirt, aware in such a confined space of how absurd was her impulse to modesty.

She clambered out and was shifting herself around to reach back down for Clancy, who seemed mobile, although he had yet to utter a sound. The car rocked as she moved. Again, shifting tactics, she slid down to the ground. Putting her shoulder to the chassis, she set the car rocking back and forth until gravity yielded and it rolled slowly over onto its back.

It was fairly easy, then, to sit back on the ground and kick out the remaining glass that was hanging in place like cheap plastic. She dragged out Clancy, and together they reached in and withdrew Linda through the back window opening. She was still whimpering in shock as the three of them struggled down the driveway, away from the house that was roaring now like a blast-furnace inferno, with a cloud of black smoke spiralling high into the blue of the morning sky.

At a safe distance they settled onto the ground beside the drive. Sirens wailed in the distance, reminding them they were not the last people left in the world.

Clancy still said nothing. But he seemed fully aware of what was happening and tried to comfort Linda, whose agonized cries seemed to be not from the pain of the explosion itself but from knowing her husband's body had been shredded and scattered with the blast.

As the sirens closed in, Miranda suddenly remembered Elke and Tony. She started running up the drive, back toward the raging fire, the pavement tearing at her bare feet — she did not remember when she lost her sandals; they must be in the car, which was now engulfed in flames.

She raced around to the back. The walls showed gaping cracks and smoke billowed through, but no flames. A trickle of smoke rose from the hole in the garden earth where she had crawled out.

She lay down on her stomach and called into the darkness.

There was no answer.

She listened for the sirens, trying to judge how far away they were. Too far.

Looking frantically around her, as if trying to embed the bright blue of the sky in her mind, Miranda swung about and slid feet first down into the hole, and darkness closed around her.

At least she knew the room. As her eyes adjusted to the murky gloom she could see a body on the bed, two bodies. She shook the one closest to her. It was Elke.

Miranda tried to lift her, but she was a dead weight.

She felt for a pulse at her neck. She was alive. She rolled her over part way, pressed her lips to her mouth, and exhaled, feeling the other woman's lungs expand, fall, expand.

Elke choked. "Miranda?" she murmured.

"Get up, Elke, get up. The house is on fire."

"Miranda, I can't."

"What?"

"I'm handcuffed."

"You're what?

"Tony, he's dead."

"Okay, let's go."

"He bled to death."

"Come on, we've got to get out of here. Now."

"He handcuffed us together."

"Oh, Jesus," said Miranda. Something crashed over their heads. A fissure opened in the ceiling and molten light dazzled from the fire upstairs. The heat surrounding them was becoming overwhelming, and the air was depleted of oxygen as it was sucked up into the flames and out through the burrow into the outside.

"'Get me out, or we die together,' he told me. But I couldn't move him, Miranda, and I think he's dead."

Miranda felt for Tony's carotid artery. A scrambled image of herself in bed with a corpse flashed through her mind. There was a pulse.

"The bastard's alive. What did he do with the key?"

"I don't know!" Elke said frantically. "Miranda, you go. Get out of here. Go, go."

Miranda wheeled away, leaving Elke shaking beside Tony on the bed. Miranda raced into the bathroom, felt in the darkness for a towel, wrapped it around her arm, and in a familiar gesture smashed the mirror with her elbow. She grasped a clam-sized shard of glass in the towel. Back in the bedroom, she felt around through the murky light, choking as she moved, and found the steel bar.

Back beside Elke, she spoke, then slapped Elke on the face until the other woman responded. Then she dragged her around onto the floor so that Elke screamed from the pain as the steel of the cuffs embedded in her wrist. With Elke's arm outstretched and Tony's arm draped across the bed, Miranda found a ragged slab of cement and jammed it under between his elbow and wrist. She braced her legs firmly as the fiery light danced from the overhead veins of flame, and she brought down the steel bar against Tony's arm with all the force she could muster.

Elke screamed as Tony's arm quivered in spasm. Miranda swung again and again until she had shattered the bones in his forearm. It would have been more efficient at the wrist, but then she would have smashed Elke's wrist as well. She picked up the shard of glass with the towel wrapped across one edge to protect her hand, and she carved into the flesh of his arm, sawing through bone fragments and sinews.

Suddenly, she felt Elke fall away. She was free. Miranda hauled her to her feet, Tony's battered arm still hanging from her wrist.

There were voices at the hole in the wall.

"I'm coming down," a man's voice shouted into the thick darkness.

"Stay there," Miranda screamed at him. "I'm passing her up. Grab hold, grab her."

Miranda got her arms under Elke, around her thighs, and heaved. The bloodied stump of Tony's severed arm slapped against Miranda's face as Elke's weight pulled away and she was drawn out through the hole.

"There's another one," Miranda shouted.

"Get out of there, lady," a fireman ordered in a shrill but resounding voice.

"Yeah, yeah, " she mumbled to herself as she crossed back over to Tony's inert body. "Yeah, yeah, lady, fly away home, your house is on fire, your children are gone."

Miranda hauled on Tony, who she imagined was still alive.

A fireman in breathing gear appeared beside her. He held out his mask to give her a breath. She wrenched it away.

"I told you not to come in," she screamed into his face.

"Lady, it's okay." He forced a mask at her again and she took in a deep breath of pure oxygen, and another, and more as he walked her through the rubble to the hole.

"Now, you stay here," he shouted at her. "Don't move a frickin' muscle, lady. We don't want anyone else down here, having to haul us both out, we don't want to die."

Miranda shuddered, suddenly exhausted.

"Stay!" he yelled, but with affection, like giving an order to a unruly and beloved old dog. "You! Stay!"

In no time he was back with Tony and had him secured in a harness. He called up and Tony was hauled out through the burrow, momentarily eliminating all light from the room except the dazzle of flames licking down from upstairs.

Then Miranda was pulled out, and the fireman followed.

Away from the house, she leaned against the fireman like they were spent lovers.

"You're gonna be all right, lady," he said through a wheezing cough.

"Miranda," she said.

"What?"

"Not 'lady,' Miranda."

She looked around, trying to penetrate the bustle, to make the frenetic activity resolve into a coherent scene. She was drenched in blood. She was shoeless and limping as particles gouged at her feet. Medics got to her and were at first confounded because, despite the blood, they could find only a few abrasions, no open wounds.

"Where's Elke?" she said to the fireman.

He looked around. "The other woman? I don't know. She made it, she'll be fine."

Clancy walked over to where Miranda and the fireman were being fussed over beside an ambulance. He stared at her. The detective from Toronto, so far out of her own jurisdiction, was covered in a shroud of blood and filth. She looked like a disaster victim, but she was alive, on her feet, talking.

"Where's Elke?" she demanded.

"Don't know," said Clancy.

"You can talk!"

"Yeah. Didn't before. Had a lot on my mind." He grinned almost shyly. "Linda Sebastiani has a few bruises. She's hysterical about Carlo ... you know."

"Where's Elke?" Miranda declaimed again in a loud voice, anxiously looking around, trying to focus on someone who might answer her question.

A policewoman approached. "The woman with the arm? Is that who you want?"

"Yes, where is she?"

"We got the arm off, it just pulled through the cuff."

"Where is she?"

"The cuffs came off easily with snips — she got a ride to the hospital, just to be checked out. She's okay."

"She's gone!" Miranda declared.

"Yeah, lady," said the policewoman. "An ambulance took her. She said to tell you thanks. She sent you her love."

"Her love!"

"Yeah," said the policewoman. "It ain't up to me."

Miranda could not even begin to imagine what was going through the other woman's mind. She turned to Clancy. "Did anyone find my sandals?"

"What sandals, where?"

"My Cole Haans. They were in the car."

"Car's gone, the whole house is ablaze," he said, realizing he was saying the obvious.

"She's gone."

"She'll turn up," said Clancy, "sooner or later."

Miranda pivoted around and looked down the drive, smiling to herself. To the others she appeared like a smashed apparition, inconsolably sad.

"Yeah," she said, "she'll turn up. She does that a lot."

She could hear Carlo Sebastiani inside her head. The Château Mouton was a fake. She could hear her own voice coming from a long way off, she could hear her father, whispering in her ear.

Miranda turned to Seymour Clancy and smiled wanly then collapsed against him as she passed out, but he was too surprised to catch hold as she slid to the ground.

17

London

The unmistakable smells of a hospital swarmed into Miranda's mind as she came to a sense of herself before she opened her eyes. She could also sense the close presence of David Morgan, who was leaning over her, almost low even, to kiss her on the forehead, as if he were communing beyond words or perhaps quietly praying. In fact, he knew she was just recuperating from exhaustion and stress, and he was admiring her pores. He had never noticed before, because of her robust demeanour, how smooth her skin was, like porcelain.

Shyly, he reached out and touched her cheek with his fingers.

"Morgan?" Her eyes were still closed.

He withdrew his hand with a start. "You're awake."

"Yes. Have you been here long?"

"A couple of hours. I flew in early this morning. They wanted you to get a good sleep."

"What time is it?" she asked, opening her eyes, trying to get oriented.

"About eleven."

"In the morning?"

"Yeah."

"What day?"

"Day after yesterday. You've only been out since yesterday noon. They shot you with sedatives."

"Really?" she said dreamily.

"I think so. It's Friday."

"Already?"

"Yeah. How're you feeling?"

"Good. Where am I?"

"In New Jersey."

"I know, in a hospital. What kind of hospital?"

"Not psychiatric. Convalescent."

"Does OHIP pay?"

"What?"

"Does the umbrella of socialized medicine reach this far south?"

"Don't worry about cost. It's all right."

"Says you! Who's paying, if the Ontario government won't?"

"A friend."

"Morgan, I can tell by your voice that it's Francine Ciccone. I don't need any favours from your Mafia friends, old girlfriends, you, or anyone else. I'll pay my own way."

"Feisty, aren't we?"

"Don't speak in the precious plural, it doesn't become you."

"And we're pedantic as well. Why did you think Frankie was involved?"

"I don't know. Is she?"

"Not directly."

"Morgan?"

"Yeah?"

"Thanks for coming down."

"No problem."

"I feel disconnected, you know what I mean?"

"In the hospital, or in New Jersey?"

"In the States, I guess. I'm *at* home, here, but I'm not home. The proverbial stranger in a strange land, only the land isn't strange."

"Why don't you rest. I'll go grab a coffee and come back in a bit."

"Black. No double-double, no doughnuts."

Morgan chortled to himself as he walked out of the room. He was naturally fit but she watched over him as if he had an eating disorder. And perhaps he did. They had been together so long, for over a decade, since she finished three years with the RCMP right out of university and joined the Toronto Police. He could not be sure if his dietary habits were his own or shaped by his partner.

Miranda sank back against her pillows, feeling gravity mold flesh to her bones as she ran a leisurely inventory in her mind, checking out her body from the inside. Everything seemed to be intact. She knew about ghost limbs providing sensation to amputees, but she couldn't think of anything missing.

She could taste smoke and realized her throat was scorched in the fire, and then she remembered that Elke had disappeared from the scene. She was anxious to ask Morgan if he knew where she was and waited, feeling strangely bereft, for him to return.

* * *

Morgan sat in the hospital cafeteria, looking out over the manicured grounds. He had received a call after he landed in New York, telling him to cancel his hotel reservation and take the day flight to London. He assured his superintendent there was not enough time. He was already en route from Manhattan to the hospital in New Jersey.

Alex Rufalo knew he was lying, that he was still at JFK, but he acquiesced.

"Take the overnight, then. And give Miranda my best."

"Yeah, of course."

"You have your passport with you, right?"

"For sure."

"Check to make sure she doesn't have hers. Make the point, make it stick. She's not going with you. When she's rested, I want her back here."

"She's not gonna like that."

"Morgan, I don't give a damn. She's too much involved on a personal basis in this whole affair, there's no way I'm going to compromise a conviction because one of the principals was travelling the world when she should have been home."

"Okay, I'll tell her that, those exact words."

"You tell her she's lucky she's not in shit for going to the States."

"Yeah, she owes you. What's with London? Is this a vicarious thrill thing, where I check out all your old haunts?"

"I've never been to London. We always go straight to the Continent."

"Really?" said Morgan, surprised. "Good, then I'll go to my own favourite places."

"What you will do is get in touch with New Scotland Yard when you get there."

"And say what?"

"Find Alistair Ross. He's your man."

"In what sense?"

"Elke Sturmberg, Morgan. She's in London. She arrived this morning."

"Really! Right, Guv. I'll give Miranda your love."

When Morgan returned to Miranda's room, she was up and dressed in her filthy clothes that she had retrieved from a bag by the bed. Her feet were bare; her toes on the terrazzo floor looked embarrassed.

"What do you think you're doing?" he demanded.

"I'm going to hunt down Elke, and then I'm going to … I don't know what. Get clarification."

"That'll scare the hell out of her. She's in England —"

"The bitch!"

"Because?"

"Because she isn't here. She's bad, Morgan, she's playing with fire."

"Literally. But she's gone, like the ladybug, she's flown away home."

"How did you know about the ladybug?"

"The rhyme, ladybug, ladybug, you remember, fly away home."

"Yes, I do. Morgan, she's going to burn."

"That's pretty dire."

"Morgan, she's connected to the Sebastiani family, probably to the mob in Toronto as well."

"The superintendent talked to Clancy at NYPD. I heard about her and the mob. He wants me to back you up on this."

"Well, good." She paused. "In what sense?"

"Sorting out how she fits in. Spivak and Eeyore are in a holding pattern. They can't resolve the Philip Carter thing until we sort out the context. And for that, Elke Sturmberg is the key."

"Good, we'll work together."

"After you've had a chance to rest, maybe changed your outfit, and cleared out your lungs."

"I'm not hanging around here, doing nothing."

"Yeah, you are."

"Morgan, you can't do it without me. I know her. For God's sake, I've slept with the woman."

"Really?"

"Really."

"I didn't know."

"You know what I mean. Literally. We've shared the same bed, the same bedroom. To go to sleep with another person, we're talking trust — and then betrayal. She's ..." Miranda could not think of an appropriate epithet. "She's a manipulative manipulator," she concluded.

"No doubt."

"I just want to look the absolute bitch in the eye."

"And?"

"That's it. My smug self-righteous double whammy will reduce her to a puddle of nothing."

"Well, maybe I'll do that on your behalf. I'm on my way to London tonight."

"You're not!"

"I am."

"Me too!"

"No way."

"Way."

"No."

"Says you!" she exclaimed.

"Says Superintendent Alex Rufalo of the Toronto Police Service, Homicide Squad, your boss."

"I'll go on my own time."

"There's no such thing. You're on the payroll again."

"Good! And what better way to earn my pay than bringing Elke Sturmberg back to Canada?"

"You've got a point. Do you have a passport?"

"No."

"Good."

"Good?"

"You can't go. I promised Rufalo."

"You are beneath contempt."

"Really?"

"Yes, really. You go. I'll stay here. I don't care."

"Miranda, take off those ridiculous clothes, crawl back into bed. Spend a couple of days, get a good rest. Go home."

"I was never off the payroll. I just wasn't working."

"I know."

"Give Elke my love."

"For sure. How 'bout I go away now and buy you some clothes."

"Yeah, maybe some sandals. Cole Haans. I'll settle for Nikes. You don't even know what I'd wear, you don't know my size, none of my sizes."

"You'd be surprised."

"You're gonna buy me underwear?"

"You bet."

"Have fun imagining."

"I do."

"You do!"

"I will — see you later." He grinned at her lopsided smile and wheeled out of the room, intent on finding a store with a saleswoman who occupied space in exactly Miranda's proportions.

Riding the tube in from Heathrow, Morgan struggled with exhaustion. He hadn't slept on the red-eye, but he was too tired to doze off and too unsettled by the barrage of memories from two decades before, when he had last been in London. He lived there for a couple of years after university, travelling back and forth to the Continent with England as home base. It all seemed familiar, the smells of the carriage, the sounds of the wheels on the tracks, and, especially, the familiar and resonant names. Piccadilly Circus, Trafalgar Square, Covent Garden, tube stops on the underground map, cultural capital echoing through his mind from earliest childhood, from songs, movies, books, history lessons, and lectures, the latent colonialism of Cabbagetown.

Miranda in the States felt she was a stranger in a familiar land. She was not overwhelmed but uneasy. It was different for Morgan in Britain. He felt at home, but the world surrounding him seemed more substantial than his own presence in it. He felt it would be easy to lose himself here and stay forever.

That's the power of memory, he thought. His mind swarmed with clusters of images, mostly of himself with the girl he lived with in Knightsbridge for the better part of a year. He tried not to think of her when he was at home, because he should have married her and not Lucy.

She had flown to Canada to console him for the choice he was making, just before his wedding, being prescient enough to know marrying Lucy would lead to disaster.

He lost track of her after that. He had not fallen in love with her until after she had exited from his life, stage left, as he thought, and he knew that by then she was likely no longer in love with him. Their relationship was theatre of the absurd, something by Ionesco or Sartre — in love, but in different dimensions of time. He tried to envision her now, and her life. But she was still twenty-two in his mind, with copper-red hair, forgiving eyes, and the lips of a compromised angel.

Morgan rode the Piccadilly Line through to Russell Square, then wandered down into Bloomsbury and found a small hotel close by the British Museum, past Needlenose Court on Thackeray Street. He was enthralled by the names, like redolent snippets of poetry that shaped how he saw wherever he looked.

At the Vanity Fair Hotel, he slept for a couple of hours, then went down to the lobby for a coffee and used the phone at the desk to call New Scotland Yard, only to discover that Alistair Ross was in the country for the weekend but would be available for consultation on Monday at nine.

It's Saturday, Morgan thought. *Time is a gift.* He had two whole days to relax, to subdue the gnawing effects of jet lag and act the tourist, renew old haunts, and take in some culture. *Lovely,* he thought, and went back to sleep until four.

When he woke up, he was famished, but he was not sure which meal he craved. After cleaning up, he walked over to a small Italian restaurant in Soho where he and

Susan had once shared a frugal dinner, both of them being poor at the time, he because he was saving travel money from his job in a pub and she because secretarial wages were miserable. It was still there, exactly the same, across from the Windmill Theatre with its anachronistic slogan emblazoned across the marquee: WE NEVER CLOSED. The Windmill was a burlesque theatre that stayed open right through the Blitz, two decades before Morgan was born.

He changed his mind and walked west for an hour, ending up at The Bunch of Grapes on Brompton Road. He devoured two meat pies with a pint of Guinness and tried to picture how it used to be, the same setting, twenty years ago. This was their regular pub. Everything seemed as it was, everything in place, yet he was sure it was different.

He retraced his steps back up Brompton Road past Beauchamp Place and turned into Beaufort Gardens, a cul-de-sac with two rows of flourishing trees down the centre boulevard. He knew at a glance that things had changed. Jaguars and Mercedes lined the street. When he and Susan had lived there, in fifth floor walk-up adjoining bedsitters, not all of the buildings had yet been converted to leasehold condos. It was one of the few places in Knightsbridge where you might encounter a Morris or an Austin.

Walking along the east side of Beaufort Gardens, Morgan puzzled about which set of steps leading up from the sidewalk between pair after pair of identical white pillars had been theirs. At the end, he crossed over and walked back toward Brompton Road, peering through the trees at the handsome colonnade across the boulevard. He marvelled that he could not tell one entryway from another.

Staring off in reverie, he stumbled into a woman climbing out of a sleek sedan.

"Excuse me," he mumbled, doing a two-step, trying to let her get by.

"Stand very still," she said. "I'm going due west. We should be able to manage this."

"Sorry," he said, nodding to her as he ambled on toward the traffic on Brompton Road.

"Not at all," she said as he moved away. Her voice lingered with a familiar cadence, but when he allowed himself to look back she was gone, swallowed up through one of the doorways.

He shook his head, trying to get a grasp on the moment. Surely, he thought, she had copper-red hair. But that was twenty years ago. Susan Croydon has long since settled into the sweet life she deserved, and this other woman, this was a ghost, nothing more.

By the time he reached the South Kensington tube station he was tired, but he walked on, cutting up along the Fulham Road. The woman who might have been Susan had faded like a dream on awakening, and he could only remember what he thought he had seen, not the encounter itself.

Half an hour later, when for the first time he was beginning to feel lost, he turned a corner and came upon a massive exhibition hall. There were flags all around, flapping in the evening breeze, some familiar but most intimating parts of the world that had been renamed so many times in their surge toward sovereignty, he would not have been able to find them on a map. There were faces of every hue, and most of the people wore military uniforms of one sort or another, some resplendent, some even more resplendent.

From the posters displayed in the close vicinity, Morgan determined that there was an Arms and Armaments show. He walked up to an entrance.

"Sorry, sir," said a uniformed bobby. "You can't go in there."

"Isn't it an exhibition?"

"You might say that, sir. It's more what you might call a sale."

"I've never seen anything like it," said Morgan congenially.

"Nor have I, sir. I'm afraid it's not open to the public."

"Thanks anyway, Constable," said Morgan as he prepared to walk down the steps and find a pub before taking a taxi back to the Vanity Fair.

"Excuse me," said the bobby. "You're a Canadian, aren't you?"

"Yes, I am."

"I have a brother in Toronto. In Ontario. I haven't seen him in twenty years."

"Toronto's a big place."

"But you might know him. You ever run into a Donald Smith?"

"No, I don't think so."

"He's a policeman with the city police."

"Really?" said Morgan.

"Yes he is. He works at the Headquarters, a lump of a building all granite and glass. He sent me a postcard."

"That's where I work," said Morgan. "It's rather a nice building."

"You're a policeman, are you?"

"Detective. I work in Homicide."

"Well then, this is the exhibition for you."

"Donald Smith?" said Morgan, trying to decide if the bobby's features were familiar. "There's a Don Smith, he's been around for a long time, he works on the desk."

"He's older than me, Guv. He's been gone twenty-five years. Came back once for a visit, just a year or two after he went. I was still a little gaffer, but I know my old man was proud he was a copper. So there you are, and here I am."

"I do know him, " said Morgan. "Yeah, sure. I'll say hello."

"Thank you, I'd appreciate that. Tell Donnie his brother Ronnie sends his regards."

"I will."

"You over on business, Guv?"

"Yes, I am. Just arrived. I'm still a bit jet-lagged."

"You carrying credentials?"

"Yes."

"And no sidearms?"

"No."

"Then why don't you slip on in, Guv, and look around."

The bobby shrewdly took Morgan at his word about having police credentials and carrying no guns and waved him through.

Inside the cavernous exhibition hall, Morgan was overwhelmed by the sounds of hell: the clatter of military hardware, the clacking of lethal keyboards, and most ominously, the cheerful conversations about demolition potential and kill-power. People seemed as enthusiastic about death as attendees at an undertakers' convention. They stood in groups beside displays of weaponry, from rocket launchers to hand grenades, as shills declaimed the kill-to-cost ratios and hostesses recruited from east-end hair-dressing salons demonstrated intricate mechanisms and fluid operational modes, sealing in the minds of potential buyers the direct correspondence between female breasts and the capacity of men to destroy.

Morgan was fascinated, and cynical. He stood close to a man who was describing to several Arabs in flowing white robes how his particular version of a bunker buster known as the Jolly Roger could surgically penetrate cement, steel, or rock, and once inside burst into a paroxysm of orgasmic intensity, scouring the interior cavity with shrapnel guaranteed to leave no survivors. *Sounds like a monstrous spermicide*, he thought.

Another display featured a young woman narrating a computer-generated display of an exploding cluster bomb, cleverly called a Weapon of Masses Destruction, that would break up just before impact into a thousand small bomblets that could rip flesh from the bodies of people spread over the space of an entire city block with minimal collateral damage to surrounding buildings and infrastructure. The young woman explained to the small crowd gathered around her that the advantage of their WMD was it could be launched from a plane no larger than a crop duster with suitable adaptation.

Picking up a free coffee in a Styrofoam cup, Morgan ambled through the crowd, falling deeper and deeper into a curious sense of dissociation, as if he were unreal within his own skin. Here was an array of destruction, the arms, the armaments, the personnel, that could demolish the world. Yet it was all so carnivalesque. There was virtually no security; generals of ancient democracies mingled with aspiring terrorists, liberation fighters with the henchmen of dictators, almost exclusively men. They all leaned in to hear the spiel, to observe breasts tumbling over oiled steel.

Here was the world being saved or destroyed — it was impossible to tell the difference. He felt claustrophobic, sick to his stomach. He made a sustained lunge for the nearest exit and found himself standing beside Constable Ron Smith.

"All right, Guv?"

"Yeah, thanks," said Morgan, drawing himself upright against the knot in his gut. "I just need a pint."

"Try Guinness, they say it's good for you."

"Yeah," said Morgan as he walked down the stone steps away from the exhibition hall. "I'll say hello to your brother," he called back over his shoulder.

"Goodnight, Guv."

"G'night, Constable."

When Morgan arrived back to his hotel on Thackeray Street, there was a message waiting for him. He was to call a room number at Claridge's.

"It's probably a joke, now, isn't it?" said the concierge when she gave it to him. "I doubt that you nor I would know anyone staying at Claridge's, would we, or we wouldn't be here in the Vanity Fair?"

Morgan smiled and went to his room to phone, then returned to the desk in the small lobby.

"There's no telephone in my room," he said.

"No sir," said the concierge. "There's a television, though."

Morgan searched for an appropriate response. None came to mind. "Well, could I have one put in," he said.

"A telephone?"

"Yes."

"No sir. We'll take messages for you. Privacy assured, we're very discreet."

"That phone over there?"

"In the kiosk?"

"In the kiosk."

"That's for the public, sir, you could use that one if you wish. It's an outside line."

"As opposed to what?"

"The house phone, sir. That's the red one over on the table."

"Which connects you to where?"

"To me, sir, at the desk. Or you could use this phone here, but there's no privacy then, is there?"

"And you can't connect to the rooms."

"No, sir. But you could leave a message, like your lady friend did."

"It was a woman who called?"

"It was a woman, your caller, yes sir."

"Thank you," said Morgan, "you've been a great help."

As he stepped into the kiosk, he noted the red telephone no more than two strides away from the front desk. *The English do things differently*, he thought as a wave of nostalgia swept through him. *The past is a presence here, and that's lovely.* There was an infectious resistance to modernity that both charmed and appalled him. *It's a good place to live, but you're not always comfortable visiting*, he thought, turning the conventional axiom on its head.

Morgan dialed Claridge's Hotel and asked for the room number he had been given.

Elke Sturmberg answered the phone.

Morgan was so thrown he didn't respond.

"Silence," she said. "It must be Detective Morgan."

"It is. And why would the elusive Elke Sturmberg be calling me? I'm supposed to be tracking you down."

"I hope you're not disappointed?"

"Not yet."

"We need to talk," she said.

"That's an understatement. I'll be right over."

"Morgan! Morgan, don't hang up."

"What?"

"You don't know where I am."

"Claridge's."

"It's the technology thing again, Morgan."

"What do you mean?"

"Things aren't always what they seem, *et cetera*. I'm not at Claridge's. I am at, as they say, an undisclosed address — a friend answered at the hotel, patched me through. Even she doesn't know where I am."

Morgan felt his heart sinking. He had been irrationally annoyed she had turned up so quickly; now he was irritated she was being difficult to pin down.

"So where do we meet?"

"Meet? I said talk," she responded.

"Elke, listen to me. You've got to help us sort this out. We start with a corpse in my partner's bed and end up with a suicide bomber in New Jersey."

"How's Tony?"

"Tony, well you wandered off with his arm, how do you figure?"

"He's okay?"

"Do you care?"

"Yes, and I care about Miranda. I heard she's in hospital. Just smoke inhalation, I hope?"

"No thanks to you."

"I owe her, I owe you both."

"Well, it's payback time. I want a face-to-face meeting."

"You're not exactly in a position to insist."

"Practically, no. But morally, I think I am."

"And what makes you thing I care about your sense of morality?"

"Because I saw you at Miranda's. You weren't faking it. Because we steeped in the same marinade together and were shot at, and when you got out, you reached down and hauled out Miranda. Stuff like that. We're not so different, Elke. You're not convincing as a bad guy."

"God, Morgan, what a terrible thing to say. I'll meet you on London Bridge at midnight. How's that? The middle. Alone. Is that dramatic enough?"

"See you there, then."

18

London Bridge

Morgan took a taxi down to the Thames and walked along the Embankment. When he got to the bridge, he admired how the towers cast columns of shadow into the air from light reflected off the water roiling below. Before he reached halfway, he knew she wasn't there. He walked right across then back to the middle. He checked his watch. It was almost twelve.

He stared up into the convoluted planes of darkness and light, marvelling at the stolid weight of the towers even in the dead of night.

He felt apprehensive. A trickling of cars went by, a few taxis. He was very exposed. He wondered how he was able to reconcile the violence this woman spawned all around her and his trust. She had killed at least one man, the kid under the bridge, and she had, perhaps, manipulated the death of her ex-boyfriend. She had attended the explosive deaths of others on two occasions. Even if she were innocent, he realized, she was a magnet for danger.

Miranda, who trusted Elke from the beginning, felt completely betrayed. She would be annoyed with him right now. Morgan suspected he was setting himself up for a fall. Perhaps it was just as well if Elke didn't turn up.

He leaned against a low stone wall of the bridge and gazed upriver at a sequence of other bridges spanning the rippling surface of the Thames.

"London Bridge is falling down," he hummed in a sonorous rumble. "London Bridge is falling down, falling down...." He didn't know the next line. No longer aloud, he let the words play over and over in his mind. He gazed up the broad sweep of the river. Westminster Bridge, London Bridge — suddenly, he realized, he was on Tower Bridge! Tourists were always getting it confused with London Bridge. He should have known better. *Damn*, he thought, *damn, damn, damn*.

Morgan seldom swore, but he rarely felt such a fool. If she slipped away because of his stupidity, he would return to the church of his childhood and become a cleric, all for absolution in the eyes of an absent God. *Damn, please God, let her be there*.

His desperation surprised him. He knew he'd catch up to her sooner or later. She wanted to connect. It was feeling stupid that oppressed him in religious proportions.

Clocks all over London began to chime and peal and toll and clang, marking the stroke of midnight, and Morgan began to run.

He ran along the Embankment all the way to the real London Bridge, where she was visible in the middle of its sleek expanse from the river's edge. Why meet here? There was no place to hide. *Precisely*, he thought. *She's making certain neither of us will ambush the other.*

"Slow down," she called as he approached. "I've waited this long, there's no hurry."

When he drew up beside her and doubled over, trying to catch his breath, she said, "I've been watching you, Morgan. You have the makings of a runner. I've watched your progress almost from Tower Bridge. I knew that's what happened when you weren't here on time. Everyone does it. There's no way you'd have been intentionally late. I'm your whole objective for being in the U.K., right?"

"I know the difference between Tower Bridge and London Bridge," he mumbled between gasps. "I lived in this town, I know it better than," he clutched at a stitch in his side, "better than parts of Toronto."

"Morgan, if I wanted to escape your clutches, I imagine I could outrun you at this point."

"Not in those shoes."

She held out one foot for him to admire her sandal. "Thank you. Actually, these are understated preppy chic Cole Haans. I figured if Miranda could, so can I. I bought them at Harrods. And for anything short of a marathon, they'd be first-rate."

"If Miranda could what?"

"They're expensive. It's good to see you, Morgan."

"Miranda sends her love."

"I doubt it."

"You really did a number on her, you know."

"Walking out? I had no choice."

"No, the whole business with the Sebastianis."

"She's right, I did."

"Did you set up your boyfriend?"

"Ivan Muritori? Not to be killed. He was a moron, walking out into a street full of armed police waving a gun in the air."

"So much for speaking ill of the dead. It wasn't the police who killed him, you know, it was a sniper."

"Morgan, I was there. That doesn't make him less of a moron." She paused. Perhaps for a moment she was letting good memories breach the protective shell of disinterest. "I had no reason to want him dead."

"Not because he turned you over to the cops, because he sent you north into the jaws of hell?"

"I've never heard Canada described that way. No, I understood what I was doing."

"What *were* you doing?"

"In Rochester, Buffalo, Niagara, Toronto?"

"Take your choice. Why not start with the Sebastianis, how do you know them, what's the connection?"

Elke leaned against the bridge railing and gazed down the Thames in the direction of Tower Bridge. The lights of the city glimmered through the trees along the Embankment and sparkled on the south bank, where most of the buildings had been reconstructed since Morgan was there last. Elke's blond hair shimmered in the light summer breeze. Morgan stepped back to consider how she had changed. He had not seen her since the night she had disappeared under the portico of The Four Seasons, bedraggled at the end of a long and difficult day.

Her accent had migrated a little. In Toronto she sounded North American, from Michigan or southwestern Ontario, with a slight Scandinavian inflection that could have come from an immigrant parent. Now there was a touch of upper-class English. Not aristocracy, he thought, but well-educated. Strange, she seemed more Swedish here, but a Swede who obviously moved in the right circles, among people who appreciate fine vintage wines.

In the perpetual twilight of the urban night she looked surreal.

Eventually, she spoke, ignoring his questions. "Morgan, I won't be coming with you, you know, not just yet."

"And the wheels of Canadian justice grind to a halt until you condescend to pay us a visit?"

"If you like."

"I've been sent here to take you back. New Scotland Yard is on side. You can come willingly, or not. It doesn't matter."

"Oh, it does matter. Morgan, I have things to do. When they are done, I am all yours. Until then, enjoy London."

He reached out and touched her on the arm, gently but with authority.

She smiled again, but this time with a disarming ambivalence. "David, if you care to glance downwards, you will find I am holding a diminutive but powerful gun in my hand. It is in firing mode. I promise, I will shoot only to wound. I will be, might one say, quite surgical. How cruel that word is, in a context like this. Please back away just a bit."

Morgan could not see her hand in the shadows, or the gun. But her voice left no doubt of her sincerity. He released his grasp on her arm and stepped back. The aura of menace made her seem even more attractive.

"Then why this meeting?" he asked.

"I owe you, David. I heard you were in London. I assumed you were looking for me."

"Then perhaps you could answer a few questions before disappearing again."

"Possibly."

"What in the hell is going on? How's that for starters."

"As I have said over and over, nothing is quite what it seems. And much is."

"Riddles! Elke, I need answers."

"You *want* answers. To need is something else. All I can tell you is this, you'll have to be patient. And yes, I did know the Sebastiani family, yes, I do know a lot about wine, and no, I did not betray your partner. In fact, she left me a prisoner."

"In the house of your friends."

"I told you I knew them, I did not say they were my friends."

"And?"

"And what?"

"Like, who do you work for?"

"I don't work for anyone, Morgan."

"Come on, everyone works for someone."

"How very cynical."

"Even freelancers work for someone. Is that what you are, an independent agent? Independent from whom? The wine syndicate? Is there a connection with drugs? The Mafia? What?"

"Morgan, I'll tell you who I'm not working for."

"Who?"

She handed him her gun, slipping the safety on as she did so.

"Them." She nodded toward the Embankment. There was a car in shadows at the end of the bridge. It was rolling slowly in their direction.

"Who are they? What's with the gun?"

"The gun is to prove we're on the same side. And them? They followed you."

"Why?"

"To get to me."

"Why?"

"Morgan, in ten seconds they're going to break out of the shadows, then watch the rubber burn, they're coming to get us. Perhaps we should leave."

"One car, two directions. They can't get us both."

"Very gallant, Morgan. They don't want us both. They could have taken you out anytime. Here they come."

As the large sedan at the end of the bridge suddenly accelerated, Morgan and Elke both looked around them. There was nowhere to hide. Morgan could see what looked like the barrel of a sawed-off shotgun protruding from a window of the onrushing car.

"Come on," he yelled above the engine roar.

They both swung over the rail of the bridge, dangling precariously below the stonework, ducking their heads as the shotgun exploded. Another shot, and another shattered the air.

The car screeched to a stop. Car doors snapped open and slammed. Morgan and Elke exchanged desperate glances.

They reached out and grasped hands, released their grip on the bridge and leaned into the air, plummeting toward the water, falling down, falling down, and the air above them rained shot pellets all around.

When they hit, their grasp on each other was torn by the force of the fall. Morgan went deep and could see up through the murky water the radiance of London's night sky, and he could see Elke's legs flailing above him. He grabbed hold of her ankle and hauled her under, touching her body to reassure her it was him.

She stilled in his arms, and they drifted underwater. Finally, both desperate for air, they surfaced. London Bridge was receding. They could see figures at the centre, but there were no more shots. The water was cold, but for northerners, a Swede and a Canadian, it was not a shock, and they swam gently so as not to attract attention, and came ashore at stone steps leading down from the Embankment close to Tower Bridge.

When they stepped up out of the water, Morgan was incredulous to see Elke had clasped firmly in one hand her new shoes from Harrods.

Nothing could have redeemed her more in his eyes than this wonderfully irrelevant gesture of an inveterate survivor.

"Now what?" he said, acquiescing to her superior knowledge of the situation. He did not have any idea who was trying to kill them. She obviously did, and was not surprised.

"Do you have money?" she asked.

He felt for his wallet. It was still in his hip pocket.

"Yeah, did you lose your purse?"

"It's okay. There was nothing in it. We lost the gun, I imagine."

"No," he said," as he struggled to fish it out from where it had slipped down into his pants. When he retrieved it, without thinking he handed it to her. She held it in her open palm.

"No," she said, handing it back to him. "You hold on to it for now. I've nowhere to put a gun."

He looked at her in the mottled illumination from a light standard. Her clothes were wet and slick to her body. Even as she pulled them away to create a layer of warmth close to her skin, the cloth slumped back in a clammy caress, leaving no place on her form not fully defined.

"We'd better get you out of those clothes."

She looked up at him with a wry smile. "And you out of yours?"

"Honestly," he said, feeling awkward, "you can get hypothermia in the middle of summer. Water drains away body heat forty percent faster than air."

"Morgan, you are a sweet man. Miranda was right."

"Miranda? What did she say?"

It did not matter what she had said. Bringing her into the scene, Elke aroused in Morgan a feeling of constraint, the sexual intimations suddenly inappropriate. Still, as he began to shake, and as Elke shivered, he could not help but respond to her radiant and dangerous allure.

"Come on, Morgan. We can't go to my place, and yours isn't a good idea, they'll be watching the Vanity Fair. Let's grab a taxi, explain we've tipped our canoe, and get him to drop us at a comfortably anonymous hotel by Victoria Station."

In the morning, Elke was gone. They had washed their clothes in the small bathroom at the Excalibur Hotel, using the hair dryer to dry them. Elke towelled her hair after a long, hot shower. Morgan let her towel his hair dry as well. No one had done that since he was a child. Sometimes his father used to. He did not remember his mother touching him, except for the occasional cuff, although he had long since forgotten why.

He was not surprised she was gone. Nor did he regret not following her or trying to prevent her from going. They had flagged down a taxi with no trouble, in spite of looking like they had just emerged from the Thames, and the driver had been very English and pretended not to notice. The only thing the concierge asked when they checked in was how long they were staying. As they climbed the narrow stairs, Elke giggled that Morgan had answered only one night. She explained he was being asked how many hours. It was that kind of hotel.

He glanced around for the note he knew she would have left. Beside his wallet, he found a scrap of paper on which she had written, *I.O.U. £10. Taxi Fare. Thanks for a good night. Elke.* There was no other evidence that she had been in the room, apart for a lingering fragrance that clashed as he inhaled with the stale tobacco smell emanating from the furnishings, although the room was designated a non-smoker.

He lay back on the bed with his head propped on both pillows. They had had a restless night, touching at arm's length, the nerve ends in fingertips burning, and then careening into each other, soaring and humping and roaring their pleasure in each other's bodies and minds. They dozed, wrapped in one another's arms, desperate to avoid falling away. Each brought out in the other something of the loneliness and longing that no one else had discovered. And then they fell deeply asleep, and then she was gone.

Coming into the room they had made straight for the bathroom and helped each other out of wet, clinging clothes and into the shower as casually as if they had been lovers for years. They washed and rubbed with soap and hot splashing water until their skin, sallow from their swim in the Thames, glowed pink and flush, and they dried off in a flurry of towels and suddenly, stepping into the bedroom, they became shy and climbed into bed quietly and touched each other with tentative and gentle deliberation — not with the innocence of virgins, he thought, which is another name for not knowing what you are doing, but that different kind of innocence that comes only from experience, making love with the full knowledge of how much they could do for each other.

She was gone and it was Sunday. He had nowhere to go. He would spend the day walking through London the way he had when Susan would go home for the weekend. She used to invite him but he always resisted. Meeting her family might somehow bring an end to his adventure, and he still had too much to do. He was in the process of losing and finding himself, and she, with her copper-red hair and her full lips and her eyes filled with hope and forgiveness, was perfect, as long as she wasn't too real. Parents and bedrooms and kitchens and siblings were more reality than he could deal with, back then.

Now he missed her. He wondered if the woman he had bumped against in Beaufort Gardens could possibly be her? He wondered where Elke Sturmberg had got to, and how Francine Ciccone was getting on in her splendid and solitary widowhood.

Morgan never envisioned himself a lady's man. In fact, he was rather contemptuous of the notion. He was certainly not a man about town nor casual in his occasional affairs. Since Lucy, he had had no lasting relationships with women, apart from Miranda. Now, in a few days, he had made love with a beautiful friend of his childhood and with a stunningly dangerous blond who had exploded into his life only the week before, with whom he shared no other past and virtually no chance of a future.

He wondered about Miranda, whether she was recuperating or back in Toronto.

From the end of Thackeray Street, Morgan could see a large dark car parked in front of the Vanity Fair. He had no choice about returning to his room and caught the tube from Victoria Station up to the British Museum. His clothes, his passport, and his notes on the Humber Bridge shooting and the Ciccone execution were there. He was not about to leave them behind because some maniacs were trying to kill Elke.

It's all about why, he thought as he walked slowly up the street toward the parked car. *We know who killed the kid under the bridge and who killed Vittorio Ciccone and who killed Philip Carter. We even know who killed the old lady, Mrs. Peter Oughtred at Bonnydoon Winery. But we don't know why. When we do, maybe we'll know who killed the ex-boyfriend in New York, and who killed Carlo Sebastiani, and who tried to kill Elke and me.*

Morgan had Elke's little pistol tucked into the front of his pants, with his shirt out to hide it. He rapped on the closed window of the parked car. It rolled down. A man sporting a neat mustache gazed up at him with an annoyed look on his face.

"May I help you?" he said to Morgan in a tone suggesting they could not possibly have anything in common.

"You tell me," said Morgan.

"I am sorry," said the man. "There seems to be some mistake."

The car window started to roll up. Morgan lifted his shirt so the gun showed. The window stopped halfway.

"See here," said the man, "I really am awfully sorry, I don't think I can be of much help. I've never even talked to an American before, not on the street."

Morgan could not make sense of the man's statement.

"Roll it down," he demanded.

The window descended. The man's face glowed a deep red. His mustache twitched. "Perhaps I could pay you," said the man.

"What for?" Morgan asked.

"In lieu of whatever it is you want," said the man.

"What I want? What I want is to know what you want."

"My dear fellow, I want nothing more than to leave. Providing you don't shoot me."

"You're waiting for me, right?"

"I'm waiting for Flo."

"What flow, what the hell are you talking about?" Morgan nudged his hand against the gun through his shirt.

"Flo, my dear fellow. Florence. She is my friend, she is up for the weekend."

"Your friend?"

"Yes, my 'friend.' You know, in quotation marks. Are you here from my wife? Is she behind this? Good God, she hired an American."

"Canadian."

"Canadian? I didn't know you people carried guns."

"We don't."

"You are."

"It's not mine."

"Here's Flo. Perhaps you wouldn't mind. Thank you. Flo, this gentleman and I have been chatting."

"Hello," said Flo.

"Hello, Flo," said Morgan as Flo walked around and slipped into the passenger side.

"It's been nice meeting you," said Morgan to the man with the mustache. "I'm not from your wife. I've never met her."

"Well, good for you, old chap. It's not something one easily forgets. If I may, we have an engagement...."

"Yes, of course, tally-ho," said Morgan. He waved them off and stood in front of the Vanity Fair, gazing up and down the street, trying to see if there were any other people sitting in parked cars. Then he decided he did not care and went in.

Morgan decided to have a pub dinner in The Bunch of Grapes and then, although he had walked all the way over from his hotel, he decided on a postprandial stroll up and down the length of Beaufort Gardens. Several times. But of course a woman his own age with copper-red hair was nowhere to be seen. He left, trying to put Susan Croydon out of his mind.

Morgan slept soundly through the night. When he woke up and had breakfast in the small dining room of the Vanity Fair, he was feeling himself for the first time since arriving in England. He looked forward to his meeting with Alistair Ross at New Scotland Yard.

As he walked over past the British Museum and down Charing Cross Road, he passed one of the pubs where he had worked some twenty years earlier, but he did not glance in. He was done with nostalgia, and he had a job to do. It amused him that he was not certain what his job was.

It was still early when he reached Trafalgar Square and sat down on a bench to watch the fluttering of pigeons. Horatio Nelson looked dapper on the top of his column, staring off into the distance at the oncoming French and ignoring the gathering of tourists below.

Morgan was having what he thought of as an existential moment. Everything around him was defined by his own position in the scene. On a corner to his right was Canada House. Behind him, the steps leading up to the National Portrait Gallery, behind to the left, St Martin-in-the-Fields, then down on the left, The Strand, leading to Fleet Street, and straight ahead, past the lions, Whitehall, with Big Ben barely visible, and hidden to the right, past Pall Mall and Canada House, just a narrow garrison of buildings away, were St. James Park and Green Park and Buckingham Palace.

So familiar was the panorama, he knew every aspect without looking. He felt very much alive, surrounded by the substantiality of things. Paradoxically, he also felt ephemeral, knowing if he were not here, everything would be exactly the same. Being and non-being, he thought — you can only deal so much with things like this, then you go mad or get bored.

At New Scotland Yard he was given complicated instructions on how to find his way through labyrinthine corridors to a door marked ALISTAIR ROSS. *At last*, he thought, as he knocked with the assurance of a man who had achieved his goal, *it is all going to make sense*.

Ross rose to meet him as he entered a surprisingly nondescript room. Morgan strode forward and thrust his hand out in greeting, aware as he did so that there was someone else in the room, revealed behind him as the door swung shut in his wake.

"Ross," said Alistair Ross, "liaison."

Morgan wheeled around without shaking hands and stared into the eyes of Elke Sturmberg. She had changed into a light cotton dress and looked almost demure.

"Detective Morgan," she said.

"Ms. Sturmberg."

"You two know each other? Good," said Alistair Ross. "That should make things easier. Perhaps between the two of you, you can explain what's going on, what you want me to do. New Scotland Yard is at your service — within reason, of course."

19

Cambridge

On Saturday, Seymour Clancy came to visit Miranda. It was after lunch and she was sitting outside, wrapped in a hospital gown that in both fabric and cut was generically cheery. He brought her a small bouquet of spring flowers, although it was the beginning of summer. When she saw him approach, she settled low in her chair and gazed up through lowered eyes.

"Help me, help me," she said plaintively.

"What? Are you all right?"

"Yes, of course," she responded, sitting upright. "Help me break out of this joint. They're all so bloody nice, it's making me sick. It's time to go back to Kansas."

"Kansas?"

There's no place like home, but she didn't want to go home, just somewhere else.

"It's time to move on," she explained.

"Yeah, lets see if we can't get you out of here."

New Jersey seemed happy to release her into the care

of a New Yorker, and she was out within an hour. Only after they were on the road did Miranda remember she'd left the flowers behind.

On their way through the Henry Hudson Tunnel, she closed her eyes and did not open them until they emerged in Lower Manhattan.

"We're right near the Best Western I was staying at," she said. "I can stay there."

"You want to get your clothes from Elke's?"

"Sure, let's go there first."

The building superintendent let them in when Clancy identified himself as a cop. Opening the door into Elke's capacious loft, Clancy whistled.

"She was doing all right in the wine racket, wasn't she?"

"You think she was part of the scam?"

"No, I don't think she was part of the scam. I think she got in over her head precisely because she was not part of it. She was an expert, and that made her dangerous."

"To whom?"

They sat down on an improbably long sofa, then Miranda got up and went into the kitchen area and returned with a couple of imported beers.

"From the bottle okay?" she asked.

"Sure."

They settled in side by side on the sofa. Both put their feet up on the coffee table, sliding a couple of heavy wine books and a stack of *Vogue* magazines to the side.

"Why don't you stay here for the night," Clancy suggested.

"You think so?"

"Why not. You were here as a legitimate guest. You're not breaking any laws just because she's taken off.

If she's a felon, it's on your turf, not ours."

"How's Tony doing?"

"He lost his arm."

"I remember."

"He's lucky to be alive. What about Elke Sturmberg?"

"What about her?"

"She might have done it. I understand it wouldn't be her first."

"Her first hand! Tony's forearm was shattered and hacked, the hand in the bag was severed with a single blow at the wrist."

"A definitive distinction."

"Probably by the nefarious Mr. Savage. We told you about him, and I think he was sending a message."

"To you?"

"No, I don't know what the message was and I don't know to whom it was being addressed."

"To whom? I've never heard anyone say 'to whom' before."

"You don't suppose Elke is one of the good guys?"

"Like, working for the CIA, the Mounties, INTERPOL? No, we checked her out. If she does, she's undercover, so deep her own people don't know she exists."

"That is an existential paradox," said Miranda.

"What?"

"Nothing," said Miranda. For some reason she thought of Morgan. "You know what?"

"What?"

"I feel like I'm inside a connect-the-dots puzzle, where you draw lines and a picture appears. But because we're inside on the two-dimensional page, we can't see all the dots. If you can't see the dots, how can you draw the picture?"

"We need perspective...."

"Yeah, literally...."

"You want to watch *Buffy*?"

"What?" said Miranda.

"There's a twenty-four-hour *Buffy the Vampire Slayer* marathon. One of the New York channels is playing the whole of season four back-to-back. It's for charity. You ever watch *Buffy*?"

"Yeah, Clancy, I am a devoted fan, although I avoid trying to articulate why."

"Wit, some of the funniest lines, irony, irony about irony, and moral density, psychological complexity, profound silliness, silly profundities. No, it's like trying to explain Monty Python and the Ministry of Silly Walks. Either you get it or you don't."

"Clancy, I am genuinely relieved to know you watch *Buffy*. It makes you more human."

"You were doubting."

"Yes, no."

"So, why don't we order in Chinese food and watch *Buffy* until dawn."

"I'm with you, Clancy. And what happens at dawn?"

"I'm off for a few days."

"And you want to hang out?"

"Actually, I was thinking of leaving you here for a bit, going home and picking up some clothes."

"You're not moving in!"

"No? No, I have no intentions of moving — in, or otherwise. I was thinking of driving you home."

"Home?"

"Toronto. I've never been to Toronto."

"Ever been to Canada?"

"No."

"Mexico?"

"No."

"Not well-travelled, are we?"

"The Gulf, Desert Storm, does that count?"

"Marines?"

"Marines."

"It figures. Yeah, thanks."

"For what?"

"The ride. Thanks for the ride to Toronto."

By the time Miranda awakened, late Monday morning, Morgan was having tea with biscuits in Cambridge. She and Clancy had watched television in Elke's apartment until they were saturated with vampires and tired of reiterating appreciative responses like two old hippies sharing a joint. Coming down made them edgy and they set out on the road before sunrise. Since there was no hurry and only Sunday traffic, they decided to have a late breakfast in Boston, which was significantly out of the way.

When they got to Faneuil Hall in the Boston Market, they were famished and they grazed from one stall to the next, eating bagels and waffles and baked beans and whatever appealed in the moment, throwing away what they could not eat or did not like. Miranda confided she felt like an ecological terrorist, wanton with waste, and they donated twenty dollars each to a street musician busking in the morning sun.

They forced themselves to walk for an hour, over to Boston Common and around through the narrow streets of Beacon Hill, until the vaguest pangs of hunger returned, then drove across the Charles River to pay homage to Harvard on their way through to Concord, where they had already determined they would have a picnic lunch beside Walden Pond, and a swim if it was possible, legal or otherwise. Miranda chattered to Clancy about Waterloo County, filling in details she had not mentioned at dinner with Elke. She had grown up in a village called Waldron, she had a friend called Celia, she still owned the family home, although it was empty, she had a few relatives, stragglers from generations older than her, living across the Grand River Flats in what used to be Preston, which along with Hespeler and Galt were now swallowed up in an amalgamation without any centre called Cambridge.

They drove through Harvard Square and parked off Massachusetts Avenue near the gates of Harvard itself in the heart of Cambridge Mass, as she called it, and walked among the red-brick buildings and towering trees for an hour. She wondered about Morgan in London. It would be Sunday dinner by then. Was he washing down a meat pie with a pint of draft Guinness in The Bunch of Grapes? She had never been to London, but he had told her about his local, implying he had been a frequent visitor and not usually alone. She could not remember what his friend's name was, but she knew she had copper-red hair.

"Do you think this job is easy?" Alistair Ross demanded of Morgan and Elke. "It is not easy, I assure you. It is not easy at all."

Morgan glanced around the room, looking for a brollie and bowler. He was gratified to discover both on a stand by the door, just behind the chair where Elke was sitting like a truant schoolgirl, waiting out the headmaster's rant.

Ross got up and walked rapidly three paces toward Morgan, then veered so as not to collide. He wheeled upon Elke and strode by with such bluster he nearly tripped over her outstretched legs, which she withdrew just in time to avoid calamity.

"They put me here, liaison, you know. It is a French word, as if we don't have enough of our own. I am not *the* liaison officer, I am *a* liaison officer — do you see the distinction? Well, what is it you expect? Speak up, one of you, one at a time."

"Perhaps you should sit down," said Elke in a soothing but sombre voice, abandoning her passive role for something more dominant as she rose to her feet and began slowly to back him into the far wall by the curtainless window, from which point he had only one safe retreat and that was behind his desk into a sitting position, which he assumed with relief as she closed in. She leaned over and smoothed the lick of hair draped across his forehead.

"Now then," he said, his confidence apparently restored by her ministrations. He looked past Elke to address Morgan as if she were no longer there. "What is it I can do for you, sir?"

"Nothing," said Morgan. If this man was meant to arrange his meeting with Elke Sturmberg, his purpose had already been accomplished. It seemed unlikely he would lend further clarity to the situation.

"Good," said Alistair Ross. "Then, if you will excuse me, I have a lot to do."

"Have you?" said Elke, moving into his line of vision. "Are you expecting visitors?"

"Actually, I am. How did you know?"

"Lucky guess."

"No, it was deduction, you must be a detective."

"Wine expert."

"Whine? What, what?"

Elke glanced over at the umbrella and bowler and smiled at Morgan. "Mr. Ross," she said, "were you expecting a detective from Toronto?"

"Apparently I was."

"That would be him over there, Detective Morgan."

"But you arrived first, you take priority. Detective Morgan will have to wait."

"No, I'm here to meet Detective Morgan. Morgan, help me."

"We're here to meet each other," Morgan explained.

"Then why bother me?" said Alistair Ross. "I am a busy man. It is not easy being *l'officier liaison*."

"I thought there were several," said Morgan.

"What?"

"Liaison officers."

"We are a special cohort — how many of us, I am not prepared to say."

"More than two, less than twenty," said Elke.

"How did you know?"

"Elke," said Morgan. "I think we could take our leave now, without causing offence."

"Elke, is it? I'm waiting for someone called Elke," Ross observed. "It is not a common name, what?"

"Thank you," said Morgan, motioning to Elke with a nod in the direction of the door. "If we see her, we'll send her right on."

"How very kind."

"Not at all," said Morgan as they slipped out the door and left Alistair Ross to his own devices.

A clerk looked up from her desk and winked. They walked on, not daring to say a word. Emerging onto a side street, they cut through several laneways and came out on Whitehall not far from Downing Street. There was no sign of anyone following them.

"Well, what do you think that was all about?" said Elke, finally allowing herself to laugh as they walked toward Westminster Abbey.

Morgan shrugged, indicating he was pondering the question with great gravity.

Inside the Abbey, in the Poet's Corner, surrounded by the mortal remains of so many cultural luminaries, he at last found the words.

"The guy was a clinical fruit bar."

"I think the English are charming and strange."

"I think my people and your people, whoever they are, used the office of Alistair Ross as a rendezvous. He wasn't supposed to understand what was happening. And I think he's whatever the police equivalent is of shell-shocked. I'll bet there are others throughout New Scotland Yard; they're harmless enough, waiting for their pensions to kick in. It's bountiful eccentricity, much better than consigning the poor sods to an institution or early retirement watching re-runs of *Coronation Street*."

"Does that happen often with police?"

"Possibly it does in all jobs, I don't know. Do accountants burn out? I expect they do."

"But you deal with death."

"So do morticians. Do you suppose undertakers look after their own walking wounded, or maybe send them off to dig graves?"

"Morgan, what are we doing in Westminster Abbey?"

"Where would you rather be?"

"Cambridge."

"Really?"

"Yes, I need to go there. I'd like you to come."

"To Cambridge? Why not? Providing you answer a question."

"Sure."

"Who are you … and all that that implies?"

"A big question. I can tell you some things, not everything. Let's take a pew, I'll try to explain."

Morgan breathed a deep sigh. From where he was sitting, he could see the sarcophagi of numerous kings and queens of the realm. What fascinated him more were the spidery lines of architectural stonework, solid and beautiful, mysterious and ephemeral. He looked at the woman beside him. She was not necessarily going to tell him the truth, but at least she was about to talk and maybe he'd see through the lies.

"Carlo Sebastiani contacted me."

He was surprised she chose to start there, but pleased she was making a start.

"Yeah?"

"Yes. I got to know Tony."

"One-armed Tony? What do you mean, got to know him?"

"I got to know him. Tony Di Michele. He's not a bad guy."

"Yes he is."

"Well, not in the sense I mean. He's intelligent, ambitious —"

"And a drug-dealing gangster."

"He doesn't sell."

"Yes, he does. He sells to the sellers. That doesn't make him less responsible for the misery and degradation."

"Morgan, don't lecture. Carlo heard about me from Tony. Carlo called and we had a meeting."

"A meeting?"

"Yes."

"The blond, the gunman, and the godfather. Go on."

"It was Ivan Muritori who introduced me to Tony. When Ivan tried to unload the wine through me, Tony got upset. So did Carlo."

"Why?"

"Okay, Morgan. Follow this. I used Ivan to get to Tony to get to Carlo. *Capiche*?"

"This was not a chain of coincidence."

"No."

"Why?"

"Why what? Why was my connection with the Sebastiani family not a coincidence? Or why am I telling you this?"

"Both."

"I'm bringing you in because it's not safe for you on the outside."

"On the outside of your own very hazardous world?"

"Exactly. Trust me. Morgan, I knew about the wine scam long before Ivan exposed it to Beverley Auctions and, theretofore, the world."

"Thereafter. You don't mean *theretofore*. I've never heard a living person utter the word, except maybe a lawyer."

"Miranda was right."

"About what?"

"You really are pedantic. Mind you, she meant it in the nicest possible way."

"So, what was Ivan's crime that he died for?"

"Not for knowing me. And not for blowing the scam. He knew other things."

"Like what?"

"Well, for starters, he crunched numbers and came up with discrepancies."

"When?"

"When I told him the wine was bogus, he started snooping into weights and measures and the importation of Lebanese wine into Canada. He got into the Bonnydoon Winery accounts. Not the secret ones. The public records. Trust Ivan, he found minute discrepancies that could only be accounted for if something else had been shipped in the casks along with the wine, before they were dumped into the blending tanks."

"And for this he was killed."

"Morgan, the mob was pissed off but the mob did not kill him."

"What was in the barrels?"

"The casks, they were from Lebanon."

"Yes?"

"Drugs. A lot of drugs on a regular basis from Afghanistan, via the white powder road through Iran, Iraq, Syria."

"The dangerous complexities expand exponentially. So who do you work for? If you knew all that, why wouldn't the Sebastianis, the Ciccones, and every other gangster, biker, and street corner pusher want to kill you?"

"Carlo Sebastiani was attempting to save my life."

"You believe that?"

"Absolutely."

"Why?"

"Not yet."

"What? You're going to keep me in the dark? Is this some kind of a game?"

"You might say so. Trust me, Morgan. Sebastiani had the best of intentions — in regard to my well-being and Miranda's."

"Let's take another direction. Why did you go north?"

"To Canada? To Rochester. Carlo arranged for a contact but I was intercepted and taken to Buffalo. From there it was pretty much like I told you. Except I wasn't blindfolded. No one saw the need — I was a dead woman from the moment they nabbed me. They stuffed me into the back of the plane, but I got to see Niagara Falls from the air, and a memorable view of Niagara-on-the-Lake. It looked like an architect's model."

"So, you've seen our Mr. Savage face to face. That's why they want you dead."

"That's part of it, yes."

"But I've seen him too, and they haven't killed me."

"They needed you, Morgan, to get to me. On London Bridge, they had us together. They missed a grand opportunity."

"They're still after me and you let me go back to the Vanity Fair? Thanks."

"I didn't think they'd do it. They were counting on you leading them to me a second time. They needed you alive."

"You were speculating with my bloody life."

"But you survived. We're here now, together."

"Exactly. I wonder if they respect the sanctuary of the Church."

"I would be certain they do not."

"Then let's get the hell out of here," said Morgan, suddenly seeing every shadow moving inside Westminster Abbey as a possible assassin.

Boarding the train from King's Cross Station for Cambridge, Morgan and Elke found an empty compartment. They sat opposite each other as the train lurched into motion. Morgan covertly gazed at her bare legs, which were considerably revealed by the way she sat, and he surreptitiously glanced at the maddening way she wore the strap of her large handbag over her far shoulder, even though she was sitting, so it crossed between her breasts, accentuating their individuality. *Damn*, he thought, *do women know when they're doing that? What?* he asked himself. *Doing what? That. Making their breasts stand out.*

As the train rolled out into the countryside north of London, he became aware that he was slouching so his slacks bound up against him. *Damn*, he thought, as he adjusted himself, *do women notice things like this?* Her eyes were half closed, but he swore she was watching when he raised himself upright and tried without drawing attention to make himself comfortable.

The door slid open and a man carrying a trench coat stepped in, nodded to them both when they looked up, and sat down beside Morgan. He had the unhealthy skin of someone who avoided the sun and a full mustache. Middle Eastern, perhaps. Not Arab, perhaps Persian, and class-conscious, preferring unhealthy pallor to the working-class ravages of desert sunlight. The man stared at Elke's legs, at one point bending his head to the side to afford himself a better view.

When he caught Morgan observing him, he smiled as if they were conspirators. Morgan resented his presumption and scowled.

The man sat back, appearing to doze. All three of them seemed lulled almost to sleep by the clackety rocking of the train. Morgan started suddenly, shaking his head to wake up. He glanced at Elke. Her eyes were on his. When she caught his gaze, she lowered her eyes to one side. Morgan glanced casually in the direction she indicated and saw that the man was holding a semi-automatic in his lap, covered by his coat. Only the snout was visible, but the bend of his arm made it clear he had his finger on the trigger.

When he saw they both knew he was holding a gun, the man spoke. "Do not move, please, Mr. Morgan, Miss Sturmberg —"

"I prefer Ms."

"Miss Sturmberg, you will kindly shut up."

"No," said Elke. "What do you think, Morgan?"

She seemed entirely nonplussed. Morgan was impressed.

"He doesn't have a silencer," said Morgan. "So he's not intending to shoot until we pull into Cambridge."

"My judgement exactly," said Elke. "You are very stupid," she said, addressing their prospective assailant.

"Shut up," said the man, at a loss about how to deal with two such people who seemed indifferent to their imminent demise.

"Perhaps," suggested Morgan, "we should simply disarm him."

"No," said Elke. "He is a very committed young man. He will have to be killed. That's all right, though, Morgan. He wants to die."

"He does?"

"I do?" said the man. "You misunderstand, of course. It is better to live."

Morgan marvelled at the absurdity of the situation. Elke seemed to be enjoying herself. Perspiration on the man's face gathered in droplets. With his free hand he rubbed his eyes. Suddenly the door slid open and two girls in school uniforms they had pretty much outgrown trounced in and plopped down opposite Morgan and the man with the gun. Morgan glanced at Elke. She looked concerned.

"So where are you three going?" said one of the girls. They both giggled as if a great joke had been made.

"Piss off," said the other girl to her friend. "They don't know each other. This guy clutching his lap, he's a loner. Those other two, they're estranged lovers."

"Estranged?" Her friend giggled. "How did they get estranged?"

"They're just not right for each other."

"Why don't you shut up," said the man. "Get the fuck out of here."

"Get the fuck out of here, get the fuck out of here." They both mimicked him. "Get the fuck out of here."

"Go on —"

"Or what? What you got under your coat?"

His hand with the gun twitched.

"He's wanking, he's getting off on the blond and her lover's enjoying it."

"You watch what you got in your crotch," said the other girl. "It's gonna explode. Come on, Crissy, let's go."

They left as suddenly as they had arrived. The door slid closed. Morgan, Elke, and even the man with the gun seemed to relax a little.

"You sure you want sixty-six of those?" Elke taunted.

"What, what?"

"Or is it seventy-seven or ninety-nine. Morgan, hold on to your hat."

"What?" said the man. "What hat?"

"It's an idiomatic expression, my friend. It means you're a dead man." She smiled. She uncrossed her legs and extended one out, admiring the expensive sandal.

"Do you know what that is?" she said to the man.

"It is a shoe. Sit back, sit up against the seat."

"Or what? You will shoot me? It is a very expensive shoe. Cole Haan. Have you ever heard of Cole Haans? Oh dear, we seem to be slowing. I think we're coming into Cambridge."

Her forward leg shot out like a piston and jammed him straight in the groin as she pivoted forward on the other leg, lunged, propelling herself across the carriage, and knocked him off balance as he tried to rise. Morgan swung his arm across the man's face as the gun clattered to the floor, and the man's head snapped against the seat.

Elke scooped up the gun and retrieved the sandal that had got tangled in the man's coat. She sat back, holding the gun on the man, and reached down, putting her miscreant sandal back on, extending both legs to admire her sandals as a pair — which she had refurbished with care after their stint in the Thames.

"So, my friend," she said. "You lose."

He said nothing.

Morgan regarded Elke in a new light. She wasn't a wine expert who had been seconded by an agency or syndicate. She was a pro.

Elke rose and pulled down the blinds. She did not seem concerned with keeping the gun on the man. He knew he was defeated and sat impassively, waiting.

The train lurched to a stop. Morgan glanced at Elke, nodded, and opened the door to the carriage, looking along the platform for police as he stepped out.

Suddenly there was a single explosive crack behind him, as if someone had slammed a carriage door, and then Elke was beside him, taking his arm, and they walked rapidly past the ticket-taker and out onto the street.

"Where's your wanker friend?" shouted one of the schoolgirls from the window of a car pulling out of the parking lot.

Elke winked.

"Hey, you want a ride? Hey, hey," she shouted back into the car, "these are my friends, they need a lift."

Morgan looked away. He knew Elke had executed the man in the carriage. He did not know what his own response was. She was walking briskly with a jaunty gait, the weight of her bag drawing the strap down taut between her breasts. He was horrified, angered, and strangely impressed by her emotional detachment, her clinical efficiency.

"Yes," said Elke, turning to the car. She clambered into the back seat, drawing Morgan in after her. The driver, the girl's father, seemed not at all pleased to be alone in the front.

"Where's your friend?" the girl repeated.

"Where's yours?" asked Elke.

"Her father met her, we're both in trouble. We took the day off."

"The day off?"

"From the Perse School for Girls and Young Women. We went down to London for a one-day sabbatical but Daddy had my uncle meet us at King's Cross, and the old queen sent us back on the next train."

"Crissy! He is not an old queen," said her father from the front. "My name is Pumphrey. Where may we drop you?"

"Hello, Pumphrey," said Elke.

"Mr. Pumphrey," said the driver. "I am not the bloody chauffeur. I own this car."

"Anywhere along King's Parade would be lovely," said Elke.

Morgan observed Elke like he had discovered a new species of bug and did not have the specialized knowledge to know what it was. He was amused. He was appalled. She was beautiful and as lethal as a black widow spider.

They were dropped off by the market and cut through to the Parade. Morgan was charmed by the splendour of King's College set back from the street and the row of storybook shops facing it. During his two years in England, he had seldom been outside London, except to go to the Continent. Looking around at the resplendent tranquillity, he realized London was another country.

They walked along to a shop opposite the Fitzwilliam Museum and ordered tea and biscuits.

"You don't think they'll be looking for us?" he said.

"No, why would they? No one saw us together but those two girls. It will be a while before the news gets out. They won't say anything, anyway. Those two would love to be part of a life-and-death conspiracy. I'm betting they'll keep it their guilty secret."

"Are you MI5?"

"Good heavens, no."

"CSIS?"

"Who is CSIS? Oh, Canadian intelligence. No. And not the CIA."

"Why are we here?"

"In Cambridge? Or is that an existential question."

"In Cambridge."

"To see an old professor of mine."

"An old professor? You went to Cambridge?"

"Yes."

"You never mentioned it."

"Why would I?"

"Usually, people who went to Cambridge let you know. Same as people who went to Harvard. It comes up."

"Well, I did go to Cambridge. I even graduated."

"And then you travelled the world and learned about guns and wine."

"I learned about wine right here. Most of the colleges have wonderful cellars. This professor I want to see, he was my mentor. He is a Muslim but paradoxically he is a great connoisseur of fine wines."

Morgan looked into her deep blue eyes then let his gaze run over the length of her long blond hair. He took in the fine regularity of her Scandinavian features. He had a hunch.

"In your travels …"

"In my travels?"

"Did you ever go to Israel?"

"Yes."

"Yes what?"

"Yes, I spent some time in Israel."

"It's interesting. You say Israh-el."

"Do I? As I said, I spent some time there."

"Elke, you carry a Swedish passport. But you are an Israeli. You are Mossad. You are an agent working for Israeli intelligence. You have been trained to kill. You killed the man in the train. One shot. You killed the man under the bridge. Six shots to make it look like panic, calculated for our benefit, because you needed us."

He paused.

She said nothing.

"I just don't understand why."

"Milk?"

"What?"

"Sugar?"

"I take it clear."

"And so do I."

Miranda and Clancy slept in. They had not left Walden Pond until four in the afternoon, after having a swim in homage to Thoreau, and it was midnight by the time they crossed the Thousand Islands Bridge into Canada. It was 4 a.m. when they pulled in front of Miranda's condo on Isabella Street, and the sun was broaching the horizon by the time they got to sleep.

After breakfast in the Starbucks where College meets Carleton at Yonge, Miranda took him up to the office to introduce him around. No one was more surprised to see him than the superintendent. Like most of their colleagues, he could not imagine her with anyone but

Morgan, even though he was fairly sure they were professional partners only.

"Business or pleasure?" asked Alex Rufalo, immediately embarrassed by the implication.

"Just being a tourist," said Clancy. "I've never been to Canada before."

"And what do you think so far?"

"So far, so good, as the man says."

"Which man?" said Eeyore Stritch, who had been listening from the edge.

"It's an expression," said Spivak, who was trying not to show his provincialism by being impressed at talking to an NYPD Captain of Detectives. "You know, Eeyore, 'the man.'" He broke into a hacking cough.

"Are you telling me it's black slang?" Eeyore whispered. "How am I supposed to know that?"

"No," Spivak wheezed with barely stifled condescension. "I mean, the man, a person, someone — jeez, Eeyore, it's a saying."

Spivak looked around and realized the others were listening. "So, what are you doing in our jurisdiction?" he said to Clancy in a tone that was both collegial and challenging.

"Like I said, I'm a tourist."

"You heard what the man said," said Stritch, allying himself with the American.

"You ought to quit smoking," said Clancy to Spivak.

"I did. Two days ago. Lungs haven't recovered from the shock."

"Perhaps we could talk in my office," said the superintendent, implicitly inviting Miranda and Clancy, excluding Spivak and Stritch.

Once they got settled, he addressed Clancy, making it clear this was business. "You people know things we need to know."

"And vice versa," said Clancy.

"You should know, first, another body's turned up. In Buffalo. The guy was an illegal, a Frenchman."

"Let me guess," said Miranda. "He was a master wine blender."

"Yeah, something like that. The Americans are sending the file through to us once they get it together."

"The Americans?" said Clancy.

"The FBI. The guy was dropped from a plane."

They spent the next hour exchanging information, and when they were finished, neither the Canadians nor the American knew more than they had started with.

"Okay," said Miranda. "I think the problem here is we don't know the right questions to ask. We've got gangsters and wine, killings, contract murders, explosions, and betrayals. What's missing? I'd say there have to be drugs in the scenario, big time, to make it all worthwhile."

"That's a safe assumption," said Rufalo. "There must be a drug connection."

"Agreed," said Clancy. "But what is it?"

"Well, there's one way to find out," said Miranda. "We'll go straight to the horse's mouth."

"Is that a pun?" Clancy asked.

"What?"

"The horse's mouth. H, heroin, it's called horse on the street."

"Yeah," said Miranda without conviction, "it was a pun."

"So who, where?" said Rufalo.

"Why not ask the bad guys?"

"Such as?"

"Well, the Sebastianis are reorganizing right now to cover for the loss of Carlo, so I imagine we should talk to someone in the Ciccone family."

"I don't think they'll have much to say," said the Superintendent. "They're still dealing with Vittorio's … passing."

"What about Frankie?" said Miranda.

"Morgan knows her? Maybe when he comes back…."

"When is that? Has he caught up with Elke Sturmberg?"

"It would be hard to say," said the superintendent. "Our contact in London seemed a bit addled."

"Addled. As in, not all there in the head?"

"He was very pleasant. A secretary of some sort who put me through insisted both Morgan and a blond woman met in his office, but then he completely denied it."

"They've gone undercover," suggested Clancy.

"It seems likely," said Rufalo.

"What do you mean 'they'?" said Miranda. "I thought you sent Morgan over to haul her ass back to this side of the pond."

"Do I sense antipathy?" said the superintendent.

"A whole lot of antipathy." She turned to Clancy. "How did she know the Sebastianis? Tell me that!"

"Maybe she really is one of ours. If she's working on the drug angle, maybe she's a good guy."

"Well, I don't know whose," said Rufalo. "We've checked with the FBI, with the RCMP, New Scotland Yard, INTERPOL. Nothing comes up from prints or pictures. According to them, she doesn't exist."

"Of course," said Miranda, "if she is covert, whoever she's working for wouldn't claim her as theirs, not if it risked blowing her cover."

"But why would Carlo Sebastiani want to protect her?" said Clancy. "And who from? From whom?"

"Mr. Savage," said Miranda.

"Or she could be working *for* Savage," said Alex Rufalo.

"In which case, she is a very, very dangerous person to be with," said Miranda. "And she is!"

"Somebody killed Sebastiani," said Clancy. "We can assume it was the same people who wanted to kill you and Elke. The same people who wanted Carlo to call a meeting of the bosses."

"What meeting, what bosses?" demanded Rufalo, realizing he was missing some pieces.

"That was what got Sebastiani blown up. It was supposed to be a mob safe-house," Miranda explained. "He was supposed to call a meeting of mob bosses."

"With Savage?"

"We can only assume."

"Okay, Miranda. You're back on the job. Catch up with Spivak. Good meeting you, Captain Clancy. Enjoy the rest of your stay." With executive flair, Rufalo rose and casually backed them out through the door of his office. "Take care," he said and closed his door behind them.

They sat down near Spivak and Stritch, Clancy at Morgan's desk, Miranda at her own, which seemed alien territory. The three men chatted about sports, but she tuned them out and started riffling through the accumulated papers on her desktop. There was a letter from the medical authorities. She was clear of HIV. *Thank God for* big *mercies*, she thought. She switched on her computer. There was an email from the Medical Examiner's office.

"I wondered when you were going to get to that," said Ellen Ravenscroft, who had approached from behind and was reading over her shoulder. The others glanced up but kept on talking about the Jays, Leafs, Raptors, or Rock.

"Just passing by," said Ellen. "Thought I'd check out the action. Things are dead over at the morgue, love." She lowered her voice to a whisper. "Who is *he*? I want to meet him? I mean, Miranda, I *want* to meet him. Is he yours?"

"I brought him all the way from New York." Miranda smiled coyly. "No, he's not mine."

"His name is Clancy," said Clancy. "Seymour Clancy." He rose to his feet and walked around the desk. "And you are? You're not police, no, I'd say you're a lawyer, no, a doctor. And very serene in a flushed sort of way. I'd say you are a medical examiner. Am I right?"

"You have astonishing powers of deduction, Mr. Clancy."

"I overheard your crack about the morgue."

"You have astonishing powers of hearing, Mr. Clancy."

Miranda's telephone rang and as she picked it up the two new friends moved away from her desk to continue in animated conversation. Ellen winked at Miranda over Clancy's shoulder. Miranda winked back.

"Is that Detective Quin?" said the voice on the phone.

"It is."

"This is Francine Ciccone."

"Yes, Mrs. Ciccone —"

"Francine."

"Yes, what can I do for you?"

"I tried to reach David Morgan."

"He's out of the country."

"I know where he is."

"You do?"

"I'm sorry to impose."

"Not at all. What can I do for you?" It struck Miranda as almost comical. This seemed more like the exaggerated formality between upwardly mobile matrons soliciting each other for charities, not a gangster's widow and a detective.

"We've met."

"Yes, briefly. What can I do for you?"

"You were very kind to my husband."

"Please accept my condolences, but no, I was not kind. It had nothing to do with kindness, Mrs. Ciccone."

"Frankie."

"Yes?"

"Someone is going to kill me."

"Mrs. Ciccone. I do not mean to be presumptuous, but I believe you have your own people. I'm not sure what it is you think I can do."

"I need to talk to you."

"Go ahead."

"In person."

Miranda did not respond. For a few moments the two women listened to each other breathing.

"I can tell you about the winery."

"Bonnydoon?"

"Yes."

"About ChâteauNeuf-du-Pape?"

"The Ninth Chateau, yes."

"Where are you?"

"At home."

"Are you secure right now?"

"Yes, right now."

"I'm on my way," said Miranda.

She put down the phone. Clancy, who was obviously more comfortable flirting with Ellen Ravenscroft than talking with Spivak and Stritch, sidled over to her desk, Ellen close behind.

"What's up?" he asked.

"What's up? How do you know anything is up?"

"I have been to Walden Pond with you, I know everything you're thinking."

"I doubt it. But how about hanging out with Ellen for a while. I've got things to do."

"For the rest of the day?" said Ellen, hardly able to contain her glee.

"Yeah," said Miranda. "Can you two amuse yourselves?"

"Can we amuse ourselves? Oh yes," said Ellen, "without a doubt."

"You need backup?" asked Clancy.

"No," said Miranda. "Anyway, you're out of your jurisdiction. You two have fun."

"That's like — you're telling us, have fun?" said Ellen.

"Yeah."

"Come on, love," she said, taking Clancy by the arm and leading him toward the elevator. "See you all later."

Miranda was surprised by the lack of security when she passed through the walkway gate in front of the Ciccone house. She had picked up her semi-automatic from the superintendent, which had been evidence in Philip's death and then held while she was on suspension, but she did not say where she was going. She swung the large brass lion's head knocker on the door and, incongruously, could hear chimes ringing inside. After a delay and some fumbling with the latch, the door swung open.

Tony Di Michele bowed his head slightly in greeting.

"I'd shake your hand," he said, "but one of mine seems to be missing."

"It happens," said Miranda. "I'm surprised to see you up and about."

"I'm surprised to see you alive."

"No one wants to kill me any more," said Miranda. "Unless you do. A life for an arm? Not your style?"

"What makes you think I have style? What makes you think there aren't people out there who want you dead?" He led her toward the kitchen. "Frankie's in here."

"Tony." She stopped him. "Sorry about the arm."

"Me too. But fair enough. I nearly took down your friend."

"Why? Why kill Elke?"

"It was die or be dead. I thought she'd get me out of there. And if not, then not. You got us both out — I owe you."

"Very cryptic."

"So why do you think you're safe?"

"I can hear you two," said a voice through the door. "Come in here and we'll all talk."

Frankie Ciccone turned from the sink where she had been cleaning vegetables and wiped her hands on her apron before reaching out to greet Miranda.

"Excuse the domesticity," she said. "I've let Maria go, just on holiday, until things settle down. Tony, be a good boy and get us a couple of drinks. Make them weak, it's still early."

When Tony left the room, she turned to face Miranda squarely, assessing her openly, as one might a prospective daughter-in-law.

"Tony lived with us when he was at university. Sometimes he stayed at the fraternity, sometimes here. Vittorio was very close to Tony."

"Why is he here? What about his arm?"

"You don't think we've got doctors in Toronto? He told me you did that to him, that it had to be done. As soon as I heard, I said he should come for a visit."

"So he's not here as a bodyguard?"

"What bodyguard? He's only got one arm. I've been talking to Linda Sebastiani. She's sorry it went so badly. Her Carlo, you know he was trying to help you."

"That's what everyone keeps saying."

"And you don't believe it?"

"How is Mrs. Sebastiani?"

"She's all right. She's staying with family. That was a good thing you did, saving her life. Tony's too."

"Her husband saved her life."

"Yes, he did, but so did you and Captain Clancy."

"Do you know Clancy?"

"Not really. Carlo knew him."

"Really?"

"Not like you think. I mean, we all know police, sooner or later."

Tony brought in the drinks and the two women settled in at the breakfast table. "You want me to stay?" he asked.

"No."

"I'll be watching TV."

"Keep it low."

"Before we get down to true confessions," said Miranda, "can you explain why Carlo Sebastiani would want to protect us, and from whom?"

"Carlo was a patriotic American."

"So he said, and was your husband a patriot, too?"

"Yes, I suppose he was."

"What's going on, Frankie?"

"I heard you talking to Tony. What makes you think you're not in danger?"

"From whom? Good grief, Frankie, who the hell is causing the mayhem?"

"We're at war."

"Who is? The mob? A gang war?"

"No. There's us and there's them. We were business associates, but it hasn't worked out."

"Who's them, Frankie?"

"The enemy. That's the problem, it's hard to say who they are."

"Have you ever heard of collective paranoia?"

"Was it delusional? They've killed so many already. They're very real."

"Is it about drugs?"

"Yes. No. You have to understand, we operate like any business — both inside and outside the law. They are different. They sell us 'goods' from the source. They bring in …" she paused, then shrugged, "… heroin … from Afghanistan. We buy it here. It's good for them, good for us. Except they are not businessmen. It is not money that drives them but power, the destruction of power."

"Come again? The destruction of power?"

"Yes."

"You're saying these are not revolutionaries but terrorists."

"Yes, you understand, there is a difference." Francine Ciccone smiled. She seemed relieved. "They are impossible to fight, even for us," she continued. "They are innumerable — literally. And they are not afraid of death. That makes them dangerous, even to us. Especially to us."

"Especially?"

"They know if we die, society applauds."

"But why kill you?"

"Because, as Carlo told you, we are patriots."

"Carlo and Vittorio discovered where their money was going, and the Mafia wanted out, yes?"

"The Mafia wanted out. Yes."

"And there is no getting out."

"There is no getting out. Your worst enemy is someone who once was your friend."

"Are they punishing you for turning against them, or are they afraid you'll blow their network open?"

"Both, I think. They are afraid because they need to remain invisible to be effective. They are not a network, they are a cabal of zealots spread through the world, like Coca-Cola, like cocaine, they are everywhere. The ultimate multinational. And they are waiting, building their resources and waiting."

"For what?"

"For the end to begin."

"And when will that be?"

"We'll know when it starts. Vittorio was horrified —"

"Like Carlo —"

"Like Carlo."

"Because it would be bad for business. If the world as we know it collapses, they're on the street."

"You are a very cynical woman."

"No, I watch *Buffy the Vampire Slayer*."

"I beg your pardon?"

"There is a character named Spike who recognizes that the end of the world would be a bad thing, even for bad people. While he personally might survive the Apocalypse, since he is already undead, there would be an extreme shortage of blood, and he's a vampire."

"You have a very strange mind, Detective. I have never watched *Buffy*, but I understand the concept."

"Of the Apocalypse?"

"Of the aftermath. And that is why Vittorio died, that is what Carlo died for. And that is why these people would like you dead as well."

"And you?"

"Yes, of course. I know everything about their interests. They are afraid of me. They would like me eliminated. I would imagine they know you are here right now. They watch this place, but they assume my home is a fortress. For the time being we are safe."

"How long would that be?" said Miranda.

"Until night."

"We'll call in reinforcements."

"Against what? These people fade like a fart in the moonlight and gather from nowhere like maggots."

"Very poetic. Tony said he was trying to take down Elke. Why? How does she fit in with all this?"

"Carlo thought she was on our side. Tony didn't trust her. When Tony was shot by the bomber, he figured she was behind it."

"Why would Carlo think she was on your side?"

"Good question."

"What do these people want?"

"*If you need to ask, you cannot understand.* That is a direct quotation."

"From?"

"Mr. Savage."

"So much for understanding Armageddon. How does the wine scam fit in?"

"These terrorists, they moved heroin from Afghanistan across to Lebanon."

"And shipped it for the North American trade inside the wine casks?"

"Yes."

"It was win-win for you, you made money on the wine, you made money moving the drugs, buying them cheaper than you could bring them in on your own."

"Yes," said Francine. She was amused to be talking openly about business to a cop. "The enemy of my enemy is my friend," she said and smiled.

"No," said Miranda. "It's not as simple as that. We're allied in a common cause right now, you and I. But don't kid yourself, Frankie, we're not friends. You are a pillar of society and you are the scum of the earth. So much for society."

"Well, perhaps I don't like you as much as I thought. Righteousness is unbecoming."

"Have you ever gone down into the streets to see what wretched lives —"

"I was born there," she snapped. "For me, Morgan's family was upper crust."

"Yeah?"

"There's a way things work, Detective. There are you guys and there's us. It's not always pretty, but for the most part, society keeps on track. You're always going to have losers and winners, and good guys and bad guys. And it's not always easy to tell who's who without a scorecard."

"But your new partners, they screwed up the game."

"Something like that. You've got to know the rules, to respect the rules, otherwise nobody wins. You know that line about anarchy. *Mere* anarchy. It's Yeats, I studied literature at U of T, Yeats is talking about the banality of absolute chaos, he says:

Things fall apart, the centre cannot hold,
Mere anarchy is loosed upon the world."

There was an edge of defiance in Frankie's voice. "Isn't it great what an education can do?" she said, then continued, as if she had just made up the words: "'And what rough beast ... slouches toward Bethlehem to be born.'"

In spite of her righteous outrage at the source of Frankie's opulent lifestyle, Miranda admired the woman's feisty intelligence. In other circumstances, they might have been friends.

"If you're worried they'll close in after dark, perhaps we should be planning an escape," she suggested. Frankie nodded her agreement.

"What's going to bring this all to an end?" Miranda asked. "I mean, if we don't call in reinforcements, either from your side or mine? And I see your point, if we do, they back off and wait. It's catch-22. If we get backup, we won't need it; if we don't get it, we're in deep trouble. But the alternative isn't appealing."

"What alternative?"

"A showdown."

"Miranda, they are fanatics. Nothing would please them more. And do you seriously think you and Tony and I could take them on?"

"I thought you had someone living over the garage."

"Harry and Thelma are on holiday."

"Holiday!"

"You don't think we take vacations? Come on! And Maria, I told her to stay away for a few days. Then I called you."

"Thanks."

"You're the cop, you decide on our strategy."

"If we make a break for it, what's going to stop them from waiting for us to come back? We can't stay in hiding forever."

"Someone has to take down Savage," said Frankie.

"If he's gone, things fall apart."

"Yes and no. Think of him as a catalyst. No, think of the terrorists as a virus, and he's a point of infection. When he goes, his cohorts are still deadly but they go into dormancy."

"And the rest of us go into remission. Okay, first things first. We get out of here. My car is on the street. If they're watching —"

"They *are* watching!"

"What about your car?"

"Sure, we have several."

"Good. Tony can't drive. I'll have to do it."

"Miranda, that's what Tony does. One arm or two, he's the best in the business. He drives."

"Okay. We'll shake them, right? I have a place near Cambridge in a little village called Waldron. We'll go there. You'll be safe."

"We?"

"I have some business that needs taking care of." Miranda smiled. "Meanwhile, we wait until dusk."

"Another drink?"

"No thanks," Miranda responded. "So, you knew Morgan's wife?"

"Lucy? Not well. She wasn't right for him. Everything he liked about her was for what she wasn't."

"Sorry?"

"She wasn't working class, she wasn't stupid, she wasn't summer camps and country clubs, she wasn't big city, she wasn't homely, and she wasn't too flashy. She was safe, from Scarborough, a suburbanite then and now."

"Now?"

"She's married to an engineer. Two-point-four children. They vacation at Club Meds. Plural. A different Club Med every year. Without the kids."

"How do you know all this?"

"I knew her before Morgan did. They didn't really connect until after he came back from finding himself … on his so-called European tour. We talk sometimes. I'm her guilty secret, just knowing me, that's as wild as it gets for Lucy these days. Don't get me wrong, she was tough. A bully, really, and manipulative. Still is tough, about small things, I guess."

"Did he?"

"Find himself? I doubt it. He came back and found her."

"Which was another way of losing himself."

"Yeah, I think being a cop, that was his best move. And leaving Lucy."

"You know a lot about Morgan."

"He's the man I didn't marry. Know what I mean?"

"You think you might have?"

"We'll never know. You and him, rumour has it, you've got something going."

"No!" Miranda blushed and realized they were talking like friends at a sleepover. "Not that way," she clarified. "He's, he's important, he's my partner."

"You'd have done a lot better with him than the dead guy."

"Philip?"

"Yeah, Philip Carter," said Frankie, "that was the name he used."

Miranda felt her blood stirring, and she leaned forward in her chair. She reached across the table and took the other woman's hands in her own.

"Francine, what can you tell me about him?"

"Does it matter?"

"Yes, of course."

"Did you love him?"

"That's not the point. No, I did not love him. How can you love an illusion? Even when we were together I knew he wasn't real. But I wanted to think it was because he was married. I wanted him to be terribly unhappy, I didn't want to risk being a diversion. It's easier if you're an alterative."

"I wouldn't know," said Frankie with a sly smile that Miranda took not as a judgement but a companionable gibe. By opening herself up for a nasty comeback, the gangster's wife was making herself vulnerable. Miranda understood that.

"Francine, the man was murdered in my bed, right beside me. I was supposed to take the fall. But the killer was too meticulous. One set of prints, mine, on my own gun. Not likely. There should have been layers of my prints. And he left proof I was drugged, in my blood. And proof I was raped —"

"Raped! Savage raped you?"

"He fucked me. I was unconscious."

"My God, what a cretin."

"How do you know it was Savage?"

"It was, Miranda." She drew in a deep breath. "I arranged to have the man who murdered my husband turned over to Morgan. We picked him up above Lake Superior, and he was heading for Minnesota. Things fell apart. He was killed by Savage. Morgan had a narrow escape."

"So I heard."

"We talked to the man, the Albanian, before we took him to the warehouse. I talked to him personally."

"Talked?"

"You don't want to know."

Miranda looked across the table at Frankie Ciccone, trying to imagine the other woman interrogating the man who had made her a widow. She could not put images to what she was thinking, but she shrank within herself, knowing how demeaning it is to inflict pain. And then her stomach churned as she remembered what she had been told about the man's penis being lopped off and stuffed in his mouth. Maybe Francine wasn't there for that part.

If a severed hand was meant to be a signal, this was more so, but of what, to whom?

"And?" she said.

"Branko, that was his name. He *clarified* Savage's role in your lover's death. He explained who your lover was."

"Philip? Who?"

"Philip Carter was another Albanian. His name was Mohammet Jousef. He was an Islamic extremist. Many Albanians are Muslim. He worked for a group called al-Qaeda, and they paid for his education in the United States."

"Al-Qaeda? The terrorists behind the American embassy bombings in Africa? You're telling me he was one of them? Come on."

"Yes."

"He was utterly convincing as a corporate lawyer from Oakville."

"Is that a judgement on lawyers?"

"Possibly."

"Why shouldn't he be convincing? They have the advantage. We are a society built on rules and mutual trust, which makes us vulnerable. Even people in our business, we are not suspicious enough."

"Philip Carter was a terrorist." Miranda had trouble getting used to the idea.

"Mohammet Jousef was a terrorist, Philip Carter was an illusion."

"But why kill him if he was one of theirs?"

"They wanted Vittorio out of the action. The wine, the heroin, Vittorio wanted to close them down. When they found out — Carlo Sebastiani, my Vittorio, whether you like it or not, they died as patriots."

"It would have been neater for the terrorists to have Vittorio in jail — but I was in the way."

"Yes. Your friend Mr. Carter, he was your watcher. When it seemed your testimony was going to set Vittorio free, it was time to dispose of you."

"Why not Vittorio?"

"Too risky. It might draw too much attention. Ultimately, they took the chance."

"The man with the ring, the man in the vat with the hand chopped off, he was sent to kill me."

"He was sent to instruct Mohammet Jousef to kill you. Mohammet refused, in spite of the ring-man's assistance — it was the ring-man who drugged you."

"That was him, not Philip? And Philip refused to kill me?"

"Exactly, Miranda. For what it's worth, that cost him his life. And he took the man with the ring down with him. The ring-man reported back to Savage. Savage was not pleased. He drove to Toronto and took care of business himself."

"Took care of business!"

"And when he returned to Bonnydoon Winery the next day in time to meet Ms. Sturmberg, he executed the man with the ring. First he cut off his hand. He wanted it known that the ring-man betrayed their cause by backing down when your Mr. Carter tried to protect you. There is no room for disobedience with such people."

"But amputation is the punishment for thievery."

"The ring man, he insulted al-Qaeda, he dishonoured their merciless God," said Frankie, rising and going to the sink, where she picked up a lethal-looking knife and resumed preparing vegetables. "We'll take along a snack when we make our escape. Carrot sticks and celery. The failure of his mission, Miranda, that was the theft of honour. We too have a code, I understand that. Chopping off the man's hand was symbolic."

"Not for him."

"His execution, that was real. He will not go to heaven and be cosseted by sixty-six virgins. He will simply spin through eternity with only one hand."

"Sixty-six? I thought it was seventy-seven. I wonder what heaven Philip is in?"

20

Rubik's Cube

"Tony wants to blow them away," said Frankie, looking out the kitchen window as dusk settled over the slate rooftops and silvery trees of Rosedale. "I told him, 'No, not in this neighbourhood.' He's not so sure, so I told him, 'You think about it, we have quarrels, we take out a few on each side, there is a truce, and we get on with business.' That's how it is with us. But I told him, 'Tony, with these people, it's never over.'"

"I walked out and looked through the hedge," said Miranda. "There are half a dozen cars parked along the street. They're empty. I think we can relax."

"That's when they get you," said Frankie. "Trust me, they're watching. They know you are here and they're coming. They're waiting, and they're coming. Getting rid of you will be a bonus."

"Have you packed enough food for a week?"

"Tony did that already. The car's loaded. We've got

clothes. We've got DVDs. Your TV is working, right? I mean, what's to do in a village?"

"Read. Take a few books. There are books there. And walk. I phoned Mrs. DeBrusk at the general store, the whole village knows by now I'm having guests. You can get basics from her."

"But you're not staying."

"No. You'll like Waldron."

After Tony climbed in behind the wheel and Miranda slid in beside him with Frankie in the back, he started the car and eased out of the garage, letting it roll into the light of the street, then he gently accelerated, turning west. Half a block along they passed a side street and a car started, catching them briefly in its headlights. It pulled out behind them, making no effort at stealth.

Tony drove nonchalantly. He turned a number of corners, and then for a moment the following lights were gone and he gunned the car and spun around another succession of corners.

"Careful," Frankie shouted from the back. "Don't hit anybody. These are my neighbours."

"Rosedale hasn't seen anything like this before," exclaimed Miranda. Tony swung the car in and out and around the labyrinthine roadways of Toronto's most prestigious location. Then suddenly he was on Yonge Street, heading south, their car indistinguishable among the carnivalesque traffic in the late evening rush of gawkers cruising Toronto's most garish and inelegant strip.

By the time they got settled into the house in Waterloo County, Miranda was tired. She decided to stay the night. They all went to bed early.

Miranda lay awake in the room that was her sanctuary and refuge through childhood, when her father was her ally and her mother and sister were allied against her. Staring into the darkness, she realized how absurd it was to have drawn lines like she had, but after her father died, it seemed she was alone.

She heard a stirring and got up to see if her guests were all right. Frankie was coming out of the bathroom.

"Frankie, the kid who was killed under the bridge, was he one of yours?" Miranda was not sure where the question came from. Her mind was working on several levels; on one, trying to sort out the details of crime, on another, reliving her childhood as she did every time she came into this house. She had not slept here since her mother died several years ago.

"Gianni, yes, he did jobs for us. He was not a regular. I think he went over. He wanted to belong, and I guess we didn't let him in. He wanted to devote himself to something, to anything. In another life, he might have been a monk."

"Some people are born zealots, aren't they," said Miranda. "See you in the morning."

"And some lives are so empty, only unreasoning belief fills the vacuum."

"Amen," said Miranda.

During the night three messages were left on Miranda's answering machine in her Isabella Street condo, waiting for her to access them in the morning.

Miranda, it's Seymour Clancy. Listen, I have to get back to New York. Thanks for everything.

I'll never think of Thoreau the same way ... not that I spend a lot of time thinking about Thoreau. But Walden was memorable. The drive was memorable. You're a good person, Miranda. Let's keep in touch. And thank you for showing me a bit of your Canada. It's the same and yet different from what I expected ... like being at home but you're not who you thought you were. I'd love to spend more time there, some time. Call me if you're coming to Gotham. You take good care. Click.

Miranda, it's Ellen Ravenscroft. Thank you, thank you very much. Your Captain Clancy is a dreamboat, love. We had a wonderful time together. Of course, you did not mention he was gay, but then why should you have mentioned he was gay? More interesting, let Ellen Ravenscroft find out Captain Clancy is gay all on her own. Did I make a fool of myself? You will never know, my love. I'm sure Captain Clancy won't tell. He's much too discreet. Maybe he decided to try out the alternative, wink wink, nudge nudge, you'll never know. I hate you, love. Call me some time. Click.

Miranda. Where the hell are you? If I can't count on you being at home in the middle of the night, then what's the point ... You're okay, I hope. Listen, I should be back later today.

Nothing's resolved but I've got a lot to tell you. Elke and I are staying the night in Cambridge. Twin beds — not that I'm explaining myself. We're going to see an old professor of hers in the morning. Very important, apparently. She's got an agenda, Miranda. She's not the enemy. I'm not sure she's a friend, either. I called Alex Rufalo earlier. He said Clancy drove you back from New York. You be wary, now. No new very, very close friends without me checking them out. Bye now. Click.

After a breakfast of kippers, fried tomatoes, stringy bacon, and cold toast Morgan and Elke strolled along King's Parade, down past Magdalene College and across the River Cam — nothing more than a stream, Morgan thought, or a creek or a brook, he wasn't sure which. Growing up in the heart of Toronto meant his experience of moving water was mostly in ditches during rainstorms or thaws, or in historical references, rivers as geographical boundaries. Elke's college was beside a stream of its own, beyond the inner city but surrounded by ancient houses, belying its medieval origins when it was cloistered away from the intellectual thrum at the centre.

As they walked, Morgan asked her, "How did you know I was coming to England? Where I was staying?"

"How did you know I was here?"

"Intelligence, I assume. The superintendent must have been on the phone to MI5 or New Scotland Yard. Perhaps it was our friend, Alistair Ross."

"Or else we let him know."

"Did you?"

"Yes. And, Morgan, you were tracked from Heathrow. It wasn't difficult."

"You have agents everywhere."

"Not everywhere."

"And meanwhile, the bad guys are tracking you."

"And you. You led them to me."

"And they are exactly who?"

"In due course, Morgan. I have to give you a context for it all to make sense."

"I feel like an actor who's wandered into the wrong movie."

"Brought in, not wandered. You were brought in, you and your partner."

Morgan looked up. The sky was a brilliant blue and it had started to drizzle. *Anything is possible,* he thought.

When they reached the college, the porter rang ahead. They clambered up an impossibly narrow set of stairs to find Elke's professor waiting at the open door of his study. He and Elke shook hands vigorously then he ushered them into a room with leaded casement windows opening onto a quadrangle of intensely green lawn. A gesture was made for Morgan to sit down. He looked around appreciatively. The walls were books and the floor was carpets layered in haphazard profusion.

The professor was old, with a luxuriant white beard and piercing black eyes. He wore a skullcap, possibly to keep long wisps of the little hair remaining on his head under control. He should have been a mullah, not a professor, Morgan thought. And immediately he countered himself by wondering why these were mutually exclusive. On the other hand, how many mullahs were wine connoisseurs?

When the effusive greetings between student and mentor subsided, Elke introduced Morgan, who again rose to his feet and the two men shook hands.

"Professor Ali Rashid Izzadine Al Sayyed," said the professor, repeating his name several times, bowing graciously as if to acknowledge the worth of someone outside the academic profession.

"David Morgan," said Morgan, repeating his own name and returning the gesture.

"To what do I owe this very great pleasure?" said the professor, turning to Elke after motioning to Morgan to resume his seat.

Elke responded with casual banter about being in the area, not wanting to pass up the opportunity, honouring her mentor, sharing wine reminiscences, having a chat about life in Cambridge, ever changing and always the same.

Professor Sayyed exchanged pleasantries with his young protégé, but Morgan could see he was waiting. He expressed neither patience nor urgency, but it was clear to all three that this casual informality was a prelude — to what, Morgan wondered? When Morgan asked Elke their purpose, she had been coy. He would have to wait and see.

My goodness, he suddenly thought, *she's here to kill him!*

No, the professor did not look like a man about to die. But with her you never know. Morgan surveyed the room, his eyes falling again and again on the rugs, his mind getting caught up in the details of colour and design.

Professor Sayyed interrupted his conversation to address Morgan. "I see you admire my carpets, Mr. Morgan."

"I do."

"They are mostly from Persia — I am an expatriate, you see, in time as well as space. I belong to an Iran of an earlier era, when it was still a remnant of the great Persian Empire."

"Iran?"

"Yes."

"I would have guessed you are from Kurdistan."

"You would?"

"Aren't most of these carpets Kurdish? I imagine they are a reminder of home. Perhaps Iran, but definitely, I would have said, from the Kurdish north."

"You would have said, would you? Excellent, Mr. Morgan, you are very observant. Mostly these rugs are made by Kurds, yes. They come from Turkish Anatolia and Iran and Iraq and Afghanistan. My people cannot be contained by national borders."

"I was right, then, you're Kurdish?"

"My family is originally from the mountain country of northern Iraq."

"Where Saddam Hussein used chemicals on his own people in '88?"

"His own people! Tens of thousands of my people have died, not just in 1988, not just from Saddam — so many Kurds have died under the rule of outsiders." He smiled, as if to acknowledge that his vehemence showed a lack of social grace. "These rugs are from the villages of my childhood. That one is from Duze, my father's village." He pointed to a small prayer rug with stylized handprints.

"You brought them with you?"

"No, when I departed from Tehran I travelled lightly — I was on the faculty of the American University. I was no friend of the Shah's, but even less of the Ayatollah

Khomeini — I carried only what was inside my own head … and several degrees, of course, from the Sorbonne, Yale, and Oxford."

"One could argue you were carrying a good deal."

"Some might argue that knowledge in this world weighs heavily upon us, so we cannot look up and see God. And therefore we place carpets beneath our feet as reflections of his presence above."

"You have much to reflect upon."

"Yes, yes, but these carpets, they were all purchased here. Such is the legacy of empire, my dear Mr. Morgan. These poor remnants of our tribal life, they fetch astonishing prices at auction in London. There is not, perhaps, such a market for Kurdish carpets as for those from the Qashqa'i and Loris of the south."

"Of Iran! And you represent yourself as Iranian."

"It is easier at this brief point in our history. Iraq is a pariah, Iran is merely a renegade."

"But you are neither, you are from Kurdistan."

"Which does not presently exist. It is as easy to be from one as the other, and more convenient right now to be from Iran. And how do you know about carpets?"

"I have read a little. That one," said Morgan, pointing to a carpet of finer weave and more formal design partially covered by others, "that is an Akstafa. It is Caucasian."

"Indeed it is. A gift from some wealthy friends, and it is beautiful, is it not? The peacocks, they are splendid, the blue as deep as the night."

Elke shifted in her chair and both men looked in her direction. "I'm sorry about Gianni," she said to Professor Sayyed, making it clear she wished the conversation to swing to more serious matters. Morgan suspected there was nothing more serious for the old man than a discussion of his ancestral roots and the ways they had been pruned back and stifled. But Sayyed turned to Elke with focused attention.

"You have to understand," she continued, as if they were in the middle of a debate, "it was either him or me."

"Yes, I am sorry too," said Professor Sayyed. "And I'm sorry it had to be you."

"Gianni?" said Morgan. "The kid under the Humber Bridge."

"He wasn't a kid, but, yes, he was working for Professor Sayyed."

"Not for me, my dear Elke, not for me."

"For your people."

"What are you talking about?" Morgan asked almost peevishly.

"His father was an Italian, his mother was a Kurd," said the old man in a way that suggested no further explanation was necessary.

Morgan rose to his feet and motioned to the others to remain where they were. He was an old hand at informal interrogation, and it was his turn to be in charge. Or so he thought. In fact, it became immediately evident that Elke had not relinquished control, and Professor Sayyed himself was more than a venerable tutor from an out-of-the-way corner of the world.

"I really would appreciate an explanation of your relationship," Morgan began.

"You would?" said Elke.

"Yes."

"Ho, ho," said the professor. "I am an old man. We do not have a relationship."

"I think you know what I mean."

"What do you mean?" said Elke.

"A wise old Muslim, a beautiful Israeli, it is not the most likely combination."

"This is a very cosmopolitan university," said the professor with a glint in his eye.

"Okay," said Morgan. "Let's try — an agent from Mossad and a militant mullah."

"A-ha," said the old man. "Such assumptions! I am merely a professor of mid-eastern cultural studies. Hardly a militant."

Morgan looked around and thought how wonderful it must be to sit in these gloomy and exhilarating chambers day after day, surrounded by books and carpets, with inquiring minds dropping in for conversation and a glass or two of port or Madeira. It would be easy to forget the world of conspiracies and oppression.

"Perhaps you are what you seem," said Morgan. "Certainly all this is a long way from the mayhem that travels with your protégé, here, like a constant companion."

"The mayhem that led you here," said Elke. "Sit down, please, and let us talk. It is important."

"Yes, Mr. Morgan. You are an essential part of the story," said Professor Sayyed.

"The story?" Morgan sat down.

"You have been drawn into a complex tale," the professor continued. "In this tale there are an infinite number of stories. Do not expect a resolution or closure. This tale will outlive us all. Perhaps we should both listen."

"Morgan," said Elke, "the money from the drugs was being distributed throughout North America to bankroll terrorism." Her face was in shadow but she leaned into the light. "There is an infection of religious fanatics that is spreading throughout the world."

"They operate under the banner of Islam," said the old man, also leaning forward. "It is not the Islam I know, it is not the Islam of my ancestors, but they proclaim themselves Muslims."

"When the Tri-State drug lords and the Ontario mob learned what the money was for," said Elke, "they declared themselves an enemy of the cause. Good business, perhaps. They cannot thrive without a stable society. But something more, call it patriotism, call it the primal need to survive, something else brought them on side."

"You told them?" said Morgan. "They didn't know their suppliers were terrorists until you let them know?"

"My job was to infiltrate through the wine operation. They had to believe they were discovering the truth by themselves. We had to work on assumptions about honour."

"Business and honour are not incompatible," said Professor Sayyed. "Patriotism is good business even when the business itself is corrupt."

"We were right," Elke continued. "Your Vittorio Ciccone, however, his arrest was a complication. We would have preferred to have him in a position of power to bring them down."

"The terrorists, is this the bunch that calls itself al-Qaeda?"

"Yes," said Elke. "Among other things. Think of an insidious contagion. There is no single leader, it is not a finite organism, it is a virus. We can only fight on a contact basis."

"And Bonnydoon Winery was one such contact."

"Exactly."

"Then what are we doing here?" he demanded. "The three of us — is the professor one of yours?"

"Professor Ali Rashid Izzadine Al Sayyed is not with Mossad, if that is what you are thinking." All three of them laughed at the incongruity.

"Let me explain," said the old man. "I am, you might say, a magnetic pole in the distribution of forces at work for the eventual sovereignty of a free Kurdistan. Is that too lofty a way to say it, Mr. Morgan? I am not a leader in the political sense and I am not a mullah, although I take it as a compliment to be thought so. I am here, and it seems Kurdish nationalism in some modest way draws from me directions and force. Whether we will be successful, we shall see."

"But your sympathies as a Muslim, are they with al-Qaeda? How the hell does Mossad fit in? Isn't Israel your enemy?"

"Israel is the enemy of Palestine, yes. And I am for an independent Palestine, of course. As a Kurd, I am opposed to the regimes in Iraq and Iran and Turkey, although they are Muslim and I am a Muslim. There are many sides. You think we are strange allies, an old man and a girl, a Jew and a Kurd. The university is a wonderful place, Mr. Morgan. In the ivory tower, we were mentor and protégé. It was simple. We provided each other a cover of academic privilege."

"Were you with Mossad as a student?" Morgan demanded of Elke.

"Yes, of course. Think of me as a scholarship student supported by my people. Professor Sayyed knew that when I came to him."

"We explored our common causes. The Jews are scholars as well as warriors," said the old man. "They want to understand. And Muslims, we have a scholarly tradition. We need to understand as well. Intelligence and the university environment are not inimical, Mr. Morgan." He paused, then added a satisfied, "Ho ho."

"And why me, why am I here in the middle of this?"

"There is not a contest between opposing forces, Mr. Morgan. We are all caught up in the machinery of the universe." He smiled beneficently, forgiving himself the cliché. "Think of a Rubik's cube. Each time one facet is adjusted to a common colour, the coherence of the others breaks down, until you solve the puzzle and then it is just planes of colours, not very interesting at all. But, but, but, we are not on the outside of the cube, we are on the inside. Think of that. Inside the Rubik's cube there are tensions and alliances constantly shifting as the facets on the outside are moved about. We are on the inside. Tensions and alliances, Mr. Morgan, tensions and alliances.…"

"And I am here because?"

"The enemy of my friend is not necessarily my enemy."

"You mean Israel?" Morgan paused to consider the implications of the old man's assertion.

"And the enemy of my enemy is not necessarily my friend," said Professor Sayyed.

"Al-Qaeda!" said Morgan. "And the moral of the story: Do not place your faith in aphorisms."

"Ho ho, Mr. Morgan," said Professor Sayyed. "You understand, very good."

"You are here," said Elke, turning to Morgan, "because I want you here, because we need you here. We need you to understand."

"What, exactly? What you've told me? What difference does it make whether I understand or not?"

"We need you to understand your role in all this."

"Go on." Morgan admired these strange allies, gathered here in academic chambers with their fingers on the pulse of the world.

"You and Miranda, we needed to use you to bring down the al-Qaeda operation in Canada. Vittorio Ciccone, he was our instrument, but he was compromised. In the States, the Sebastiani family declared war on the terrorists. It is a war they could not win, no more than you can win a war against drugs. You cannot fight a virus with swords — or with guns."

"But they're out of business."

"Temporarily, yes. They'll steer clear of the Mafia now. We have slowed the contagion but by no means conquered it. They will shift alliances, perhaps consolidate, mutate into more virulent strains. And then they will strike, and they will strike again and again until they have dissipated their strength or destroyed the world."

"That is not rhetoric," said Professor Sayyed. "They do not have to blow us up to bring us to ruin. They can force us to change our laws, shift our values, compromise our most fundamental beliefs, and we will destroy ourselves, Christians and Jews and Muslims alike. If we are not careful, we will become the cause of our own destruction — the inoculation will be worse than the illness."

"And in Canada," said Morgan, "you think the terrorists still have the upper hand?"

"Until the man known as Mr. Savage is terminated," said Professor Sayyed.

"And that is where I come in," said Morgan.

"Yes," said Elke. "Savage must be quietly eliminated."

"Quietly?"

"We cannot risk a trial," said Elke. "It would send the terrorists into deep cover. We would lose too much, trying to flush them out and hunt them down. And the Mafia, they cannot be compromised."

"You must be joking," Morgan exclaimed. "Why not? They do more damage than all the terrorists in the world."

"Mr. Morgan," said Professor Sayyed, "we are not here to have a discussion about moral relativity. Terrorists strike at the foundations of civilization. Gangsters, they eat away at the edges. The difference, perhaps, between skin cancer and a tumour in the vitals; both virulent, but one is on the surface and the other buried deep within."

"I make no promises," said Morgan.

"Of course not," said Professor Sayyed. "It is important for you to know what is at stake. I am sure you want this Mr. Savage brought to justice one way or another. It is a terrible thing that he did to your partner."

"You know about that."

"Are you surprised?"

"Nothing surprises me at this point."

"Do you see, Morgan?" said Elke. "Israeli security and the dream of a Kurdish homeland, these are not so far apart. The professor and myself have causes in common and, of course, profound differences. But these terrorists, they will destroy any possibility of an independent Kurdistan, just as they will reinforce the Hezbollah extremists."

"You leave yourselves open."

"To argument, yes. To terrorist atrocities, yes. And you will be as vulnerable as we are, perhaps more so, because you will not be prepared."

"By you, you mean us?"

"Exactly, Canadians, Americans, who live beyond the fear of attack or the logic of dreams. You think I don't know all the arguments: how can we be in favour of a homeland for the Kurds but not for the Palestinians? Israel brutalizes the Palestinians, the Kurds must be subservient to the Islamic authority of Baghdad, Tehran, Ankara. Fine, let us argue — but not be awash in the blood of the innocent."

"Elke, are you an agent for Mossad, an apologist for Israel, or a champion for the Kurds against fundamentalist oppression?"

"These are not mutually exclusive," the old professor interjected. "Rubik's cube, Mr. Morgan. If we could see all the tensions and alliances inside, the puzzle would lie in pieces, each facet a meaningless fragment."

"A final question?" said Morgan.

"Shoot," said Elke.

Morgan looked at her through narrowed eyes. "Why Miranda and I, why not you, Elke? This is your line of work."

"Al-Qaeda knows me. When they picked me up in Rochester, it was the end of the line. Carlo Sebastiani asked me to go there as a mediator with the terrorists, to let them know it was over, to broker a peace settlement. Their response was pretty much what I've told you. They figured out I wasn't there as a wine expert. I met with a cell in Rochester and we drove to the distribution centre in Buffalo. Their people were not happy so they took me to Canada to allow Savage to resolve the problem. No problem. Kill me. Unfortunately for Gianni, it didn't happen that way."

"Why us?"

"You were already on the inside. Miranda was involved in Ciccone's trial and she was sleeping with one of theirs — Philip Carter, really an Albanian Muslim extremist by the name of Mohammet Jousef. She was a perfect connection between terrorists and gangsters. She was already in position, and you were a bonus."

"So you were faking it when you turned up at her place?"

"Faking it? No, I was distressed. But yes, I was in control."

"You peed on her floor!"

"What?"

"On purpose, you peed your pants."

"Yes, I did."

Morgan gazed at her in amazement.

She smiled.

Professor Ali Rashid Izzadine Al Sayyed busied himself adjusting the corner of a carpet with his foot.

Miranda glanced out her bedroom window as she was getting dressed. The trees had grown since she was a child but she could still glimpse the river behind the houses across the road. Looking down toward The General Store, the name *Millers* displaced by a definite article, she caught sight of a car parked just at the edge of her line of vision. Ominously, it was not in front of a house.

As she finished putting on her clothes, she called out to Frankie walking by in the hall to the bathroom.

"We've got company."

"No!" Frankie exclaimed and strode into Miranda's room. "Where? Who? Damn it. I'll call Tony." She strode back out the bedroom door.

The three of them gathered in the living room. The drapes were still closed. Privacy was harder to come by and of greater concern in a village than in the city. Miranda's mother had always kept the curtains drawn from dusk until mid-morning.

"I wouldn't count on them waiting until dark, not this time," said Miranda.

"How did they know we're here?" said Tony. "If they've been there all night, why didn't they take us out in the dark?"

"Because they just arrived," said Miranda. "They waited until office hours. They must have someone on the inside at Police Headquarters, someone who would know I owned a place here."

"Who would know that?" asked Frankie, implying that it seemed very personal to know her family home was in Waterloo County.

"Yeah, maybe, okay, they went through my mail. I get bills for this place sent to Toronto. The bastards had better not have broken into my apartment."

"That's the least of your problems," said Tony.

"Yeah, right." Miranda walked to the front window and peered through a slit in the drapes between the folds of dark velvet so old the colour was an indeterminate bluish-brown-green.

"Still there?" asked Tony.

"No," said Miranda. "They decided we're too tough."

"Can we call for reinforcements?" asked Francine.

"Cops. You want me to call in the police. Lovely, Francine. The irony's almost worth the risk."

"Can we?"

"Sure, but I guarantee these guys aren't going to wait."

"How many of them are there?" said Tony.

"I don't know. Two, I think."

"Okay, our car's in the drive. Miranda, you drive. Give me your Glock. I've got my own. Vittorio wouldn't let us keep guns in his house, but I'm carrying, I picked it up in Toronto." Tony took out a shiny semi-automatic, and grasping it awkwardly between his stump arm and his ribs, he slid the action back and forth, then he took Miranda's gun, checked it, and tossed her the car keys.

"So much for village life," said Tony. "Let's get out of here."

They slipped out the back door, out of sight of the parked car. Miranda got behind the wheel. Frankie climbed in beside her and Tony got in the back and rolled down the window.

"They facing this way?" Tony asked.

"Yes," said Miranda.

"Then drive straight at them. And miss. It'll take them a minute to get their shit together. Let's go, we're off."

"You're a good boy, Tony," said Frankie.

"Thank you, Francine. Let's go!"

Miranda peeled out of the driveway and barrelled down the road, dead set to hit the parked car, then careened around it, jamming the gas, sliding, roaring past The General Store in a whirl of noise that brought Mrs. DeBrusk, disgusted, to the door. The other car wheeled around and followed in roaring pursuit, no more than ten car lengths behind.

Tony was gazing through the rear window, waiting for a good shot.

"For God's sake," Miranda shouted, "don't fire in the village."

"You know this road," he yelled back. "Take it to the floor."

"It's a straightaway," she yelled. "A few hills, no turns, they're gaining."

"Tony," said Francine with authority that penetrated the noise as she rolled down her window. "Give me one of those guns."

He started to protest. She glowered at him.

"You've only got one arm, give me your goddamned gun, Tony."

He handed her Miranda's Glock. She leaned out the window, and the shrill whistle of a bullet made her flinch but she did not withdraw. Holding for a steady aim, she waited then fired.

"You got them," shouted Tony. "Got the windshield. Damnit, you need mushroom shells, Miranda. It just made a neat hole and missed the guy's head."

Tony leaned out and took a couple of shots. The oncoming car swerved without slowing, as if they were dodging the bullets.

Miranda could not wring any more speed out of their car. She knew this road along the river like the back of her hand. Over the next rise there was a sudden dip. If she braked when they dropped for a moment out of sight, she could swerve through a gate into the trees. Then what? The only thing for it was to maintain the gap, if she could, until they reached Galt city limits, then try to lose them, oh God, on residential streets. That wasn't the answer.

Suddenly she heard a loud crack and a thump and the car swung crazily side to side. A tire had been shattered. She kept her foot down on the gas, rose up over the hillock and dropped down, wheeling sideways into the wooded lane.

As the car shuddered to a stop among trees within sight of the road, Frankie fired off a couple more rounds into the other car as it skidded to a halt. Tony leaned out and fired. There was another thump and Tony twisted violently, slamming against the back of the seats.

"Tony!" Francine screamed.

He was alive and reached out to her. "Give me your gun," he demanded. She reached to hold him. "Give me your goddamned gun. Now get the hell out of here, you two. Go, go, go."

Miranda reached back and brushed her hand against his face. "Thanks, Tony."

"I pay my debts. Go, take Francine, go on."

The shrill sounds of gunfire pursued the two women as they ran among maple trees, then cedars, toward the river. Suddenly there was a deadly silence, then a single shot. Both women knew what it was, but they kept running.

On a small rise, they slowed and Miranda looked back. She could see the assassins making their way through the underbrush. She turned toward the river. This was familiar terrain. A sheer cliff dropped off ahead, but she knew where there was a cleft among the cedars that led down to the water. She grasped Frankie's hand and drew her along like a friend through a treacherous obstacle course.

"The Devil's Cave," she said, and Frankie nodded acquiescence, as if Miranda was making sense.

Miranda used to come here with her father. Her sister always stayed home, but she and her father would clamber down through the fissure in the cliff and walk along to a bit of rubble that betrayed the cave in the limestone wall above. They would climb up, and her father would tell her about Foxy Smith, either a bank robber or a war veteran and homeless derelict, depending on which story he chose, who used to live in the cave. And that made the cave seem bigger than it was.

They would hack open a tin of Libby's pork and beans and warm them in the can with a small fire on the cave floor, then eat them with their fingers, and they would wipe their hands off on their clothes and share a tin of Allen's apple juice down to the dregs. Miranda would imagine that the great caverns and catacombs she had seen in *National Geographic* could not have been more thrilling than this shallow cave overlooking the Grand River and the fairway of the golf course on the far side.

Not long after her father died, she came here with her friend Celia, who stole a full package of cigarettes from her mother, and they smoked the whole pack in an afternoon. Celia was fine, but Miranda threw up on the way home and never had another cigarette, ever.

Now, as she gazed up at the opening of the cave, she shifted her attention back to the matter of their survival. There was a rope hanging down from a bent cedar on the ledge above; kids had obviously found a new way in from the top. She clambered partway up the rock, then carefully backed down until she was standing beside Frankie again.

"We've got a choice," Miranda explained. "Those guys are coming, there's nowhere to go except up or across." She motioned toward the river. It was churning, murky and ominously wide. Miranda shrugged. "I'd opt for the river, but if they see us, we're sitting ducks. They can run along faster than the current and pick us off from the top of the cliff. I'd say we're better here." She tilted her head back, looking up at the mouth of the cave.

"How deep is it? Won't they find us?"

"Yes, they will," said Miranda. "Sooner than they think. We can't hide in there, but we can catch them by surprise. If they check it out, they'll assume we're in deep. We'll get them on the way up."

"You think it'll work?"

"Guaranteed."

"Good," said Frankie.

"Let's climb."

The cave was only twenty feet from the rubble at the base, but it afforded a spectacular view of the river valley. A couple of golfers stopped their cart on the fairway opposite and waved excitedly across to them.

"What the hell," said Miranda, and waved back. "I guess we won't count on not being found."

Frankie waved as well. "They're women," she said. "They must identify with us as intrepid spelunkers or something. They certainly are making sure we see them. Maybe our friends won't risk killing us in front of witnesses."

"Don't count on that," said Miranda, leaning out to spy along the trail running the base of the cliff. "Here they come."

"Miranda," said Frankie. "Thanks."

"Sorry about Tony," said Miranda as she reached around and dislodged a chunk of limestone the size of a stack of dinner plates.

"He was a good boy," said Frankie. "Vittorio loved him like a son. Maybe more. Me, I'm a mother, a stepmother, I liked him almost as much. So, what do you want me to do?"

Miranda reached out and grasped the thick rope dangling in front of the cave. She pulled on it, testing its strength. Then she pushed a short length of it into a crevasse so that it caught where she could reach it. She looked at the other woman and could not help but admire what dignity she had, even in these circumstances, covered in the fine dust from the cave floor that had caked them as they clambered inside.

"Morgan, you know," she began. "He, he thinks you're special."

"Funny thing," said Frankie, "He thinks you're special — in a different way, I'm sure."

"So Morgan, *morituri te salutamus.*"

"Grade ten Latin. You don't sound like you were any better at it than I was."

"'We who are about to die, salute you.' I might have the cases wrong? Yeah, it's nice when a good man thinks you're special, whatever it means."

"Yeah, so what do we do?"

"Grab hold of that other slab. Okay, we crouch low. When the first one pokes his head over the top we stand and we throw. Don't use it as a club. Bash his head in from where you are or you'll go over the edge. And don't hold back."

"Gotcha."

They squatted low in the shadows to the side and waited. After a few minutes they could hear shuffling among the boulders below and low voices. Then there was silence and they knew at least one of the men was climbing up. Briefly they could see a flash of dark hair.

It disappeared, then suddenly he surged upright with his gun pointed into the cave. Simultaneously, they rose, screaming, and heaved their slabs of limestone at his head. His revolver went off as his skull split open and the bullet ricocheted around them as he fell straight out away from the cliff.

"That's one," Miranda whispered.

Frankie smiled.

"A qualified triumph," Miranda said. "There's still one to go. He's not about to give up."

They crawled around in the thick dust and charcoal detritus on the floor, trying to pry loose more rocks. Nothing yielded so they leaned back into the shadows.

"My dad and I, we used to come here," said Miranda. "There was an old guy, before my dad was a kid, who lived in this cave. Foxy Smith. He was a dangerous bank robber."

Frankie looked at her in amazement. She could not imagine a past rich in memories like that with her own father.

"Okay, he's coming. Now here's what I want you to do. Stay perfectly still. You're going to be all right, I promise you, Frankie."

Miranda reached over and dislodged the rope very gently so that someone looking up would not notice it moving. She grasped it firmly in one hand and slowly moved back into the shadows.

"Frankie," she whispered. "When you see him, nod."

They both stayed absolutely still — then Frankie nodded, Miranda exploded from her crouching position, leapt forward, swinging out on the rope over the man's head, then she relaxed her grip and let the rope burn through her hands as she dropped on top of him, sending him spiralling down onto the boulder rubble, his gun clattering away. Miranda dangled for a moment but her burned hands would not hold and she dropped, hit boulders, and rolled to the side.

Frankie screamed as she stared down at Miranda, who was splayed between the man with his skull split open and the other man, who was moaning but not moving. Miranda opened her eyes, gazed up at Frankie, and winked.

"Oh my God, you're okay," shouted Frankie. She scrambled down the rock face. "My God, my God, do you want me to kill him?"

Miranda struggled to her feet and lurched toward Frankie, who was raising a boulder over the groaning man's head.

"No, Frankie."

Frankie held the boulder poised and gazed into Miranda's eyes. She wanted to smash in his skull for Tony and Vittorio, for Carlo and Linda, maybe even for Gianni, the kid who sold out.

"No," Miranda repeated emphatically. "We're being observed." She said this as if otherwise it might have been acceptable. She was looking across the river and Frankie followed her gaze. There were three golf carts now and a cluster of people all watching them. A couple of elderly men were playing through, obviously annoyed by the distraction.

"We should tie this guy up," she said.

"Around the neck with a noose."

"All in due course," said Miranda and surprised herself by wincing in pain. She looked down at her hands. The flesh of her palms and the insides of her fingers was burned raw from the rope. She had not noticed until now. Her back hurt and her ribs ached but as she ran a quick inventory of her various pains and contusions, she decided nothing was broken.

Stones dropped onto the rubble beside them. There was shouting from across the river. Both women looked up and could see a man leaning over. He fired a shot but they were in too close to the rock face and it went wide. He fired another and then slipped out of sight. On the far shore, several people were shouting and gesticulating wildly.

Miranda turned directly to them. She raised her arms and swung them down in a spontaneous attempt at semaphore. The wild gestures stopped. Then a woman stepped forward out of the crowd. She turned and yelled something at the others. Then signalling Miranda, she pointed to the clifftop and slowly moved her arm, marking the third man's progress. *Damn*, Miranda wondered, *how could we have missed him? He was in the back seat. We missed him.*

The woman across the river dropped her arm sharply, raised both her arms high, and swung them downwards. The man was descending the cleft. Miranda looked upriver and down. In the direction the man was coming from, the cliff base widened out into a field in the distance, but they could never get by him. In the other direction it narrowed to nothing. Water swirled and eddied against the rock.

"Where's the gun, Frankie, do you see the guy's gun?" she demanded.

"It went down between the rocks. I can see it." Frankie sprawled across the boulders and tried to reach into the crevasse.

"Not even close!"

"Then it's the water," said Miranda. "Let's go!"

"Miranda."

"Yeah."

"We didn't have swimming pools in my part of Cabbagetown."

Miranda stared at her incredulously.

"You got it," said Francine. "I can't swim."

Miranda looked across at the woman on the far shore. She was flapping her arms to signal flight. Or perhaps just telegraphing her own fear.

"Well, you're going to learn."

"No."

"Yes," said Miranda and grasping her arms around the other woman, hauled her to the edge and heaved both of them into the turgid water.

Francine sputtered and thrashed. When they came to the surface the current thrust them apart. Miranda moved close as Frankie went under. When Frankie came up, Miranda swung out with her fist against the other woman's jaw as hard as she could. Frankie swirled away and sank back. Miranda grabbed her hair. If she lost her grip, she would never find her in the dark muddy water. Frankie came to the surface gagging and swinging at Miranda, trying to sock her in the face. *Damn*, thought Miranda, *she's a fighter. We're gonna make it.*

The power in Frankie's muscles dissipated and Miranda rolled her onto her back, then, getting a grip under her chin, started kicking toward the far shore as the current swept them out of their assailant's range. Several times Frankie wrenched herself free and Miranda went under but she never released her grip and gradually

Frankie relaxed, finding she was floating above Miranda's legs kicking vigorously beneath her.

When hands grabbed her by the shoulders, Miranda gasped in shock and went under. Half a dozen men and women had waded out downriver and extended themselves in a human chain into the current. They had to pry her hands free from Frankie. They hauled and then carried the two women up onto the shore. They were a long way from the golf course, almost within what used to be the city limits of Galt. The man on the far shore had disappeared.

Morgan caught the train south from Royston. Elke thought it would be better to stay away from the Cambridge train station, just in case. She borrowed Professor Sayyed's car and drove him over. Morgan was anxious to talk and fill in the details, but Elke was quiet. She assured him she would come back to Toronto to assist in drawing their various investigations to a satisfactory conclusion, but he knew she would not.

"Where are you going from here?" he asked as they pulled into Royston Station.

"After I leave Cambridge? Back to Israel, I expect. Maybe to Sweden. I'll let you know."

"Will you?"

She smiled enigmatically. "I must reinvent myself, Morgan. I've reached the end of my usefulness to Mossad."

"Maybe you'll retire to a kibbutz and grow old and grey, surrounded by grandchildren."

"Perhaps."

"Or build a cabin by a crystal lake in northern Sweden and live out your life in solitude, writing poems about pine trees and peace."

"People like me do not live to be old."

"That's ambiguous, Elke. You do not live in order to become old or you do not survive to old age?"

"Both, I think."

She waited on the platform with him. Her blond hair gleamed in the sunlight. Her eyes were the blue of the afternoon sky. He felt empty, sure he would never see her again, and yet relieved. She was a dangerously complicated person to know.

"In Toronto," he said tentatively, "are there many in your line of work?"

"Mossad? Other agencies? Yes, of course. On all sides, it is a very cosmopolitan city. Many are part-timers. They are the eyes and ears, and professionals, people like me, we are the legs."

"And the brains. Mossad in Toronto?"

"Morgan, you didn't really think I begged money on the street to get back to New York?"

"When you skipped out? Yes, I did, it seemed possible you could do something like that."

"Well, maybe I did. Here's your train. And here's the ten pounds I owe you. I owe you a lot."

She reached up and kissed him passionately, then suddenly turned away and strode off to the car. By the time he looked out the window of the train, she was pulling out of the parking lot, up onto the road back to Cambridge.

In London, Morgan contemplated picking up his few things at the Vanity Fair, but he was travelling light. He had all his papers with him and there was nothing he was not prepared to abandon. It wasn't like leaving things in foreign territory. London was not like that; it was home and yet not quite familiar, like home in a dream.

He took an indirect route to Heathrow, stopping in at The Bunch of Grapes for a farewell pint of Guinness. He dawdled until the last minute then left in a hurry, with a couple of inches still in his glass. On his way out he strode by a bulletin board and had he not delayed so long in tearing himself away, he might have noticed a folded slip of paper with his name on it pinned to the cork. The bar woman remembered a lady with copper-red hair posting it earlier in the day, but she did not connect that woman with the rumpled American who gazed morosely into his Guinness for an hour and then bolted.

The Cambridge Police were very accommodating when Miranda explained who she was. Since the events along the river road from Waldron to Galt and at the Devil's Cave fell under the jurisdiction of the Ontario Provincial Police, they arranged for her to meet with the OPP after her hands were treated at the Waterloo Memorial Hospital adjacent to the golf course.

The only anomaly in the story Frankie and Miranda told the investigating officers was their inability to account for the bullet through the skull of the man at the base of the cliff who, when last they had seen him, was moaning but alive. The third man had obviously executed him at such close range the victim's brains had muffled the shot, then fled in the car, which he had probably dumped back in Toronto by the time the two women and a small squad of OPP forensics people got to the scene.

Miranda did not attempt to make a connection for the OPP between what had happened here and the mayhem at Bonnydoon Winery, which was being investigated by another detachment. Nor did she explain that Tony Di Michele was a gangster from New Jersey or that Frankie was the widow of Vittorio Ciccone. All that would come out, but for the time being it was easier to gloss over complexities. She wanted to get back to Toronto. She still had business to take care of, especially now. Mr. Savage was going down.

Standing at the top of the cliff, where she had directed the crime scene investigators to the Devil's Cave, Miranda looked over to the golf fairway, where play had resumed, even though the more curious slowed in their game to observe the police activity across the river and to gossip. She glanced at Frankie's bruised jaw and moved close enough to feel the other woman's warmth. They had been through a lot together, but Frankie's thoughts were entirely her own, probably circling around her grief and the loss of Tony as well as Vittorio. For Miranda, time briefly collapsed and she thought she could hear her father's voice. She glanced sideways at her friend, expecting for a moment to see Celia, smoking, with a conspiratorial grin. Instead, it was Frankie Ciccone, wearing a borrowed windbreaker from the Cambridge Police Department and looking thoroughly bedraggled but somehow poised. *She's a survivor*, thought Miranda. *We're survivors*.

When Morgan's flight arrived in the late evening, he felt disoriented. It was different than jet lag on the way over. *When you fly opposite the earth's rotation, you're thrust into the future*, he thought. *A little faster and you could land before you left.*

When he reached home he called Miranda.

"Hey," she said. "What's up?"

"You know," he said.

"Yeah."

"It's good to be home."

"How was England? Did you bring Elke back?"

"No, I saw her. She sent her love."

"I'll bet she did. Did you give her mine?"

"Yeah, sort of."

"What does that mean?"

"I don't know. She's not what she appears."

"None of us are."

"No, I mean, really."

"So do I."

"What have you been doing?"

"I spent some time with your old friend Frankie Ciccone."

"Frankie? You did?"

"Yeah."

"Doing what?"

"You know, this and that."

"With Frankie?"

"Yes."

"Want to tell me about it?"

"Tomorrow."

"Tomorrow?"

"I'm on my way into a nice hot tub."

"What time is it?"

"Ten, maybe."

"My body is totally confused. I don't know whether it's much later or much earlier than ..."

"Than what?"

"Than it is. My head, too."

"That doesn't leave much."

"What?"

"That isn't confused. Your body, your head, what's left? I don't want to know."

"You don't?"

"No."

"Do you remember the Rubik's cube?"

"Which one? Yes, of course. I was good at it."

"Getting the colours lined up?"

"Yes."

"Did you ever think about what holds it all together?"

"Hooks and elastics? Swivels and tracks?"

"I suppose. I'll call you in the morning."

"Toronto time."

"Yeah."

"Morgan."

"Yeah?"

"It's good to have you back."

"Yeah. It's good to be here. Enjoy your bath, sleep well."

"Call me in the morning."

"G'night."

21

Toronto the Good

"**A**mazing!" Morgan exclaimed over morning coffee. "If even half your story is true, you're an Amazon. And Frankie, you and Frankie fighting the bad guys together? That is a truly formidable team. They didn't have a chance. My role was more passive, it was Elke in charge. She's a trained agent, she kills for a living. Or knows how to kill. My goodness, Miranda, we're supposed to find dead people and solve murders, not be there for the killing or get ourselves killed."

"That about sums it up, Morgan."

They had been talking for two hours in Tim Hortons near the Summerhill subway station. She accepted his sympathy for her hands encased in surgical gloves full of ointment. She smiled broadly at his account of Alistair Ross, the liaison officer at New Scotland Yard, and shared his admiration for the venerable mullah of Cambridge. She thrilled to his description of dodging shotgun pellets in the turgid waters of the Thames, and was pleased to match his escapade with her own, fleeing bullets in the roiling waters of the Grand. She was perplexed by Elke's cool dispatch, executing the man in the train, until she connected it to the shooting of Gianni under the Humber Bridge. But what really threw her was discovering that the night Elke had presented herself at her apartment, she had been faking dementia from shock and intentionally peed on her floor. Miranda was disturbed but fascinated by the inevitability of their friendship.

Morgan laughed at her recital of the phone messages from Clancy and Ellen Ravenscroft. The fact that Miranda had not herself realized Clancy was gay he found strangely satisfying. He did not mention his brief trysts with either Frankie or Elke. He and Miranda seldom talked about sexual intimacy, although not from shyness, for they were both very open about other details of their lives. Once, Morgan had had a lurid encounter with two young women from the secretarial staff at Headquarters, and he had not even told her about that — but it was because he suspected they had used him as a fantasy toy rather than because he felt incredibly shallow and enjoyed it.

"We're at an impasse," said Morgan.

"The focus has tightened tremendously," said Miranda.

"Yeah, Mr. Savage, we get him and it's over."

"We bring him in, Morgan. Alive."

"Is that what you want?"

"It's what's going to happen. Agreed?"

"We'll see." He had not told her about his commission to eliminate Savage with a minimum of legal theatrics; he had not decided whether it was, in fact, his mission.

"Your people want him dead even more than I do," she said, reading his mind.

"They're not my people. And I'm certainly not theirs."

"A secret agent."

"Two secret agents. I don't work for them."

"But they were pretty convincing."

"They each have their causes. Both find radical fundamentalism offensive. She thinks the terrorists will strike at her homeland, he thinks they will prevent his homeland from being established. Me, I'm a homicide detective like you. I'm not an agent for anybody."

"Well, for all the terrorist implications of what we're into, Morgan, and a visceral need on my part to see his balls on a platter — I think we'd better concentrate on finding him and let the system look after the rest."

"So let's go."

"Let's."

Since they had absolutely no leads, they took the subway down to College and Yonge and walked over to Police Headquarters. Inside, manning the desk in their division, Morgan recognized Don Smith, the brother of the Bobby at the Arms and Armaments Show in Earls Court. He saluted the older man and got a cheery wave in return. Morgan walked over to him. All he could think of to say was, Ronnie sends his regards. It wasn't much on which to start a relationship.

"You'll never guess who I was talking to," said Morgan.

"My brother Ronnie, I imagine."

Morgan grinned. "How on earth did you know that?"

"Simple deduction, my dear Watson."

"Well, Mr. Holmes, perhaps you would edify."

"I heard you were in England, Detective. On the desk, I generally know where people are when they're away. And your eagerness, 'you'll never guess?' It had to be someone special, and the incredulity suggested uncanny coincidence. That pretty much narrowed it down to my brother or the Queen Mother."

"Well, he's a good man," said Morgan. "He broke the rules and let me go where I shouldn't."

"Good men question the rules, Detective Morgan. Great men break them. We'll have to have a pint sometime."

"I look forward to it," said Morgan.

Alex Rufalo was in his office and motioned them in. Spivak and Stritch were busy with paperwork as they walked by but glanced up. Detective Bourassa nearly bumped into Miranda and smiled shyly. His huge face was still swollen from where Morgan had popped him.

"Shut the door behind you," said the superintendent.

Miranda and Morgan settled into chairs facing him and all three of them waited expectantly.

"Well?" the superintendent finally said.

"Well, what?" said Morgan.

"You two are back on track?"

"Yeah," said Morgan. "How about you?" As soon as he spoke, Morgan realized the indiscretion. If occasionally he and Alex Rufalo shared a few drinks and exchanged confidences, it was outside the office. Nothing secret, but outside the office.

"Yeah, sure, we're on track," said Morgan before Rufalo had a chance to respond.

"You want to fill me in?"

"There's nothing much to tell," said Morgan. "I think Elke Sturmberg has disappeared. She wasn't much help, anyway. I'd say she was an innocent victim caught up in a series of unpleasantries. She handled herself well, and she's gone. We don't need her."

Miranda was stunned. Morgan was leaving the superintendent out of the loop. Was this strategy? Did he think they needed to work outside the law — or was he buying in to his reluctant role as a counterterrorist? Either way, he had clearly, and so far as she knew, spontaneously, chosen to exclude the Toronto Police from his plans. Not that he had any plans.

"What about you, Detective?" said the superintendent, turning to Miranda. "You and Frankie Ciccone, what was that all about? Racing around Rosedale! Who is or was Tony Di Michele? Mafia, for God's sake, from New Jersey. How did you get yourself caught between sides in a gangster bloodfest? This isn't good for business, this kind of publicity."

Miranda looked to Morgan. He stared back expressionless. She took her cue from that and simply shrugged.

"Okay, then," said Rufalo, "go out there and do something."

"For sure," said Morgan as he and Miranda rose to their feet.

"I want the whole story," said Rufalo. "I want the pieces to fit."

"We'll do our best," said Miranda.

"It's us and the OPP and the Mounties and God knows who else. I want a nice neat package we can all take home."

Morgan winked as they walked out Rufalo's door. She knew he was thinking about the impossibility of taking one package to multiple homes, about the proliferation of stories without closure, about the mechanism inside a Rubik's cube.

They sat down at their desks, which opposed each other,

back to back. They flipped on their computers and started riffling through accumulated paperwork. Miranda would have to complete her account of her Waterloo Country adventure with sufficient detail to satisfy the Cambridge Police and the OPP, as well as her superintendent. Morgan had to justify an expensive trip to England that was apparently a waste of resources. They worked quietly for the rest of the morning without looking up or comparing notes.

Lunch in the food court under the old Eaton's College Street department store with Spivak and Stritch and a few others from the office, including a sheepish Bourassa and his partner, was a raucous affair. It was rare that they ate out together, but this was an occasion. Bourassa had picked up a lead from a contact in New York and closed down some bikers who had knocked off a runner for the mob. No arrests, but the bike club had picked up and gone back to Quebec. This was as close to a celebration as Homicide cops generally allowed themselves, at least during the daylight hours.

"I met a guy in New Jersey who knows you," Miranda said to Bourassa while trying to negotiate a collapsing taco shell stuffed with chili. "He used to. He's dead."

"Yeah, I've known a few down there."

"You get around, don't you?" said Spivak.

"Yeah," said Bourassa. "Some."

"You too," said Spivak to Morgan. "Gawd, everyone gets around but me and Stritch."

"Speak for yourself," said Stritch in his most funereal voice. No one knew quite what he meant, but it seemed funny and everyone laughed.

"Did you really go to law school?" Miranda asked Bourassa.

"Where'd you hear that?"

"Where did you go?"

"Columbia."

"The country or the university?"

"New York," he said.

"And?"

"And what?"

"Did you graduate?" As soon as Miranda asked, she was annoyed with herself.

"Actually, I did. Third in my class. So what?"

"Oh," she said with relief. "Did you practice?" It seemed unlikely, but it seemed politically correct to inquire.

"I came home. I would have had to do the Ontario bar exams. Wasn't interested. Saw enough in law school, I wanted to be a cop."

"Did you ever tell anyone you failed out?"

"Yeah, sure. There've been times when it's better being a dumb lawyer than a cop."

"Even a smart cop?" said Miranda.

"He fakes it," said Spivak, uncertain what his point was.

"There's too much moral ambiguity being a lawyer," said Bourassa in the most coherent statement he had ever made about police work. "I prefer enforcing the laws, not seeing how far I can bend them."

"The law's loss, our gain," said Morgan.

The subject shifted from Bourassa, to everyone's relief. Morgan sat back in the molded plastic seat and surveyed the scene. He was homesick for The Bunch of Grapes and at the same time pleased to be back. These were people he admired. They worked hard and they were good at what they did. Each would go off to a different life at the end of the day, some solitary and some to families. Some of them were solidly working class and some were professionals. They all earned pretty much the same, they spent money and time in different ways. That's what he liked about being here, rather than England where class still prevailed, or the States, where the job defined who you were.

"Hey, Morgan, wake up," said Spivak. *He likes opera*, thought Morgan. *His partner plays hockey, always the only black kid on the team.*

"Morgan," said Bourassa, then turned to the woman beside him, "you know, Morgan should have been a lawyer."

"Yeah," said Morgan, blowing on his knuckles, "the defense never rests." He laughed. *Bourassa collects, indiscriminately, for every charity going, walking desk to desk, door to door. His partner, Audrey, is a chess master.*

Miranda rubbed her gloved hands gently together, trying to spread ointment into the sore parts. She and her partner didn't hang out much, but it was just what she needed, to get her mind off the case. *There is no case*, she thought. *There's Savage. Once he goes down, the details look after themselves.*

Suddenly she was restless but she didn't know which way to turn. Morgan sensed her agitation. He stood up.

"We've got to go," he said. "We've got an interview downtown."

After they were out of earshot, she whispered her thanks.

"Let's walk for a while," he said. "Try to relax. Say anything that comes into your mind."

"Anything?" She glanced sideways and caught him in profile. "You think we already know where he is, don't you?"

"He's here."

"Where?"

"In Toronto."

"What makes you think so?"

"His cuticles."

"His cuticles?"

"Did you notice the hand with the ring?"

"Notice it! Yes."

"It was like Savage's hand. The cuticles were inordinately neat."

"Inordinately?"

"Yeah, you wouldn't expect a man wearing a macho ring like that to have manicured nails."

"That was a vanity ring, Morgan. I would say he was exactly the type who would go to a professional."

"Whatever. Savage's nails, they gleamed like talons. Same manicurist. And I'm betting that means they both hung out in the city."

"There are manicurists everywhere, Morgan, even small towns."

"Not ones these guys would go to. Culturally, they would find it offensive to hang around with women in a beauty salon. They'd go to, maybe a barbershop, big and fancy, where the clients get their nails done as a bonus, with a shave, and a Cuban cigar is thrown in at the end. Toronto. Big hotel, downtown."

They wandered south on Yonge Street then cut west on Dundas and back up University Avenue.

"Okay," said Morgan. "Try this for logic. The old lady, Mrs. Oughtred, she told us Mr. Savage sometimes drove to Bonnydoon and sometimes flew in by 'aero-plane.' I'm betting when he flew, it was from Buffalo — that's how they brought Elke up — and when he drove, he wasn't crossing any borders."

"Okay."

"Okay, and he had an extravagant house at the win-ery, very west coast postmodern. He and his cohort like to live well, much better I'm sure than their minions working the trenches."

"The trenches?"

"Toilers in the vineyard — bad analogy. The guys working at newsstands, taxi-cabs, variety stores — mur-derous hours, low pay, keeping watch — how do you think they track us so easily? They're everywhere."

"Morgan, that's xenophobic."

"No. They're not all foreigners."

"Or immigrants."

"No, okay, I take it back. But Savage, he likes to live well. He has a fabulous house in the country, only it's ashes and dust now. He commuted. From where? From a great place in the city … it stands to reason. He fancies himself cosmopolitan. He'll have a suite in a hotel in the heart of Toronto, yes!"

"You are not being monitored by every kiosk selling lottery tickets."

"The lottery outlets, I hadn't thought of them."

"Shut up."

"Do you know Mrs. Oughtred's husband and I, we might have been distantly related?"

"What are you talking about?"

"I have a family hope chest that belonged to a Haun from the Niagara area, at least two hundred years old.

The old lady said her husband was a Haun on his mother's side."

"It's sad. She didn't tell us about her own ancestry, only his. She was a woman of her era, I guess. Ninety-six years old. What an absurd way to die, blown to ashes and dust."

Walking north past the Ontario Legislature at Queen's Park, they each experienced brief encounters with nostalgia evoked by university buildings visible through the trees on either side of them. Avenue Road stretched out ahead, a canyon between condos running all the way to the tower at Upper Canada College, where it diverted around the playing fields of the privileged.

"That's it," said Miranda, suddenly. "Not a hotel, a condo. We're looking for a condo. Philip's nails were immaculate, too — did I tell you his name was Mohammet Jousef? He was Albanian."

"You told me he was an Albanian. I don't think you told me his name."

"Mohammet Jousef. He was educated in the States. Morgan, his nails were manicured."

"No big gold rings?"

"No, he was a corporate lawyer."

"Miranda —"

"I know, Philip Carter was the corporate lawyer, not Mohammet Jousef. He told me once it was an occupational thing."

"Getting his nails done?"

"Washing his hands, you know, Pontius Pilate, Lady MacBeth."

"Ah, don't we love lawyers. So, do you think Mr. Savage is Albanian as well?"

"Morgan, we're not looking for a barbershop. We're looking for room service manicurists."

"At a hotel. You think these guys lived at The Four Seasons."

"Not necessarily. But I'm betting if we check out the manicurists in a few of the better hotels around here, we'll find one who provides off-premises room service."

"Let's give it a try." They were within easy reach of several expensive hotels, but it seemed an arbitrary undertaking.

"I'm betting Savage lives in one of these condos," said Miranda, gazing up Avenue Road. "He wants to be at the centre of things. This is it. There aren't many condos by the big hotels closer to the lake. Except down at the harbour. We'll try there next."

"You think you know this guy."

"You're chasing down a killer, Morgan. I'm after a nightmare. I know him, yes."

"And you think he's somewhere near the corner of Bloor and Avenue Road."

"Toronto has any number of centres, right? But this is the centre of refined decadence. This is where he needs to be — to observe all that is dissolute about the world he wants to destroy, to revel in the richness of its inevitable demise. He'll fuck it, the world he fears and can't have. That's how this guy thinks. He'll lift its skirts for a peek, feel it up publicly, fuck it by stealth."

"Nasty," Morgan responded. She was handling herself so well emotionally, he was taken off guard by the revelation in her crude language of how much she was hurting inside.

They walked into a palatial hotel lobby, past service

personnel in livery, straight to the beauty salon near the Unisex Health Club.

"Police," said Miranda, flashing her ID at the mascara-afflicted receptionist. "We're looking for a manicurist who works off premises."

"No one here like that," said the receptionist, her voice indicating she had taken offence. "We're not allowed."

"You send people up to guests' rooms, don't you?" Morgan leaned past her desk to look through the door of the gym, over which there was a large sign reading GUESTS ONLY."

"Yes, we can keep an eye on things here. But no one goes out. We're not an escort service."

"No," said Miranda. "That's not what I heard."

She was bluffing but she had pressed the right button.

"That was months ago. It wasn't us, just one of the girls. She worked independently, she was a pro."

"As in prostitute or fingernails."

"And toenails. She was both, I suppose."

"And where would we find her?"

"She was murdered."

"What?"

"Two nights ago. Someone found her in a dumpster."

"I heard about that," said Miranda. "Bourassa's case, he's working with Audrey Slocombe."

"Pardon?" said the receptionist.

"I was talking to my partner. So, what can you tell us about her?"

"The same pretty much as I told the other cops, yesterday."

"Did they leave a card?"

"Yeah, the big guy did. Here it is. His name is Detective Bourassa."

"Like I said, do you know who her customers were? Did she have regulars?"

"This is a clean operation. You'll get us thrown out of the hotel. I never talked to her for months. I hardly knew her name. Rhoda something, she was a part-time blond. Good looking, with roots. Not too smart. I know she had regulars in that condo across the street. Over there, top floor. She had every guy up there on the string."

"On the string?" said Miranda. "She was working them."

"Yeah, there are three or four really large condos on the top floor. She'd spend a whole day there, once every week."

"A whole day?"

"Like I said, she was a pro."

"But you didn't keep track of her."

"We'd better call Bourassa," said Morgan.

"Thanks, for now," said Miranda to the receptionist, whose eyelids drooped under her makeup, her lashes solid gashes of deep blue. Then as they stepped out into the corridor she said, "No need. I heard them talking at lunch. It was a domestic quarrel. Her old man beat her up. She climbed into the dumpster herself and died there. You got to figure she felt like garbage. The bastard, he lived on her money, hated her for it. And she hated herself, probably for loving him. It's a funny old world, Morgan."

"It's a hell of a way to die."

"Yeah."

He pointed to the massive new art deco building across from them when they emerged onto the street. "Do you think Philip Carter lived there?"

"He had to live somewhere," she said.

They crossed over and rang the buzzer for the building manager.

"Sure," he said, when they asked him. "Philip Carter, he's a lawyer. Top floor. Condo fees paid up until September. Haven't seen him around much." The elderly man's nose twitched and his small eyes glistened. *Some people look guilty*, Miranda thought. *Not for anything in particular, it's just the way they are. He looks furtive, like a squirrel after the first snowfall.*

"What about the others?" asked Morgan.

"What others? He lived alone."

"Was he friends with the other residents on the same floor?"

"I don't know, I mean how would I know? These people, they're polite, but they keep to themselves."

"These people?" said Miranda.

"Yeah, single guys with a lot of money. You don't want to ask."

"What does that mean?" Morgan demanded.

"Hey, I don't know. It means nothing." He paused, looked at them. He plainly did not want trouble from the police.

"Speak," said Morgan.

"Single guys, lots of money, no parties, you don't know what to think."

"Well, try," said Morgan.

"Maybe drugs?" said Miranda.

"You just don't want to know. There are three of them up there. I guess they know each other. They have the same interior decorator. Very expensive, nothing personal, you know what I mean. No photographs. Generic collectables."

"Generic collectables, where'd that come from?" said Morgan.

The man's nose twitched. "I read it," he said. "It's in a magazine. Generic collectables. What's the matter with that? I wasn't snooping, just doing routine maintenance."

"Is there anyone up there now?" asked Morgan.

"I don't know, I could ring."

"No!" said Miranda. "Don't do that. We'll want to surprise them."

"You sure you're cops?"

"Yeah, we like surprises."

"On them, eh? Not on yourself." The man with the squirrel eyes chuckled.

"What are the names of the other two?" Morgan asked.

"Besides Mr. Carter, there's Mr. Johnson."

"Does he wear a gold ring?" said Miranda.

"Johnson? Yeah, a big honker. And the other one is Mr. Savage."

"You're kidding," Miranda exclaimed.

"He's registered as *Savage*?" said Morgan, incredulously.

"He's the owner, he owns it. Yeah. He banks offshore."

"How do you know that?" said Morgan.

"I see the mail. I take it up to their foyer, that's part of the service. Funny thing, the other two don't get any mail. They must do their banking by phone."

"He can't be that brazen," said Miranda. "All we had to do was look him up in the phone book."

"No, you couldn't do that. His number's unlisted."

"Unlisted?"

"I tried to call him myself about something, can't remember what. Unlisted. If he's into drugs — do you think he's into drugs?— a young guy like that with money, he's going to be very particular who has his number."

Morgan leaned into the man's space. "He's not that young."

"To have enough money to live here, yes he is. Do you want me to go up with you?"

"We'd appreciate if you'd go to your own place, please. Stay there. We'll let you know when you can come out."

"Yeah, sure," said the squirrel-faced man, looking disappointed that he wouldn't be there when they confronted Savage. He had not seen the other two around lately but he was fairly positive Savage was home.

"Fourteenth floor?" said Morgan.

"Yeah. Here, you'll need this key. The elevator stops at thirteen, then you turn the key and it goes the rest of the way. They pay extra for that."

Miranda took the key and turned to the elevator button. Morgan stood close beside her as the building manager retreated to his own quarters.

"You okay?" Morgan asked.

"Sure. You?"

"Yeah. You armed?"

"Yes. You?"

"Yeah. Press it."

When the elevator door opened, they stepped into a mirrored cage, like a shower stall in a bordello. Only the floor was not mirrored. No matter which way they looked, they saw reflections and refractions of themselves.

The elevator stopped at the thirteenth floor. Miranda inserted the key, the doors closed again, and after a brief whirring opened into a marble foyer with a great crystal chandelier and three doors leading to the separate condo apartments. One door had a brass label by the buzzer that read PHILIP CARTER. Miranda felt a twinge and Morgan touched her on the arm. The next read, JOHNSON. An unlikely name for the man with the ring.

Poised in front of the third door, which had no nameplate, Miranda suddenly turned around and looked up. Concealed within the intricate armatures of the candelabra were three small cameras. She pointed them out to Morgan.

"We're expected, I imagine," he said.

"He must have another way out — a private exit leading down to the fire stairs, a service elevator."

"I don't think he's going anywhere," said Morgan. "He can't be sure we don't have backup waiting at ground level. And he's not the kind to run."

"You admire this guy, Morgan!"

"No way. Like you said, I know him. Not the way you do, but I do. He shot a man in the head right in front of me. He knew we would meet again. Some things are unavoidable. He's waiting for us."

"I am, Mr. Morgan," said the disembodied voice of Mr. Savage.

Neither Morgan nor Miranda whirled around. Both turned slowly and stared up into the lens of the camera aimed in their direction.

"You have come to pay me a visit, Ms. Quin. How very thoughtful. And you, Mr. Morgan, I have been expecting you. I have been expecting you both."

Locks snapped on the door behind them and as they turned back it swung open. The voice urged them to enter.

"No need to draw your guns. There is no point," said the voice. "Much of the weaponry at my disposal is already directed toward your vital parts. If I wished the flesh flayed from your bones by bullets and shrapnel, it would already be done. But that is not discreet, and I believe it is better if we keep our business discreet for the time being. Do come in, make yourselves comfortable. I shall be out in a moment."

There were mirrors here and there along the walls of the entryway and in the two-storey living room, behind which, it was safe to assume, there were arms and armaments poised for the destruction of unwelcome visitors. They heard an electronic bolt slide on the door behind, locking them in. Looking around, Miranda and Morgan could see how this opulent if uninspired residence could well be a fortress, bristling with instruments of death.

Everything hidden. Morgan had no doubt the entire place was rigged for lethal impact. And yet, gazing out to the balcony, he marvelled at the serene view of Toronto that would be accessible, lounging among the summer palms that flourished in an oasis of huge plastic buckets, looking down Avenue Road to Queen's Park.

A door to the side swung open and Savage stepped into the room. He was wearing a light blue linen suit, rumpled in just the right way to accentuate the clean lines and expensive cut. His eyes were dark but lively with highlights from the light of the day streaming through the two-storey living room windows. He nodded graciously and motioned to them to sit. He sat opposite.

"Let us be civilized," he said. "It is good to see you again, Detective Quin."

"I don't remember our first meeting," said Miranda. "I wasn't all there."

"Indeed you weren't, but I assure you, the pleasure was mine."

She refused to show emotion, apart from a hint of contempt in the curl of her upper lip. There was too much at stake to let him take the lead.

"It's over," said Morgan. "Whatever your name is, do you have a name of your own? It is over."

"For me, perhaps. But it is not over. As they say, Mr. Morgan, my name is legion. It is a long way from over."

Miranda opened her handbag and slowly removed her diminutive Glock semi-automatic. She pulled back the action and grasped the gun firmly in one hand with her finger on the trigger.

"You will shoot me now, Ms. Quin? That is certainly an option."

Miranda raised the Glock to a firing position, bracing one hand with the other. She aimed at his forehead, then lowered her sights until the gun was pointed directly at his crotch.

"That seems a reasonable course to take, Ms. Quin. You were humiliated, so humiliate me. It will be very painful, and that will give you great satisfaction."

"Miranda," said Morgan emphatically.

"What? You think I would give this twerp the satisfaction of directing his own retribution? If I kill him, Morgan, it will be on my terms."

"In that case," said Savage, crossing his legs, "perhaps we should talk."

"Talk," said Morgan.

"Well, you see, Mr. Morgan, if I may just open my

jacket, there, you see I am wearing a belt with little gadgets and wires. What will happen, if I slump over, shall we say, with a bullet or bullets in my head or my groin, these wires will detonate materials in the bedrooms with an explosive equivalent to approximately fifty tons of TNT. I am afraid the damage to this part of Toronto would be quite extreme. But such is life. If it is time, it is time. I had been hoping to delay the inevitable. I have come to enjoy your city a great deal. It is very cosmopolitan, Toronto the Good — isn't that what you call it in your very smug way, Toronto the Good?"

"Hogtown," said Morgan. "Closed on Sundays. That's all in the past. We're world-class now."

"How sad. A city that defines itself as *world-class* never is."

"You're not too good on irony, Mr. Savage."

"Oh, but I am. Do you see? I live very well, I will die for a cause I no longer believe in. Do you see the irony? Death has no meaning, Mr. Morgan. Only life is worth dying for."

"So are we at an impasse once again, Mr. Savage?"

"Not this time, I'm afraid. It is no longer about just you and me and the very attractive Ms. Quin. I am quite serious about the damage to be done. This is not a standoff, it is a rout. You will place your weapons on the coffee table, please."

"Morgan?"

"He means it. I'm guessing these condos are an upscale warehouse. This is their arsenal. This is where the money has gone, into weapons of imminent destruction."

"Very wise, Mr. Morgan. But only a small part of our income from the vineyards of corruption went into armaments. Much is being banked for future use, when Armageddon shall come to the Western world."

"I thought you weren't a believer."

"I am a leader. Leaders cannot afford to believe."

"Well, you've led yourself into a dead end," said Miranda. "Literally," she added.

"Quite possibly I have. And I do see the irony. But this is just one of innumerable roads to the same end. There are other roads, others to travel them."

"We all die?" Morgan asked with apparent disinterest.

"You die, Mr. Morgan. Your deaths will be heroic, I'm sure. For myself, there may still be time. We shall see."

Miranda reached over and retrieved her Glock from where she had placed it on the coffee table. She cocked it and pointed it again at Mr. Savage.

"I understand your logic, Ms. Quin. If you are to die, at least you can take me with you. However, if you will think for a moment, it is not that simple."

"You think for me."

"Indeed I will. If you shoot me, a thousand people will perish in the flash of an eye. But if you let me go, there is a chance you may avert disaster. Perhaps you can disarm the explosives, perhaps you can evacuate the buildings in this vicinity — I warn you, you will need to clear a very wide radius. But no, I do not think there will be time. Disarming the explosives is probably your best bet. Except you know me too well, you know I will not allow this stockpile to go to waste. Therefore, it is logical, you shoot me and our bodies explode into each other. Imagine that."

Morgan rocked back and forth on the sofa and Miranda passed her gun from one hand to the other, without taking it off Savage.

"It is possible, just possible," said Savage, "if you let me go you might be able to do something to save yourselves and your beloved world-class city. People like you cannot resist grasping at the chance to survive, no matter how miserable the odds."

"He's playing with us," Miranda said with disdain.

"No," said Morgan. "It's a game. We're playing each other."

"It's not a game of chance," said Miranda. "Chess, not poker. I'm betting we win."

"And if you don't! Of course, there is another possibility," said Savage. "Since I am the detonator, you have to be wondering, if I leave the premises, will my little gadgets broadcast this far? Now there is an irony, indeed. For me to reach safety, my weaponry might be disarmed. It is possible. Then you will be safe as well. Of course, knowing me as you do, you know there might be no explosives at all. But is there time to look? That is the question."

He stood up.

"I really must go. At the very least, my departure will delay certain death by a few minutes. It has been a pleasure, once again, Ms. Quin." His dark eyes flashed and she felt a chill to the bone. "Goodbye, Mr. Morgan."

Morgan stood up.

The two men faced each other, less than an arm's length apart. Morgan leaned to the side and picked up his semi-automatic. He held it in the open palm of his hand. Both men examined it as some sort of fossil, extinct and useless. He tossed it onto the sofa beside Miranda.

"Mr. Savage," said Morgan. "We prefer you stay for the signing."

Savage looked at him quizzically then pressed his lips in a sneer. "The signing, my signature, of course. Blood on the walls, an interesting diversion. This particular version of the Apocalypse should undoubtedly carry my name."

"Miranda," Morgan said, "use my weapon, it's bigger. Shoot Mr. Savage in the right leg."

Both men held their ground. Miranda tucked her own gun into the waistband of her skirt and moved on the edge of their range of vision. The eyes of the two men locked, as if they were in deadly combat without moving a muscle.

Suddenly a shot exploded from the gun in Miranda's hands. Mr. Savage lurched but remained standing. Morgan stood close enough to feel the man's minty breath on his face.

"This is an interesting turn of events," said Savage, grimacing from the pain in his thigh. "Perhaps we shall die together, then." He drew in a deep breath. "Mr. Morgan, I'm sorry about your friends. It was unavoidable."

"My friends?"

"In England. Miss Sturmberg? I believe she was a friend of yours. And the old mullah, Professor Ali Rashid Izzadine Al Sayyed, you visited his chambers in Cambridge. I believe you spent several nights with Miss Sturmberg, one in a sleazy hotel near Victoria Station and then in a rather pleasant B&B in Cambridge, with twin beds. From that I surmise you were lovers for a night and thought better of it the day after."

"What about my friends?" Morgan demanded.

"Ah, yes, it is difficult to be dispassionate when you do not have the training, Mr. Morgan. Your work is so much different from ours, Miss Sturmberg's and mine. We had much in common, I think, though she was a

Jew. I had more in common with her than I did with the venerable Kurd. He was a true Peshmerga, a samurai, a knight. He was a Muslim and a scholar, he believed with his brain and his heart. I believe nothing. He was not trained, so he had to rely on education and passionate intelligence. That is not enough, or too much, perhaps. Still, he died without flinching. They held him by the beard and slit his throat. Ms. Sturmberg, on the contrary, she went down like a fighter. She died first, but she murdered two of ours in the process. There are many ways to be brave, I suppose. Cambridge chambers will never be the same. I'm told it was all quite messy. It is difficult to wash blood from such beautiful rugs."

Morgan remembered the rugs. "Miranda," he said.

"Do nothing, Ms. Quin. We will be dead soon enough. Then your flesh and mine will be one, once again."

"Savage," said Morgan, "Disarm the bomb."

"It is many bombs."

"Miranda, shatter his kneecap."

Another shot exploded and the room shook like thunder. Savage whirled, and as he did so Morgan flung his arms under the other man's flailing arms, pinning him against his own body so the man could not fall to set off the detonator.

Miranda lunged forward and held Morgan's Glock to Savage's forehead.

The man sneered through the pain. "Too late," he said. "We are dead."

"Not yet. Miranda, would you mind cutting in?" She looked at the two men, embraced in a tottering *danse macabre*.

"What do you want me to do?"

"If I've learned one thing through all this, it's that high tech is limited by the mind that controls it."

"Morgan?"

"Under his jacket, the Batman utility belt, Velcro. I'm betting it comes off easily. Don't tilt it."

"You're betting!"

"Yeah, go for it. He's a dead weight."

Miranda crouched down and fumbled around, then found tabs, but with her hands still encased in greasy surgical gloves she could not get a grip. She leaned forward, clasped a tab between her teeth, and pulled. Then another pull and the belt released.

"Keep it upright, keep it upright."

"Morgan, I am. I've got it, you can drop him."

Morgan let Savage slide to the floor. The man rolled over on his side and lay still. Morgan took his gun back from Miranda. He was tempted to finish Savage off but thought better of it. They might need him, and he wasn't going very far.

"What do I do with this?" Miranda demanded. She held the ominous contraption between them, examining the wires and webbing and tabs. Morgan reached out and touched a wire.

"It's always the red one," he said.

"What?"

"In the movies. It's always the red one. The hero gets set to cut blue or yellow, then in a leap of intuition at the last second switches and cuts the red."

"Morgan."

"Yeah."

"There are four wires and they're all red."

"You know what?"

"What."

"Drop it."

"What, the belt? Don't be insane."

"Give it to me." He took hold of it but she would not release her grip.

"Morgan, what are you doing, for God's sake?"

"Don't swear."

"Pardon."

"Don't swear."

"Shit, Morgan. If there was ever a time —"

"It's a decoy."

"You think?"

"Yeah."

"Here, you take it, you put it down — if we go up in a fiery inferno, it's your fault."

He took the belt and gingerly set it in an upright position on a chair.

"I thought it was a fake?"

"Just in case it isn't. So far, so good. So, what now?"

"You're asking me? You seem to be reading the situation pretty well."

"Miranda, I'm guessing there's a real detonator. Savage knew we were coming. He monitored us in the lobby or out in the foyer. I think we're inside a time bomb. I think that's what we've walked into. And he set it going when we came through the door. He might have tried to escape but it isn't his style. This Mr. Savage is all about style. I'm guessing we're on a short fuse — he knew he wouldn't have time to get away. He decided to pay us the ultimate compliment of sharing our deaths."

"How nice."

"Very good," said Savage from the floor. His voice was surprisingly clear, as if he had dissociated from the agony of his shattered knee, as if they were friends in a conversation he had just dropped out of for a few minutes.

Miranda looked down at him with utter contempt, not spitting because she knew from her mother's knee it would reflect badly on her own self-respect.

"We've got about four minutes left," said Savage.

"Why so long?" said Morgan. "Why not just press the button and take us out from the start?"

"Because I did want to talk to you both, to renew my acquaintance with Ms. Quin and to chat about old times with you, Mr. Morgan."

"Morgan," Miranda snapped, "don't you believe him. You're wrong about style, he's gutless. He still thinks he can get out of here. The service elevator is closed, I'll bet you anything. The emergency stairs are sealed off. They did it themselves to protect their storehouse. He needs time to get by us. If we're inside a time bomb, I'm betting it's got fifteen minutes to go, maybe more. He needs time to get away."

"I am not afraid of dying, Ms. Quin. Surely you know that."

"Bullshit, you're petrified."

"Miranda?"

"He likes to believe he's no longer human, he's one of the Borg — but he is a leader. Those are not compatible."

"The Borg? You're talking *Star Trek*? We're counting seconds."

"The Borg are an inexhaustible corporate entity, they absorb personalities —"

"What about Seven-of-Nine?"

"Barbie with brains, every man's nightmare."

"Excuse me," said Savage, straining to suppress his pain. "Have you lost track of what's happening?"

"Have you?" snapped Miranda.

"No, no, Ms. Quin. I am human, yes, serving an unstoppable cause. And it, not we, not me, but it, will prevail. As the Borg say, Ms. Quin, *resistance is futile*. You now have approximately two minutes."

"You are al-Qaeda, the Borg in real time. But you think for yourself, Mr. Savage, and that is dangerous."

"For whom, Ms. Quin?"

"For you. Morgan, this man is a pathological bully, he is pathologically terrified of women, he is a pathological coward. I'd say he has allowed himself time to negotiate."

"In that case, Ms. Quin, we will cut to the end. I will make a deal with you," said Savage from his twisted position on the floor. "I will tell you how to disarm the detonator. I will unlock the door. It is steel and it is bolted. We will leave. It is over. I disappear. There is no hole in the heart of Toronto. You two become heroes."

"Morgan, it's us he's trying to disarm. I say we have lots of time, if there's a timer at all."

"Let's resolve the confusion," said Morgan, motioning for her to check one of the bedrooms while he checked another. The first room Morgan went into was piled high with materials parcelled in ominous crates beside stashes of weaponry.

"Morgan," Miranda called from a study off the master bedroom, "in here!"

"Yeah," said Morgan, hurrying down the hall to her side. "He wasn't bluffing." They stood looking at a computer monitor with a digital display of numbers, counting down.

"But I was right about having more time than he said," Miranda offered.

"Twelve minutes to go. Yeah, you were right about that," said Morgan. "Let me fiddle with this — you think he's a coward, maybe torture will work? Shoot him in the other kneecap."

"Maybe I should bring him in here first."

"Whatever."

Miranda rushed back to the living room to drag Savage into the study.

He was nowhere in sight.

She raced down the hall to the entry door but it was still solidly secured. Returning to the living room, she stopped and looked at the carpet where he had fallen. A smear of blood narrowed like a wedge in the direction of the two-storey window.

He's stopped the bleeding, he's on the balcony.

But she could see the entire balcony. There was no one there.

She slid the glass door open. Squat summer palms rustled in the afternoon breeze. More blood, some on the railing. She stepped forward and leaned out.

Savage was hanging over the side from the rail at the base of the balcony, fourteen storeys above Avenue Road. Technically, thirteen, since he was dangling below his own level.

"Hello," said Miranda.

Savage took a deep breath. He clearly had intended to swing out and then in, onto the balcony below, but once in position he must have realized his arms against the edge of the balcony would throw his weight away from the building and he would fall. He gazed up at her, waiting for something to happen.

"No gun?" said Miranda. "No, I have the gun. No time left? You're right about that. Still, I'd rather blow up than fall down, down, down, thinking the whole way about what it's going to be like to hit bottom. A nasty business, Mr. Savage."

"Najim."

"What?" said Miranda, leaning over.

"Najim Mustafa Tanimi."

"Really. Najim Mustafa Tanimi. Is that your name, Mr. Savage?"

"If you help me," he gasped, the weight of his body compressing his lungs, "you will have righteousness on your side for rescuing me in spite of what I did to you."

"And if I do not, Mr. Savage, Najim, there will be righteous satisfaction in seeing you fall to your death, thinking about me all the way down."

"Please."

"What, Mr. Savage, what do you want?"

"Help me. Shoot me. Do not let me fall."

"Perhaps you could explain how to stop the countdown. That would be very helpful to all of us."

"Yes, yes. I cannot. It is started."

"You can't stop it?"

"No, yes. Maybe I can. Help me."

Miranda braced herself and reached over. She extended one arm downwards and Savage released one of his hands from the rail, flailing upwards, and his fingers clenched around the glove on her lowered hand, and the ointment oozed and the material slid away from Miranda's flesh in slow motion, and their hands pulled apart, his with the glove grasped desperately limp as his weight swung onto his other hand, down and away, and his fingers on that hand opened and, gazing up into Miranda's eyes in astonishment, his mouth open in a silent scream, and he fell back into the air.

Miranda walked almost casually back into the study. Morgan was staring at the monitor. Three minutes and twenty-eight seconds left, twenty-seven, twenty-six....

"I take it you didn't get very far with Savage. Did you kill him?"

He turned away from the screen and looked into her eyes. He could not recognize anything familiar. And yet she was there, not a stranger. He shuddered with an odd feeling of grief, realizing that she would not survive. His own death was more difficult to imagine.

"Ring around the rosy, Morgan ... husha, husha, we all fall down."

"Don't worry," he said. "You did what you had to do. I don't think he knew how to stop this thing anyway. My dad used to say the bombardier can't call back the bombs."

"Was he in the war?"

"World War Two? No. Korea."

"Morgan, it's the end of the world as we know it."

"It's the end of our knowing it — husha, husha — what would Buffy do now?"

"Buffy?"

"Buffy."

"Morgan."

"Yeah."

"You want to have sex?"

"You think there's time?"

"I don't know, you might not respect me in the morning."

"Let's chance it."

"I'll settle for a hug."

"Me too."

"You ready for the world's biggest orgasm?"

"Yeah."

"Me too."

He stood up and they held each other for the first time like lovers. They rocked gently together. He smelled nice. She looked by him at the screen. Fifty seconds, forty-nine, forty-eight.... She glanced down at the tangle of cords under the computer. She looked back at the screen. Twenty-nine, twenty-eight.... she had lost ten seconds. Twenty-four, twenty-three, twenty-two.... *It's always such a viper's nest*, she thought. *High-tech, and nobody thinks about the mess.* Eighteen, seventeen —

"Morgan."

"Yes."

She leaned away from him and smiled. "Let go."

"What?"

"Let me go."

"Okay."

"You know the problem with all this electronic stuff?"

"Yeah." He kissed her. She rose to the pressure of his lips then pulled away quickly and dropped to her knees. She called up to him.

"Morgan, if you hurry, you can get in the last word."

"Miranda?"

She squirmed under the computer console, grasped two cables plugged into an electric outlet and yanked. She lay perfectly still, waiting.

"Boom," said Morgan in a soft voice. "You did it."

"I did?"

"We're ten seconds past Armageddon."

"Lovely. Get me out of here. Can you believe it?"

"Yeah, I believe it."

He helped her to her feet and she leaned against him to extricate herself from the tangle of wires, then remained leaning against him. He drew her close and they breathed deeply in unison.

"I don't suppose you've replaced your broken cell-phone," he said softly into her hair as if he were mouthing endearments.

"I imagine yours is at home," she responded against his shoulder, without looking up.

"What do you think the chances are there's a working telephone here?" he asked.

"One line, unlisted. Disconnected from this end, I imagine," she answered with incongruous warmth.

"As in, unplugged?"

"As in, ripped out of the wall. A precaution when he knew we were coming."

"Yeah," said Morgan, still whispering. "He needed us to find him. Somehow we became witnesses to measure himself, even if he intended to blow us up."

"But he figured he would survive."

"Otherwise the dummy detonator he was wearing doesn't make sense."

"Well, we witnessed his death." She breathed deeply. "Actually, we didn't," she whispered. "You were in here and I didn't wait to see him hit bottom."

"Ouch."

"Morgan?"

"Yeah."

"You're still holding me."

"I thought you were holding me. Do you want to stop?"

"Not really."

They maintained a close embrace until their breathing slowed to normal, then pulled apart shyly, neither prepared to say anything that would destroy the intimacy, yet each recognizing the world had not come to an end and time was back to its normal flow.

They walked into the living room arm in arm. Morgan noticed the door out onto the balcony was ajar. He saw blood on the carpet smeared in that direction. He said nothing. She would explain if she wanted. He turned to her and kissed her forehead. She reached out, bent his head down, and kissed him on the forehead with a loud smack. It was an expression of affection and a parody of what he had just done.

"He did know we were coming, didn't he?" she said.

"Morgan, I think he's known we were coming for a long time. People on the inside can see more than those of us playing the outside of the cube. He knows what's in there, doesn't he? Intersecting tracks, swivels, and pivots. Agents for this and for that, there's not much difference among them. Tensions and alliances, Morgan. Swivels and pivots. I prefer it on the outside, lining up what you can see."

"Amen," he said.

"You all right, Morgan?"

"For sure. I knew you were, too, when you called him a dweeb."

"Twerp, I called him a twerp."

"Yeah, and that's when I knew we had him beat."

"Morgan — a sleazy hotel near Victoria Station?"

"Pardon?"

"Sorry. I'm sorry about Elke. We were friends in a way. And the old man, I'm sorry about him, Morgan. The wise old man in the ivory tower, he shouldn't have suffered like that. Morgan, why do I keep saying your name?"

He smiled. "I don't know, Miranda."

"You never use my name. I'll bet you don't, even when you think of me."

"How do you know I think of you, Miranda? The old man, he was a warrior. I expect death was a reasonable price for his dreams, I imagine that's what he thought when he died. And Elke, she didn't believe she'd ever get old."

"And for us, this is as far as we go, isn't it?"

"How so?" Morgan asked.

"Rufalo wanted a nice neat package. This is it. Savage is dead. All the details connect. Lots of leads for CSIS and the CIA and MI6 and God knows who. But there won't be any convictions. The enemy is amorphous. It dissipates, lies dormant, mutates, regroups, who knows? If it doesn't come back as al-Qaeda, it'll be something else."

"That's sad," said Morgan. "Truly sad. So many died and nothing is changed."

"Oh, but it has, Morgan, changed utterly. Each act of terrorism takes us little by little farther away from the world we know and closer and closer to anarchy."

"And what rough beast slouches towards Bethlehem."

"You know your Yeats, too."

"Who else?"

"Besides me?" She looked at him thoughtfully. "You know, others. Come on, let's get out of here."

"How? I guess Mr. Savage made quite a splash on the street. Toronto's finest will be up here, sooner or later, we just have to wait."

"I wonder what his real name was," said Morgan. "I suppose we'll find out soon enough."

"Perhaps he didn't have a name," said Miranda. Najim Mustafa Tanimi. She didn't say it out loud. "He was the man who never was."

"Wouldn't it be nice to think so?"

"Nice? Even necessary."

Morgan tousled her hair and she shook off his condescension with a friendly flourish.

"Here," he said, hoisting a marble pedestal to chest height, after setting the vase that was on top of it carefully on the floor, "let's test out the building code. I've got a theory that walls are conventions."

"Me too," said Miranda.

Morgan swung the pedestal like a battering ram against the wall beside the heavy front door. It jarred violently, sending spasms of pain through his shoulders.

"But, but," said Miranda. "You want to find a soft spot, Morgan. I think you just hit solid cement. Try over a bit to the left."

"You try," said Morgan, flagging his arms through the air, trying to make the pain fade away.

"Can't," she responded, holding up her injured hands.

"Where's your glove? You've lost one of your gloves, did you know that?"

"Yeah. Come on, heave the marble, let's get out of here. I'm betting —"

"Between the two of us, we've been betting a lot —"

"And coming up winners. Morgan, I'm betting the wall right here is non-supporting, it's six-inch cement blocks. They'll crumble on impact. Try it again."

He hoisted the column back into the air and swung it

with all his might, this time releasing his grip just before it hit the wall. It penetrated out into the marble-walled foyer, a marble slab dropping whole to the floor. Another couple of swings and there was a hole big enough for them to crawl through. After what seemed an interminable wait, during which they exchanged embarrassed glances as if they were lovers, the elevator opened. There was a uniformed cop on board with a key in his hand. He was refracted into multiples of himself as he stepped from the mirrored interior. Morgan recognized the officer who had insisted on seeing his ID in front of Frankie's in Rosedale the night he turned up in her bedroom.

"Good to see you." He nodded.

"Yeah, Detective Morgan. And Detective Quin? You two see anything funny going on up here?" He looked past them through the dust-laden air to the hole in the wall and the marble slab lying aslant on the floor.

On the street where the body of Mr. Savage lay splayed like a dropped sack of blood, a crowd had gathered behind a cordon. The body had been covered, but Ellen Ravenscroft was holding the sheet away for a better view.

She looked up when Miranda and Morgan moved around Spivak and Stritch, who were interviewing the building manager by the front door. The man's nose twitched and his beady eyes brightened when he saw them.

"How are you two?" said Ellen. "You know anything about this guy?"

"No," said Miranda.

"Not much," said Morgan.

"Has he got a name?"

"I don't know," said Morgan, looking at Miranda.

"Not really," said Miranda.

"Strange," said Ellen, crouching down and removing a crumpled surgical glove clutched in his grip. She glanced up at Miranda's hands.

"You must have dropped this," said Ellen. "I heard your hands got burned pretty bad."

"Yeah," said Miranda, taking the glove. It was flecked with blood. "We'll talk. I'll call you. I'm going home now. I've had enough for one day."

She leaned gently against Morgan. No one but Ellen from her crouching position would have noticed.

"Come on," said Morgan. "Talk to you soon, Ellen."

"Please," said the medical examiner. "I wait by the phone every night."

They walked off down Avenue Road. When they got to Bloor Street, Isabella was to the east and the Annex to the west.

"You want a shower?" said Miranda.

"Your place or mine?"

Back in front of the condo, Ellen Ravenscroft rose to her feet above the smashed body on the pavement and let the cover drop over what was left of the face. She looked south and saw Morgan and Miranda, turning west. She glanced down again. She knew exactly who the dead man was, even if he had no name.

Acknowledgements

Miranda and Morgan and I are fellow travellers; I'd like to thank them for being such challenging company along the way. Writing novels is a paradoxical endeavour. It is a solitary pursuit, populated with engaging characters doing interesting things, and a sedentary pursuit, writing for hours that merge into months with a computer on my lap, living and reliving forays through Toronto streets, Muskoka haunts, and favourite destinations around the world. It is a wonderfully rewarding pursuit, where reviewers seem friends, whether hostile or enthusiastic — I have friends who are both — and where other writers and readers are co-conspirators and publishers are actual people, working on the same side of the fence. After a full career doing other things, I am grateful to have found myself here, doing this. I share my passions with my wife, Beverley Haun, who is a writer herself, and I owe her so much, words can't begin to convey. I'd like to express my deep gratitude to my daughters, Julia Zarb, Laura Moss, and Beatrice Winny, for their unstinting critical and editorial generosity. Once again, I'd like to thank my friend Jack Morgan for his indefatigable patience and keen critical intelligence.